PACIFIC THREAT

Book 4 of the Falcon Series

Novels by C. H. Cobb

FALCON SERIES:
Falcon Down
Falcon Rising
Falcon Strike
Pacific Threat

OUTLANDER CHRONICLES SERIES:
Outlander Chronicles: Phoenix
Outlander Chronicles: Pegasus

STANDALONE:
The Candidate

NON-FICTION
A Prayer of Moses

PACIFIC THREAT

C. H. COBB

Published by Doorway Press, Greenville, OH, USA
doorwaypress.com

Copyright 2020, C. H. Cobb. All rights reserved.
Find C. H. Cobb on the web at chcobb.com
or on Facebook as C. h. Cobb.

Print version is available on Amazon.com.
Signed copies are available by ordering from chcobb.com.
A Kindle version is available from Amazon.

ISBN-13: 978-0-9848875-7-6
Library of Congress Control Number: 2020912743
First Edition, 2020

Cover design by Doris Cobb
Cover photo by Mass Communication Specialist 2nd Class
Devin M. Langer, and is in the public domain. It was accessed
at https://www.navy.mil/management/photodb/photos/
180804-N-LI768-1033.JPG

Scripture quotations taken from the
New American Standard Bible® (NASB),
Copyright © 1960, 1962, 1963, 1968, 1971, 1972, 1973,
1975, 1977, 1995 by The Lockman Foundation
Used by permission. www.Lockman.org

The quotation from George H. W. Bush's inauguration speech
was accessed at https://www.inaugural.senate.gov/about/
past-inaugural-ceremonies/51st-inaugural-ceremonies/in-
dex.html#oaths.

This is a work of fiction. Names, characters, businesses, organizations, places, events and incidents are either the products of the author's imagination or used in a fictitious manner. Any resemblance to actual persons, living or dead, or actual events is purely coincidental.

This novel was written using OpenOffice 4 and LibreOffice 6.

Dedication

I am a navy brat, as are my siblings. As a child I remember Dad being away for months at a time. He was in the Navy from 1942 to 1966, serving as a fighter pilot (Grumman F6F Hellcats) in the Pacific during World War 2, on flying boats during Korea, then in A-3 Skywarriors, in one of which he re-fueled John Glenn on his record-setting flight across the US, and finally as the nuclear weapons officer aboard the USS *Ranger* (CV-61) during Vietnam.

I can remember listening to Christmas greetings from him on reel-to-reel tape when he was in Japan and we were in Albuquerque. During those times he was gone, Mom carried the burden of us four kids, plus a cat and a dog, all by herself. It was very hard on her, but by diligent effort Mom and Dad made it work, and I grew up in an excellent, stable family. Commander Lewis M. Cobb, USN, ret., passed away in 2011 having survived the front lines of three hot wars. I'm thankful my mom is still with us, as of this writing.

This tale is dedicated to the military families, the warriors and their spouses and children, who make such huge sacrifices and give such large parts of their lives to serve our country. Their service is a sacred gift, and I am thankful for them.

Preface

From August 18-22, 1991, the rapidly dissolving Soviet Union experienced a coup attempt against Mikhail Gorbachev, General Secretary of the Communist Party. The conspirators included an assortment of high government officials who were conservative communist hardliners: the vice president, the prime minister, the head of the KGB, the minister of defense, the interior minister, and other miscellaneous powerful figures. While there were many sources of discontent that led to the attempt, the most fundamental were reactions against Gorbachev's programs of *perestroika* (restructuring) and *glasnost* (openness).

On the 18th, the coup plotters flew to the Crimea where Gorbachev was on vacation in his *dacha*. They demanded he declare a state of emergency to allow the coup plotters to "restore order" to the country. Gorbachev refused and so they bottled him up in his *dacha*, cutting off all his communications. Returning to the Kremlin, they declared a state of emergency on their own authority and began maneuvering troops in place to overthrow the government.

The tide began to turn on the evening of the 19th with a broadcast of President Yeltsin, a Gorbachev loyalist, standing on a tank defending government offices and addressing a crowd of citizens, urging them not to support the coup. The following day, while mixing with the crowds, the commanders of the Alpha and Vympel elite special forces realized the pulse of the citizenry was against the coup plotters. They urged that the planned assault on the government buildings be canceled.

On the 21st, the Taman Guards infantry fighting vehicles were called up to begin the assault on the government buildings. Three Soviet citizens tried to block their approach and were killed. The deaths horrified both sides, and the coup quickly fell apart.

Among the principal reasons for the failure of the coup, aside from the lack of support from the average Soviet citizen, was the divided loyalty of the military. Their hearts were really not in it—they were not willing to shed Russian blood.

Pacific Threat is a fictional prelude to the 1991 coup. The planning and activities of the plotters span 1988 and early 1989. They know a coup will not be successful without the unified support of the military. The US response to their plan to attain that support comprises the heart of this tale.

While *Pacific Threat* can be enjoyed as a standalone book, it follows seamlessly the first three books of the Falcon series (*Falcon Down*, *Falcon Rising*, and *Falcon Strike*).

Please note that three helpful appendices can be found at the back of this book, followed by the acknowledgments.

> *Appendix 1: Cast of Characters*
> *Appendix 2: Special Terms and Acronyms*
> *Appendix 3: Russian Terms*

Chapter 1

January, 1988

Crosswinds buffeted the massive Boeing 747 as it made its final approach to LaGuardia, threatening to tug the big jet off course. The pilot struggled to keep the widebody lined up with Runway 22. A major nor'easter was pummeling the Atlantic Seaboard with high winds and snow; the flight from London was the last to land before the airport closed. The pilot jammed the aircraft down firmly, ensuring that the wind gusts couldn't blow it off the runway. Though the landing was hard, it was right on the centerline.

The jolt woke Jacob Kelly, also known as Falcon, from a deep sleep. As the 747 taxied to the terminal, Kelly rubbed his eyes and prepared to gather up his things. The last seventy-two hours seemed like a dream—only Kelly wasn't sure whether it was a good dream or a bad one. Detained by the KGB in the Moscow airport and then unexpectedly released, his outlook had gone from the graveyard to the mountaintop. He was glad to be back on American soil. He reached into his suit pocket. The tiny box was still there. He pulled it out and opened it up. The three rings—one engagement ring and two wedding bands—glistened under the cabin lights. Kelly grinned. *A good dream*, he decided as he closed the box and returned it to his pocket.

After passing through Customs, Jake checked the monitors for his connecting flight to San Francisco. Boarding was supposed to be in four hours, but with the winter storm he figured he'd probably be spending the night in the airport. Plenty of time for a good meal and a good book. He strolled into one of the shops on the concourse and bought a copy of *Patriot Games*, Tom Clancy's latest blockbuster.

As he left the store he noticed that two men in dark suits fell in alongside of him. He stopped, pretending to study the departures monitor, and they stopped, also looking at the monitor. Kelly glanced around and spotted two more suits, one leaning against the wall, the other across the concourse standing in line at a coffee shop.

He continued in the direction of his gate, wondering what was going on. Had Anatoly Geredin lied to him? Was the Soviet GRU still after him? Did they intend to kill him after all? His escorts stayed with him just out of reach on either side, pretending to pay no attention to him. Falcon weighed his options. He had no doubt that he could dispense with the two goons, but the resulting scene would end in his arrest by airport security. And that would mean they would discover the handgun under the false bottom of his briefcase, which would really create problems.

He was about to duck into a darkened restaurant lounge full of patrons stranded by the weather when the matter was decided for him. A fifth man in a dark suit stepped in front of him. "Major Jacob Kelly, CIA. Would you come with us, please?" It was an order, not a question. The other two suits joined up, and the five men surrounded Kelly as they exited the concourse through an unmarked door into a narrow hallway.

This was as good a place as any to make his stand, as the hallway was narrow enough to prevent all five from laying hands on him at the same time. He looked in both directions and was relieved to see no security cameras.

He stopped. "Wait a minute, gentlemen. Before I go any farther, I want to know who you guys are."

A gruff voice behind him said, "We told you, Major. We're CIA."

"Let me see some credentials."

"There's someone who wants to talk to you. You can see our credentials when we get there."

"No. I will see them now," Kelly insisted.

The man behind Falcon barked "Move!" and shoved him. Rather than resist Kelly went with the momentum, colliding with the three in front, knocking them down like pins in a bowling alley. He pivoted and kicked the man behind him in the groin and struck him with a karate chop to the neck when the man bent over in agony. The agent following the downed man started to reach into his jacket.

Falcon, in a fighting stance, growled, "Buddy, if you pull

out a gun I swear it's the last thing you'll ever do."

A sharp command from further down the hall brought Falcon up short. "JAKE! Stand down!"

The agent slowly removed his empty hand from his jacket. "Relax, man. No gun, okay?"

Kelly turned around and saw Bill Jensen, his friend and mentor. Jensen called out, "It's okay, Jake. These men are with me." Jensen was a special assistant to the Deputy Director for Operations (DDO) of the CIA. He had also been the best friend of Kelly's father, Clancy. The men were so close that when Clancy died of cancer, Jensen flew back from a special assignment in Australia to attend the funeral. After Jake's mother, Galina, died the following year, Bill and Susan Jensen took Jacob Kelly under their wing and treated him as their own son.

As the three agents in front untangled themselves and stood up, Kelly bent over to help the man he'd laid low. "Sorry, friend, I don't take well to being pushed. I was afraid you guys might be with the opposing team."

The man groaned as he stood, rubbing his neck, his crotch still throbbing with pain. "Seems to me, Major, that you're a whole team all by your lonesome."

"Sit down, Jake. Let me have your briefcase," Jensen said when the whole group had gathered in a room off the hall. Kelly handed the briefcase to his friend, who turned it over to the leader of the team that had corralled him. The man popped open the latches, removed the false bottom as though he knew exactly what to look for, and retrieved Kelly's handgun. He deftly ejected the magazine, cleared the chamber, and pocketed the ammunition. He handed the weapon to Jensen, who placed it on the desk.

"Gentlemen, leave us please. The things I must speak with Kelly about are private. You needn't worry, Major Kelly is my friend." The five agents stepped outside and shut the door.

****

"So who is that guy?" asked Paul, the agent whom Kelly

had downed. He was still hurting.

"Kelly is a pilot in the air force. Sorry, Paul," said the team leader, Roger Carson. "I know the man, or know of him, anyway. But he doesn't know me. I should have shown him my credentials out in the concourse—would have saved some hassle. Apparently, he was expecting trouble. He seemed loaded for bear."

"A pilot? What a weenie. If I'd been ready for him I'd have taken the punk to the mat," responded Paul, trying to repair his wounded pride.

"Um, actually no, you probably wouldn't even be able to lay a hand on him. Kelly could have taken the five of us down separately or together and not even wrinkled his shirt. He's one tough customer. He's not just a pilot, Paul. He's also a special forces operator, USAF Combat Control Team (CCT). Those guys are like Navy SEALs. You want to ruin your day, try picking on one of them."

"How do you know about him, Roger?" Paul asked. "Jensen didn't tell us anything, gave us nothing more than a picture and a name."

"Jimmy and I," Carson said, pointing at one of the other agents, "were on a case up in Alaska back in October, trying to protect the guy from a pair of hit squads that the Sovs hired."

"The Soviets were trying to kill him? On American soil? What was that all about?" Paul asked, his interest piqued.

"It's quite a story. What I'm about to tell you doesn't go outside of the Agency. The only reason I'm telling you now is because the five of us are going to be detailed as security for Kelly. There's some concern that the Russkies are still trying to bump him off. We're even going to cover his wedding whenever that happens. So you need to know. I was preparing to brief you boys this morning, but then we got news that Kelly was on the flight from Heathrow. We had to drop everything and race up here to intercept him."

"We're covering his wedding? You've got to be kidding."

Carson shook his head. "I'm very serious. Several years ago the Sovs decided they were going to do science on the cheap—particularly, science related to weapons development. So they started kidnapping top scientists from around the world—Brits, French, Indian, Americans. The plan was to interrogate them to fill in the gaps in Soviet research and development. If the scientists didn't agree to switch sides they would eventually be executed and buried in some unmarked Siberian grave. No one would ever know what happened to them.

"Their grab teams were very good—nobody saw the snatches. There was no evidence of foul play. The result was nothing more than a bunch of missing person reports at local police stations.

"And then they decided to cop Kelly. Bad move, very bad move. Kelly was the top test pilot for a secret F-16 weapons development program, a mission that required him to receive full CCT training. Apparently, he aced the training. Well, the Russkies had no clue about that part of his resume. They actually shot him down over the Bering Sea while he was on a test flight. He ejected and they snagged his parachute and reeled him in."

Carson chuckled. "Those poor people had no idea who and what they'd just tied on to. Within a couple of weeks he'd escaped, nearly burning down the whole interrogation facility in the process. For the next fourteen months thousands of Soviet soldiers chased him across Siberia. Every time they got within shouting distance they'd lose equipment and men. He's that good. He finally got to the northeastern extent of the Chukchi Peninsula and paddled back to the US in a kayak."

Carson stopped when a door opened farther down the hall. Several uniformed airport security men walked toward them.

"What are you doing here?" asked a burly fellow suspiciously.

"CIA," Carson said, flashing his ID. "We're cleared by your shift supervisor to be back here. We've got another team in that room," he said, motioning to the door. "Check with your supervisor."

The man turned away and radioed the security office. He

looked back during the conversation and verified, "You Carson?"

Roger nodded.

The man finished his conversation, then clipped the transceiver to his belt. "Okay, sorry, buddy. Just checking. Nobody is supposed to be in this hall."

"No problem."

When the security men exited the hall to the concourse, Paul exclaimed, "You're not serious! A kayak?"

"Yep. Well, it seems that when Kelly escaped, the career of the GRU officer running the facility, a fellow by the name of Chernikov, went into the toilet. Chernikov decides that he wants revenge, so ever since Kelly got back to the states last fall, Cherny has been trying to off him. I suspect that's why Falcon—Kelly's nickname—was so on edge tonight. Probably thought we were GRU agents intent on killing him."

"So if he escaped from the Soviets, why in the world did he go back?" asked one of the other agents.

"Scuttlebutt has it that he went back as a private citizen to assassinate Chernikov in order to put an end to the Russian's vendetta. That's why Jensen needs to talk to him. We may wind up having to arrest him. If Kelly bumped off a high-ranking Soviet officer, all you-know-what is about to break loose."

****

"Can we speak freely, sir?" asked Falcon, looking around the room.

"Yes. I had the room swept a few minutes ago, there are no listening devices," assured Jensen.

"What's this all about?" demanded Jake. "Why did your guys stop me?"

"Jake, I'm sorry, but I have to interrogate you and I'll probably have to detain you. You could conceivably face charges. We might even be forced to extradite you to the Soviets. I did everything in my power to keep you from traveling back to Moscow to assassinate General Chernikov, but you would not listen. Now you've put us all in an extremely difficult position."

"Mr. Jensen," Jake responded heatedly, "I had to do it. It had become personal for Chernikov—he would have never stopped pursuing me. I would have been looking over my shoulder for the rest of my life. Since it had become personal for him, I had to make it personal for me."

"I understand, son, but when you assassinate a top officer on the Soviet General Staff's intelligence arm, it's not the same thing as popping some neighborhood thug. It's huge. Wars are started this way, Jake! They can't let it go and we can't let it go."

"Well, sir, you don't have to worry about that," Kelly said, smarting under his mentor's rebuke. "I didn't do it."

"You didn't kill him?" Jensen said, relief spreading over his features.

"No."

Jensen shut his eyes and exhaled noisily. He dropped his head and breathed, "Thank You, Lord." He was silent for a moment then put his hand on Kelly's shoulder. "Jake, we'll assign security to protect you. That team outside the door will be shadowing you as long as necessary. We'll keep you and Galina safe—we won't let Chernikov harm you."

Jake shook his head. "Not necessary, sir, he's dead."

"What? I don't understand."

"I broke into his *dacha* and was waiting for him. No one else was there, I think his wife lives in their other home. When he arrived I held my gun on him, was planning on torturing him before I killed him, like he tortured me. Had the soldering pencil hot and everything. As we walked through his living room, a bullet came through the window and hit him right in the head. Killed him. I had nothing to do with it, although in another ten minutes it would have been my bullet in his skull."

"Who do you think did it?" Jensen asked, mystified.

"I know who did it. It was the KGB."

"How could you know that?"

"Because the director of the KGB, Anatoly Geredin, told me so. He intercepted me as I was about to board my flight out of Moscow. He told me they'd had a sniper ready to take Chernikov down. They even knew I was in his house, though I was not aware of them. Geredin said that their man pulled the trigger precisely to avoid the kind of complications I would have caused had I killed him.

"Geredin told me to bring a message from the Politburo to our government. I suppose telling you is telling the government. He said, *Tell them, we take care of our own problems. There will be no retaliation for your SEAL raid. Chernikov needed to be killed a long time ago and his recklessness finally caught up with him. His project never should have been allowed to exist. It was a mistake.* Those are his exact words."

"Oh, thank God," Jensen sighed with relief, rubbing his face with his hands. "That is the best news I have heard in a long time. The president will want to hear this. Now maybe we can finally close the door on that whole terrible episode." Jensen put the empty handgun back in Jake's briefcase, replaced the false bottom and snapped the case shut.

"Is there anything else, sir?"

"Nope. That's it. I am so glad you are home safe and sound. Susan and I have been praying for you since the day you flew to Moscow on your mission of revenge. We were praying that you would not do it—and you didn't. It's great to see you, Jake. It's a relief."

"It's good to see you, sir," said Jake, smiling for the first time in the interview. "I'm beginning to think there's more to this providence stuff than I originally believed."

"God's real, Jake. You of all people should know that by now."

"Well, you've got me thinking about it, Mr. Jensen, I'll say that much."

"What do I have to do to get you to call me *Bill*, Jacob? You're an adult now! No more of this *Mr. Jensen* stuff."

****

During Jake's escape he was sheltered from the brutal Siberian winter by an illegal timbering operation near Sidima in the Sikhote-Alin mountains in the Khabarovsk Krai. The operation was managed by Galina Toporova and her brother. Jake was attracted to the woman, not only by her beauty and character, but also because she had the same name as his mother—Galina.

Jake had broken his arm fleeing Soviet soldiers in Khabarovsk, and though he'd forcibly commandeered her vehicle while escaping the soldiers, Galina felt compassion for him and took him in, intending to hide him until his arm healed. However, during the winter the two fell in love. When Jake fled the approaching door-to-door search in the spring he promised Galina he would return for her and take her as his wife. Shortly after Jake fled, Galina was captured and arrested by the KGB for her part in harboring Kelly.

But as it happened, Galina was protected by a high-ranking anonymous benefactor in the KGB. Rather than being tortured, interrogated and then executed, she was exiled to China. She eventually made her way to San Francisco and was unexpectedly reunited with Kelly through an odd combination of circumstances Bill Jensen labeled as "providential." But Kelly didn't want to marry her until he had settled matters with Chernikov, fearing that he would be putting her life in danger. Now that Chernikov was dead, the couple could move forward with their plans.

****

"Gorbachev is a traitor," groused Admiral Konstantin Grigoriyevich Shukshin, the deputy commander of the Red Banner Pacific Fleet. "*Glasnost* is dangerous. The Party must never be subject to criticism—especially not from the common laborer and certainly not from journalists. And *perestroika* is foolish. No matter how Gorbachev tries to paint it, *perestroika* is a repudiation of Marx and Lenin." Shukshin stubbed out his cigarette in the overflowing ashtray. "Our dear general secretary must be restrained before he destroys the *rodina*. And destroy it he will, if comrades of good character do not unite to stop him."

Captain First Rank Boris Sayanovich Mirov frowned. "But sir," he objected, "you must not speak that way. Surely there are ears everywhere." He glanced at the political officer sitting next to him.

The *zampolit* grinned and took a long drag on his cigarette before responding. "No worries, Borya. I am in complete agreement with the Admiral."

Shukshin smiled. "Relax, Boris Sayanovich. Your quarters are not bugged. And I have discussed this subject at length with your *zampolit*," he said, nodding at the political officer. "We see eye to eye on this. Gorbachev must go. He's done little about that provocateur in Gdańsk, Lech Wałęsa, and his mewling followers in Solidarity. If he does not crack down and force Jaruzelski to get rid of Wałęsa, Poland will soon cease to be a reliable buffer against NATO. Afghanistan is a disaster—the hard fist of Stalin would never have allowed that situation to get so out of control. The Baltic States are becoming restless. There's trouble in Azerbaijan. The *rodina* requires a firm, iron grip over the citizens and the *soviets* and our allies. Mikhail Sergeyevich Gorbachev does not have such a grip. I repeat, Captain Mirov, Gorbachev must go."

Mirov's two companions sat across from him in the cramped space of the captain's quarters on the K-263, a Projekt 971 boat known to NATO as an Akula-class nuclear attack submarine. On the fold-down table between them sat three glasses of vodka and a bottle, the half-empty container a testament to their celebration of the fulfillment of another excellent mission. Three hours earlier the *K-263* had returned to Vladivostok from a "combat service" deployment (i. e., a forward-area, blue-water patrol) in the Pacific.

There was a tap on the door. "Enter," responded Captain Mirov.

The chief engineering officer, Captain Third Rank Ilya Germanovich Fedin, poked his head into the cramped cabin. "Skipper, the reactor is secure and we have completed the necessary shutdowns in the engineering spaces. With your permission, sir, I will relieve the propulsion watch with the portside watch complement."

"*Da*, Ilya. You may relieve the watch. Your people have been outstanding on this cruise. I will note it in my report."

"Thank you, Captain. I serve the Soviet Union," the man replied with enthusiasm before he shut the door. To receive praise in the presence of the deputy commander of the Pacific Fleet was a rare treat!

"So where do you stand, Borya? Are you content to let the Soviet people suffer while Gorbachev tries his little experiment with capitalism? Will you stand by while the Union falls apart?" asked the admiral, studying Mirov intently.

Captain Mirov felt like he was the subject of a psychological x-ray, fearful that his most closely guarded inner thoughts were subject to exposure under his superior's relentless gaze. But he was a man of integrity and gave an honest answer. "I cannot counsel a new revolution, comrade Shukshin, if that's what you're asking. I will not stand against Gorbachev. I think we should allow more time to see what his efforts to restructure the economy will produce. On the other hand, I cannot condemn your concerns, Admiral. I know you love the motherland. I suspect everyone is struggling with the changes, especially when there are lines for everything—bread, potatoes, sugar—and the supply runs out long before the line does."

Shukshin shrugged. "We must agree to disagree then, Captain. Perhaps the Pacific Fleet has its own version of *glasnost*," he chuckled. He stood up and stowed the bottle of vodka in his attache case. "Wouldn't want anyone finding that in the captain's quarters, now, would we?" He opened the door and stepped into the passageway, then looked back at the captain. "When you have completed the change of command and filed your reports, I want you to go home to your family, Borya. Take a couple of weeks off. That's an order."

Mirov brightened, "Thank you, Admiral!"

Shukshin shook his head dismissively. "It's not generosity, Captain Mirov. I'm sending you out again, sooner than I should, on a another deployment. Russia needs all of its sons in the present crisis. So go to your family while you can."

It was snowing heavily as Admiral Shukshin walked down the gangway to his waiting UAZ-3151 jeep. He pondered the conversation with Mirov. *I think I just found my sacrificial lamb. But not in that boat—can't afford to lose that one.*

Planning a military coup in the Soviet Union is riskier than playing Russian roulette with five of six cylinders loaded. But that's precisely what the deputy commander of the Red Banner Pacific Fleet had in mind.

****

Captain First Rank Boris Sayanovich Mirov was an icon in the Soviet submarine service. Born to a diesel mechanic working in the rail yard machine shop in Irkutsk, Mirov began his career with no patrons and no political pull. During his secondary schooling he'd distinguished himself with nothing more than a good mind, fearless character, and hard work in the Young Pioneers. Eventually he was noticed by the local administrator of the Voluntary Society for Cooperation with the Army, Aviation, and Fleet, otherwise known as the DOSAAF. As a young teen Mirov was inducted into the DOSAAF where he quickly mastered a set of specialties that qualified him for advanced training in the Soviet navy, particularly the submarine service. Natural ability combined with diligence eventually won him a spot in the coveted Leninsky Komsomol Highest Naval School for Submarine Navigation in Leningrad. His performance in that institution opened the doors for additional advanced officer training, until he finally found himself commanding his own submarine.

Mirov's exploits included penetrating the inner ring of a US carrier battle group ASW screen with an improved Kilo diesel attack submarine, locating and tailing multiple US ballistic missile submarines, and completing the closest undetected approach of any Soviet submarine ever to the US Naval Submarine Base Bangor, the only home port of the *Ohio*-class Trident ballistic missile submarines on the Pacific. When one of Mirov's commanding officers retired and was appointed to the Duma, he gained an important ally in the upper echelons of Soviet politics, as well as a backchannel of information for news affecting the submarine service.

Mirov's fame around the fleet grew even larger when his nuclear attack submarine experienced a disastrous reactor failure while on a combat service patrol, far from any assistance. Although three seamen died from radiation exposure, the boat and the rest of the crew was saved. His actions demonstrated that he valued the life of his crew over the preservation of the boat, though he was ultimately able to secure both. This brought him much admiration from the lower levels of the fleet even though his priorities didn't sit well initially with the Soviet brass. A board of inquiry later vindicated him, determining that his command decisions were exactly what the emergency required.

Mirov's service record combined with his ability to mentor junior officers who later became excellent commanders in their own right made his the most popular and coveted command in the submarine divisions of the Pacific Fleet. It also placed the man on the radar of both US Naval Intelligence and the CIA.

****

Anatoly Geredin, head of the KGB and General of the Army, should have retired long ago. Because of his arthritis, his pain was ever present. One could still see in his seventy-eight-year-old body the fading signs of a man who'd once been muscular and vigorous, but those days were long past. He'd developed a perpetual cough which he feared might be a consequence of too many cigarettes and cigars, but he'd elected not to have it checked out by his physician. Death would one day have its prize, he acknowledged, but the old atheist refused to live in fear of it. If cancer was growing in his lungs, he didn't want to know about it.

Geredin was a man alone. His wife had passed away years earlier and their marriage had produced no children. He'd been for many years the secret guardian of the children of his best friend, a man who'd willingly sacrificed his own life to save Geredin years earlier in a botched covert operation in Syria. A double agent had given away their presence to the Israelis, resulting in a firefight with the IDF, a battle from which only one of the two men could escape. Geredin had vowed to his friend that his children would be well cared for. It was a promise Geredin kept all of his life. But now his charges, Boris and Galina Toporova were beyond his care, Boris having died two years earlier and Galina about to be married in the US.

He sat at his desk in his mahogany-paneled office in the Lubyanka. The high ceilings tended to steal all the heat in the room, so a fire was blazing in the fireplace. He slowly sipped his tea as he perused the morning edition of *Pravda*, not wanting to get into the mundane stack of administrative problems sitting on his desk. Gorbachev's *perestroika* had left large parts of the KGB without much to do. On the other hand, the KGB was now busy keeping an eye on the rumblings of potential coup attempts—something they'd not had to deal with before. Aging conservatives and communist hardliners were becoming agitated under Gorbachev's innovations. Portions of the military in particular were particularly worrisome, especially those branches that controlled nuclear weapons—such as the strategic submarine divisions.

"Enter," he said, responding to a knock on his door.

Colonel Vladimir Leonidovich Dobrynin opened the door. "A minute of your time, Anatoly?"

Geredin waved him in and set down the newspaper. Dobrynin was chief of the Third Directorate in the KGB, responsible for the political surveillance of military officers. It was quickly becoming one of the busier divisions of the intelligence service. "Tea?" the KGB director inquired.

"*Nyet, spasibo.*" Dobrynin sat down. "Admiral Shukshin landed in Leningrad two hours ago on a military transport."

Geredin raised his eyebrows. "And why is this a concern?"

"According to my source on his staff there's nothing on his schedule. What would cause him to fly 7300 kilometers on a military transport on his own initiative? That's why I'm concerned. We know that Shukshin has been agitating against Gorbachev."

"Hmm. You have him under surveillance?"

"From the moment he stepped off the plane."

"I want to know about everyone he meets and everywhere he goes. See that something happens to his driver—nothing serious, just make him unavailable. Perhaps a temporary stomach bug. Put one of our men in his place."

Dobrynin nodded and left the room.

****

Three months later, on a beautiful day in the middle of May, Bill Jensen sat in the second row of a Presbyterian church in San Francisco. Jake and Galina's big day had finally arrived, and the wedding was scheduled to begin in fifteen minutes. He whispered into his microphone, "Showboat, this is Professor. Report."

The quiet voice of Roger Carson came through his earbud. "Blue Team is in position, Red Team is in position. No visible threats, Professor."

Although neither of the soon-to-be newlyweds were believers, they wanted their ceremony in a church. They asked the pastor of the Chinese Presbyterian Church Galina had been attending with her host family to conduct the ceremony. Even though Chernikov was dead, Jensen insisted on bringing a security team over Kelly's objections, knowing that there were many fallen stars in the Soviet Union who would like some payback against Jake.

An old man studied the church from across the street, watching the guests arrive. Along with the civilians who were entering were many military men in full-dress uniform. The man sighed. *These silly Americans and their preoccupation with religion. Why can they not see that their God is nothing more than a myth?*

He turned to his security team. "I will not need you in there—I'm not in any danger, and I'm afraid you would draw the sort of attention that I don't want. Don't be obvious, but take up positions out here just in case. However, Pavel, I will need your help crossing the street and climbing those stairs. My arthritis is especially bad today."

He leaned heavily on his cane and tried not to grimace in

pain as he hobbled across the street, his bodyguard taking him by the elbow. After the security man left him at the entrance he made his way painfully into the church and sat on the back row.

Geredin was immediately recognized. Jensen happened to be looking back when the old man entered. He stiffened. *Why is the head of the KGB here in San Fran at Jake's wedding?* he wondered. *It can't be good!*

He whispered into his microphone, "Bogey on the back row. Old man with a cane, just came in. He's KGB." Several members of the Red Team inside the church moved casually into position behind Geredin, standing in the back of the church. The Blue Team, outside the church, had no need of subtlety and they sprinted to cover the exits and entrances of the building.

The Soviet security team observed the activity and casually walked across the street, trying not to give themselves away, taking up positions to counter the Americans if things started happening. Nonetheless, Roger Carson spotted them.

"Professor, this is Showboat. Looks like the bogey brought a team with him. I count five potential hostiles. If we watch the exits then they'll have us boxed. Requesting instructions."

"Red Team, this is Professor. Stand by, repeat, stand by for a possible Code Red. The northwest exit is the extraction point. Blue Team, concentrate there. Have a vehicle ready."

The Soviet team observed the agents racing around to the far side of the building. Now they began to fear for Geredin's safety and started for the main entrance of the church. The team leader sent two men to observe the American agents, then radioed Geredin, who directed him to stay outside the church but remain ready.

Jensen looked at his watch. *Ten minutes before the ceremony begins. Got to get Jake and Galina out before any more guests arrive.* He quietly stood and left the sanctuary, headed for the room he knew that Jake and Galina were waiting in. Two of his men were standing outside the door. "Don't let anyone else in. I've got to talk to Jake."

"Mr. Jensen," exclaimed Kelly, "thank you so much for

coming!" Kelly looked dignified in his air force blues dress uniform.

"Would not miss it for the world, Jake. Galina, you look absolutely stunning," he said, hugging the young lady all dressed in white. He was careful not to crush the bouquet of roses in her hand.

Jensen pulled Jake into the corner of the room while Galina's attendants put the finishing touches on her dress and veil. Keeping his voice down, he said, "Listen, Jake, we've got a complication. Anatoly Geredin just walked in. He's sitting in the back of the church and has a team of agents outside the church. I fear that we need to get you both away from here. I have a security team and vehicle waiting outside the northwest entrance. I think it best if you two come with me."

"Geredin? Here?"

"Yes. We need to move you two, now."

"No, sir. You are mistaken—his intentions are the best. I'm sure of it. I've never really told you his part of the story. He is the one who protected Galina and got her safely out of the country. He's kind of like her godfather, only without the God part."

"Are you sure of this?"

"I'd stake my life on it. Years ago, when Galya's father was dying, Geredin bound himself by an oath to protect her. All these years he's been faithful to it. He's not going to harm her. In fact, I'm going to ask him to be part of the wedding."

Mollified, Jensen spoke into his microphone. "This is Professor. Red Team, Blue Team, stand down but remain vigilant. The bogey is not a threat, repeat, not a threat."

Jake went to Galina. "Honey, I think we have someone to walk you down the aisle and give you away. Anatoly Geredin, the man who was your father's best friend, the same man who gave us the rings—he is here, right now. If he is willing, would you have him walk you down the aisle?"

"Mr. Geredin is here? He came to our wedding?" she asked, surprised. When Jake smiled and nodded his head, she cried, "Oh, yes, yes, please! All those years he stood in my father's place, and I never knew it until you told me. Please ask him."

While Jensen returned to his seat Kelly entered the sanctuary and sat down next to Geredin. "Mr. Geredin, I am surprised but overjoyed to see you. You are very welcome here."

The old spy nodded. "Thank you, Major Kelly. My men inform me that your wedding nearly became an international incident a few minutes ago. Do these troubles follow you everywhere?"

Kelly laughed. "Well you must admit, sir, that honoring us with your presence is, shall we say, a bit unusual."

"That's the problem with being a spy at the top of the food chain, Major. You don't get to live a normal life. Not even when you're as old as I am."

"Mr. Geredin, would you do us one further honor? We have a tradition in America of the father of the bride escorting her down the aisle and giving her away. As you know, Galina's father is not here. Would you do us the honor? Both Galya and I would love it if you would."

The request caught the old spy by surprise. His chin quivered, and he swallowed hard several times. He clasped Kelly's hand and squeezed. Not trusting his voice, he nodded vigorously.

Several moments later the music began and Major Jacob Kelly and the pastor walked out onto the platform. The wedding march began and a radiant Galina began walking slowly down the aisle, arm in arm with the General of the Army of the Soviet Union, Anatoly Geredin. His smile was broad and genuine, even as tears coursed down his old face.

"Who gives this woman to this man?" asked the Chinese pastor in heavily accented English.

"*Ya*, I do," came the vigorous response from Geredin in both Russian and English.

Before taking Galina's hand in his, Jake helped the old spy to a seat next to Jensen. As Geredin sat down he thought of Galina's father, Yevgeniy, and his act of self-sacrifice so many years ago that had saved his own life, and he remembered the vow he made. *Yevgeniy, my old friend, I have fulfilled my vow. Your daughter is in good hands—the best of hands. You would be very proud of her.* Geredin would later write in his memoirs that walking Galina down the aisle that day was the very high point of his life.

Chapter 2

Early August, 1988

"Comrades, the current situation cannot be tolerated, it cannot be allowed to continue," cried Alexander Ivanovich Pushkaryov, pounding the lectern with all the pathos of a camp-meeting preacher appealing to his choir.

Pushkaryov was the vice president of the Soviet Union. He was speaking to fifty of the top civilian and military leaders of the country. The meeting was billed as a problem-solving forum addressed to the challenges of the USSR's collapsing economy, rising inflation, and critical shortages in the food and consumer goods sectors.

Gorbachev's policies of *perestroika* and *glasnost* were creating havoc for a populace not accustomed to taking personal initiative. Moscow was doling out a limited amount of new liberties and the New Soviet Man was having difficulty adjusting. Farms and factories were missing their production quotas. Some weren't producing anything because the managers and overseers were paralyzed for fear of making a mistake for which they'd be called to account.

The gathering was Pushkaryov's brainchild and had the official approval of the premier, Nikolai Kosygin, and the general secretary of the Communist Party of the Soviet Union (CPSU), Mikhail Sergeyevich Gorbachev, neither of whom were present. Their absence was by design—Pushkaryov's design. The two leaders were told that their presence might intimidate the attendees into making safe suggestions instead of bold, creative ones. It was hoped that by gathering a group of innovative and dynamic leaders a Moses would arise with ideas that could lead communism out of the economic wilderness and into the promised land.

But what neither Kosygin nor Gorbachev was told was that the published agenda of the group was a sham, a cover for a budding insurrection of which Gorbachev was the target and Pushkaryov the intended beneficiary. At least, that was Pushkaryov's intention.

Every attendee had been quietly vetted as to their political leanings and loyalties, and only communist hardliners who were angry with Gorbachev and his innovations were invited. The KGB minders in attendance were the usual "security" team assigned to Pushkaryov, a team whose actual purpose was less security than KGB-ordered surveillance. Unbeknownst to their bosses in the Lubyanka, however, the team of agents was wholly owned by the vice president through a combination of blackmail and bribery. He had cleverly compromised them by enticing them into a weekend of sexual indiscretions during a trip to a UN conference in New York the year before. Ever since then he'd had them by the short hairs, threatening to expose them to their superiors if they didn't play ball. It didn't take much more than that plus a little cold hard cash to purchase their loyalty. Pushkaryov knew that the agents would dutifully report the names of all who attended, as well as several hours of scripted discussion that never actually took place.

"Mikhail Sergeyevich has betrayed our glorious revolution!" Pushkaryov shouted. "What? What? Shall all the pain, the necessary pain that the *rodina* felt at the hands of Stalin be wasted? Stalin was a stern father, but a good one. He did what had to be done. We needed to feel his loving lash. We needed to be purged of the elite, the rich, and the bourgeois who were oppressing and exploiting the workers."

"Hear, hear!" cried his enthusiastic disciples.

"But, comrades, we endured that necessary painful period and we emerged on the other side a mighty and powerful nation, ready to carry the message of liberation to the workers of the world! It is a matter of scientific inevitability, a matter of economic evolution as certain as tomorrow's sunrise that capitalism will fall before the science of socialism. Having endured those painful years, shall we now betray the glorious revolution by adopting capitalism? Shall we throw our progress away? But evil capitalism is exactly where the general secretary's policy of *perestroika* is taking us! It's a betrayal of all we stand for, comrades! Shall we go back? I say, No! No! We shall not go back! Not now, not ever!" Pushkaryov paused and mopped the sweat off his brow with a handkerchief. Looking around the room, he knew he had his audience in the palm of his hand.

Confident that none of his speech would be reported, Pushkaryov spoke for ninety minutes, seeking to whip the attendees into a frenzy. He concluded by assuring his audience that plans were being formulated to save the Soviet Union, and one day soon they would be called upon to stand shoulder to shoulder with the workers of the country to preserve the Revolution and their way of life.

After the meeting a small select group met at Pushkaryov's *dacha* to continue the discussion. "Valentin, will the military stand behind us if we move against Gorbachev?" asked Pushkaryov, addressing Valentin Valentinovich Aristov, the defense minister. "Who can we count on?"

"My sense is that they won't tolerate any blatant violence against the general secretary, not at first anyway. We'll need a way to get Gorbachev off the scene, out of the public eye, and limit his communications—isolate him without looking like we are isolating him," Aristov answered. He turned to Kirill Ilyich Yegorov, chief of the general staff of the Soviet armed forces, and asked, "What do you think, General? Will the army unite around a coup, or at least enough of them so that it becomes a fait accompli for the others?"

"I think we can count on the Alpha and Vympel special forces units, comrade Minister. Their commanding officers are unhappy with things as they are at present. Most of the lower ranks of the KGB will stand with us. The top echelon will not. Geredin rules them with an iron fist. He hates Gorbachev's policies but he will not support a coup—he's made that clear.

"As far as armor goes, I know we've got the 2nd Guards Motor Rifle Division in our pocket, along with the 4th Guards. Beyond that, I'm not sure."

"Is that enough, comrade?" Pushkaryov asked.

Yegorov looked at his hands and chose his words carefully before replying, knowing that being as deep in the conspiracy as he was, it would probably mean his death if he did not appear to support it. "It's enough to hold the Kremlin and essential parts of Moscow for thirty-six hours, forty-eight at the most. But if significant parts of the army don't fall in line with us we could not hold the city any longer than that. We could all be looking at firing squads, comrades, if we launch this without adequate support from the military."

"How about the navy, Shukshin? Will they stand with us?"

The deputy commander of the Pacific Fleet was indulging in private fantasies that it would be he, not Pushkaryov, who would take the helm of the country when the coup happened. He responded with careless confidence. "The surface fleet is not an issue, comrades. It really doesn't matter what their loyalties are. If we hold the capital, they'll fall in line. They will support whoever signs their paychecks. No, comrades, it is the submarine force we must concern ourselves with. Our ballistic missile submarines and the fast attack boats that protect them —these are the ones we must win. I'd say right now that we're looking at fifty-fifty. We must do better if we want this project to succeed."

"I don't understand, Admiral. Why are the submarines so important?" asked the interior minister, Yulian Semyonovich Churkin.

"Because they control such a large portion of our nuclear forces, comrade Minister," answered Aristov, the defense minister. "We cannot be in control of the government if we are not in control of the nukes."

"*Pravda.* I think what I am hearing is that we aren't yet ready," observed Pushkaryov.

Most of those gathered nodded agreement.

Aristov spoke up. "*Da.* In order to ensure our success, we should wait until we are confident of the military's support. Once they are behind us we can pull it off and probably without bloodshed."

"But how can we get the united support of the military? It sounds like the loyalty of our officers are divided between the general secretary and his imperialist *perestroika* on the one hand and the Revolution on the other. How can we get them to pull together?" asked Churkin.

"I know how. So does Yegorov," Shukshin claimed quietly.

All heads turned toward him.

"Please continue," said the vice president.

"Military men pull together when they are under attack," Shukshin said. "They need a common enemy. Not an enemy within our borders, because then you'll have the problem of divided loyalties. No, it must be a common enemy outside of our borders. Afghanistan won't do—everyone is sick and tired of dealing with those crazy *mujahideen*. It needs to be an enemy who presents a legitimate threat to the country."

"Are you saying we need to start a war, Admiral, because I will not be in favor of that!" warned the interior minister.

The defense minister frowned. "*Da*, I'm not sure I'm comfortable with what you are saying either, Konstantin Grigoriyevich. What exactly are you proposing?"

"Just hear me out. We need to create a brief and limited engagement with an external foe—a conflict that can be concluded with diplomacy. This will create a period of high emotions and patriotic fervor within the country. The coup attempt must happen during that period. I guarantee you, even the Gorbachev loyalists in the various services will unite before a common enemy on the outside—even if they are unhappy about the coup."

"He's right about that," affirmed General Yegorov. "There's a loyalty comrades-in-arms experience that goes even deeper than national or political loyalties. The military will unify under this sort of situation. The admiral's reasoning is sound.

"And this provides another possibility, now that I think about it. If we can isolate Gorbachev and cut off his communications, we can present it to the people as though Gorbachev himself has chosen to step down for health reasons exacerbated by the crisis. It won't even appear to be a coup. And who cares what people find out after the fact? What's done is done."

Pushkaryov considered this. "And who would we create that fight with? Certainly not a member of NATO. A weaker nation without firm alliances? The Philippines, perhaps? I hear that the negotiations between them and the United States pertaining to the naval base at Subic Bay are not going well—they very well might find themselves standing alone."

"No," Shukshin responded firmly. "Not the Philippines. It has to be a nation that poses a legitimate threat. Nothing less will pull our military together so that we can act as one."

"Whom did you have in mind, Admiral?" queried Aristov, fearing that he'd already guessed and desperately hoping he was wrong.

Shukshin hesitated. Then he admitted quietly, "I propose we create a conflict with the United States."

"Are you crazy?" shouted Yulian Churkin, leaping out of his chair. "Are you seeking our destruction?"

"Absolutely not!" Aristov shouted. "Do you want to start World War 3? You're looking into the abyss, Admiral, from which no winners anywhere will emerge. That's complete lunacy!"

Pushkaryov slapped the table with his palm. "Comrades, calm yourselves! It *is* a crazy idea, but I want to hear the admiral's thinking, nonetheless," he said, voice raised. He turned back to Shukshin. "This does sound suicidal, Admiral, but I have a feeling you've been thinking about it for a while. Perhaps there are mitigating factors, such that it's not as fanciful as it sounds. Please explain your idea."

"*Spasibo*, comrade Pushkaryov. It's not as dangerous a proposal as it sounds. For all our rhetoric to the contrary, the United States does not want a war with us. Do the imperialists love empire? Certainly they do. But war is expensive and they love their money even more than they love empire. When they are engaged in a conflict anywhere around the globe, many of their legislators in Congress, their Hollywood celebrities, their academics, and most of their media outlets agitate for a quick resolution, preferably a diplomatic one. My idea is counting on this fact.

"Assuming we can start a limited conventional conflict, as long as we don't back them into some sort of win-lose corner they'll bite on the offer of a diplomatic resolution. The engagement will be very bloody but very, very brief. Both sides will lose some assets, but I am convinced we will meet at the negotiating table very rapidly. But this, my comrades, just might be the price of saving our country from the disasters that Gorbachev is wreaking on us."

The gathered men sat in silence considering Shukshin's idea. It was a dangerous roll of the dice—a frightening proposal. It would initiate a hot confrontation with the world's other superpower. If they miscalculated it could easily go nuclear—a catastrophe in which there were no winners, only losers. Since the end of World War 2, a direct confrontation with the United States was precisely what the leaders of the USSR had been trying to avoid. It was one thing to conduct operations through proxies such as the North Koreans or the Nicaraguans, it was another thing entirely for Soviet units to face off directly with those of the United States.

Shukshin spoke up again. "What I propose is baiting them into an engagement between one of our submarines and one of their surface groups. We'll play it up in our media and stir up our citizens, *the imperialistic capitalists are acting as an international pariah, but the USSR will not be cowed.* Once there's been a little shooting, we'll explain it was all a mistake, that one of our commanders misinterpreted the intentions of a US vessel and launched a weapon. We'll propose that both sides stand down and cease fire. End of story; Gorbachev is gone and Pushkaryov becomes our new leader." Shukshin actually thought of himself as taking over but he was not about to say that. Perhaps a little accident could be arranged for Pushkaryov, or maybe he could be an unintended casualty of the coup.

"In your plan, do you anticipate any losses?" Aristov asked.

"Yes. I would expect a potential loss of one of our submarines—not a missile boat, mind you—and one of their surface combatants. A trade, if you will. But comrades, we could not expect such a plan to succeed without loss. What the *rodina* would gain would far outweigh the loss." What Shukshin did not say is that the surface combatant he had in mind was an aircraft carrier.

Pushkaryov stared at the navy man, considering the idea. It

was definitely risky. There were a hundred things that could go wrong. But there was also an attractive simplicity to the plan, and Pushkaryov had seen the country pull together before during times of crisis.

They discussed the proposal but decided not to pursue it at the present time. But the defense minister encouraged Shukshin to order the Pacific Fleet's submarines to take a more aggressive posture during their patrols. Perhaps the United States could be provoked into starting something.

****

Jake Kelly parked his new red Chevy pickup in the driveway of his one-story brick rancher and hopped out. Galina stuck her head out the door of the house and inquired, "Did you accomplish your mission?"

He grinned at his wife. "Mission accomplished, General. Where do you want this thing?" He'd been to the local Home Depot to pick up a barbecue grill.

Galina had taken to being a military wife like a fish to water. She was proud that her husband was serving her new country, a country she'd fallen in love with. She'd wanted to paint the American flag on one of the walls of their rental—thankfully, Jake had been able to talk her out of that and now it was a nice, fresh white. Every task was a "mission," as far as she was concerned.

"The back porch, of course, *Sokolov*," she teased, using the name Kelly's adversaries had given him during his escape from the Soviet Union. *Sokolov* meant falcon in Russian.

"Yes, sir. I mean, ma'am."

He lifted the big box from the bed of the pickup and carried it around back. Pulling a box cutter from his pocket, he sliced the box open and then groaned. Confronting him were multiple plastic bags of parts. He stood up and hollered at his wife who was in the kitchen with the window open, "Hey Galya, you might want to do the steaks in the oven. It's going to take me until midnight to put this thing together. It's got more parts than an F-16." He groaned again and went into the garage for his toolbox.

After the wedding Jake and Galina had taken an extended honeymoon in Florida. One of Galina's dreams was to visit Disney World. She'd heard fantastic stories of the Magic Kingdom when in the USSR and couldn't wait to see it. The reality outperformed the rumors. She was agog at the colors, the rides, the displays, the flowers—the entire scene. For a solid week they visited the resort until she'd finally had her fill. Next they spent several days at the museums in Cape Kennedy. They'd both hoped to witness a space shuttle launch but the craft wasn't scheduled to return to flight until September, having been grounded after the *Challenger* disaster in 1986. The remainder of their honeymoon was spent exploring the west coast of Florida all the way down to the Everglades.

On return to active duty Jake got his wish: he was reassigned to the "Rude Rams," the 34th Fighter Squadron stationed at Hill AFB, Utah. After a month of reacquainting himself with the F-16 and taking several checkrides, he was cleared to rejoin the squadron. Shortly after that the squadron leader was promoted out of the group and Kelly took his place.

The first three months after their wedding were pure bliss for the couple. The stress and heartache of the preceding two years was ebbing away, and they felt as if things had finally improved for good. They couldn't be happier.

Over a tasty meal of steak, potatoes and corn, the two lovers chatted happily about their new home and the amazing sequence of events that brought them together. Their improbable reunion, when Galina had lost all hope of ever seeing Jake again, made both of them think seriously about Bill Jensen's claims of divine providence. Then the conversation turned to what Galina wanted to do and see. Her first task was to secure a position teaching advanced mathematics at one of the public schools in the area. At the top of her list of things to see was a visit to the Grand Canyon and the Hoover Dam. Jake adored the fact that Galina was enthusiastic about everything. It made him see his country with fresh eyes, and he loved it.

After Jake cleared away the dishes, Galina brought out a small gift-wrapped box. She sat in his lap and gave the box to him.

"What's this, babe?"

"It's a gift, *Sokolov*. Only it's not for you."

He looked at her, confused. "Okay, what would you like me to do with it?"

"Open it, of course, silly," she said, eyes sparkling.

"But you just said it's not for me," he objected.

"That I did. Open it anyway."

He shrugged and tore away the wrapping paper. Inside were two tiny white baby shoes.

He stared at them for a moment before it hit him. He looked at Galya with mixed love and wonder, and asked, "Really?"

With an expression of pure delight, she nodded, "Really!"

****

The lethal black shadow glided silently two hundred feet beneath the cold waves of the Bering Sea. The USS *Honolulu*, SSN-718, was returning to Pearl after a long deployment. Twenty-four hours earlier the *Los Angeles*-class fast attack submarine had been stalking a Soviet ballistic missile submarine, hiding in the Delta III's baffles where the Russian's passive sonar could not detect her presence. Twelve hours ago the *Honolulu* broke off contact and ascended to periscope depth. After raising her AN/BRA-34 antenna and transmitting the contact report on the SSIXS (Submarine Satellite Information Exchange Subsystem), the *Honolulu* dove and continued the long transit back to Pearl.

Captain Roscoe Raines nodded at his XO (executive officer), Commander Larry "Bubba" Baker. "I'll be in my quarters, XO, pushing a pencil. You have the conn." Raines was a twenty-year veteran of the submarine service. His wife jokingly claimed that he had two brides, herself and the sea, and she came second.

Captain Raines's career was highly distinguished, a point

which led to the odd and contrary fact that a man of his rank and reputation was still commanding a fast-attack submarine —a job normally occupied by an O-5 (a commander), not an O-6 (a captain). But because of retirements and a shortage of submarine-qualified officers, Raines had been able to use his seniority and service record to request that he remain as the *Honolulu*'s captain for two more deployment cycles—this after he'd already completed two full deployments on the boat. In what qualified as a major miracle for the navy, his request was granted. Though he'd told no one except his wife, the day that he was promoted to a desk would be the day he'd put in for retirement.

"Aye, Skipper. I have the conn. Enjoy your report," Baker responded, snickering. Writing patrol reports was a stultifying exercise—at least, you wanted it to be. Exciting reports were usually associated with deployments on which very bad things had happened.

Baker looked over the busy control room team with great affection. It was a young crew—the first deployment for many —but they had performed well. The patrol and training objectives had been completely fulfilled, and the qualification goals for the enlisted men had been accomplished, plus some. The captain would have a stellar—if boring—report to submit to COMSUBPAC when they returned to Pearl.

"Conn, sonar. We've got an intermittent contact, bearing two-two-eight. Molly says the tonals sound like a submarine."

"Sonar, conn. Can you give me a probable range?" Baker asked.

"Negative, sir. It's too weak."

Captain Raines was in his stateroom working on the patrol report when the messenger of the watch tapped on his door. "Captain, the XO sends his respects and asks if you can come to the sonar room."

Raines stepped into the crowded sonar room and glanced at Baker. "What's up, XO?"

Baker motioned to the sonar operator. "Tell him, Molly."

Isaac Mulholland had acquired a well-deserved reputation for ferreting out submarine noise from even the faintest acoustical signals coming through the sub's various hydrophones and acoustic arrays. A concert-quality virtuoso on the cello, Mulholland was rumored to have perfect pitch. His sensitive hearing gave him a natural edge in sonar. Several years before, while the young man was acing every test at sonar school in Groton, he'd had an instructor who couldn't master the pronunciation of Mulholland, and thus the nickname "Molly" was born.

"Captain, up until three minutes ago we had seven surface contacts: four merchantmen, a Soviet trawler, and two small fishing vessels. But when we came off the sprint and began our drift, I picked up faint tonals along bearing two-two-eight. I think it's coming through the convergence zone, so it's probably a long way off. It's very faint, sir, but it sounds like a sub to me."

"Okay. How does SAPS identify it?" asked Raines. SAPS was the Signal Algorithmic Processing System software running on the BC-10 computer system, which analyzed underwater noises and sought to identify them. The navy maintained a growing database of the acoustical signatures of submarines, and SAPS had evolved to the point where, with good data, it could identify the class of a submarine contact and often the identity of the submarine itself.

"It's still chewing on it, Captain. The signal was probably too faint and too intermittent for the computer to get a handle on it."

"So, let me get this straight. SAPS can't figure it out, but you're sure it's a sub?"

Mulholland blanched. "Um, affirmative, Captain. It is a sub."

Raines grinned at the nervous sonar man. "Relax, Molly. Just checkin' to see if you're certain. You've not been wrong yet. Designate it and send it to fire control tracking."

"Aye, Captain. Designating as S-37, and sending it to fire control tracking."

Raines and Baker returned to the control room. Raines announced, "I have the conn, Commander Baker has the deck."

"I have the deck, aye, Captain," Baker acknowledged.

"Quartermaster of the Watch, have we cleared Stalemate Bank?" Raines queried. Stalemate Bank is an undersea bank sixty miles east of Attu Island in the Bering Sea that rises to within a few meters of the surface. The *Honolulu* skirted it to the east, but Raines wanted to make sure he had maneuvering room, if necessary.

"Affirmative, Captain. We cleared it," Petty Officer Yates checked the log, "about two minutes ago and are now transiting Stalemate Canyon."

In the sonar room, Petty Officer Mulholland pressed his headset to his ears as he studied the sonar display. He fiddled with a few knobs but finally shook his head and muttered to the sonar officer, "Lost him, sir."

"Conn, sonar. We've lost contact with S-37. Last bearing was two-three-zero."

"Sonar, conn, aye. Stay on your toes, I'm going to get you guys a little closer. Let's figure out who this guy is." Raines hung up the sound-powered phone and turned to Baker. "We're above the thermocline, XO. If we're hearing a signal that weak, then S-37 must be above the layer too."

"I agree, Skipper."

"Well, let's go deep and see if we can sneak up on him." Raines turned back to the control room. "What's the depth beneath the keel?"

The quartermaster of the watch checked the chart. "Nine thousand feet plus, Captain."

"Very well. Diving officer, make your depth six hundred feet."

"Six hundred feet, aye," answered the diving officer. He turned to the planesman. "Fifteen degrees down-angle on the planes."

"Fifteen degrees down, aye, sir."

After a moment the diving officer reported, "Our depth is six hundred feet, sir."

"Aye. Helm, come right to two-one-zero, all ahead flank."

"Coming right to new course two-one-zero, all ahead flank, aye, sir," replied the helmsman.

Raines turned to Baker. "XO, give us a thirty-minute sprint

on this heading, then drift and ease above the layer once you've streamed the TB-23 towed array. Let's see if we can pick up that contact again. I'll be in my stateroom pushing a pencil as you say. You have the conn."

"I have the conn, aye, Captain."

Thirty minutes later Raines returned to the control room just as Baker was issuing commands to begin the drift phase.

"Helm, all stop. Clear the baffles."

The helmsman brought the submarine to the right forty-five degrees until sonar reported the baffles clear.

The one place a submarine is deaf to the sounds of the sea as well as to potential enemies is directly behind it—a cone of silence known as the baffles. In order to detect threats directly to the rear, submarines will "clear the baffles," meaning they will periodically turn far enough off their course heading to listen along their back-trail, to see if they're being followed. If they are being stalked by an opponent who is following too closely, clearing the baffles can be a dangerous maneuver resulting in a collision, with the following submarine "rear-ending" the target it was following.

"Stream the TB-23," Baker commanded.

The TB-23 towed array is a passive sonar receptor on a very long tether. It is stored on reels in the ballast tanks, and can be towed a half mile behind the submarine. The tether includes an embedded coaxial cable carrying multiplexed data signals from the array's many hydrophones and other sensors to the submarine's sonar signal processing systems. The TB-23 provides the submarine with greatly enhanced underwater "ears," the only hitch being that aggressive maneuvering can damage it. If it's towed too slowly in shallow water, it can also snag on the seafloor. To prevent the possibility of unnecessary damage, the towed array is normally housed when a submarine is coming off patrol and transiting back to its home port.

Baker noticed the captain and nodded, acknowledging his presence, then directed, "Helm, resume course two-one-zero, make revolutions for three knots."

"Resuming course two-one-zero, making revolutions for

three knots, aye, sir."

"Diving officer, make your depth two hundred feet."

Slowly the submarine ascended through the thermocline, a horizontal layer created by a sharp change of seawater temperature within a relatively minor change in depth. The difference in temperature creates an acoustical barrier, such that weak sounds on one side of the layer don't pass readily to the other side. Submarines typically use the layer to hide.

The control room crew was silent, as though each man was holding his breath. Though they were not at wartime conditions, sneaking up on a Soviet submarine was always fraught with danger.

"Conn, sonar. Contact at bearing two-four-zero. I'm sure it's S-37, sir. It's definitely an Akula."

"Range?"

"Working on it, sir. Calculating by triangulation."

Baker shot a brief look at the captain and winked at him. Even though they were headed for the barn, the contact would give them an opportunity to exercise the crew one more time. *Practice makes perfect*, Baker thought to himself. "Battle stations, torpedo. Fire-control tracking party, I want a TMA (target motion analysis) on S-37 and a firing solution."

Raines pulled out a stopwatch and started timing the response. The tracking party hurried to their stations and began updating the Mark 117 fire-control computer with data from the target motion analyzer, itself being updated by the latest sonar data.

"Conn, sonar, based on the screw revolutions I have him at three knots. Reactor noises confirm that he's an Akula."

"Sonar, aye." Baker looked over the control room crew with satisfaction. They were professionals doing their job—no panic, no confusion, just quiet competence.

Raines stepped close to Baker, and whispered, "If he's just doing three knots, then he's up to something, Bubba. Either he thinks he's heard something—probably us—or he's trailing one of our boomers."

Baker nodded, and whispered back, "Or, we could have stumbled into the middle of a Russkie exercise."

"True."

"Sonar, report all contacts," Baker commanded.

"Conn, sonar. Three of the seven surface contacts have disappeared. I still have three noisy merchantmen, S-30, bearing zero-zero-zero, range twenty-seven thousand yards, S-31, bearing zero-four-five, range thirty-three thousand yards, and S-32, bearing zero-seven-three, range twenty-five thousand yards. The fishing vessels are off the scope, and the trawler is growing faint. He's S-29, bearing zero-one-zero, range estimated at fifty-five thousand yards. The only reason I can still hear him, sir, is because he's got a bad bearing on the prop shaft. All ranges are estimates by triangulation, sir. I have only one subsurface contact, S-37 at bearing two-four-zero. Still working on the range, sir."

Raines looked at Baker. "Not likely a Soviet exercise, XO. I think we'd be hearing more vessels."

"Aye, Skipper, I expect so. The Akula must have heard us as we were coming off our sprint."

The fire control coordinator turned in his seat toward Baker. "XO, S-37 is at range seven thousand yards, bearing two-four-zero. Target speed is three knots, sir, heading zero-four-five, depth one hundred eighty feet. I have a firing solution."

"Well done, tracking party," Raines said. "That took just," he paused as he examined his stopwatch, "ninety-three seconds. Very well done."

The men in the control room grinned at each other. Praise from the captain was hard-earned.

"Conn, sonar. Aspect on S-37 is changing. He's turning, sir."

"When he settles into his new course, give me a new firing solution, fire control," Baker said.

"Aye, sir."

"Meanwhile, let's try to hide. All stop."

"All stop, aye, sir" replied the helmsman.

Baker looked at the COB (chief of the boat) and said, "COB, rig ship for ultraquiet. Pass the word."

The momentum of the 6,000 ton attack submarine slowly

bled away, and the vessel came to a stop in the water.

"XO, S-37 is at range seven thousand yards, bearing two-three-eight. Target speed is three knots, sir, new heading is one-three-five, depth one hundred eighty feet. I have a firing solution," reported the fire control coordinator.

"He's on an intercept course, XO. He wants to get in behind us," murmured Raines.

"Aye, Captain," agreed Baker. "If we just hang loose and make like a hole in the water, he'll cross in front of us and we'll be on *his* tail instead."

The OOD stood next to Baker and said, "He must be flying blind, sir. He obviously can't hear us, because he wouldn't continue on this course if he did."

Baker nodded. "Good thought, OOD. The Akula has a towed array, but maybe his skipper doesn't have much confidence in it. Or maybe he doesn't trust his sonar operator. We're not moving and not making any noise, but he's acting like we're maintaining course and speed. Go figure."

For the next ten minutes the fire control tracking party continually updated the firing solution on the Akula as it proceeded on what its captain apparently thought was an intercept course.

And then what every submariner feared happened—unexpected noise. In the auxiliary machinery space aft of the torpedo room, a compressor on the air conditioning system which cooled the sonar equipment had a catastrophic failure. Suddenly it began making a noise like a small jackhammer. A crew member monitoring the equipment in the room shut it down within eight seconds, but the damage was done.

"COB, find out what that racket was, and see that it doesn't happen again!" growled Raines.

"Conn, sonar. Aspect on S-37 is changing again. Screw count is dropping. I think he's turning toward us, sir."

"He must have heard us," offered the OOD.

"Obviously," Baker said dryly. "He'd have to be deaf not to."

Suddenly a series of five pings reverberated against the hull.

"Conn, sonar. S-37 has gone active and is pinging us."

"Aye, Molly, I heard it. He's getting a fix on our position for his own firing solution," Baker replied. He turned to Raines, "He knew we were here, he just didn't know exactly where. Now he does."

Raines nodded without replying.

"XO, we have a new firing solution on S-37. Target's range is six thousand eight hundred yards, bearing two-three-six. Speed is zero, no doppler. Last known heading was one-three-five, depth one hundred eighty feet." reported the fire control coordinator.

"Conn, sonar. I'm picking up transients from the Akula. He's flooding his tubes and opening his outer doors."

"Sonar, conn. Molly, please verify that last." Baker's voice was calm and professional, but he was surprised. The Soviet's actions were extremely provocative: they'd stuck the revolver in *Honolulu*'s face, spun the cylinder, and the finger was slowly tightening on the trigger. Or to use another metaphor, it was a game of chicken and if no one blinked death and disaster would soon ensue.

"Conn, sonar. Aye, confirming that S-37 has flooded his tubes and opened his outer doors, sir."

Mulholland's voice carried a note of anxiety. Baker looked around the control room. Everyone was looking at him. Though they were each at their stations, ready to execute whatever orders were given, there was a hint of fear in the air. It was at times like this that their training kicked in and took over.

Raines stepped further into the control room. "XO, I have the conn."

"Aye, Skipper, you have the conn." As much as he tried to hide it, the relief on Baker's face was palpable.

"Fire control, firing point procedures tubes one and two. Match bearings on S-37. Flood tubes one and two, but do not, repeat, do not open outer doors," barked Raines.

"Flooding tubes one and two, aye, sir. Outer doors remain shut."

For a moment the control room was dead silent other than

the environmental systems and cooling fans on the equipment. The fire control officer, perspiration beading on his brow despite the comfortable temperature of the control room, stood looking at the captain.

Raines spoke very quietly, addressing the whole control room. "The captain of the Akula knows that we have an accurate firing solution, and he knows we have flooded our tubes. But if we open the outer doors, gentlemen, we just might start a war without meaning to. It's almost as though this character wants us to do just that. But we're not going to do it. No, we just sit tight."

A drop of sweat was forming on Baker's nose as the quiet continued in the control room. He wiped it off with the back of his hand. He was thankful Raines was in command. While Baker had played cat and mouse with the Soviets multiple times, his opponent had never taken such an aggressive posture.

Raines waited three minutes, then queried, "OOD, what are his and our positions relative to the thermocline."

"We're both above it. The layer is down at three hundred feet, Skipper."

"Very well. Let's get under the layer and see if we can disappear. Helmsman, come left to one-seven-zero, make revolutions for three knots. Make your depth six hundred feet. As long as he doesn't use his active sonar again, he'll think we're still right here—but we'll be long gone."

Once the *Honolulu* dropped below the layer, Raines secured from battle stations and set a new course for Pearl.

Chapter 3

Late August, 1988

Bill Jensen was sitting at his desk at CIA headquarters in Langley, Virginia, studying a classified analysis of the Soviet Union's economy. The report was written by Sam Bergman, the CIA's foremost analyst on the USSR. The most compelling part of the brief were the conclusions. Bergman was predicting that the unity of the Warsaw Pact countries was beginning to fracture as a result of Moscow's diminishing foreign aid handouts.

Bergman's take was that the inherent economic inefficiencies of communism were finally catching up with the Soviet Union—food and consumer goods were not the only thing in short supply. So was cash. The USSR had its own problems and found itself no longer able to prop up the dozen or so economies that were relying on its foreign aid packages.

The part that caught Jensen's eye was the paragraph in which Bergman speculated what the Politburo's response would be to the splintering union. Bergman was predicting a new era of military adventurism for the massive superpower, on the principle that even a fractious family unites when there is an external enemy.

Jensen reached for the phone and dialed the analyst's number. "Hi, Sam. Bill Jensen here. I just finished reading through your latest intelligence estimate on the USSR, and I was wondering if you had a few minutes to come up to my office and talk about it. You do? Good. See you in a few."

A few minutes later the analyst was standing at his door. "Come in, Sam. Coffee?" Jensen asked, pointing at his personal percolator. Technically he was not allowed to have his own office coffee maker, but it was one of those mind-numbing, petty, bureaucratic rules that Jensen ignored.

Bergman's eyes lit up. "Oh, you've got the good stuff! Sure, I'd love some. I see you're tired of the brown water from the dispenser down the hall."

Jensen poured them both a cup and then said, "Your analysis of what's going on with the Soviets is pretty impressive,

Sam. Where are you getting your data?"

"Much of it is open source, Bill, culled from *Pravda* and other newspapers in the major cities, especially the heavy manufacturing centers. I did use a detailed report of the Soviet Union's total manufacturing output for last year. It was prepared for the CPSU's central committee and contained data from across nearly every sector of their economy. I haven't a clue as to how we got our hands on it, but it was in the files and was very helpful. That's pretty much the only classified source material in my analysis." Bergman spooned some sugar into his coffee and took a sip.

"How about your conclusions, Sam? What led you to suggest that they might try to handle this problem by getting into some sort of military conflict?"

"That was an exercise of logic, Bill. The Soviet Union is collapsing on itself. The way their economic system is structured, they can't even feed their own people even though they have some of the richest farmland on the planet. But a collapse means that their entire ideology is flawed. Their economic structure is supposed to be several evolutionary steps advanced down the road from capitalism. If the USSR dies an economic death, it's pretty much a repudiation of their philosophy—something their hardliners will never accept.

"So, what are their options to keep the union from imploding?" the analyst asked rhetorically as he set his coffee mug on the end table. "Gorbachev is trying the smartest option. He's liberalizing and reducing the centrally planned control of the economy, granting more freedom and local control. That's what his *perestroika* is all about. But it's not going to work because he has two problems. First, it's too little, too late. Moribund socialist economies lack the dynamism to turn around quickly. Second, they haven't the foggiest idea how to manage—or better, how to get out of the way of a non-scripted supply-and-demand, profit-based economy. Rather than the producers responding to what the consumers want, they have a layer of elite bureaucrats telling the consumers what they *should* want. Their every instinct is central control, and so most of their adjustments made after *perestroika* was in place wound up being poison pills.

"So, Gorbachev's *perestroika*, while it's going in the right direction, can't work fast enough to save the union. What's left, then, is a military option. Military engagements are often used to distract a population from other problems. They can create a superficial, temporary unity that will last as long as the conflict does—so long as the conflict does not go on too long. If the conflict is large enough, it even holds the possibility of restructuring the belligerents in significant ways. For example, the US economy in the 1950s roared as a result of WW2 and Korea.

"In my opinion, a military engagement is probably the direction that Soviet hardliners will drive their nation." Bergman stopped and took a sip of his coffee.

"Who's the other party to the conflict? Who does their military engage? Us?" Jensen asked.

"I don't know. Probably not us. I think even their hardliners would realize that tackling the US would not be a good idea."

Jensen didn't respond at first. He sat staring out the window and then turned back to the analyst. "But what about Gorbachev? As the general secretary of the CPSU he wields enormous power. Under his direction their military is trying to extract itself from Afghanistan. There's not been any public saber-rattling. Their military has even been talking to our military on almost friendly terms."

Sam shook his head. "I fear for Gorbachev. I don't think he will last very long. People have a way of disappearing in the Soviet Union—even top leaders. I'm guessing that one of these days we'll hear that he's having 'health problems,' and he'll disappear from the public eye. Permanently."

Jensen nodded. "Yeah, I can see that happening. It's happened before." His intercom buzzed, and he picked up the handset. "What is it, Marge? No, I can't talk to him now. Tell him I'll call back. Make sure you get a number where I can reach him. Thanks."

Jensen turned back to Sam Bergman and asked, "So when do you think we'll see this military conflict?"

"I don't know. Hopefully I'm wrong about that."

"You're not wrong. You may be wrong about the *who*, but not about the *what*. You'll be interested in a call I received this morning from the director of the Office of Naval Intelligence (ONI). Seems that our sub drivers in the Pacific are reporting that Soviet sub drivers in the Pacific are getting very, very aggressive. ONI wants to know why, and they're wondering if we know anything."

****

The pain was excruciating—it felt sciatic. Anatoly Geredin knew that it was caused by the advance of his arthritis, but knowledge of the cause didn't ameliorate the pain. He groaned and rubbed his right hip. *I am but a shadow of what I used to be*, he thought dismally. He reached into his nightstand for the bottle of Ibuprofen and downed four of the extra strength pills. As a member of the *nomenklatura*, Geredin had a ready supply of American medications. It was one of the few privileges of his position that he did take advantage of.

There was a day when he was hailed as the most competent and dangerous field agent in the KGB. That day was long past. On the other hand, the vigor, strength and daring of his youth earned him a reputation that steadily elevated him in the ranks until he finally found himself at the top of the heap, directing the KGB.

He swung his legs over the bed. A cry of pain escaped his lips. He shook his head, ashamed of it, and struggled to stand. His bed was empty of any companion. His beloved wife had died suddenly eight years ago, and he'd never had the heart to take another woman. They were childless, and so Geredin was alone. *Not alone*, he thought. *Now I'm married to the* rodina, *and I shall die having been faithful to both my wives.*

Geredin was a man of rare integrity. Utterly incorruptible, he was a loyal Soviet patriot whose love of country, love of order and love of the communist political ideology ruled him and his actions. Geredin himself could not be bought, and he did not tolerate bribes, corruption, or the abuse of office. He was ruthless in the pursuit of his duties. His companions in the Politburo feared him for precisely this reason.

He was thought to be utterly cold. If the good of the *rodina* depended on the removal of someone standing in the way, Geredin would set up the assassination and never give it a second thought. His first loyalty was to the *rodina*, always the *rodina*.

But he was not cold. Geredin's second streak of unbreakable loyalty was to those who served him faithfully, to his friends, to his wife while she was alive. With these he was warmhearted, generous, tender, even sentimental. And such emotions were genuine for the man—they were not something for mere display, for public consumption.

On those terrible days when his two loyalties collided, the *rodina* always won. But if he had to sanction someone in his inner circle of loyalty, his first option would be exile. If exile was not workable, in Geredin's odd calculus of morality he would ensure that the death was as painless and merciful as possible. Murder with mercy. At some level it made sense to him—perhaps as the lesser of two evils.

He hated Gorbachev's policies. But he remained loyal to the man because he was convinced greater damage would be done by removing the general secretary. As a consequence, his top priority became protecting Mikhail Gorbachev from any threat to his leadership. It was a priority that would soon lead him to do something he never envisioned himself doing.

Geredin grasped his walker and stumbled toward the bathroom to begin his morning ablutions. No one but his housekeeper knew he used a walker, and she was sworn to secrecy. He needed it for the first hour or so after he arose until his old bones limbered up. After that he was able to get along with only his cane. An hour and a half later his driver was depositing him at the Lubyanka, and he took the elevator to his third-floor office. The steps were out of the question.

As he passed his secretary's desk, he barked, "Victor! I want to see Colonel Dobrynin immediately. Get him for me, please." He'd not meant to be so abrupt, but the pain had him in a bad mood. He disappeared into his office, closing the door behind him.

A few minutes later Colonel Vladimir Leonidovich Dobrynin, the chief of the Third Directorate, knocked on his door.

"Come in, Vlad. Tea?" Geredin asked.

"*Da. Spasibo*, Anatoly. What can I do for you, sir?"

"Give me your latest on our traitorous friend, Admiral Konstantin Grigoriyevich Shukshin. Have you been able to figure out what he is up to?"

"*Da*. We've known since his trip to Leningrad last winter that he is evaluating various naval officers for their political loyalty, with a special emphasis on the men who are working in the submarine service. But we did not know why he is doing this. Now we do. There is a group of high ranking leaders that are beginning to discuss overthrowing the general secretary.

"Two days ago a man in this cabal apparently got cold feet and contacted one of my agents. Not only has he told us what he knows, but he's agreed to continue participating in the plot as our informant."

"Who is it?"

"Yulian Semyonovich Churkin," Dobrynin sighed.

"Churkin, the interior minister?" Geredin asked, raising his bushy eyebrows. He'd not expected this.

"The same," Dobrynin affirmed. "And that's not all, sir. Shukshin appears to be something of a bit player. This plot goes much deeper, comrade. The leader of the group is none other than Pushkaryov himself."

Geredin set his tea down, surprised. He was about to respond when the pained look on Dobrynin's face told him that he hadn't heard the worst. "Speak, Vladimir. There's more to this, isn't there?"

Dobrynin nodded. "*Da*, Anatoly. They had a meeting last month that the premier approved—in complete innocence, I might add. He was told it was a problem-solving session. What he wasn't told by Pushkaryov was that the problem they were solving was Gorbachev. Fifty top men met, including the defense minister, the interior minister, the chief of the general staff of the armed forces, and Shukshin with a handful of top officers."

"How come I haven't heard about this before? We own Pushkaryov's bodyguard. Why aren't they coming forward with this information?" Geredin exclaimed, angry at this latest revelation.

"We believe they have been compromised, and then bribed by Pushkaryov, sir."

"Bring them in," growled Geredin. "I'll shoot them myself, right in this office."

"I don't think that's the best idea, sir. If we do that the whole movement will go underground. It's probably best that Pushkaryov doesn't know we are aware of his group."

Geredin sipped his tea, considering Dobrynin's response. Finally he nodded. "*Da*, you're right, Vlad. Besides, we have that lamb Churkin. He'll tell us everything."

"Well, there's a problem there, too. Although Churkin is in the inner circle of plotters, he suspects there is a smaller, closer group of advisors that meets with Pushkaryov. Churkin feels that he does not know all of their plans. We have no informant among that tighter group."

"That is a problem," Geredin agreed. He tugged at his lip, considering the matter. After a minute he turned back to his subordinate. "Contact Churkin. Tell him we need him to be the most loyal, enthusiastic member of the cabal. Tell him to attempt to work his way into the innermost circle. Is there anything else I should know?"

"*Da*. I was getting to that. The concern of the larger group, as of the last meeting, was that the military is not united and cannot be depended upon to support a coup. They plan to unite the armed forces, sir, by initiating a violent but limited engagement with the United States. Once that engagement happens, they believe the armed forces will draw together under their officers with the result that the plotters will have enough support to overthrow Gorbachev."

Geredin closed his eyes and shook his head. "These men are hooligans, Vlad, street thugs in cheap suits. Do they really think they will be able to start a shooting war with the United

States and control its outcome? They are idiots."

"The plan was Admiral Shukshin's, sir. Apparently he thinks it is possible. Churkin said that the group did not approve of Shukshin's plan—not yet, anyway. But they did decide to instruct the captains of the Pacific Fleet to show more aggression against the US navy. Churkin also said Shukshin would be delighted if they could provoke the Americans to fire a shot."

The two men discussed the problem for another twenty minutes. As they concluded, Geredin stood and placed his hand on his deputy's shoulder. "Vladimir Leonidovich, trust no one. These men have created a cancer and we have no idea how far it has spread. You handle Churkin yourself, as his case agent. Do not let anyone else take him into confidence. Identify ten agents you can trust with your life, men who will follow your orders without question. Don't brief them—just in case—but keep them close. Replace my entire bodyguard—driver included—and yours as well, with these ten men. See that they sweep our homes, offices and cars daily for bugs. I suspect our regular staff has already been compromised, so just reassign them to cases unrelated to this one.

"This is going to require me to disappear for a week. I need to recruit some help that I can trust, and I know just the man. Make preparations for a vacation, a week-long fishing trip to somewhere on the Chukchi Peninsula, somewhere remote. Invite me, publicly, to go with you. Just you and me—no staff."

Dobrynin grinned. "Anatoly, why do I get the feeling that I'm going to be fishing by myself on this trip?"

Geredin just smiled at him. "Vlad, I believe you have a lot of work to do. Best get at it."

****

Jake trotted down the flight line to his F-16C as the eastern horizon blazed orange with the sunrise. He walked around the fighter and inspected the weapons loadout. Four of the hardpoints contained Lockheed Martin wind-corrected munitions dispensers loaded with the *Hydra* anti-tank guided cluster munitions, an experimental weapon system for which Kelly had been the chief test pilot. Another hardpoint contained a battle-damage-assessment camera pod. The rest were empty.

The *Hydra* weapon was just entering production, and Kelly's unit was flying a training airstrike on four squadrons of M1A1 Abrams tanks maneuvering on the Barry M. Goldwater Air Force Range, in the south of Arizona. The shaped high-explosives had been removed from the munitions, and each was loaded instead with a bladder of paint to mark its strike.

Kelly performed a walk-around of his fighter to ensure that the weapons pods were each painted with an orange stripe, signifying that they were harmless test munitions. The rest of his squadron were conducting the same inspection of their fighters.

"Good morning, Major," his crew chief greeted him.

"Morning, Joe. Did you check the oil and rotate the tires?" Kelly kidded.

"Always, sir. Your windshield wipers are looking a little worn, though. We're running a special deal on them—only cost you about $2000 to change 'em. What do you say, sir?"

Kelly made a show of craning his neck and checking the blue sky overhead. "Naah. Not gonna rain today. Maybe next time." Kelly enjoyed the light-hearted banter with the technical sergeant serving as his crew chief. Joe Ryder was one of the best—nothing escaped his careful eye. Kelly had complete confidence in him. "Everything check out okay, Joe?"

"Yes, sir. We replaced the ejection seat yesterday—the ACES II pitch stabilization unit looked a little flaky under test, so we yanked the whole assembly and replaced it. Everything else looks primo, Major."

"Excellent." He checked his watch. "Time to saddle up. No rest for the wicked, Joe."

Ryder laughed. "No, sir."

Kelly walked around to the boarding ladder, slung his flight bag over his shoulder and started to climb. He was at the third step when his peripheral vision began shimmering. It made him dizzy so he stopped climbing and hung on to the ladder. Suddenly there was a loud roaring in his ears, and his whole body started shaking.

Ryder noticed Kelly's hesitation. "Sir, are you okay? Major Kelly?" He stepped to the foot of the ladder just in time to break Kelly's fall. Both men fell to the ground. Kelly was jerking and shaking uncontrollably. His eyes were wide open, but he was unseeing and completely unresponsive. Ryder realized the man was having a seizure of some sort and radioed for an ambulance.

Kelly came to in a bed in the base infirmary. The room was crowded, Galina was seated at his side holding his hand, and a doctor and three nurses were attending him. He had an IV drip, was connected to a heart monitor, and had some sort of sensor attached to his head. He was confused—the last thing he remembered was climbing the boarding ladder.

"What happened?" he croaked.

"That's what we want to know, young man. As of this moment, we don't have a clue other than to say you've had a seizure. Your blood pressure is high and your pulse rate is a little fast, but everything else looks normal. I've ordered blood tests and a CAT scan. Until I get the results back, you're staying right here, Major."

****

The phone on Jensen's desk rang. He groaned and set down the report he was reading. "Jensen here," he said crisply.

"Bill, I need you to come up to my office," said the voice on the other end. It was Paul West, the Director of Central Intelligence (DCI). The tone of his voice was so serious it made Bill wonder what was up. Whatever it was, it couldn't be good.

"I'm on my way, sir." Jensen hung up the phone, gathered the classified material from his desk and locked it in his safe.

"What's up, Paul?" he asked as he entered the DCI's office.

"Shut the door, Bill, and have a seat. As you know, Murphy McCallister has been on vacation this week. He was playing tennis with his wife this morning and had a heart attack. I got a phone call an hour ago, Bill. Murph is dead."

McCallister was the Deputy Director for Operations (DDO) at the CIA. A former field agent who spent many years undercover in various Soviet bloc nations, McCallister's name was near legend. A terrible injury ended his field service, but it wasn't long before McCallister had worked his way up to the office of DDO, a position he occupied for over twenty years. He was loved because he cared for his people and never abandoned an agent in the field, mounting daring extraction operations to retrieve his agents if they found themselves compromised or exposed.

When Jensen turned in his resignation ten years before, it was McCallister who talked him out of it. Jensen had spent years managing field agents and highly placed contacts spread across Cambodia, Vietnam, Thailand, and China. He'd landed in more secret, short landing strips in the jungles of southeast Asia than he cared to remember. Fluent in Russian, Chinese, Vietnamese and Hindi, Jensen was regarded as a high-value operative. When he turned in his resignation, he was planning to devote himself full-time to his first love—teaching political science at Georgetown University.

But McCallister could not bear to lose him, and so had created a position out of thin air just for Bill Jensen—Special Assistant to the DDO. In that role Jensen would work on selected black projects for the DDO. McCallister had assured him he'd be able to teach at least half-time. The Agency would use his professorship at Georgetown as his non-official cover. Jensen bit on the offer and had stayed with the CIA ever since.

"Dead?" Jensen repeated, shocked. "It can't be! He was just three months from retirement."

"I know—it's terrible. Why does it seem that the paper-pushers retire and live forever on fat pensions, but the patriots who sacrificed so much and gave heart and soul to the country don't even get to enjoy a well deserved rest? It's just not right." West shook his head. After a moment of silence, he added, "I've sent a plane to pick up Dorothy and the body. It's the least we could do."

Jensen nodded. He fought the lump forming in his throat. "Yeah. Good of you, Paul—it will mean a lot to Dorothy. And both Murphy and Dorothy know Christ, Paul, so he's with Jesus. That will be some comfort to her."

Paul looked down at his desk, reluctant to bring up the next matter so soon after McCallister's death. "Bill, I know this is a terrible time for you. I know you and Murph were really close, but I need you here. Even while we grieve Murphy's passing, the bad guys are still doing their thing and this old world is not running on kindness. I need you here, Bill, at the Agency."

Jensen looked up, confused. "I'm not planning on leaving the Agency anytime soon. You don't need to worry, Paul."

"Good, because I am appointing you acting DDO, effective immediately. I expect the president to approve the appointment when I get a chance to speak to him, and at that point you'll be the permanent DDO."

Chapter 4

Early September, 1988

Geredin and Dobrynin stood next to a small pile of luggage in the Sheremetyevo International Airport in Khimki, about eighteen miles northwest of Moscow. Fishing rod cases and duffel bags of outdoor gear were mounded around their feet.

"I cannot walk far, Vlad. I trust you have found us a spot near the water," Geredin commented as he watched a pair of skycaps tag the baggage and carry it off.

"Better than that, Anatoly. I've secured a place with a boat. You won't have to walk. It's the perfect spot—the trout will jump into your net. You won't even have to wet a line."

Geredin had already spotted two tails who were attempting to look like normal travelers but doing an exceedingly poor job of it. He murmured to Dobrynin, "There's a pair of minders behind you. One at the newsstand and the other sitting on a bench pretending to read a paper."

Dobrynin guffawed loudly as though Geredin had told him a joke. He leaned in and whispered, "I know. We've been tailed ever since we left your flat."

Geredin chuckled, keeping up the appearance of mirth. "Those arrogant young pups. We could lose them through fieldcraft, or I could just accost them and send them home."

"It would be more fun to confront them."

"*Da, davay!*"

Geredin hobbled over to the newsstand as though to buy a paper, and Dobrynin walked down the concourse, passing the man on the bench as though headed for the men's bathroom.

As the old spy looked over the racks of publications, he casually stepped closer to the minder. When he was only a few feet away he turned to the man and flashed his credentials.

"KGB. May I see your papers?"

The color drained from the young agent's face and he stammered, "Certainly, comrade." He nervously felt his pockets and pulled out his cover identification, not his true KGB identification. Geredin glanced at it and then called out sharply, "Security!"

One of the ubiquitous *militsiya* rushed over and demanded, "What is going on here?"

As soon as he saw his companion accosted, the other young agent sprang off the bench and tried to disappear into the airport crowd. Dobrynin was waiting right behind the bench and caught the young man's arm. "Not so fast, comrade. Come, take a little walk with me over to the newsstand, and let's see what the excitement is all about."

Geredin turned to face the policeman and displayed his credentials. "I am General Anatoly Geredin, the chairman of the *Komitet Gosudarstvennoy Bezopasnosti* (KGB). This is Colonel Vladimir Dobrynin, chief of the Third Directorate of the KGB. I suspect that these two men are foreign intelligence agents. They have been following us since we left my house this morning. Arrest them and take them to the Lubyanka for interrogation."

"No!" protested one of the men. "There has been a mistake! We, too, are agents with the Committee for State Security."

"Indeed? Then who ordered you to follow us?" Dobrynin snapped. When the men did not respond, Dobrynin said to the police officer. "They probably do possess forged KGB credentials. Take these men out of our sight. Do not let them communicate with anyone. Turn them over to the KGB."

As the two were marched away, Dobrynin grinned at his companion. Geredin said, "You know that we'll have new ones on us as soon as we land in Khabarovsk."

"*Pravda.* We'll shake 'em, Anatoly."

And shake them they did. That evening as Dobrynin flew to Sokol, Geredin boarded a flight for Tokyo on false credentials. After passing through customs he boarded a flight for Melbourne on a different passport, and from there to Detroit. Once through customs in Detroit he flew to Dulles posing as an American citizen.

****

Galina heard Jake's truck pull in the driveway, which was odd because it was only nine-thirty. He wasn't due home until after five-thirty. It became odder still when, ten minutes later, he'd not yet come in the door. When Jake failed to appear she walked into the living room and looked out the window. Jake was sitting in his truck, head down.

Curious, she walked outside to the driver's side window. "*Sokolov*," she asked softly, "are you okay?"

"Yeah," he answered, looking away, "I'm okay." His voice was flat, his face rigid, and he wouldn't look at her.

"What's wrong, honey?"

"Nothing."

She walked around the truck and entered the passenger side. He turned his face away. She reached out and caressed his shoulder, and felt the tension in his muscles.

"Tell me," she said, gently pulling his face toward hers.

"They revoked my flight clearance for medical reasons, because of the seizure I had last week."

"What does that mean?" she asked.

"It means I can't fly! What do you think it means?" he snapped.

She drew back as if struck. "I am very sorry to hear that, Jacob. When you can speak to me politely, come inside. Otherwise, please stay in the truck." She exited the vehicle and went into the house, stiff with hurt and anger.

An hour later he entered and stood silently at the kitchen door as she washed dishes. Neither of them said anything until he said softly, "I'm sorry, babe. I should not have spoken to you that way."

"No, you should not have, Jacob. Whatever is going on, it's not me you're angry at, and I will not have you speak to me that way." She busied herself for a few more minutes, ignoring him.

Finally she relented. "Sit down," she said, setting a glass of ice water in front of him. "Tell me what happened, and then tell me what it means."

"Not a whole lot to tell. When I got to the base this morning the wing commander called me into his office and said my flight clearance was being revoked for medical reasons. He said it was for my protection, as well as for the safety of others. If I had a seizure like that in the cockpit, I'd crash and kill myself and anyone on the ground who happened to be in the way. If I was flying in formation, I could bring down the aircraft flying with me." Kelly sighed, and took a long swallow of water.

"Sweetheart, I don't know anything about flying, but those sound like reasonable concerns."

He smiled grimly at her. "That's just it—they are reasonable concerns. I could do all kinds of damage if I lost it over a city. I have no argument against the concerns. I just can't stand the thought that I'm grounded. If they can't figure out why I had that episode I'll be grounded permanently. That's both air force and FAA regulations. I'm finished, Galya, I don't know what I'll do."

"They're going to make you leave the air force?" she asked.

"No, no, they won't do that. But I'll be reassigned to a desk job, probably in squadron operations. I don't want to fly a desk, fill out forms, push paperclips. I'll go nuts. I can't do it, Galya."

"*Sokolov*, you won't know if you hate something until you try it. At least give desk duty a chance," she urged.

He shook his head, staring distantly out the window. "No," he said. "If I'm grounded permanently, I'm going to resign my commission, find something else to do."

****

It was a sunny Saturday morning in late September. The leaves on the sycamores, silver maples, and tulip poplars lining the old C&O Canal towpath had not yet turned, but they were already taking on a more dusky color. There was a bit of a snap to the early morning air as Bill Jensen finished his eight-mile run and walked back to his car in the Great Falls Visitor Center parking lot. He toweled the sweat off his face and retrieved his thermos of coffee and the morning newspaper from the car. After locking it he walked over to a bench on the towpath.

Jensen poured himself a cup of coffee and opened the *Washington Post*. When he looked up, standing in front of him was an old man with dark, bushy eyebrows. The fellow was leaning on a cane.

"Good morning, Dr. Jensen," the old man said pleasantly.

"Anatoly Geredin!" Jensen exclaimed. He stuttered for a moment, trying to recover from the shock at seeing his nemesis, the director of the KGB, standing right in front of him. "I —I must say, ah, this, this is most unexpected. I did not know you were in the country."

"Indeed. I did not intend for your people nor my people to know where I am, Dr. Jensen. Spies are such nosy people, are they not? Perhaps you and I could keep this visit as our little secret, eh?"

Jensen shrugged. "Perhaps. Why are you here?" He hadn't meant to sound abrupt. He was still trying to collect his thoughts and make sense of Geredin's surprise appearance.

"Are you going to invite me to sit down? My arthritis makes it difficult to stand for long periods."

"Oh! Forgive me, I am forgetting my manners. Please, do be seated. So, what brings you to Great Falls this morning, Mr. Geredin?"

"I wanted to meet you here, Dr. Jensen, where we could talk freely—without any prying ears."

"Meet me? Well, then—I'm somewhat confused. Why is the head of the Soviet KGB calling on a lowly professor of political science?"

"Dr. Jensen, shall we dispense with pretense? You are not a 'lowly professor of political science,' as you put it. You are the new deputy director for operations, CIA. Or, I should say, *acting* DDO. Congratulations, by the way, on your promotion. It is well deserved."

Jensen dipped his head in acknowledgment of the compliment. "Thank you, sir."

Geredin added, "I was truly sorry to hear of comrade Mc-Callister's untimely death—he was a worthy opponent. The passing of my enemies tells me that my time, too, must be drawing near."

A sad smile creased Jensen's face. "He was a great man and a good friend. I shall miss him."

The two men sat silently on the bench, enjoying the morning sun. Jensen's mind was racing. Geredin knew too many details about what was going on at the Agency. Then, in retrospect he realized, *No, most of what he's mentioned today he could find in the papers. Still, I wonder how he arrived in Washington undetected. In any case, it's not every day I have immediate, unfiltered access to Geredin. Let's ride this horse for a while and see where he's heading.*

Jensen turned and nodded at the old man. "Okay, you win, Mr. Geredin. No pretense. Given the level of information you already possess, I suppose asking how you found me here would be a superfluous question."

"Oh, we know all about you and your habits, Dr. Jensen, down to the flavor of your favorite ice cream."

"Really? What is it?"

"Chocolate."

"Ah. Correct. So, are you hoping to turn me by the offer of a lifetime supply of chocolate ice cream?"

Geredin chuckled as he painfully straightened his left leg. "I wish recruitment were that easy, Dr. Jensen. No, I am here on much more serious business. I'm here to stop a war—a war between your country and mine."

"I hadn't heard that we were at war, sir. But you've got my attention—please explain."

Geredin sighed. "Perhaps I'd best put all my cards on the table, as you say in your country. Dr. Jensen, let us not kid ourselves: enemies we are and enemies we shall remain. I would betray your trust in a heartbeat if I thought it would help my country. I am here to preserve my country from madmen. I must talk to someone I can trust, which explains my visit today. I trust you as my enemy, in the sense that I trust you will do what is best for your country, even as I will do the same for mine. In this particular matter the true interests of our countries are aligned; they are, in fact, the same."

"Why can't you trust your own people, Mr. Geredin? You are, after all, at the top of the heap. You're a member of the

Politburo, one of the *nomenklatura*, and the head of the KGB. People live and die at your command."

Geredin was silent for a moment, then sighed. "My own intelligence community is badly divided over the question of Mikhail Gorbachev's reforms. As you know, Dr. Jensen, Gorbachev represents a liberalizing element in our country. Some welcome this. Some hate it. *Perestroika* and *glasnost* are not seen as good things by many in the Soviet Union. The KGB itself is split, as is the Politburo. No one really knows where anyone else stands. This is why our meeting must remain secret. Even the powerful head of the KGB would be executed if others thought he was betraying the *rodina*. You must understand, Jensen, I am *not* betraying the *rodina*, I am trying to save it."

"Why would you think I have any interest in helping you 'save' the Soviet Union, Mr. Geredin? While I wish no ill to the Russian people, it is my fondest dream that the Soviet government will collapse."

"You should be more careful what you wish for, my comrade," Geredin rejoined sharply. "Surely you realize what would happen to thousands of Soviet nuclear warheads should my government cease to exist? My country would become the world's largest and most lethal weapons bazaar, selling tanks, ships, aircraft, submarines, missiles, warheads and arms of all sorts to the highest bidder. Is that really what you wish for, Dr. Jensen?"

"Of course I realize that, and no, I don't want to see the USSR turned into a giant arms market. But given the state of the Soviet economy, that's going to happen even if your government does not collapse. The unchecked proliferation of lethal weaponry will create a whole new set of challenges for the United States, not to speak of the whole world. The moral responsibility for that problem will rest on your shoulders, however, not ours."

"I did not come here to debate morality with you, Dr. Jensen," Geredin snapped. "I came to warn you."

"Yes, of course—forgive me. Please continue, Mr. Geredin."

"Amidst the turmoil in my country, a significant faction has begun plotting the overthrow of the general secretary. They have the support of significant elements of our military. That's why I had to come to you myself and could not send this message through channels. If it were intercepted, I would be a dead man. I cannot afford to show my hand in my country."

Jensen looked at his opponent and shook his head. "You're not really expecting me to believe you, are you? I might be new in this position but I'm not exactly wet behind the ears."

"Of course not! I expect you to verify everything through your own intelligence channels. But even with well placed assets that will take time, and by then it may be too late."

"So what's the message that brought you here, the message that's so explosive you can't even entrust it to normal channels?"

"The submarine commanders of the Soviet Pacific Fleet have been instructed to aggressively engage your navy in the Pacific. They are under strict orders not to fire first, but they are to do everything possible to provoke your ships and submarines into firing. The conspirators believe that if the US engages our ships, the Soviet military will pull together, the general secretary's ideas will be exposed as dangerous, and the coup plotters will have the unity they need to overthrow Gorbachev."

Jensen blinked. The matter of the recent aggressive behavior of Soviet fast-attack submarines in the Pacific was exactly what the ONI was puzzling over. It was particularly odd that their compatriots in the Atlantic were not following suit.

"I see," Jensen responded noncommittally. "So, why are you telling me this? What's your angle, Geredin?"

Geredin exhaled noisily. "Dr. Jensen, I do not like comrade Gorbachev's policies myself. I believe they are damaging the *rodina*. But I fear much greater damage to the country if he is overthrown. And if a conflict with the US begins, unlike the coup plotters, I do not believe it will be so easy to confine it to a few ships in the Pacific. If these men pull off what they intend, the result will surely be far more destructive than they intend—we'll be staring down the barrel of World War 3.

"My angle, as you put it, is to stop this madness—I'm trying to stop a war."

Jensen stared at the man. If Geredin was telling the truth about the plot against Gorbachev and the manner in which it would unfold, then he was also right about the ultimate result.

Geredin grabbed his arm and urged vehemently, "Dr. Jensen, the US navy must not fire first! You must get this word to your naval commanders!"

****

Jensen sat in his vehicle and picked up the handset of his car phone. He dialed Sam Bergman's number.

"Sam, this is Bill Jensen. Look, I know it's Saturday, but I need you to drop whatever you're doing and meet me in my office in thirty minutes."

When Jensen arrived, Sam was waiting outside his office door in a pair of ragged jeans and grass-covered sneakers. "Sorry, Bill, I was mowing the lawn when you called."

"Don't worry about it—I'm still in my running gear, as you see." He unlocked his office. "Come on in. Have a seat." He sat down behind his desk, and shook his head. "You're not going to believe this. I'm not sure I do. Guess who I just met at Great Falls."

Bergman shrugged, "Well, it must be somebody big. Umm, the president?"

"No. Anatoly Geredin."

"No way! I didn't even know that he was in the country."

"Neither do his own people."

Bergman raised his eyebrows. "Really? Okay, this has got to be good. I'm assuming you called me here to tell me the story."

"He just confirmed nearly every point in your intelligence estimate, Sam. He claims the government—including the KGB—is split between pro- and anti-Gorbachev factions. The anti-Gorbachev faction is going to pull off a coup against the general secretary—but they don't feel they have enough support from the military—yet. So in order to unite the military around their agenda, they're going to start a limited engagement with the US navy in the Pacific. At least, they're hoping it will be limited. Their sub drivers have been ordered to get aggressive—to do everything short of launching a weapon. He says they're trying to provoke us into shooting first."

"Which confirms what the ONI told you."

"Precisely."

Bergman laced his fingers together behind his head, sat back on the couch, and stared at the ceiling. He was silent for a moment, thinking. "You said not even his own people know he's here. Why?"

"He says his life would be in danger if they knew he was talking to me. If the KGB itself really is split over Gorbachev, then he's probably right. If they're going to knock off one guy in a high position, why not two?"

Bergman nodded. "Okay, I can buy that. But didn't our people pick him up when he entered the country?"

"Nope. I'm not surprised he got past us. He's a wily old bear. Geredin is one of the best in the business."

"So, do you believe him?"

Jensen turned and looked out the window. "Don't know. He's insistent that I warn our commanders not to respond to the aggression. Geredin says their boys won't launch, and he's begging me to tell our boys not to launch either.

"In some ways his story matches what we're hearing from ONI, but that could all be one big charade that Geredin is orchestrating. He could be mesmerizing us with the left hand so we don't notice the right hand picking our pocket."

"That's definitely possible," agreed the analyst. "For disinformation to be effective it must not only appear to be true, most of it must, in fact, be true."

Jensen chuckled. "Is that Sam Bergman's *First Law of Intelligence Analysis*?"

Sam smiled. "As a matter of fact, it is."

Jensen turned back to the window. "A trusting soul might figure that Geredin is being a good citizen of the world, warning us about a nefarious plot that aims to trick us into starting a war. A more cynical soul—such as myself—would wonder if Geredin and the Soviet navy are trying to work themselves into a position to take a free shot at one of our ships—such as an aircraft carrier."

"The same thought crossed my mind, Bill."

"What to do?" murmured Jensen, staring out the window. He was silent for a moment, then turned back to Bergman. "Sam, let's put that analytical brain of yours to work. I'll give your boss in the Intelligence Directorate a call and get you freed up to work with me on this. That okay with you?"

"Sure. It's an an interesting project with potentially huge consequences. I'll be glad to work with you on it."

"Good. If I get the okay from your boss, I want you to comb through all the data you can find, especially from the Pacific Fleet's submarine bases at Vladivostok, Sovetskaya Ga-van, Magadan and Petropavlovsk. See if anything turns up.

"Are you still, um, hanging around with that translator in the NSA? What's her name?"

Bergman blushed. "Stinson, Evelyn Stinson. Not really. She's had a lot going on since last December, and so have I, and, well, . . . no. I've not had much contact with her."

"Would it be a problem for you to work with her again, would that make you uncomfortable?"

"Oh! No, not at all," Bergman responded, a little too quickly.

A hint of a smile flickered on Jensen's face, and then he looked grave. "Well, it really wouldn't matter anyway. This is a critical project. I'll call her supervisor—I want her to focus on transmissions coming from those submarine bases. I want her to contact you directly with anything—and I mean anything—coming from the Soviet Pacific Fleet.

"In the meantime, I'll bring this to the attention of the DCI. He'll have to take it to the president and the National Security Council. What they do with this information is above my pay grade."

Chapter 5

Late September, 1988

Geredin's meeting with Jensen kicked over a hornet's nest in the CIA, with the result that an emergency session of the National Security Council (NSC) was called. The NSC is normally chaired by the president himself, but the president's developing health concerns made it necessary for him to delegate that task to the vice president.

"Mr. Vice President, council members, an extraordinary meeting—an unplanned meeting—took place the day before yesterday. Put the slide up, please . . . thank you. This is Anatoly Geredin, the head of the Soviet KGB. At some point in the last few days he was able to enter our country undetected, obviously under false credentials. Two days ago he sought out the acting DDO CIA, Dr. William Jensen, while Jensen was at Great Falls. Geredin delivered a message to him, the content of which explains this emergency session of the National Security Council. With the permission of the vice president's chief of staff, I've invited Dr. Jensen here to relate that message to us. Please proceed, Dr. Jensen." Paul West, the DCI, took his seat and motioned for Jensen to take the podium.

"Thank you, sir. As each of you know, Mikhail Gorbachev has implemented two major policy changes in an effort to revitalize the faltering economy of the Soviet Union: *perestroika* and *glasnost*. These policies are opposed by the communist old guard and as a consequence are beginning to split the Soviet *nomenklatura* into pro- and anti-Gorbachev factions. Geredin came to warn me that this division has become critical, to the point that the anti-Gorbachev faction is seriously plotting a coup. While Geredin himself aligns with the communist old guard and not with Gorbachev's attempt to liberalize Soviet policy, he believes a coup will do far more damage than good. He's completely opposed to it.

"According to Geredin, the cabal plotting the coup does not yet believe they have sufficient support from the military to pull it off. Therefore, acting on the assumption that a military unites when it's under attack, the insurgents are planning to create what the KGB director described as a 'limited naval engagement.' They believe the Soviet armed forces will unite around the putsch if they come under a foreign threat.

"Even if Gorbachev is deposed and the hardliners take over, other than sending relations between our countries back into the deep freeze, the effect on the US would be negligible. We can afford it; they cannot. Their economy is in a shambles. However, this delusional thinking about a 'limited naval engagement' poses a real danger."

The vice president held up his hands. "Whoa! Stop. I feel like I've just stepped from reality into the twilight zone. Let me get this straight: you're saying that the head of the Soviet KGB just happens to bump into you at Great Falls, and he proceeds to sell out his country by bringing you up to date on secret behind-the-scenes machinations of different factions of the Politburo? Really?"

"Mr. Vice President, if this seems a little like Alice in Wonderland to you, imagine how I felt when I looked up from my newspaper and found Geredin studying me. It was so disorienting I had to scramble to control my reactions.

"You must understand, however, sir, that Geredin sees himself as patriot, not a traitor. He does not feel that he is betraying his country by sharing this information, but is rather saving it from madmen. He would move heaven and earth, if you will, to *avoid* any sort of hot engagement with the US."

"Wait! Did I just hear you correctly? Are you saying that the coup plotters intend to start something with the United States?" interrupted Walter Atkins, the secretary of state.

"Yes, sir, that is correct. They plan on initiating a naval conflict with the United States. That's why we're meeting today."

"That's crazy! We'll blow 'em out of the water. We'll 'limit' the engagement to the destruction of their entire rusting navy!" growled Stanton Washburn, chief of staff of the air force.

The secretary of state shook his head. "General, please. We're not facing the same Soviet navy we were ten years ago. Their capacity has been sufficiently upgraded—as Admiral

Feldstein can undoubtedly share with us. And besides, if they were to attempt such a precipitous action, we don't want to be the ones who push it over the brink." He turned back to Jensen and asked, "Dr. Jensen, do you find Geredin's message credible?"

"Mr. Secretary, the CIA is not ready to accept Geredin's statement at face value. We are putting together a team of analysts and field agents to assess the reliability of the information. We're calling this effort Operation *Zephyr*. But whatever *Zephyr* might turn up, we do have a piece of apparently corroborating information that Admiral Feldstein can comment on. Geredin said that the commanders of their Pacific Fleet have been instructed to become highly aggressive in confronting our ships. It seems they are trying to bait us into taking the first shot, to give them some diplomatic cover when and if a general engagement ensues. In other words, they want us to be seen as the aggressor. The ONI has verified that Soviet sub drivers are getting uncharacteristically aggressive. Admiral Feldstein, would you care to comment on that?"

Feldstein, who was serving as chairman of the joint chiefs, nodded. "Yes, I certainly can. We've had several contacts with Soviet submarines in which they flooded their torpedo tubes and opened their outer doors. That's extremely provocative and is generally interpreted as telegraphing the intention to launch a weapon. It is simply not done in peacetime except in war games and training, and never in proximity to a potential hostile. The fact that there's not already been an incident can be credited to the courage and restraint of the captains of our own submarines. We've also had two incidents between our surface ships that have led to near collisions. A curious point is that all these incidents have occurred in the Pacific. We are not seeing any commensurate challenges from the Soviet Northern Fleet."

"Is it possible," asked the national security advisor, "that the coup plotters are more heavily represented in the Pacific Fleet?"

Jensen answered, "Yes, sir, that is the theory we are currently pursuing. I should also add that Geredin virtually begged me to warn our commanders not to fire first. Of course, passing any such messages along to our naval officers is not my prerogative."

The secretary of defense, Melvin Smithson, was silent up to this point but now turned to Jensen and asked, "Have you considered that Geredin might be taking you for a ride, Dr. Jensen? Perhaps he's hoping that—based on his 'warning'—we will allow Soviet warships to get close enough to our own vessels, say, a carrier battle group, so that they can launch a crippling first strike?"

Jensen nodded. "Yes, Mr. Secretary, that is one of our primary concerns."

The vice president tapped his pen lightly on the table. He had a habit of doing that when he was about to speak. Everyone looked at him and waited. "Dr. Jensen, I think we are all aware of the Soviet skill in disinformation. Aside from all the reasons not to believe Mr. Geredin, do you see anything that would perhaps lead us to believe that he is telling the truth and is actually trying to prevent a military engagement?"

Jensen was silent for a moment, looking down at his notes. He knew this question would be coming and had spent several hours deciding how to respond. He looked directly at the vice president and replied, "Yes, Mr. Vice President, I do. There are three pieces of data that may—I repeat, *may*—be seen in Geredin's favor. First, he virtually confirmed a recent briefing produced by the Agency's top Soviet analyst as to the extremely weakened state of the Soviet economy. You were given a précis of that article in the Presidential Daily Briefing several weeks ago."

"Yes, Dr. Jensen, I remember it. Please continue."

"Well, sir, it is highly unusual for any member of the Soviet government to admit that the system is failing. Such would amount to a tacit repudiation of socialist economic theory. Their normal response to economic failures within their system is to charge the responsible party with either corruption or incompetence. The fact that Geredin is admitting a systemic failure makes me wonder if his warning is real. Second, as already mentioned the ONI has confirmed a ramped up level of aggression, which Admiral Feldstein has just veri-fied. At the very least, that lends some degree of credibility. But perhaps the biggest piece of data supporting the notion that Geredin's warning is real is the point that he delivered this message himself, personally. If disinformation was in play, he probably would have put it out on a compromised communi-cation channel, knowing that we would eventually get the mes-sage. Instead, a seventy-nine-year-old man who suffers from very painful and crippling arthritis, arranges to leave the USSR traveling under false papers. He takes multiple flights around the globe to hide his tracks, and catches up with me in the only place I frequent that will assure him of secrecy—Great Falls. He does all this at the extreme risk of his own life, for if his comrades knew what he was up to he'd be summarily exe-cuted, his high-ranking status notwithstanding. Who knows what he had to pull off in his own country to escape surveil-lance without raising any alarms?

"Mr. Vice President, that is why I believe we need to, at the very least, take this information seriously and work hard and fast to either finally confirm its authenticity, or disprove it. The stakes are much, much too high to simply dismiss it."

When the meeting concluded, the vice president directed Admiral Feldstein to send a general warning to all the naval commands, alerting them to the possibility of heightened So-viet aggression and directing that they promptly report any occurrences. Standard peacetime rules of engagement would continue to apply. The vice president also ordered Paul West, the DCI, to "do whatever is necessary" to confirm or refute Geredin's intelligence.

****

Sam Bergman was headed for the super-secret high-secu-rity NSA facility located in Maryland, just outside the Beltway. This location was where the NSA did most of their transla-tion work on the communication intercepts snagged by hi-tech satellites, listening posts, secret communication taps, and other classified devices and techniques.

On beautiful days such as this warm, sunny September afternoon, Bergman would park his 1987 Porsche 911 Carrera in the farthest parking space he could find from the CIA building entrance. Whether coming or going it gave him a bit of a walk in the sun, a valuable commodity for a man who spent his days in front of computer screens in a semi-darkened office. As he strolled to his car he enjoyed the near-zero humidity, a rarity for the Washington metro area. A gentle breeze out of the south trifled with the leaves on the trees lining the parking lot. It was, he decided, a truly gorgeous day.

The Porsche eagerly sprang to life when he turned the key, and in a few minutes he was doing eighty on the Beltway, headed north. Bergman was nervous. He was about to visit the most wonderful woman he'd ever met, a brilliant NSA translator by the name of Evelyn Stinson. It was exactly a year ago that he'd been collaborating with her on a project known as *Snowbird*, in which they were trying to determine whether Major Jacob Kelly was telling the truth about his experiences in Siberia, or whether he'd been turned by the Soviets.

Stinson was an honors graduate of the University of Bristol in the UK, with a Masters degree in the Russian language. During the summer of 1982 she was admitted to the PhD program at Harvard in prerevolution Russian literature. Her belongings and books were already shipped to Cambridge and she was stepping into the cab that would take her to Bristol International when a phone call changed everything. Her roommate burst out of the front door and raced to the taxi, shouting, "Evie, Evie, there's someone ringing you!" It was an NSA recruiter desperate to increase their portfolio of Russian translators. They made her an offer she didn't refuse. She took the cab but flew to DC, not Cambridge, and had worked for the NSA ever since.

A year ago Bergman believed that the developing relationship with Stinson was becoming something more than professional. But then, after *Snowbird* was finished, she stopped returning his phone calls. Finally getting the hint, he stopped calling. He was eager to see her today but also somewhat fearful. He'd pinned his personal hopes on her only to have them dashed without ever understanding why. In any case, they would be working together again on *Zephyr*.

Shepherded through multiple layers of biometric security, he was finally ushered into her office. She was facing away from the door, bending over a greenbar printout and holding a line-printer character ruler, making tick marks on a line of characters. Standing next to her was an outlandish character dressed in a Grateful Dead t-shirt, raggedy cut-off jeans, and sandals. The apparition was crowned with an unruly mop of curly hair that cascaded down around his shoulders.

"Okay, Clifton, this is the one hundred twenty-seventh character position, and you're telling me it is the end of the packet? And so I'm supposed to ignore these hundred and twenty-nine characters beyond it? But why?" Stinson asked.

"Yes, Evelyn, that's what I'm telling you. Character number one-twenty-seven there on the printout is a hexadecimal zero zero, which means it is the end of the character string. The characters that follow are meaningless. They are just artifacts left over in the buffer from previous messages. They have absolutely no bearing on this message. They aren't part of the message and were never intended to be."

"You're sure about that?" the woman asked dubiously.

"So sure I'd bet my entire collection of Joni Mitchell albums on it."

"Clifton Edwards and Evelyn Stinson. Fancy meeting you guys here, just like old times," said Bergman, smiling.

The two turned and noticed him for the first time.

"Shouldn't be too unusual to meet me here, after all it is my office. How are you doing, Sam?" she asked with a warm smile.

"Oh!" Clifton exclaimed, a grin of recognition replacing the frown on his face. "You're that CIA dude, right?"

"That's right. And you're the hero of project *Snowbird*. You're the guy that gave us the final breakthrough, discovering that that triplicate of messages would have never been seen by a single recipient. It was your work that proved we were being played by the Sovs."

"What was that all about, anyway?" Edwards asked.

"Sorry, classified. Can't say anymore than I've said. But thanks in part to you, CE, it was a successful operation."

Edwards grinned as he gathered up the printouts and the ruler. "Well, at least you know where to send the donuts," he quipped as he left the room.

"Indeed I do." Sam turned to Evelyn. "I'm fine, Evelyn, how have you been?"

Her expression changed. Though still civil, the warmth was gone. "Oh, fine, Sam, fine. You must be here about *Zephyr*. I've already been briefed on it."

Her swift transition from warm to civil stung. He'd hoped for a chance to try their relationship again, but it appeared that wasn't something she was interested in. They spent the next twenty minutes discussing what her SIGINT targets should be and the proper document custody for transferring information from her desk to his. Once during the conversation he thought he saw a certain wistfulness in her eyes, but it passed quickly.

"If there's anything you feel might be really important, give me a call, Evelyn, and I'll run right over and pick it up. There's an aspect to *Zephyr* that we're afraid is going to go down quickly. A delay of even twenty-four hours could be critical."

"We have a courier, Sam, I could just give it to him."

"No. Please, just call me. I—I like the drive. I don't get out much any more, and besides, I'll get here quicker than the courier.

She shrugged and turned away. "Whatever. Fine, I'll call you."

The return trip to the Agency somehow did not seem as sunny and beautiful.

Chapter 6

Early October, 1988

On Tuesday, October 4, Major Jacob Kelly was called into the wing commander's office and given the news: his flight clearance had been permanently revoked. It was stressed that the sole reason was the seizure—in every other respect his ability as a pilot was superlative. He was told to take the rest of the day off and to report back to the wing commander's office the next day. They would then discuss his options for the future.

Kelly walked out to his pickup, got in, then sat staring off into the distance. The windows were down, the day was sunny and warm. He could hear an F-16 on a nearby runway, spooling up its General Electric F110-GE-129 turbofan, followed by a throaty roar as the aircraft raced down the runway and took off. It was followed immediately by three more jets taking off. Kelly knew that his *Rude Rams*, the 34th Fighter Squadron, were launching for another day of training exercises.

He turned the key and considered where he was going to go. He briefly considered the Officers' Club, then decided against it. He'd find no answers in a bottle, and besides, it would be too humiliating to go there after losing his flight clearance. He sat motionless, reviewing the events of the last several weeks. He had a choice—sink into self-pity, or make the best of a disappointing situation.

"No more pity parties," he said aloud. "Adapt and overcome. That's what I'm going to do."

Kelly drove to the grocery, picked up a couple of steaks, and went home. Galina was home when he arrived. She heard his truck pull in the driveway and intuitively knew what his early arrival meant. She met him at the door.

"Jake, I'm so sorry," she said as she opened the door. She threw her arms around his neck and hugged him tightly. "You're still my *sokolov*, no matter what," she whispered.

He nodded. "It's going to be okay. I'll figure it out, and I'll survive—we'll survive." He set the grocery bags down, wiped his eyes, and gave her a long hug.

"They told me to go home for the rest of the day. Tomorrow they will tell me what my options are."

"What did you bring?" she asked, motioning to the grocery bags.

"Dinner. We're going to grill steaks tonight and celebrate. We're going to talk about this new chapter of our lives and start thinking about what's next. I've got responsibilities and obligations to you and to the air force, and I intend to keep them. I'm not going to feel sorry for myself."

That night as they lay in bed, she ran her fingertips over his shoulders. "The scars are healing well. Does it still hurt?"

"No. It's odd, though."

"What?"

"Well, that when I decided to have the plastic surgery to remove the burn scars Chernikov put on my shoulders, I went ahead and decided to have my tattoos removed at the same time. Right after that I lose my flight certification." He paused as he tried to put his thoughts together. "Strange. It's almost like it was planned to happen that way." He wrapped his arm around Galina and pulled her close. "Anyway, now that I'm no longer flying with the 34th at least the tattoos won't constantly remind me of it. I guess that's another decision Mr. Jensen would call 'providential.'"

"I'm beginning to think he might be right," she said softly.

"Yeah, I'm beginning to wonder about it, too."

"Wonder what?"

He looked at her. "What if it really is true?"

****

Admiral Pyotr Stefanovich Zelenko was the commander of the Red Banner Pacific Fleet; Shukshin was his deputy and favored protégé. Nearing seventy-five, Zelenko was on the threshold of retirement, and it had been his intention to recommend to the Admiral of the Navy that Shukshin be his replacement. But now he was having second thoughts.

Zelenko was not an administrator, he was a sailor's sailor.

He despised office work, reports, and the entangling morass of desk-bound administrative duties laid upon a fleet commander—so he simply refused to do them. He left all of that to Shukshin, who was a skilled administrator.

One look at Zelenko's sunburnt, wind-chafed face would reveal that he spent his days at sea on the bridges of his ships, not in the office. With equal facility he mixed with both enlisted men and officers and was respected by both. Zelenko was constantly evaluating, encouraging, mentoring and teaching men, drawing from his own wealth of experience and skillful seamanship. One moment he could be teaching line handling to the deck crew and the next moment helping a sweaty-palmed junior officer with ship handling on the bridge. No matter their rank, practically all of the sailors manning the Pacific Fleet could recognize the admiral by sight. Most had even had the chance to talk to him, if not singly then at least in groups. Stern with shirkers and incompetents but willing to give a man a second chance, Zelenko was genuinely loved by the sailors of the fleet.

A Ukrainian, the admiral was not from a wealthy or connected family, and he had no patron in the Politburo. He'd ascended to his high post on nothing more than his character, courage, and exemplary record. His father had been an uneducated and unremarkable potato farmer on a collective east of Odessa. The son, however, distinguished himself in school at a young age with unusual intelligence. An outstanding student, Zelenko achieved an early dream when he was admitted to the Frunze Higher Naval School, graduating in 1935. As a young officer of lower rank and a humble background, he managed to escape notice during Stalin's maniacal purge of the professional naval officer corps. The purge created a vacuum in the upper ranks and Zelenko advanced rapidly. He was involved in many bold small-boat riverine operations during the Great Patriotic War, finally emerging from the conflict with numerous decorations and awards, and a permanent but manageable limp from a shell fragment. By the middle of the 1950s he was commanding a destroyer, by the 1960s, major surface combatants. His career continued to climb until he was finally entrusted with the command of the Pacific Fleet.

His stellar reputation combined with common knowledge that he was near retirement enabled him to get away with leaving the fleet administrative duties in Shukshin's capable hands. Zelenko's superior, the Admiral of the Fleet, considered it an eccentricity he could tolerate given the fact that the old man would soon be leaving the service. However, Zelenko's choices had the consequence of making Shukshin the de facto commander of the Pacific Fleet. Zelenko didn't even sign the deployment orders that went out from his office, nor was he aware of their contents—all was left to Shukshin. Instead, he spent his time helicoptering out to deployed ships to spend time with his beloved sailors.

As Zelenko spent time aboard his ships, he began to hear that Shukshin was culling the officers, transferring good men out of the fleet. When he queried his deputy about the transfers he found that Shukshin's explanations didn't satisfy. Zelenko finally smelled a rat and returned to the office to begin looking into things. He didn't like what he was finding, and the working relationship between the two men deteriorated.

****

General Yegorov unlocked the door and turned on the lights. He set the bag of groceries on the counter and went in search of the thermostat. The *dacha* was cold and had been unoccupied for the last three weeks. It belonged to the state-owned engineering company Omsktransmash, primary manufacturer of the T-80 main battle tank. The *dacha*, fronting a lake in a heavy forest just south of Omsk, was used to wine and dine potential clients and government officials. Yegorov had secured it ostensibly to inspect quality control on the tank production line. His real reason, however, was to meet with his fellow coup plotters in a location far from Moscow's prying eyes and eavesdropping ears.

The inner circle was composed of four men: Pushkaryov, the vice president of the USSR; Aristov, the defense minister; General Yegorov, chief of the general staff of the Soviet armed forces; and Admiral Shukshin, deputy commander of the Pacific fleet. At their meeting a month ago they had decided to invite Yulian Churkin, the interior minister, into their confidence.

"We're missing one piece of the puzzle, comrades. I think we should add another voice to our little executive committee," Pushkaryov had said in the earlier meeting.

"No, I disagree. The more who know of our plans, the more risk we run of exposure—exposure before we are ready," Admiral Shukshin insisted. "It will be our undoing."

"Whom did you have in mind, Alexander Ivanovich?" asked Yegorov, ignoring Shukshin.

"Look at us," replied the vice president. "We have representatives from the navy, the army, the whole defense establishment, and a high-ranking politician," he said, looking around the room. "What essential piece are we missing?"

Aristov stroked his beard as he considered the question. He sat up and replied, "Someone who runs internal security."

"Precisely. We already know that Geredin is against us. While we have some friends in the KGB, by and large we cannot count on them. We must look elsewhere in the intelligence apparatus. Which is why I propose that we add Churkin, our minister of the interior. We know that Churkin is loyal to our vision of a revitalized Russia. With Churkin we would have the MVD and the *militsiya* in our pocket."

In the end even Shukshin grudgingly agreed that the interior minister would be an asset. So tonight Yegorov was preparing a meal for five, instead of four. Cooking was his hobby and fine dining was his passion. Singing patriotic songs to himself in a deep bass voice, he moved about the well equipped kitchen cubing and browning prime beef, peeling and dicing fat purple beets, and cutting thick slices from a fresh loaf of black bread. Borshch, black bread with goat cheese, and a bottle of Tsinandali was on the evening menu, with beef stroganoff as the second course. As the chief of the general staff put the last place setting on the table, his guests arrived.

"I propose a toast," intoned Pushkaryov after the meal,

when they were sitting in the living room of the *dacha*. The temperature outside was dropping below freezing and the wind was rising. A blazing fire in the hearth brought a welcome warmth to the room, against the chill seeping in through the cracks and crevices.

Pushkaryov stood and held up a shot glass full of vodka. His face was red and sweaty, partly from too much wine at supper and partly because he was sitting too close to the roaring fire. The others clambered to their feet, Yegorov a little more unsteadily than his companions, and held their glasses high.

"We hear much talk about the New Soviet Man," Pushkaryov said, "but what we really need is a new Soviet Union. *Za novyy Sovetskiy Soyuz!* To the new Soviet Union," he cried holding his glass high then knocking back the vodka.

"To the new Soviet Union," the others chorused and emptied their glasses.

The next morning as they discussed strategy, Yegorov served them a hearty breakfast of sausage, bliny, and thick slices of black bread and caviar.

"Comrade Churkin, what can you tell us of the MVD? How would you assess the level of support we can expect?" Pushkaryov asked, speaking around a mouthful of heavily buttered black bread.

"Comrades, I can report that we do not have control of the units of OMSDON, the Independent Special-Purpose Motorized Rifle Division of my MVD troops. The general commanding that group is a Gorbachev loyalist. I am unable to replace him at the present time without causing a great deal of suspicion. However, if I have adequate warning before we take action against Gorbachev, I can ensure that OMSDON will be away from Moscow, sent to the Siberian Far East on a training mission.

"I've been concentrating on the officers of the *militsiya* in and adjacent to Moscow. Since the beginning of September I've been replacing the unit commanders with officers loyal to me and transferring those who are not. By the end of November all the commanders in the Moscow district will follow my lead. When it comes time to depose Gorbachev, all of the police units in and around Moscow will support us."

Pushkaryov clapped his hands with glee. "You see, my comrades, I was right to admit Yulian Semyonovich to our little group. Already he shows his value, eh?" He turned to Shukshin. "And what of your report, Konstantin Grigoriyevich?"

Pushkaryov's manner irritated Shukshin and it was all he could do to control his expression and keep the ice out of his voice. The idea that he, an admiral of the Pacific Fleet who controlled the world's most powerful assemblage of nuclear weapons, should have to report to a bureaucratic drone like Pushkaryov was beyond galling. He considered the vice president to be a patronizing idiot, a pompous windbag whose chief and sole asset was the high position that he held. *I will eliminate this crude peasant at my first opportunity*, he told himself. *Just wait until after the putsch, Pushkaryov.* With an effort requiring all the self-control he could muster, he smiled at the vice president.

"Comrades, I have completed the identification of submarine commanders whose loyalty to the *rodina* is unquestioned. They are distressed by the chaos Gorbachev has brought upon us, and they will support us when the time comes. Once we have established a target date for the revolution," he paused as he said the word. It was a radical word, but one that had a good Russian history and it tasted just right coming off his tongue. *Yes, it is the right word to use.* "Once we have established the target date for the revolution," he repeated, "I will do my utmost to see that all the nuclear missile submarines on patrol are commanded by men loyal to the new Soviet Union." He could see that Pushkaryov was flattered when he used the term of the vice president's toast of the previous evening. *Yes, yes, Pushkaryov, enjoy your delusions of grandeur now. You are merely a placeholder for me, you arrogant old fool.*

Shukshin continued. "I have also identified a significant problem, however. It's Admiral Zelenko. He is a thorough-going Gorbachev loyalist, and he's beginning to become suspicious. I've been reassigning the Gorbachev men and moving patriots into the positions they've vacated. Zelenko is beginning to push back."

"That is a problem," Aristov, the defense minister, admitted.

Pushkaryov stared at Shukshin for a moment and then looked away. After the silence around the table became uncomfortable, the vice president spoke carefully. "How . . . how committed are you to our cause, Konstantin Grigoriyevich?"

"Completely committed," he snapped. "What's your point, comrade?"

"Well, then," said Pushkaryov, speaking slowly and deliberately, "it seems to me that a man committed to our cause would be able to . . . eliminate any problems that arise."

Shukshin sat back in his chair. "Meaning—what?" he asked.

The vice president merely stared at him, but did not answer. The other men were all looking down at the table. Again, the silence became uncomfortable.

Oh, I understand, you coward. You are wanting me to eliminate Zelenko, but you don't have the courage to come right out and say it. Plausible deniability if the coup is unsuccessful. All of these men will testify you never ordered me to kill Zelenko. So that's how it works? You're free and clear, and I'm left holding the bag?

****

"Churkin has made it to the inner circle," Dobrynin reported to Geredin. "And he's passed along a warning. He believes that Admiral Zelenko might be in danger. Apparently Shukshin complained about opposition he's getting from Zelenko as he maneuvers anti-Gorbachev men into his submarine commands. Alexander Ivanovich Pushkaryov never directly told Shukshin to kill Zelenko, but that was the obvious intent of the conversation."

"They're raising the stakes," observed Geredin.

Dobrynin nodded. "It would appear so, sir."

"I want you to put a security team on Zelenko. Do we have anyone we can trust in Vladivostok?"

"I know of three names, sir. But I don't think that's an issue."

"Why not, Vladimir Leonidovich?"

"Because even though the possibility of a coup is spoken of in the highest circles, it is still unknown in the lower ranks, sir. There is widespread unhappiness about Gorbachev, that is true, but I doubt the talk of a coup has spread as far as the local KGB offices. Our agents in Vladivostok would consider a protection assignment on Admiral Zelenko to be a normal assignment and would not connect it to these higher machinations at all. They probably wouldn't have an inkling of knowledge about where Zelenko stands regarding Gorbachev and his reforms, and frankly, probably wouldn't care anyway."

Geredin nodded. "*Pravda.* Good thinking, Colonel. Okay, contact Vladivostok and tell them to put a security detail on Zelenko until further notice. Tell them to stay out of sight—I don't want it to be obvious."

****

On Sunday, October 9, Jacob Kelly was sitting in his living room munching on peanuts and watching the Broncos beat the 49ers in San Francisco. The game was a low scoring affair decided by a field goal. Jake snapped the TV off, and sat staring at the darkened screen. He did not like the way his future was shaping up, but he was determined not to feel sorry for himself. On a whim, he picked up the phone and dialed Bill Jensen's number.

"Hello, Jacob, how are you and your bride getting along? It was a wonderful wedding and so good to see you both. I enjoyed sharing in your happiness."

"Hi, Mr. Jensen, uh, I mean, Bill. We're doing fine. Had a great honeymoon at Disney, and then exploring Florida. We've found a house in Ogden just off the base. Actually it's in Clinton, a suburb of Ogden. It's perfect for us. Oh! And guess what! I'm going to be a father!"

"That's wonderful, Jake! Susan will be delighted to hear this news. When is Galina due?"

"April."

"Is she having morning sickness?"

"It's getting better. She was barfing every morning, now it's down to once or twice a week. Other than that, she's fine."

The two men talked for a while and reminisced about Jake's experiences in Siberia the year before. Finally Jake spoke of his current situation.

"Looks like my flying days are over, Bill."

"What do you mean, Jake?"

"Had a seizure a couple of weeks ago. Lost my flight clearance. It does not look like I'll ever be cleared to fly again."

"Jake, I'm so sorry. I know that flying was your life. What are you going to do?"

"Haven't decided yet. I'll probably stay in the air force a little longer, at least."

The two men talked for another twenty minutes. It didn't settle anything for Jake, but it was encouraging to connect with the man who'd been his mentor for so many years.

****

At five-forty local time on 12 December, 1987, a Tsyklon-2 rocket, a derivative of the R-36 intercontinental ballistic missile, roared into the darkened sky from Pad 69 of the busy Baikonur Cosmodrome. The immediate effect of the launch was to stir the sleepy watchers in the Space Defense Operations Center at NORAD located under two thousand feet of solid granite at Cheyenne Mountain in Colorado. Until the trajectory was verified as an orbital insertion track and not a ballistic path terminating on some US city, hackles were raised on not a few necks.

Perched atop the Soviet rocket was *Kosmos 1900*, a variant of the *Upravlyaemy Sputnik Aktivnyy* (US-A) spy satellite. Powered by a two-kilowatt nuclear reactor, the satellite was designed to monitor maritime vessels using radar. It was categorized in the West as a RORSAT, or Radar Ocean Reconnaissance Satellite. Its orbit enabled it to cover wide swaths of the Pacific Ocean. The long-term effect of the launch was to deny the US navy the secrecy it desired regarding fleet movements.

Chapter 7

Sunday, October 16, 1988

A hard drizzle pelted the surface of the *Zaliv Petra Velikogo*, the Peter the Great Gulf. In the murky depths the USS *Los Angeles* (SSN-688) crept north, drawing ever closer to the highly secure submarine base at Vladivostok. When the submarine stopped it was less than fifteen miles from the heavily guarded facility. To be caught here by the Soviets would almost certainly mean death. The ship was rigged for ultraquiet: non-essential personnel were confined to their racks, all machinery was set to its quietest setting, doors in the head were taped open so they couldn't accidentally be slammed, paper and plastic only were used in the mess, no cooking was allowed. Sailors quipped that breathing was permitted only insofar as it complied with naval regulations.

The mission was conceived when a mole in the Kremlin informed his CIA handler that the Soviets would be testing an upgraded SS-N-23 Skiff SLBM (submarine launched ballistic missile) on 18 October. The Skiff was thought to be the most accurate of all the Soviet SLBMs, and American intelligence services wanted eavesdroppers in place to listen in on the test and its aftermath. One US sub would be secretly monitoring the launch in the Barents Sea. Another American submarine would be gathering electronic data from the anticipated point of impact, offshore of the Kura Missile Test Range on the Kamchatka Peninsula. The *Los Angeles* would be listening in on the ensuing telemetry and chatter around the Pacific Fleet headquarters at Vladivostok.

It was risky business. The main channel leading to the port was only two hundred forty feet deep, and that was just in spots. Most of it was shallower. In any case, the *Los Angeles* could not use the main channel lest it accidentally encounter a Soviet sub coming or going. As a consequence, the *Los Angeles* sat on the mucky bottom in a mere two hundred feet of water, three thousand yards east of the main channel.

A combination SIGINT/ELINT (Signals Intelligence/ Electronic Intelligence) radio buoy on a fiber-optic tether silently floated to the surface. The buoy was coated with a radar-absorptive paint to make it less likely to be spotted by radar surveillance. It was disguised to look like the sort of marker a fisherman might throw out to mark the boundary of private, licensed fishing grounds, something like an oversized empty clorox bottle sloppily painted with a few black Cyrillic characters, attached to a light length of anchor line.

Special "civilian contractors" (in other words, NSA employees) had taken over the submarine's communication center. Several racks of highly classified and specialized electronics, installed at Pearl for this mission, began to hungrily receive and record everything on the electromagnetic spectrum passing through the ether above the water.

Forty-eight hours later, in the black of night, the buoy was reeled in and secured, and the *Los Angeles* snuck back into deep water. A day later the submarine came to periscope depth in the Sea of Japan and uploaded the contents of its recorders to a geostationary satellite. From there the information traveled to the "Anagram Inn," the secret NSA facility housed underground at Fort Mead, Maryland along with several acres of subterranean computers that didn't show up on any official government budget nor officially exist.

There the treasure trove was separated into signals intelligence (human communication) and electronic intelligence (telemetry, data, etc.) and sent off to different sections of the facility for analysis. That's how a batch of teletype intercepts from Admiral Shukshin—unrelated to the missile test but plucked from the air while the submarine was recording—wound up on Evelyn Stinson's desk.

****

Several days earlier on Monday, 17 October, Admiral Shukshin sat at his desk working on deployment orders. Bored with the unending paperwork, he stood up and moved to the window overlooking the port. Rain beat against the glass as an autumn storm held Vladivostok in its wet, dreary grip. Off in the distance, squalls drove sheets of rain across the wharves and docks, and farther beyond he could see whitecaps on the black waters of the bay.

To his left, a Sovremennyy-class destroyer was docking. Two tugs were sidling it over to its berth as they fought against the wind and the outgoing tide. Through curtains of rain and wisps of fog, Shukshin could barely make out the maneuvering watch on the deck of the destroyer as they stood by, waiting to heave mooring lines to their counterparts on the quay.

"Enter," he called in response to a knock at his door.

"Sir, you wished to be kept informed of any intelligence on the *Vinson*?" asked Captain Third Rank Stefan Stefanovich Udom, the fleet intelligence officer.

"*Da.*"

"She's tied up at Mombasa, Kenya, at the moment. She will be replaced in her support role for Operation *Earnest Will* by the *Nimitz* at the end of the month. The *Vinson* will steam east, making a visit to Pattaya Beach, Thailand on 4 November, and then Hong Kong on 13 November. From there she heads to Subic Bay."

"Where did you come by this information? Are you confident of it?"

"*Da*, comrade Admiral, I am absolutely confident of the accuracy of this information. It came from our source in the Seventh Fleet operations office in Yokosuka."

Shukshin stroked his chin, thinking. "Then she will pass through the Malacca Strait," he murmured to himself. "If she is escorted by submarines, the shallow waters will force them to abandon her when she enters the Strait. This might be an opportunity for Operation *East Wind*."

"Sir?"

"Never mind, Stefan. Thank you for the information. Dismissed."

Shukshin picked up the phone and buzzed his secretary. "Please inform Captain Mirov that I wish to see him in my office tomorrow at 0700 hours. Contact Captains Gromyko and Fetisov and tell them to be here at 0730."

****

"You're not moping around, are you, son? Do I need to come to Hill AFB and kick your butt?" General Franks asked.

Jake laughed as he trapped the telephone handset between his head and shoulder and continued to wash dishes. *One thing about General Franks*, he thought to himself before replying, *he doesn't beat around the bush. Tact is not one of his strengths.*

"Not necessary, General. I've straightened up and I'm flying right."

"Glad to hear it. What can I do you out of?"

"General, is there some way you could get my Combat Control Team training and deployments posted to my service record? It would give me more options for the future."

When Jake had been working as the chief test pilot on the then super-secret Project *Hydra* under Franks' command, he'd been covertly trained as a CCT operator. *Hydra* required close cooperation between CCT operators on the ground using laser illuminators and the F-16 pilots in the air releasing the guided *Hydra* cluster munitions. Franks had decided that his chief test pilot would need both experiences—ground and air —in order to assist in perfecting the new weapon system.

The problem Franks faced was that if it became known that his chief test pilot was getting ground combat training, foreign intelligence services might discern the intent of the *Hydra* weapon system. So Franks had created a false identity in the military personnel database—Major John Smith. Kelly went through his special operations training and deployments as Major John Smith, and none of it showed up on Kelly's own service record. This had been one of Jake's primary advantages when he escaped from the Siberian interrogation facility two years earlier. The Soviets had had no idea of his true capabilities.

"Sure, I can manage that. You think it's time to deep six Major John Smith, now that *Hydra* is complete?"

"I do, but that's your call, General."

"Okay, give me a week or so, but I'll get it done."

"Thank you, sir!"

"No problem, Jake, glad to do it. Are you thinking about transferring into the special operations group?"

"Yes, sir. My flying career is over, but I've got four deployments downrange under my belt with the CCT guys, and I think I'd like to take that up again. It's definitely more interesting than sitting behind a desk."

The next morning Jake got up at five, laced up his running shoes and went out for a five-mile run before going in to the office. He was dismayed by how out of shape he was. He'd have to work back up to his fifteen- and twenty-mile runs gradually. He decided to run on odd days and lift weights in the base gym on even days. If he stuck to it faithfully, he'd rapidly regain his former fitness.

****

"Admiral Shukshin will see you now, Captain Mirov."

"Thank you, comrade." Mirov tried hard not to stare at Shukshin's attractive secretary. She was dressed professionally, but her clothing was a little too tight in strategic places. There were rumors drifting around the fleet that Shukshin's relationship with his secretary extended beyond the office. Mirov did not entangle himself in fleet gossip and tried to avoid those who did.

He tapped lightly on the closed door.

"Enter. Ah, Captain Mirov, welcome! Coffee? Or tea perhaps?" Shukshin glanced at the old marine chronometer hanging behind his desk. "Punctual as usual, Captain. You are an example to the fleet. I trust we will produce more officers like you."

"*Spasibo*, sir. Coffee, please."

The admiral passed the request along to his secretary and then the two officers passed the time with small talk, sitting on the couch in Shukshin's office until the coffee arrived. When his secretary exited, shutting the door behind her, Shukshin got down to business. "Boris Sayanovich, I'm placing you in temporary command of three submarines and sending you on a challenging mission. It's a mission in which I will be relying on your skill, experience, and judgment. I'll run through the strategic goals before we talk about tactical details.

"As you know, Gorbachev has been trying to strengthen our relationship with Iraq. But Saddam Hussein has been reluctant to give us increased access to Iraqi ports and port facilities. The extremely favorable financing we gave the Iraqis in last year's sale of twenty-four MiG-29s seems to be softening Hussein's position on the ports. With its immense reserves of oil, Iraq could become an extremely important client state to the *rodina*. It's a mutually beneficial relationship in other ways as well. We have weapons they need, they have cash we need.

"But the Americans are our chief competitors in this endeavor. Seventh Fleet carrier groups are providing air support for their operations protecting Kuwaiti tankers filled with Iraqi oil, as the tankers transit the Persian Gulf and exit the Strait of Hormuz.

"To the Iraqis, this means that we are not the only supplier and protector in the game. They can choose between us and the US. Your job, Captain Mirov, is to put the American navy on notice that we are forcefully opposing their naval involvement in the Iran-Iraq conflict. By standing up to the Americans, the Iraqis will see that the USSR is a powerful and reliable ally, an ally near at hand, not one many oceans distant."

So far, everything Shukshin had said to Captain Mirov was true. But what he was about to say was not. Operation *Vostochnyy Veter*, or *East Wind*, was purely Shukshin's creation, complete with forged orders purporting to come from Admiral Zelenko. Shukshin's audacity was due to his confidence that Zelenko had no interest in monitoring the actions of the fleet and would never learn of the secret operation.

"The operation I am giving you, *Vostochnyy Veter*, is highly classified. You are not to speak of it to anyone other than myself or the captains under your command. It was approved at the highest level in Moscow and came to me through regular command channels. Comrade Admiral Zelenko personally picked you to command the operation. We have a lot of confidence in you, Boris Sayanovich. Do not disappoint us."

"I serve the Soviet Union, comrade Admiral," Mirov replied. "I thank you for your confidence in me. I shall work diligently to see that it is well placed. What are the particulars of the mission, sir?"

"Not many days from now, the USS *Carl Vinson* will leave the Arabian Sea and set course for Subic Bay by way of Hong Kong, with several other stops in between. It's a typical 'show the flag' operation. Her intended ports of call will require her to transit the Malacca and Singapore Straits. The dates, ports of call and estimated course are in your briefing packet.

"As you know, the waters of the Straits are sufficiently shallow that any submarine escort the *Vinson* has will be forced to abandon her when she enters the Straits. A new submarine escort will not be provided until the *Vinson* is sailing in deep waters again. This creates a window of opportunity for us.

"Your job, Captain Mirov, will be to penetrate the *Vinson's* ASW screen and get as close as you can to the carrier. You will then load your torpedoes with a firing solution, flood the tubes and open the outer doors. But you must not launch the weapons. I want them to know you are there and that you got the drop on them.

"When the Americans complain to our embassy in Washington, DC, about your aggressive posture—and complain they will, be assured—our ambassador will make the point that we do not want the US navy involved with Iraq. Your actions will demonstrate that we are serious."

Mirov was surprised by the recklessness of Shukshin's plan and did not disguise his concerns. "But sir, that will put my boat and my crew in extreme danger! It will probably provoke the Americans to put a torpedo in the water, sir," he objected.

"I imagine that it will, Captain. I suggest you have your countermeasures ready. But the risk is not as great as you imagine. You'll be facing their airborne ASW assets, all of which employ the Mk-46 torpedo. Our intelligence confirms that an air-dropped Mk-46 performs very poorly in shallow water. It is unlikely you'll be in very great danger.

"But even if they launch a weapon, you are not, I repeat

not, authorized to fire. Do you understand? If they fire, close the outer doors and do your best to escape. That is why, Captain Mirov, we have chosen you for this mission. If anyone is sufficiently skilled to survive an American torpedo attack, it is you, Captain."

"You are sending us to our deaths, Admiral."

"You forget yourself, Captain. Anytime I send you out from this place in your submarine, I am sending you and your crew to possible death. While the responsibility weighs heavily on me, nonetheless it must be done. The privilege of command comes also with the terrible burden of command, Captain.

"It is my fond hope and expectation, Captain Mirov, that you and your boat will survive. I don't want to lose you. I want to see officers of your ability advance to flag rank. But if that promotion ever does come to you, then you too will know the heavy responsibility of command."

Shukshin stood up from the couch and walked to his desk. He picked up a thick briefing packet and dropped it on the coffee table in front of Mirov.

"I'm giving you a *Projekt* 671 boat, Boris Sayanovich, the *K-264*. She's just had the fuel in her reactor replenished, and the reactor has been overhauled. Her propulsion systems will be in tip-top condition." The NATO classification of the *K-264* was a Victor III, an advanced and very quiet boat. "Bring her back to me in one piece, and you and your crew as well, Captain."

"I'll do my best, sir. You mentioned two other boats?"

"*Da.* Captain Gromyko will have the *K-284*, a *Projekt* 971 boat. Captain Fetisov will have the *K-263*, also a 971." The 971 series were known to NATO by the name Akula. The Akula was a fourth generation nuclear submarine, arguably the most advanced and quietest in the Soviet arsenal. "As senior captain, you are probably wondering why you have the older 671 boat, and your two subordinates have the newer submarines."

"*Da.*"

Shukshin sighed. He sat behind his desk and looked down. He wouldn't meet Mirov's eyes. Finally he said, "My reasons are both tactical and practical. On the practical side, you in your 671 will be threatening the carrier. If any of these boats do not come back, it will be yours. We can afford to lose a 671. We cannot afford to lose a 971."

A long silence ensued until Mirov finally responded. "I see."

"Don't you understand, Borya? It must be this way. You are the most skilled submarine officer in the Pacific Fleet. If anyone can survive this crazy mission, you can. I am gambling on the fact that your experience, wisdom, and judgment will bring both you and your boat back in one piece."

"And your tactical reason, sir?"

"The Americans call the Projekt 971 boats 'Akulas.' They consider the Akula to be the most dangerous attack submarine we have. You must allow them to detect your two 971s, because they will draw the attention away from you. They will send their ready ASW assets after the Akulas. They do not have unlimited resources and without a submarine escort, their remaining ASW assets will be thin. That leaves you a brief window to draw close undetected and threaten the carrier."

"Have you drawn this plan up in my orders, sir?"

"*Nyet.* I am leaving that to you so that you are free to accommodate your assets to the situation. All I have specified is that you complete the operation before they dock at Pattaya Beach in Thailand. We believe the *Vinson* is sailing with only one combat-capable escort. I will be able to confirm that in several days."

"Would it be possible, comrade Admiral, to give me an 877 instead? It is much quieter and almost impossible to find in a littoral region, such as the one indicated in this mission, because of the heightened ambient noise of shallow water." The *Projekt* 877 submarine, known to NATO as the Kilo, was extremely quiet. A diesel submarine, the Kilo was virtually undetectable when sitting motionless on the bottom of the sea in shallow water. Neither active or passive sonar was able to pick it out. The Kilo's primary weakness was its need to snorkel and recharge its batteries periodically.

"*Nyet*! There are none available. Besides, we *want* the Americans to hear you. Don't look so worried, Captain Mirov. If you can keep their attention focused on your 971s, there shouldn't be anyone watching you."

Shukshin's motives were much more nefarious than he intimated. His larger plan was to initiate repeated confrontations with US carrier groups, in which the Soviets approached the group aggressively but never fired—even if fired upon. His intent was to make the American commanders relax and feel safe in the knowledge that the Soviet aggression was little more than performance art. Once that goal was achieved, he would set in motion his real plan: Operation *Tikhookeanskaya Ugroza*, or *Pacific Threat*. That's when warm theatrics would become hot warfare.

****

The fiery orb of the sun rose on the distant eastern horizon, casting a brief glow of brilliant orange in the humid ocean air. The sky was cloudless and a steady fifteen-knot wind was blowing from the northwest. Widely spaced, rolling ten-foot ocean swells marched slowly toward the southeast as the USS *Carl Vinson* sailed east toward Malaysia on the southern reaches of the Bay of Bengal. A pair of red-footed boobies circled the stern of the ship hoping the passage of the massive vessel would bring some unlucky fish to the surface.

As her escort stood several thousand yards off the starboard bow, the supercarrier slowly came about, turning into the wind to begin a launch-and-recovery cycle of flight operations. Several minutes later a combat air patrol (CAP) composed of a pair of F-14 Tomcats roared off the carrier, rocketing into the sky. They were followed by a lumbering pair of S-3A Vikings. Their job was to provide an airborne antisubmarine warfare screen. The last aircraft to launch was an E-2C Hawkeye turboprop. The Hawkeye's AN/APS-145 radar could blanket the air and surface space surrounding the carrier for three hundred miles in every direction, providing an early warning of any potential threats.

From a distance it appeared as if someone had kicked over an anthill of multi-colored ants on the flight deck as soon as the last plane was airborne, a chaotic kaleidoscope of color, alive with men in bright jerseys and cranial helmets racing aimlessly about. In fact, the act of transitioning the flight deck from launching aircraft to recovery operations was a highly choreographed ballet of crewmen engaged in an extremely dangerous job with professional efficiency. Sixty years of experience with aircraft carriers had given the navy unparalleled expertise in carrier operations. Safety of both the aircraft crews and the deck crews was paramount, and the *Vinson's* record on that score was superb.

The inbound aircraft returning from their respective patrols entered the pattern around the carrier and awaited their turn to land. Once the recovery operation was complete the *Vinson* resumed her course.

Admiral Bruce Waggoner walked over to the 1MC handset. Before he reached for it he looked at the OOD and asked, "Did you arrange to have this linked with the rest of the ships in the group?"

"Aye, Admiral. You're good to go. When you speak, it will be broadcast to the whole group."

Waggoner nodded and then took up the handset. "Attention all hands. This is the admiral speaking. Carrier Group Three has been on station for the last eighty-two days. Our air wing has been flying in support of Operation *Earnest Will* as well as several other operations. Our pilots have done an outstanding job, and I compliment all the members of Air Wing Fifteen. I also want to commend all the divisions of the entire ship for a job well done in the finest traditions of the navy. This goes for the crews of the *Texas*, the *Roanoke*, and the *Flint* as well. Whether we are talking about the air defense screen provided by the *Texas*, or underway replenishment from the *Roanoke* and the *Flint*, or air operations on the *Vinson*, we have worked well as a team and everyone's contribution was important to our record of safety and success on this mission. Largely because of the good work of Carrier Group Three the oil tankers are transiting the Persian Gulf in safety.

Today the *Nimitz* is taking our place and we are sailing east. Well done, men, *very* well done. As we wrap up our patrol and eventually return to Pearl, I am anticipating that same professionalism to continue from each of you. Thank you. Admiral out."

Waggoner hung up the handset and said to the messenger of the watch. "Locate the air group commander (CAG) and the captain, please. Give them my compliments and inform them that I want to see them in my quarters in ten minutes."

"Aye, sir."

A few minutes later the *Vinson*'s skipper, Captain Arthur Young, and CAG Captain Ross Morgan, were seated with Waggoner in the admiral's quarters. There was a chart spread on the table in front of them.

"Coffee, gentlemen?"

"None here, thanks, Bruce," said Young. "I think I've had six cups since the beginning of the Morning watch. Any more and I'll be pumping the bilges all day."

"I'll have some. Want me to get you a cup, Bruce?" asked Morgan as he walked over to the sideboard where the admiral's steward had placed the tray of refreshments.

"Yes, thanks, Ross."

Waggoner put on his glasses and stood over the chart. The other two men joined him at the table. "Gentlemen, every part of our course and operations while in transit was planned in great detail before we left port months ago. Today that plan goes out the window because the situation has changed, especially regarding the Soviet Union.

"So I want to go over the course between here and Pattaya Beach. We'll be losing our 688s once we get into the Malacca Strait, somewhere around here." He tapped the chart with his index finger. The 688s he was referring to were the pair of *Los Angeles*-class fast attack submarines serving as the carrier group's escort. "It's too shallow for 'em. We won't pick up another submarine escort until we hit the South China Sea, and that makes me feel a little naked. The replenishment ships are worthless for an ASW screen—they aren't equipped for it—and while the *Texas* has a good sonar they don't have any choppers to investigate contacts."

"Are you really expecting problems, Bruce?" asked Young.

The admiral raised an eyebrow. "Haven't you been reading the intelligence reports, Art? Ivan's been getting a little aggressive lately."

"Sure, Bruce, but that's all been far, far to the east, in the Pacific. And besides, Ivan's submarines are going to have the same issue with shallow water that we will."

"Well, sort of. Not completely. Once we exit the Singapore Strait and enter the Gulf of Thailand, there's just enough water to allow a submarine to operate submerged. But we won't be getting our escort back until we hit the South China Sea. There are enough sea miles between the Strait and South China Sea to give Ivan plenty of room for mischief."

Young nodded. "Okay, I can see that. Although I don't see it coming to this, the *Texas* does have a battery of ASROCs." The ASROC, or antisubmarine rocket, was a ship-launched ASW missile, the payload of which was a Mark 46 torpedo. The ASROC extended the striking distance of a vessel against hostile submarines.

"I'm not sure they'd be all that helpful even if it did come to a hot engagement. Do you really want to light off an AS-ROC in an area as choked with shipping as what we'll be going through? It would take just one fire control mistake and that thing would lock on to and sink a merchantman rather than the sub. If you think the *Vincennes* accidentally splashing *Flight 655* this summer was a tragic disaster, what if *Texas* sank a cruise ship?"

The three men pondered that terrible possibility, and then the admiral continued. "Okay, look guys, I am not expecting trouble. But I'm not willing to stake my career—or yours—on the hope that Ivan leaves us alone. We'll probably be fine, but if he wants to play rough he's got to know that we won't have any 688s escorting us once we hit the Strait. If I were Ivan and I wanted to mix it up with a US navy carrier group, this would be the perfect opportunity. So what can you do for me?"

Captain Young nodded. "Good point, Admiral." He

turned to the Air Group commander and asked, "Well, Ross, you've got the best ASW assets on hand. What can you do for us?"

"I think we can handle it, Art. Maintenance has been good on the S-3As, all ten of them are in flight condition," observed Morgan. He thought for a moment and then suggested, "What if we launch three Vikings per patrol, instead of two? That will give us half-again the ASW patrol coverage out ahead of our course. It will be a little harder on the flight crews, but we'll only have to do it until we pick up our 688 escort again."

Young nodded. "And if we keep up our speed, it will make it a little harder for Ivan to catch us from behind without making a lot of racket. Ross, you could put up a chopper with a dipper to check our six, make sure no one is trailing us."

Morgan nodded and looked at Waggoner. "So what do you think, Admiral? Will that cover the bases?"

"It will have to do, Ross. Just make sure we're stocked up on sonobuoys. I want 'em sprinkled like candy out ahead of us once we lose our 688s."

"Will do," Ross replied. "But with the increased flight ops this requires, we'd better call for an extra UNREP with the *Roanoke* to tank up on avgas, and I expect we'll want several fresh loads of sonobuoys from *Flint*." An UNREP is an underway replenishment in which the *Roanoke* comes along side and transfers aviation gasoline and other supplies while the two ships maintain an identical course and speed. The sonobuoys would be brought aboard via a VERTREP, or vertical replenishment, using the *Flint's* CH-46 Sea Knight helicopters.

"I'll see that both are scheduled before we enter the Straits," Captain Young said.

****

Sam Bergman tossed the latest security bulletin from the Office of Naval Intelligence onto his desk, leaned back in his chair and, interlocking his fingers, placed his hands behind his head. He stared at the featureless drop ceiling above him without seeing it, his mind focused on the report he'd just read.

What is going on in the Soviet Pacific Fleet? he wondered. *Is it more than what Geredin told Jensen? It's a mighty dangerous game they are playing. Was Geredin lying to us? Or—is it possible that someone is selling a bill of goods to Geredin? Maybe Geredin himself is a dupe of someone's misinformation campaign? Did someone over there count on him passing fake information to us over here? Are they trying to throw us off another scent? Oh, brother! When the Russkies play chess, it's always three-dimensional speed chess—they don't bother with the easy stuff.*

He got up and paced around the room, thinking. Operation *Zephyr* had so far come up with very little hard data to verify—or falsify, for that matter—the dire concerns that Geredin had expressed to Jensen at their clandestine meeting at Great Falls. *Soviet naval aggression is indeed increasing, as Geredin warned, but only in the Pacific theater*, he mused. He immediately corrected himself; the proper term was Area of Operations (AO), not theater. 'Theater' was a term of war, and no one was at war—not yet. *War is what the head of the KGB is trying to avoid—so he claims, anyway.*

The CIA analyst came to a decision. He picked up the phone and dialed Bill Jensen, the newly confirmed DDO. "Bill, what are the chances of getting some boots on the ground in Vladivostok? I need some reliable human intelligence that's not filtered through the impenetrable mind of a Soviet official."

"The chances are not good, Sam, not good at all. We've not had a reliable contact in Vladivostok for several years now, not since *Yellow Fin* was compromised and executed." *Yellow Fin* was the code name of a Russian nuclear engineer who had worked in the Petrovka Shipyard, adjacent to Vladivostok. For eight years he'd been leaving photographs and technical specifications of the newest Soviet submarines in a dead drop at Nakhodka, sixty miles east. However, about a year ago he'd been sold out to the KGB, apparently by someone inside the CIA. It had kicked off a vigorous mole hunt inside the Agency that was still going on. The CIA found itself watching helplessly as one by one its best Soviet informants were exposed, arrested and executed.

"What if we insert someone temporarily? Someone who could pass as a Russian citizen, maybe as a stevedore or merchant seaman. All we need is someone who can sit in a bar and listen. Sailors talk, especially when they're drunk. And given the political situation of the country, they'll probably be talking politics. That's liable to give us exactly what we need."

"Hold on, Sam—you're in Analysis, not Operations. You aren't talking about a CIA case officer managing a Russian— you're talking about an American pretending to be a Russian, infiltrating the country. He'd have no protection if he's caught. At least case officers working out of a consulate with diplomatic cover have diplomatic immunity. But you're asking to send someone in who'd be wholly unprotected if he was exposed. That would be a mighty dangerous mission, Sam."

"I understand that, Bill. But if you've been reading the reports the ONI is producing, we've already got a mighty dangerous situation developing in the Pacific. All we need is for someone to overreact, and we could be looking at ships sunk and hundreds dead on both sides."

For a moment there was silence on the line and Sam wondered if the connection had been cut. Then Bill Jensen responded with a sigh. "Actually, Sam, that's a really good point. Let me think on this and get back to you."

When Sam hung up the department secretary buzzed him on the intercom. "Mr. Bergman, an Evelyn Stinson tried to contact you. She wouldn't say who she was with or what it was about, she just said you would know. She asked if you could see her at your earliest opportunity."

****

Once Bergman had navigated the security gauntlet at Fort Meade, he was escorted to Stinson's office. He found her sitting at her desk translating a stack of intercepts. When he walked in she looked up. "Hello, Sam," she said, "please have a seat."

The greeting was cold and professional. The green eyes

he'd found so captivating were veiled and icy. He wondered, not for the first time, what had happened to the warmth between them last year.

"I got your message. I came as soon as I could get away." He cringed as soon as he said it. His response sounded too eager, almost needy. Actually, he wasn't sure how it sounded. He just knew he was adrift, wrestling with how to shift the relationship back to pure business, as it certainly seemed that was all the woman was interested in.

"Here. Take a look at this. Came through this morning." She slid a Russian teletype document across the desk. Stapled to it was her translation.

He picked it up and read quickly. It was an order from Admiral Shukshin to the commandant of the Petrovka Shipyard, instructing him to complete whatever essential repairs were necessary, "to ensure the safe operation of the submarines *K-263*, *K-264*, and *K-284*; work to be completed within thirty-six hours; then move said submarines to the provisioning quay." A copy of the order was sent to Captain First Rank Boris Sayanovich Mirov.

"And then there's this," she said, handing him another teletype.

It was a response from the commandant, complaining that two of the submarines had been on his dry dock for less than three weeks, and the third for less than a month. The man was complaining that there was not enough time to complete the necessary overhaul and maintenance, let alone to update the equipment scheduled for replacement.

"And finally, this."

Shukshin had responded that he was confident the "heroic Soviet workers" could complete the necessary tasks on time, and that he would be inspecting the submarines himself in thirty-six hours, expecting to find them ready to provision and deploy.

"I don't know that there is any significance to these communiqués, but you said you wanted me to call you, so I did."

He nodded. "Yes, I did. Thank you." He reread each of the teletypes carefully and then noticed something that had not occurred to him before. "Each of these is coming from or going to Admiral Shukshin," he said, thinking aloud, holding the communiqués in his hand.

"Yes," she acknowledged, furrowing her brow. "Is that significant?"

"I don't know. But I just realized that in the last twelve months of reading the Soviets' mail, I've never seen an order from the commander of the Red Banner Pacific Fleet, Admiral Pyotr Stefanovich Zelenko. They've always come from his deputy, Admiral Shukshin. Both Zelenko and Shukshin are highly regarded in the Soviet navy. But it's beginning to look like Zelenko has turned Pacific Fleet operations over to Shukshin."

Her curiosity was piqued. Working with Sam in the past had been fascinating because he'd included her in his thinking, taking her suggestions and interpretations very seriously. But given the bitterness she felt about their former relationship, she was not about to let him know that she was interested in *Zephyr*. So she just stared at him and said nothing.

"Can I keep these?" he asked, studying her face.

"Yes, I was preparing them to send to you. There's quite a bit more that I need to translate yet—it all came in this morning. I'll send them over by courier this afternoon."

"Thanks, Evelyn." He moved toward the door, then stopped. *I have to know what happened. I can't move forward with my own life until I know*, he thought.

He turned around. "Evelyn, I don't mean to pry into your personal business. But, what happened? I had thought that we were mutually moving toward a, uh, well, a very special close friendship. Why have you become so, so—cold toward me?"

Her face turned red and her pretty green eyes flashed with anger. Her mouth drew into a tight line. "Shut the door," she said firmly. When he had done so she snapped, "Why did you lead me on so? Once Operations *Snowbird* and *Thunderbird* were over, you never called me. Why didn't you call?" Her chin quivered and she angrily wiped away a tear that started to trickle down her cheek.

He blinked, surprised by her sudden vehemence. "But I

did call," he protested. "I must have called your answering machine ten times and left messages each time. *You* never responded. You never called me back—not once," he answered with irritation. He sank into the chair and looked at the floor. After a moment he muttered, "I finally figured you'd had a change of heart and weren't interested in seeing me. I didn't want to harass you, so I stopped calling. For the last eight months not a day has gone by that I didn't ask myself what I did wrong."

She sat down and said incredulously, "I don't know what your game is, Sam, but that's simply not true. You didn't call once, not a single time." She stopped and grabbed a tissue. Several more tears rolled down her face as she said, "And then, back in February, my best friend tells me that you'd called her, leaving messages on her answering machine, asking for dates, leaving your phone number, your work schedule, everything. Boy, was I ever wrong about you!"

It was his turn to get angry. "Whoa! I don't even know who your best friend is, and I certainly don't know her phone number. And besides, it was you I was interested in. Only you."

"I'm sorry, Sam, but I don't believe you. My best friend would have no reason to lie about this."

"So you think I'm lying?" he asked, raising his eyebrows. Honesty was a matter of pride for him, and he deeply resented what she was saying.

"Yes. I'd have never thought it possible of you, but I don't know what other conclusion fits the evidence."

"Very well. I'll take no more of your time, and I promise I'll never bring this up again," Sam said, standing up. At the door he turned and faced her. "I hope we can still work together on Operation *Zephyr*. It's actually a rather crucial matter."

"Oh, I can work with you, Mr. Bergman. Just—keep your distance, please."

He nodded and left the office, gently closing the door behind him. He was still trembling with anger and hurt when he got into his car.

Evelyn locked her office door and sat behind her desk, shaking with grief and indignation. She replayed the confrontation in her mind. The abject pain written on his face when she called him by his last name broke through her bitter, angry heart, and she put her head down on her desk and wept.

****

Jake sat at his desk in the squadron operations office, reviewing the maintenance logs on the Falcons flown by the 34th Fighter Squadron. He signed off on the report with a sigh and put it in a manila file folder and dropped it in the file cabinet. He was working hard on maintaining a good attitude and managed to find some significance in the fact that his work was helping keep his fellow squadron members safe. That, at least, was worth his time.

The phone rang, startling him. Only people on the inside knew the direct number to his desk. The public always connected with the squadron secretary first. He picked it up, expecting the call to be from the squadron chief of maintenance.

"Kelly," he said brusquely.

"Hello, Jake. It's Jim Franks."

"Hi, General," Jake said, brightening up. "How are things at Edwards?"

"Secret, as always," Franks chuckled. "You should know that."

"So they've got you on a new project now, General?"

There was silence on the other end.

"Aha," Jake laughed, "you just told me all I need to know. What can I do for you, General?"

"I wanted to get back to you about your requests from several weeks ago. First off, I've managed to get your complete CCT history, deployments, training, evaluations—everything —put on your service record. Major John Smith is no more."

"Great! Thanks, General. That's a relief."

"And I might as well tell you now, Jake. That CCT experience on your record has bumped you up the promotions list several notches. If I am not mistaken, you'll be a colonel by March."

Now it was Jake's turn to be silent.

"What? Aren't you happy about that?" demanded Franks. "It comes with a bump in your pay that should be mighty handy with a baby on the way."

"Yes, sir. And, well, I am happy about it. There's just one problem. The higher up the food chain I go, General, the less I actually get to do things. Instead, I'm just ordering other people to do things. I'm a hands-on kind of a guy, General Franks."

"Grow up, Jake. Derring-do is what weekends are for. But if you really want to live out on the limb, I've got an opportunity for you. That's the other thing I wanted to tell you. I can get you a slot in the 1721st Combat Control Squadron at Pope Air Force Base at Fayetteville, North Carolina," Franks said. "I think you'll discover some people in that outfit that you already know, Jake. Only they don't know you as Jacob Kelly, they know you as Major John Smith. Are you interested?"

"Definitely. Is Lieutenant Gordon Blake still with them?"

"Yes, but now he's Captain Gordon Blake. Well, you go home and talk to Galina about this and call me back."

"I don't need to talk to Galina, I already know I want the billet," Jake insisted.

"You don't know much about women, son, do you? You go home and do as I have said. In fact, I'm not going to take a call from you. If you want the job, have Galina call me and give me the okay. Being a CCT operator is dangerous stuff, more dangerous even than flying F-16s. You are a husband and soon-to-be father, Jake. That has to be part of your thinking. The air force already has enough divorces among its airmen, and I'm not going to contribute to another one. So if you want the job, Galina has to call. Got it?"

Jake sighed. "Yes, sir."

****

Kosmos 1900 hung in low earth orbit at an altitude of approximately one hundred sixty-five miles above the earth's surface. Every ninety minutes it completed another trip around the globe. As it passed overhead it bounced a powerful radar signal off the surface of the oceans, transmitting what it detected to ground stations in the Soviet Union.

So it was that the progress of Carrier Group Three was tracked through the Malacca and Singapore Straits. Using the radar-based position reports from *Kosmos 1900*, Shukshin was able to direct an intelligence trawler to intercept the carrier group as it threaded its way carefully through the heavy commercial maritime traffic transiting the Malacca Strait. The trawler obtained positive visual identification of the ships traveling in company with the *Vinson*, and Shukshin radioed the information to Mirov's submarines before the carrier group entered the Singapore Strait. The trap was set.

****

Sam Bergman had intended his final question to Evelyn Stinson to put the past to rest and to allow him to move on with his lonely, bachelor life. For a brief time ten months ago, the possibility of a wonderful future with a wonderful woman had held his hopes and dreams. No more.

But that final confrontation wouldn't leave him at peace, especially her accusation that he had lied. He reached into his pocket, withdrew his wallet, and located a small, worn, and much folded scrap of greenbar computer paper. In her handwriting, the note simply said "Me" and had a phone number on it. She'd given it to him early last December, the week before the Operation *Thunderbird* assault on the Soviet interrogation- and prison compound.

Bergman was going to be incommunicado in a secure facility until the operation was over, monitoring intelligence traffic for any sign that it had been compromised. She was in the midst of a move, as her landlord had sold her apartment out from under her. Along with the change of address came a change of phone numbers, and she'd written her new phone number down on the scrap of paper and given it to him so he could contact her at her new apartment when the operation was done.

After Operation *Thunderbird* had concluded, Bergman emerged from the secure communication center and resumed his normal work at the Agency. He'd dialed the number, gotten an answering machine with the default announcement in a computer voice, and left his message. No response. Several days later, he did it again. No response, no return phone call. This went on for a whole month before he finally interpreted her silence as her response.

He stared at the scrap, trying to be angry with her—but all he felt was great sadness and a sense of loss. But then he fell upon an idea that could explain the whole terrible fiasco. He picked up his phone and dialed Geno Bianchi.

"Geno, it's Sam. How's my favorite hacker?"

"Not doin' so good, buddy," Geno responded in his heavy New Jersey accent. Geno was a former-black-hat-now-white-hat hacker, who'd chosen a straight life in the CIA instead of a crooked life in the slammer. He'd been heading to prison as a convicted twenty-year-old computer genius caught in the act of illegally penetrating the Pentagon's most secure network, when the CIA offered him a deal he didn't refuse. That was five years ago and though the man was truly going *mostly* straight (no one who worked for the CIA was completely straight), he still possessed a panoply of talents that could get his CIA bosses what they wanted without always going through the courts for permission.

"Life is gettin' tough for people like me, capiche?"

"How so, Geno?"

"Everybody's usin' encryption, you follow? Takes me maybe an extra twenty minutes or so to crack it. Used to be everyone on the Net was talkin' in clear text. Made snoopin' a whole lot easier. So what can I do for youse, Mr. Bergman?"

"Geno, I have a simple task for a man of your talents. I've got a phone number. Could you do a reverse lookup for me, find out who has that number? I already tried but it's un-listed."

"You want that I should do this the quick way or the slow

way, Mr. Bergman?" The slow way involved a court order.

"Quick way is fine—I won't tell if you won't. I just need a name and address—that's it."

In ten minutes he had his answer. On the way home that night he stopped and bought a card. He wrote a note to Evelyn explaining that he did not want to cause her any more pain or irritation, but he wanted to defend himself against the charge of lying to her—a charge he found particularly hurtful and unfair. He included the note she had written, pointing out that it was, after all, in her handwriting. The number she gave him was the number he'd called, over and over again. He asked her, "Although I realize you no longer have any romantic feelings for me, at the very least would you please clear me of the charge of dishonesty?" The next morning he dropped it in the mail.

****

"What is the surprise, Jacob?" Galina asked, consumed with curiosity. She and Jake were headed to her favorite restaurant, a barbecue ribs joint decorated in a wild west theme, full of noise and local color.

"You'll have to wait until we get there, babe," replied Jacob, smiling mischievously.

Galina self-consciously rubbed her tummy. At twelve weeks, she was just beginning to show. Her bouts of morning sickness had diminished and she was beginning to feel somewhat normal again.

Jake noticed. "So how is Rascal today?"

"How do you know it's not Rascalenka?" she teased.

"Well, could be, I suppose. So, how's Rascalenka today? Or how is Rascalenka's mommy?"

"Mommy wasn't throwing up this morning, which is a vast improvement over last week. I've been getting a few headaches, Jake, which is not normal for me. But some of the other wives I've been talking to say that's just part of pregnancy. They told me to start eating a small snack between meals. I tried it today and it seemed to help. But I don't want to get big as a house."

"If you get big as a house I'm liable to trade you in."

"Ha. Maybe I'll trade you in first, Sokolov, and find me a rich man. Did you ever think of that?"

He laughed as he pulled the truck into a parking place.

Once they had ordered Galina reached across the table, grabbed his wrist and squeezed. "Tell me the surprise, Sokolov."

"Okay. General Franks called, says that he has located a billet for me as a CCT operator if I want it. And I do want it." Kelly's eyes shone and he looked happier than she'd seen in weeks. He continued, "That's going to be a lot more interesting and a lot more fun than sitting at a desk writing reports for the squadron."

"That's wonderful, Jacob. I can see this is something you're really excited about. Maybe it's an answer to my prayers," she said.

He looked confused. "Wait. Your prayers? You're an atheist, Galya—who do you think you're praying to?"

"I don't know, Jake. I think some of my ideas are changing, but I can't really put my finger on why, or even how right now. I guess ever since I learned there was a new life growing inside of me, it's . . . well, it's made me take a second look at things. But let's talk about that later. I want to find out about your new job. What is a CCT and how do you operate it? Is it some sort of a truck, or a bulldozer? Will you have to go to school to learn how to drive it?"

Jake laughed out loud. "No, no, no, sweetie. CCT is not a vehicle, it's part of the air force special operations group. It's kind of like . . . um," he hesitated, trying to think of something his Russian wife would be familiar with. "It's kind of like the Soviet *Spetsnaz.*"

"*Spetsnaz!*" she exclaimed. "They are elite combat soldiers, are they not?"

"Exactly. CCT stands for Combat Control Team. They are sort of like Navy SEALs, only they are air force instead of navy. I've already been trained as a Combat Controller and have deployed as an operator four times. It was all before I met you. Actually, it was that training that enabled me to escape from the Soviet Union last year."

Galina nodded, but didn't say anything. He could see that she was processing his news, and he could also see that she wasn't as excited about it as he. The waiter brought their order, and they ate in silence for a few minutes.

Finally, she spoke. "That's a very dangerous job, isn't it?"

He wiped his mouth on his napkin and nodded. "It certainly can be. Sometimes the mission is nothing more than training another country's military. That's not usually dangerous. But other missions can be very dangerous. And they are almost always classified. I won't be able to talk about where I'm going or what I'll be doing. Sometimes I won't even be allowed to say how long I'll be gone."

"I see." She poked at her meal for a few minutes and then asked, "Isn't there something else you can do in the air force, Jacob? Something . . . safer?"

"Oh, sure. There are other jobs. I could sit at a desk and write reports all day, and the greatest danger I would face would be getting a paper cut. But that's not what I want to do."

"Yes, but shouldn't you be thinking about us and not just you? We've got a baby on the way, Jacob. What about what's best for the family?" she asked, tilting her head as she studied him.

He put down his fork and sat back. His brow furrowed, and she could see that he was confused.

"But, Galina, I *am* thinking about us. All three of us. This is how I make a living, this is how I provide for my family—for us, not just for me. This is what I do."

Her voice trembled. "Yes. But what if something happens to you? What if you get killed? You yourself just said it can be very dangerous. What if you go on a mission and don't come back?"

"Galina, flying a high-performance jet fighter is also a very, very dangerous job. Just three weeks ago Randy Polter's F-16 lost its hydraulics on takeoff and he had to eject at almost ground level. No one was shooting at him, his aircraft simply malfunctioned. He broke both arms in the accident and is lucky to be alive. Flying is dangerous, for crying out loud. You never voiced a concern about me flying, even as dangerous as that is. Why are you all concerned about danger now?"

Her chin quivered. "When I married you I knew what you did for a living, and I made myself accept it. And then I got pregnant, and then, you had seizure and had to stop flying. Suddenly I knew you were safe, and that we had a much better chance of growing old together, and together seeing our baby grow up and enter adulthood. But now—" She didn't finish. She twisted her napkin as tears ran down her face.

Part of his heart broke as he observed the distress of his wife. But another part became angry, and that was the part he yielded to. "Galina, stop it! I could just as easily be killed driv-ing into work tomorrow. I am not going to sit behind a desk for the rest of my life and be bored out of my skull! I want to do this. This is who I am."

She dried her eyes and looked at him angrily. "Yes, it is, isn't it? It's *who you are*, and it's all about you, isn't it? You are forgetting something, however. When you married me, *who you are* changed. And when I became pregnant, *who you are* changed again. Now you aren't just some ex-fighter pilot, *who you are* is a husband and a father. So why do I think that doesn't seem to matter to you?" She stood up, threw her nap-kin in his face and stalked out of the restaurant.

Chapter 8

Saturday, October 22, 1988

For two days, Jacob and Galina Kelly refused to speak to each other. Finally Jake tired of the tension and unhappiness. "This is stupid, Galina," he said as he stood at the sink washing dishes. She was sitting at the table making up a grocery list. "We've got to talk this through. We can't go on like this."

"What's to talk about? You've already made up your mind, you've already accepted the assignment. Now I'm just waiting on you to tell me to start packing," she said coolly, not looking at him.

"No, I haven't accepted the assignment. In fact, I can't."

With that she looked up. "What do you mean? You said in the restaurant that you were going to do it."

"I want to do it, Galina, but General Franks put a condition on it. He's not going to make the transfer happen unless, . . ." Jake paused and pulled his hands out of the dishwater and dried them on a dishtowel.

"Unless what?"

He turned and sat at the table facing his wife. "Unless *you* call him and tell him to."

"Me?"

He nodded.

Something about the image of her calling General Franks and asking him to transfer her husband to the Combat Control Team struck her as humorous. An involuntary smile traced across her face, followed by a chuckle. In seconds, the tension of the last several days came pouring out in giggles, and soon she sat laughing uncontrollably.

He wanted to be offended but found it impossible in the face of her mirth. Soon he began chuckling and then laughing out loud. In a moment, still giggling, she came around the table and sat on his lap, her arms wrapped around him while she laughed.

"What, what, . . . haha, *what* is so funny?" he asked, wiping the tears of laughter from his eyes.

"Oh, it's just that you crossed Siberia all by yourself, all the while outwitting the entire Soviet army, but your boss makes you get *my* permission to join this CCT thing. The image in my mind is just . . . hysterical," she said, starting to laugh again. "I feel like your mother or something."

Jake chuckled. "Well, her name was Galina, you know."

They sat for a few minutes embracing each other, glad that the ice had been broken. Finally she returned to her chair. "So what are we going to do?" she asked.

"Nothing—at least, not right away. We need to talk it through without hurting each other. I want to do it, you don't want me to. But we don't have to decide anything right now—I can continue writing reports for the squadron for the time being. It's not like this will be my only opportunity."

She nodded.

He reached for her hand. "I'm sorry I lost my temper with you."

"We both did. I'll never forget the hurt in your eyes when I called you an ex-fighter pilot. That was cruel of me. I'm so sorry, Jake, it just came out."

"That did hurt," he agreed. "But what hurt even more was knowing you were right about me being only concerned with myself—with what I want. You're right, babe. I've only been thinking about me."

"Let's table it for a couple of days," she said softly, "then we can talk about it again. More calmly, this time."

****

It had been a terrible day. Evelyn Stinson was tired, angry, frustrated, and—she admitted to herself—a little depressed. It got off on the wrong foot when her car wouldn't start. The last several days she'd noticed that her headlights were a little too dim and a little too yellow. It hadn't registered that something was wrong with either her alternator or the battery, so she'd let it go.

It certainly registered this morning. The battery was too weak to turn the engine over. All she got when she turned the key was a couple of half-hearted clicks. Her AAA account had expired, so she couldn't call them. She wound up calling a cab and paying a fortune to get to work.

When she finally got to work, all the donuts were gone—and she'd been counting on them for breakfast. And the coffee machine wasn't working. And things slid generally downhill from there. She found herself unable to concentrate, hating Sam Bergman but half-hoping he'd show up so she could give him a piece of her mind.

When she finally arrived home at the end of the day (after another expensive cab ride) she talked her neighbor into jumping her car. By the time she'd driven to a garage, had the battery replaced, and returned home it was going on nine. She hadn't had supper yet and she had a headache.

Muttering under her breath, Evelyn threw a TV dinner in the oven, grabbed a half gallon of chocolate ice cream from the freezer and served herself a large helping, intending to drown her sorrows in sugar. She was halfway through the bowl when she remembered she hadn't retrieved the mail.

There were four credit card offers, a women's clothing catalog, the electric bill, and an envelope the size and shape of a greeting card but bearing no return address. She pitched everything but the bill and the card and went back to her ice cream.

She opened the card and a scrap of worn greenbar paper fell out. Retrieving the paper she saw the word "Me" and a phone number, written in her own handwriting. But the phone number was her girlfriend's unlisted number. And suddenly, without reading the card she knew what she was looking at and who the card was from.

"NO!" she wailed. The card confirmed her fears. *It was me,* she thought. *I destroyed my own future, my own happiness. It's my fault. All because I wrote the wrong stupid number! And I even called him a liar!* Evelyn began to weep. The frustration of her difficult day piled onto her grief, and soon she was racked with heart-wrenching sobs.

****

Galina slid into the booth opposite her friend. Janet Lancaster was the wife of Colonel Brent Lancaster, the group commander over the 34th Fighter Squadron. She had two teenagers and a child in middle school. In her early forties, Janet led a fellowship of squadron wives. Galina was drawn to the woman's warmth and generous spirit.

"Thanks for meeting with me, Janet. I've got a situation at home with Jacob that I don't know how to handle," Galina said, "and I'm looking for some advice."

"Happy to help," the older woman said with a smile. "But first, let's talk about you. How are you feeling?"

Galina laughed. "Everyone asks me that. I don't know—how am I supposed to feel? Excited. A little scared. Fat. Last week I started having trouble buttoning my jeans. I think they must be shrinking," she said, grinning.

"Oh, I'm sure they are," Janet said, winking at her. "Well, get used to it, honey. Another month or so and nothing is going to fit. On the top or the bottom. You're going to need a whole new wardrobe. That's just part of the drill, as they say. There's a secondhand maternity store downtown—I think all the base wives use it."

The two women talked kids, cooking, and clothes over their coffee for half an hour, and then Galina brought up the situation with Jake.

"I don't know what to do. The thought of him going into special operations scares me to death. I'm afraid that one day he won't come back."

"That's possible," Janet agreed. "It happens. It's something we have to get used to as women whose husbands have taken up a very dangerous occupation."

"But it seems so selfish to me. Doesn't he care about me and my feelings?"

"You need to be careful going down that path, Galina. It's not entirely fair. Look, let's be honest. Fighter pilots have massive egos, and they can easily fall into thinking that life should revolve around them. We've all seen it in our own husbands. And frankly, selfishness frequently seems to be the most common characteristic of someone who possesses both X and Y chromosomes.

"But it's also not as simple as that. Some men—some, not all—who take up combat roles do so because it is in their nature to be a protector. They might think in big terms, in the abstract, as in being the protector of the flag or the nation, but for most it's much closer to home. Protecting their wives, their families, their communities, their brothers-in-arms—the people close to them. The thought of danger to themselves doesn't usually register on their radar—it simply goes with the territory of being a protector. They just don't give it much thought. Instead, they are thinking about the danger to you or to the community if they fail to do their jobs. In Jake's mind when he climbed into that cockpit, it *was* you he was thinking about. You are the one he's protecting. You are the reason he flies into danger or joins a special operations command. It's you he's thinking about, not himself. I know that's true of Brent. He's thinking about me and the kids, and ensuring that we will continue to live in a safe, free community."

This was a new thought to Galina. She considered it, turning the idea over in her mind and comparing it with what she knew to be true of Jacob. And it fit, aligning with what she had observed of his character and his temperament. While he expressed himself in terms of a job that was "boring" or "exciting" she began to see that he was evaluating it in terms of his contribution as a protector.

She thought back to how they met. He'd broken his arm escaping from his pursuers in Khabarovsk. She was waiting at a stoplight in her orange ZAZ-968M Zaporozhets when he vaulted out of the back of a truck and commandeered her car. He had grabbed her arm and squeezed until she drove where he commanded her to. But once they'd evaded his pursuers he sensed her fear of him. He asked her to stop the car, and he got out and walked away, broken arm and all, not wanting her to feel she was in danger. She was his ticket to escape the pursuit, but he was willing to forfeit that rather than cause her fear.

She also remembered that he refused to marry her until he could guarantee that she would not be in danger from

Chernikov's revenge. Janet was right, she decided. Jacob's first impulse had always been to protect her, regardless of the danger to himself.

"But how do you deal with the fear, Janet? If he takes the CCT assignment I'll be afraid for his life every time he is deployed. I can't live with that."

"The way I deal with the fear, Galina, is to have confidence in someone bigger than Jake, someone that will never leave you or forsake you."

"You mean God?"

Janet nodded. "Yes, I do. I believe in a God who actually exists, who is personal, and who cares about me more than anyone else does. I believe in a God who is always good, and who is always in control of the circumstances of my life. He knows what is best for me, be it pain or pleasure, sorrow or comfort, trouble or peace, and He always does what is best."

"You seem so sure of your belief," Galina said wistfully.

"Yes. I am sure of it. I know God is real, because He has changed me in ways I could not change myself. But how about you? What do you believe?"

Galina stared out the window, looking at nothing. "For many years I have called myself an atheist. But I considered the question of God's existence the most important question I'd ever face. I mean, think about it, Janet, if God really exists it would be an error of infinite magnitude to live and die without knowing Him, without acknowledging Him, without . . . worshiping Him.

"I was confident He did not exist. Having been raised in the Soviet Union, I was taught from my youngest years all the way through my college degree in Mathematics that the notion of God was nothing more than a manipulative device to control the masses through fear. But I wanted my confidence to be grounded in a careful examination of the evidence, not in ignorance or personal bias. So I made a study of all the major religions. One by one I eliminated them from consideration. Some fell off my radar because their theology was nonsense. Others I eliminated because the official history of their religion was obviously false.

"Judaism was the hardest to eliminate. It had such a solid historical background, and the laws of the Old Testament were so enlightened when considering the era and the laws of the other ancient nations. But the rabbis kept piling on interpretation after interpretation, to the point where they turned a rather elegant body of law into something that began to seem faintly ridiculous. I finally decided that Judaism does not give me incontrovertible reasons to believe in God.

"But try as I might, I have not been able to eliminate Christianity. It has the same solid historical foundation as Judaism and the same elegant Old Testament law—minus the rabbinical interpretations. And both Old and New Testaments focus on one person of history, Jesus of Nazareth. And his words—well, it's hard to imagine how anyone could say those things. I read the four gospels and I cannot escape the sense that I am reading truth.

"I am ready to be done with my long study and move on to other intellectual pursuits. I am ready to declare myself an intelligent, informed atheist, a woman who has come to a reasoned conclusion by neither bias nor ignorance, but through diligent examination. But I find that . . . I can't. The words of Jesus just won't leave me alone."

****

Al Mercer loved his work. An employee of the National Reconnaissance Office (NRO), he described himself as an "Orbital Voyeur" which basically meant that he got to peer into other countries' business using an eye-in-the-sky that orbited approximately every ninety-seven minutes. The Lockheed *KH-11-8* satellite, code-named *CRYSTAL*, had the theoretical ability to pick out items as small as 2.4 inches in size. The useful resolution was less, of course, due to microscopic imperfections in the satellite's mirrors, electronic noise in the charge-coupled optical sensor, and atmospheric conditions. Nonetheless the detail he was able to observe in the images transmitted to earth was stunning.

One of Mercer's primary assignments was to keep track of

the surface combatants and submarines of the Soviet Pacific Fleet while they were in port. Because the satellite was in a sun-synchronous orbit, it repeated its ground track every four days. As vessels docked or deployed he reported their activities. His reports were included in intelligence briefs distributed to the CIA, the Office of Naval Intelligence, and the Seventh Fleet headquarters.

Mercer studied the latest imagery from the KH-11, recorded as it passed over the submarine pens at Vladivostok earlier in the day. As he examined the pictures he thought that the count of vessels was down from the images taken four days prior. He retrieved the paper copy of his last report and verified that the census of docked vessels had changed.

The technician mounted the surveillance tape recorded four days prior and and compared it with the current images. Two Akulas and a Victor III were missing from today's fly-over. *Aha*, he thought to himself, *where did you boys go?*

Mercer enlarged the older images and studied them intently. The piers next to each boat were occupied by several trucks and a handful of dockworkers. *They were provisioning*, he realized, *and I missed it*. Out of curiosity he switched to the infrared imagery on the earlier recording. All three submarines showed heat blooms just aft of the sail, radiating from the reactor spaces. *Yep, they were heating the kettle, preparing to sail.*

Mercer had been watching the berthing areas for the Soviet Pacific Fleet for several years, and had a good sense of their operational tempo. Something about the three departures seemed out of place. He spent the next two hours reviewing his reports and selected images from the last twelve months, and then realized what was troubling him. Two weeks ago the Victor had been moved from the nuclear fuel replenishing drydock to the quay. The normal Soviet practice would call for another two months refurbishing and updating her sensors, electronics and weapons systems before sending her on patrol again. They appeared to have skipped that step. The story on the Akulas was even more unusual. They'd just come off a patrol last month. Apparently Ivan turned them right around and sent them out again. *Something is going on*, Mercer thought to himself.

He wrote up his report, noting the unusual disappearances, and then called his supervisor.

"Hey, Barry, this is Al. I just gave the courier my latest report on the sub census at Vladivostok. You might want to call ONI and give them a heads up. Sometimes I wonder if those guys even read my reports. Well, they need to eyeball today's very carefully. There's some unusual activity in Ivan's sub pens they will be interested in."

****

"Messenger of the Watch, please inform Gator that I need his entire bridge crew, everyone who is not on watch, in Wardroom 3, the officers' mess, in twenty minutes," barked Captain Arthur Young. 'Gator' was Commander William Watson, the *Vinson*'s navigation officer.

When Commander Watson and most of the Navigation Department were assembled in the wardroom, Young began the briefing. "Gentlemen, as you know, the Malacca and Singapore Straits are the most heavily traveled shipping channels in the world. Ship-to-ship collisions happen in these waters with distressing frequency. Naval careers are ended here. I do not intend that mine will end by colliding with some hapless merchantman. I expect diligent, precise, professional navigation and ship handling tomorrow. I am confident you will not disappoint me.

"I will have the conn at 0600 and will keep it until we clear both straits. We are adjusting our current speed to put us at the choke-point of the first one, Malacca Strait, at 0800 hours tomorrow. That allows us to transit the worst parts of both straits in broad daylight. Tomorrow's forenoon watch will be extended and will last from 0800 hours until we clear both straits—I don't want a watch-change evolution while we are in those waters. Barring a mishap, we will be exiting the Singapore Strait tomorrow at 1400 hours.

"I have asked Commander Watson to double the lookouts and to use senior men, preferably Master Helmsmen. I want eyeballs who have ship handling experience monitoring the situation. Rather than sticking to the regular watch bill, Gator will handpick tomorrow's bridge crew. The revised watch bill for the forenoon watch will be posted in your mess by this evening—be sure to check it.

"The official speed limit in the straits is twelve knots. We will use that as a baseline and adjust our speed as required for safe ship handling. Our consorts will be released from normal station-keeping to maneuver as the situation requires, the *Texas* taking point and the *Flint* and *Roanoke* bringing up the rear.

"Because there isn't room in the straits to turn the ship into the wind for flight operations, CAG is transferring twelve of our Tomcats to Paya Lebar Air Base in Singapore this evening. They will fly CAP from there until we have finished the transit. He is also sending four Vikings and a pair of Hawkeyes. Tomorrow CAG will put a pair of choppers in the air to run interference for us, making sure that small craft don't cross our path or approach too close. The last thing we need is to run over some fisherman.

"There are also several land-based P-3 Orions already at work, sanitizing our course from the exit of the straits all the way to Pattaya Beach. The water's pretty shallow on that leg, so I doubt there are any submarines to speak of, but we're moving forward with an abundance of caution, as always.

"Any questions? No? Good. Remember, tomorrow is an opportunity to make a good impression on the people of Malaysia and Singapore, something we sorely need after the *Vincennes* fiasco. Make me proud, gentlemen."

****

The plan of Operation *Vostochnyy Veter*, or *East Wind*, was simple enough. So simple that there were a thousand things that could go wrong.

Based on the intelligence they'd collected, the *Vinson* was expected to sail between the Anambas Islands on the east and Pulau Tioman on the west, southeast of Kuantan, Malaysia.

Captains Gromyko (K-284) and Fetisov (K-263) would prowl above Kepulauan Anambas, the westernmost of the islands, maintaining a distance of thirty kilometers between themselves. Mirov's Victor III (*K-264*) would take up a position fifty-five kilometers northeast of Pulau Tioman. He would ease the Victor down onto the seafloor and all but shut his reactor down, creating the most minimal noise signature possible in a bid to evade detection until the last possible minute.

According to the plan, the submarines would wait until the P-3 Orions had finished sweeping the area and then creep into position. When the carrier group approached, the two Akulas would make enough noise to ensure their detection and slowly advance on the carrier. The intention was to draw the Americans' ASW resources, making it easier for Mirov's Victor to close on the carrier undetected. When the American sonar picked up the Akulas, Mirov was expecting the *Vinson* to assume a zigzag course, the basic response to a potential submarine threat. If everything worked according to plan, the first leg of the zigzag would put the flattop right in Mirov's lap.

****

Five miles off the port beam a rusty Panamanian-flagged coal collier was sluggishly steaming west as the *Vinson* approached the eastern extent of the strait. The collier was being overtaken by an equally rusty freighter and two large, glistening, white LPG tankers. Two miles off the *Vinson*'s stern the Lagoi ferry was crossing the carrier's wake. One of the SH-3H Sea King choppers was shooing away several small boats off the starboard bow that were attempting to cross the channel ahead of the supercarrier. A large luxury cruise ship seven miles ahead was just turning westbound into the strait. Her wide turn was veering the vessel too close to the eastbound shipping channel.

"Get on the horn and ask the skipper of that cruise ship to get back in his lane," the navigation officer instructed the radioman monitoring the commercial maritime bands. He wiped his sweaty hands on his trousers as his head swiveled back and forth, watching the shipping traffic approach. Though the radar was manned and he had good men serving as lookouts on either wing of the bridge, he still felt compelled to keep visual track of all the shipping traffic himself.

The *Vinson* was embedded in what for all practical purposes was a convoy of eastbound ship traffic. A mile astern was the *Roanoke* with the *Flint* following her. They were followed by a pair of merchantmen sailing abreast—never a good idea in these waters. A mile behind them was an Indonesian destroyer, a Russian trawler, and a Chinese factory ship processing anchovies, part of the fishing fleet returning from the Andaman Sea. Sailing ahead of the carrier was the guided missile cruiser *Texas* and a diverse collection of commercial vessels steaming in single file.

The commercial and military ships were maintaining a professional, orderly station with respect to each other. A three-hundred-foot luxury yacht was coming up from behind, however, cruising at sixteen knots while the rest of the traffic was maintaining twelve. The yacht was passing to the inside of the channel and making the masters of the commercial vessels going in either direction very nervous. Commander Watson directed the starboard Sea King to get aggressive with the captain of the yacht, and it finally slowed and began maintaining station off the port quarter. It was sailing too close to the carrier for Commander Watson's comfort, but at least it was no longer making a nuisance of itself. He decided to let well enough alone as long as the Sea King was monitoring the vessel.

Thirty minutes later the quartermaster of the watch announced, "Skipper, we have cleared the strait."

"Praise be," Captain Young sighed. The underarms of his uniform shirt were stained with sweat. He'd been on the bridge continuously since 0600. Young looked at Commander Watson and gave him a tired smile. "Gator, maintain this course for another thirty minutes and get us out of this cluster of traffic. Then set a course for Pattaya Beach. You may replace the navigation watch once we turn north. Resume the regular watch schedule with the first dog watch."

"Aye, aye, Skipper."

Young picked up the handset for Primary Flight Control on the deck above. "Put CAG on the phone, please," he said to the watchstander who answered.

"Ross, this is Arthur. We'll be turning north in about thirty minutes once we're free of traffic. I think we should be able to resume normal flight operations at that point. It would be a good time to recall our people from Paya Lebar and resume our normal ship-based ASW and CAP patrols."

"Sounds good, Art. We'll get it rolling," replied Captain Ross Morgan, commander of the air group.

"Thanks." Captain Young hung up the phone and turned to his executive officer. "XO, you may increase our speed when the shipping traffic has cleared. Please notify the admiral once we turn north. When we make that turn, CAG will be wanting to resume flight operations. You have the conn. I'll be in my quarters."

"Aye, Captain. I have the conn."

The Soviet trawler continued to trail the carrier group. When the *Vinson* turned north, the trawler sent a radio transmission containing its position, course and speed, as well as the positions of the *Texas*, the *Roanoke* and the *Flint*, relative to the carrier. The message was relayed via satellite to the three submarines of Mirov's command, each of which had deployed a radio buoy, anticipating the message.

Chapter 9

The S-3A Viking, call sign *Big Bird*, dropped another line of sonobuoys seventy miles ahead of the oncoming carrier group. *Big Bird*'s patrol sector was on the west side of the carrier group's intended course. East of *Big Bird* another Viking was flying a similar patrol squarely on the intended course. Further east a third Viking maintained watch over its patrol sector situated on the east flank of the group's projected path. Each Viking carried only sixty sonobuoys, so the drops were widely spaced. A trio of similarly arranged SH-3H Sea King choppers provided closer surveillance with their dipping sonar, ranging between fifteen and thirty miles ahead of the carrier and on either flank.

"Sheesh, it's noisy down there," *Big Bird*'s SENSO complained over the the aircraft's internal intercom. The SENSO, or Sensor Operator, handled the sonobuoys and the surface search radar. Noisy merchantmen plowing through the waves in multiple directions plus a lot of ambient environmental noise due to the shallowness of the water, made it very difficult to pick out individual sounds.

"Not exactly the setting for *Run Silent, Run Deep*, I'm guessing," replied TACCO, the tactical coordinator.

"Nope. It's neither silent nor deep. They could be playing the opening number to *Star Wars* at full tilt, and I doubt I could pick it out. I certainly can't hear the *Vinnie* or the *Texas*."

****

"*Gold Eagle*, this is *Crewcut*. We've got a sonar contact on the dipper. We're circling around to drop a couple of pingers. We'll try to get a firm ID on the contact." *Gold Eagle* was the *Vinson*'s call sign, *Crewcut* was the call sign of the Sea King patrolling northeast of the carrier.

"Copy that, *Crewcut*."

"*Gold Eagle*, this is *Crewcut*," came the call several minutes later. "Contact is a Whiskey-class submarine, heading zero-four-zero, speed eleven knots, depth one hundred ten feet. Designating S-35 and prosecuting. Transmitting contact information over NTDS." The Naval Tactical Data System allowed target information to be shared across vessels and aircraft. The Combat Information Centers (CIC) in the *Texas* and the *Vinson* would display the submarine contact on their ASW plot screens.

Ten minutes later *Crewcut*'s TACCO reported, "*Gold Eagle*, this is *Crewcut*. S-35 has surfaced. Visual confirmation that it is Indonesian navy, the *KRI Pasopati*, hull number 410. Breaking off contact and resuming patrol."

****

Though it was not unexpected, one of the problems the three Soviet submarines encountered was their reduced ability to detect contacts via passive sonar. They each were motionless in the water, sitting on the bottom as they awaited the oncoming carrier group. None of the three could deploy their towed arrays for fear it would be snagged or damaged on the shallow sea floor. The conformal hydrophones on their hulls were their only source of acoustic data at the moment. Consequently, the effective range of their passive sonar was greatly reduced, and they could not establish the precise bearing of acoustic contacts.

"Conn, sonar. Just acquired the carrier, sir, a strong signal. Bearing is somewhere between one-six-zero and two-zero-zero. Screw count indicates he is making twenty knots."

"Sonar, aye." Fetisov walked over to the *K-263*'s plot table and examined the grease pencil marks indicating the *Vinson*'s projected course, as provided by the last satellite communication with the trawler shadowing the carrier group. The Americans were right on schedule.

"Deploy the radio buoy, and request the latest position update from the trawler," Fetisov ordered the *michman* at the communications console. "Leave the buoy up while we await his response."

"But, comrade Captain, the American's radar will get a fix

on the buoy if it is up that long," replied the man. Going undetected was, at the same time, a submarine's greatest offensive and defensive weapon. His captain's orders went against everything he'd learned in his training.

"I know that!" snapped Fetisov. He stabbed his index finger at the man, and barked, "Deploy!"

"Aye, aye, Captain. Deploying radio buoy and requesting the latest fix on the carrier," the *michman* responded, shrugging his shoulders.

Fetisov stepped over to the communication console and placed his hand on the man's shoulder. "Relax, Yuri. We *want* to be found by the Americans. It's part of the plan," he said in a conciliatory tone. Then his voice became more severe. "Do not question my orders again. Just do as I command."

When the reply from the trawler came and the plot board was updated, Fetisov studied the tactical situation for a moment. His submarine, the *K-263*, was lying fifty-six kilometers almost due north of the *Vinson*'s present position and east of the carrier's intended course. Satisfied, the captain nodded his head. "It is time to play our part," he said to his XO.

He turned back to the control room and barked, "Helmsman, stand by!" It was an unnecessary command, but the *K-263* had been parked in one spot for the last eight hours and he wanted to make sure those on duty in the control room were alert and ready to execute his commands immediately. A showdown with an American carrier was a rare privilege, but it could turn fatal in an instant if something went wrong.

"Aye, aye, Captain, standing by."

"Communicator, send message *'the east wind blows'* on the satellite channel, then secure the radio buoy." The coded message alerted the other two submarines that the next phase of the mission was beginning.

"Aye, aye, Captain." A moment later the *michman* responded. "Message sent. The radio buoy is secured, sir."

"Aye. Helmsman, steer course one-eight-five. Make revolutions for twelve knots. Make your depth thirty meters.

"Aye, aye, sir. Steering course one-eight-five, making revolutions for twelve knots, coming to depth thirty meters."

"OOD, stream the towed array."

"Aye, aye, Captain. Streaming the towed array."

Captain Fetisov stepped back to the chart table. He unconsciously tapped the indicated position of Mirov's submarine with his index finger and murmured, "May our luck not desert us on this fateful day, Boris Sayanovich, my old friend."

****

"*Gold Eagle*, this is *Crewcut*. We've got a radar contact to the north. Going to invest—check that, *Gold Eagle*, we're now also picking up an acoustical contact along the same bearing. Investigating."

****

The sonar supervisor on *K-263* reported, "Conn, sonar. Rotary-wing aircraft approaching, bearing one-six-one."

"Sonar, aye." Fetisov turned to his XO. "If the Americans stick to their normal procedures, that's a Sea King. He'll be putting his dipping sonar down, followed by sonobuoys." He didn't have long to wait.

"Conn, sonar. We're picking up some transients. Sonobuoys entering the water. Range unknown."

"Sonar, aye," replied Captain Fetisov. "I want to know immediately when they go active." Fetisov turned to the quartermaster of the watch and instructed, "Battle stations, torpedo. No alarms, if you please. Spread the word, but do it quietly. I don't want to make it too easy on the Yankees."

After a few minutes the report came. "Conn, sonar. Sonobuoys entering the water right over top of us. They are going active, Captain!"

"Aye, sonar."

Fetisov knew that Captain Gromyko in the *K-284*, south-southeast of him, would hear the active sonar and know it was time for him to show his hand.

****

"Gotcha!" SENSO on *Crewcut* exclaimed. "He's definitely an Akula, sir."

"Concur," agreed TACCO. "And that bad boy is going in the wrong direction. He's headed right for the carrier. Designate as S-36. We'd better pass this on to the *Vinson*—especially since the Sovs haven't been very good neighbors lately."

****

The 21MC sounded, waking Captain Arthur Young out of an exhausted sleep. Momentarily groggy, he struggled to consciousness. He was in his skivvies, the sweat-soaked shirt from earlier was draped over his chair. The transit of the two straits had been draining, and he'd conned the ship for twelve hours straight without relief. He looked at his watch and shrugged. Four hours of sleep wasn't bad, especially when one was the commanding officer of a deployed aircraft carrier. He swung his bare feet to the deck, rubbed his face, and picked up the handset.

"Yes?"

"Captain, one of the Sea Kings is prosecuting a confirmed contact, an Akula, sir. The submarine is headed straight toward us. You wanted to be notified of any Soviet submarine contacts."

"That I did. I'll be right there." He hung up the handset, walked into the tiny head in his quarters and splashed water on his face. He dressed quickly and headed for the Combat Information Center.

The plot board was full of merchant ships and a handful of military vessels from neighboring nations. North of the *Vinson*'s position he saw the Akula.

"When did we first detect it?" Young asked Captain Steve Mallory, his XO.

"About seven minutes ago, Skipper. The chopper is dropping pingers all over it, but Ivan doesn't seem to care."

Young shook his head, staring at the Russian's plotted position. "Man, he's operating in mighty shallow water. If Ivan's not careful, he's gonna wipe his sail off on the hull of some supertanker."

Mallory nodded. "Either that or he's gonna leave his keel on a reef. He's headed toward us at twelve knots, Skipper. Between his speed and ours the closing speed is thirty-two knots. At this rate he'll pass under our keel in," the XO paused as he checked a digital timer on the bulkhead, "sixty-four minutes."

"Plenty of time for him to change course," Young observed, thinking out loud. "He is, after all, bounded by the Andaman Islands. Doesn't give him a lot of sea room. If he's headed south, he doesn't have a lot of choices for his course other than his current heading. I think we'll stand pat for now and see what he does." He turned to one of the enlisted men who was standing by, waiting to come on watch. "Joey, grab me a cup of coffee, will you? Fresh, hot, and black."

"You got it, Skipper. Want a donut with that?"

"Yeah, that sounds great. Get yourself one, too, on me."

Mallory grinned and turned back to the plot board. He knew that Captain Young worked hard at memorizing the name of every sailor that stood watch on the bridge or in the CIC, or in any other department of the ship where he would come in frequent contact with them. He'd had the ship's print shop make him a deck of cards with the sailor's photo on one side and name and hometown on the other. Young used them as flash cards in his quarters as a memory aid. The effort paid off in spades. There are no secrets on a ship. Sailors all over the vessel were impressed that their captain cared enough about them to learn the names of the enlisted men he worked with. It was a lesson, Mallory decided, that he would put to use when he was finally given command of a ship.

****

"*Crewcut*, this is *Shark Killer*. How many subsurface contacts are you working?" *Shark Killer* was the Sea King working the patrol sector due north of the *Vinson*.

"Only one, S-36. Why, *Shark Killer?*"

"*Crewcut*, I'm picking up a probable sub on my dipper in the far southern extent of your patrol sector, along bearing one-two-zero from my position. I was wondering if you were aware of it?"

"Negative, *Shark Killer*. Thanks for the tip. We'll check it out." TACCO looked to his left at the sensor operator. "SENSO, forget S-36 for a sec'. See if you can pick up any contacts to the south. *Shark Killer* thinks he's hearing something funky at the bottom of our sector."

The sensor operator's fingers flew over the keyboard, directing the computer to ignore the acoustics emanating from S-36, and to focus on any sounds to the south. Suddenly he cursed. "How did we miss this?" he exclaimed hotly. "Where on earth did he come from? We've got another Akula making twelve knots, headed for the *Vinson*, and this one is a lot closer to the carrier than S-36!"

****

Young listened as the new contact was reported. He shook his head and growled, "Where are those 688's when you need 'em? If Ivan can operate in this shallow depth, then we should be able to also!" He turned to the messenger of the watch, and said, "Locate the admiral, extend my compliments, and ask him to meet me in the CIC as soon as possible."

A few minutes later Waggoner stepped into the CIC. He immediately sensed the increased tension. He walked over to Young and asked, "What's going on, Captain?"

"Looks like your concerns have been justified, Admiral. We've got two Akulas inbound, and something about the situation doesn't add up."

The two men walked over to the plot board and Young pointed out the two submarines. "About ten minutes ago we began tracking S-36, an Akula that was initially picked up by the Sea King in the eastern patrol sector. S-36 is headed straight for us. If neither he nor we change course, he'll be under our keel in about fifty minutes.

"Just now, another Akula, contact S-37, was picked up—also in the eastern patrol sector. He's a lot closer than S-36—only about twenty miles away—and he, too, is on what looks like an intercept course.

"I had decided to give the first contact the benefit of the doubt. But now I'm thinking this could be a Soviet welcoming committee, so I'm recommending that the group commence a zigzag course immediately, the initial leg heading due west, away from these contacts. The water gets a lot shallower in that direction, which will make it harder for these jokers to operate without surfacing. I'll also talk to CAG about putting some more ASW assets in the air—armed, I might add. I'd like to ask you, Admiral, if you would detach the *Texas* and have him investigate the nearer contact. He's not the best ASW platform, but right now he's all we have."

"Let's do it," Waggoner agreed. "I'll get on the horn and tell *Texas* to check out S-37, and then I'll call the *Roanoke* and the *Flint* and explain what's happening."

At that moment the communications watch officer entered the CIC and gave a sealed envelope to the admiral. "Priority traffic, sir, just came in from COMPACFLT."

Waggoner opened the envelope and studied the message. He handed it to Captain Young, shaking his head. "Now they tell us. It would have been good to have this information a day ago, but from the dates on this communication it looks like it's been sitting in a stack on someone's desk."

```
IMMEDIATE PRIORITY
DTG 021305Z NOV 88

FROM: COMPACFLT
TO:   CARGRU3
INFO: COMSUBPAC           JCS/JRC
      COMSEVENTHFLT       ONI
      CINCPACFLT          DIRNSA
      CNO                 NRO
      DIRNAVSECGRUPAC
```

```
TOP SECRET
WESTPAC AO

1. ON 271430R OCT 88, THE NRO
CENSUS OF SOVIET PACIFIC FLT
SUBMARINE PENS AT VLADIVOSTOK
REVEALED 2 AKULAS AND 1 VICTOR
III SAILED SOMETIME PRIOR 4 DAYS.
2. NRO NOTES THIS IS UNUSUAL
OPTEMPO. NONE OF 3 HAD COMPLETED
REFURBISHING CYCLE.
3. IN LIGHT OF RECENT SOVIET PA-
CIFIC FLT ACTIONS, ONI IS
EXPECTING ADDITIONAL SOVIET
HARASSMENT OF US NAVAL VESSELS.
4. APPLY STANDARD ROE UNLESS UN-
DER IMMEDIATE THREAT OF LETHAL
ACTION. SAFETY OF NAVAL PERSONNEL
AND VESSELS IS CHIEF PRIORITY.
```

Young scanned the message quickly. "If these Akulas are the same two subs that disappeared from Vladivostok, then there's a mighty good chance that Victor is out there somewhere too," he suggested, rereading the message.

"Quite. You talk to CAG, and I'll contact *Texas* and the replenishment ships."

Young nodded, and switched the main circuit on the bulkhead communicator to aviation control. "This is the captain. Put CAG on the line, please."

"What's up, Art?" Ross Morgan asked.

"We've got two hot contacts—"

"I know. CIC contacted me. I'm on it. We had two choppers sitting on the deck at READY-15. They're about to take off."

"Are they armed?"

"No."

"Then would you mind slapping a pair of Mk 46s on each one before they take off? The tactical situation that's unfolding makes me think we'd better be ready for anything."

"Okay. Hold on." Morgan covered the handset and gave the necessary orders. "Done. Anything else?"

"Yeah. We just got some intelligence from COMPACFLT implying there is a third submarine out there. I think it would be wise if you got two more Sea Kings armed and ready. How much longer can the current Vikings stay on their patrol stations before we have to rig for launch and recovery operations?"

"From a fuel standpoint they're fine, although they're almost out of sonobuoys now. I was planning on a launch and recovery evolution in about an hour. If that doesn't work I can have them recalculate their bingo destination to Paya Lebar Air Base in Singapore. And if you'd like I can also dial up a couple of fully loaded P-3s out of Paya Lebar." Whereas the S-3A Viking is carrier-based, the P-3 Orion is a land-based aircraft configured as a submarine hunter/killer.

"Yeah, why don't you do that? I'd like to keep the deck clear for the Sea Kings. And I'd like to put some distance between us and these contacts before resuming air operations. We'll have to rely on the choppers for the close-in stuff."

"I agree. Our only other ASW asset is the *Texas*, and I don't think she's going to be all that helpful with her ASROCs. Too much shipping in the area to send one of those babies into the wild blue yonder. Who knows what we might wind up sinking?"

"Really. If the Sovs want a confrontation, they've sure picked the absolute best place to do it what with the shallow water and the heavy commercial maritime traffic. We don't have our 688s with their wire-guided ADCAPs. We can't even think about using ASROC around this shipping. And the air-dropped Mk-46s don't function all that well in this shallow water. It's a bit of a pickle," Young sighed. One of the primary missions of the 688s, the *Los Angeles*-class fast attack submarines, is escorting carrier groups, protecting them from enemy submarines. The 688 carries Mk-48 advanced capability wire-guided torpedoes (ADCAPs), which enable the submarine's fire control party to guide the torpedo right to its target. However, the shallow water persisting for much of the *Vin-*

son's transit to Pattaya Beach stripped away its submarine escort, and therefore the most capable part of the carrier group's ASW portfolio.

"Anyway, until we get our 688s back we need to be ready in case one of these Ivans turns out to be a really crazy Ivan. So arm everything you send up," Captain Young said.

"You got it."

****

As the *Texas* dashed towards the second Akula contact, the *Vinson* increased speed to twenty-five knots and came left to a new heading of two-eight-zero degrees. Two SH-3H Sea King choppers clattered off the flight deck, each carrying a deuce of Mk 46 torpedoes fixed to the hardpoints on either side of their fuselage. Once clear of the carrier they raced toward the contacts.

****

The *K-264* sat silently on the seafloor, undetected, her sonar operator listening intently to the sounds propagating through the water. The sound energy contained in active sonar pings travels a long, long way under water, and that was what the sonar operator was listening for.

Written on the plot board and entered into the ship's log was the exact time that he heard the active pings searching the depths for Fetisov's *K-263*, kilometers away. Below that, in neat printing was the exact time he picked up the active sonar raining down on Gromyko's *K-284*.

Based on his extensive experience hunting American naval capital ships, Captain Mirov had accurately predicted the reactions of the American vessels to the discovery of the two Akulas. When the stopwatch in his hand measured fifteen minutes from the beginning of the sonar search for the *K-284*, Mirov began his part of the engagement.

"Planesman, make your depth thirty meters."

"Aye, aye, Captain. Making my depth thirty meters."

Compressed air forced water out of the ballast tanks, and the submarine slowly rose off the bottom of the seafloor. The *michman* at the diving console kept the submarine in perfect trim as it gracefully ascended.

"Captain, our depth is thirty meters."

"Aye. Helmsman, steer course zero-nine-seven, make revolutions for ten knots."

The crew responded to his commands as a well trained team. The Victor III began gliding toward the carrier, now just seventy-three hundred meters away. It was only a matter of minutes at most before the *K-264* would be detected on someone's passive sonar.

"Quartermaster of the Watch, sound battle-stations, torpedo."

****

"Whoa, this is crazy," muttered the SENSO in *Poker Face*, the Sea King operating behind the carrier to make sure no submarines were stalking the ship. He twisted several knobs on his equipment and tapped the screen with his finger. "There's got to be something wrong with the equipment."

"What?" asked the TACCO, sitting right next to him. "Talk to me."

"I'm picking up a submarine close by, on bearing two-eight-two. It just appeared out of nowhere."

"Two-eight-two? That puts it right in front of the carrier. The *Vinson*'s headed straight for it!"

****

"Captain, *Poker Face* is reporting a probable Victor III, bearing two-seven-eight, range four thousand yards and closing."

"That's it!" Young said, making a quick decision. He grabbed the handset on the bulkhead behind him and set the channel to 1MC. "This is the captain speaking. General Quarters, General Quarters, General Quarters. This is not a drill, repeat, not a drill. The route of travel is forward and up to starboard, down and aft to port. Set material condition Zebra throughout the ship. Potentially hostile submarines."

All over the ship sailors raced to their battle stations even as they wondered what could have possibly transpired to bring matters to such a state. Watertight doors, fittings, and hatches were all dogged down.

"Captain, *Poker Face* is reporting transients from the Victor. He's flooded his tubes and opened outer doors."

"My word, he's preparing to shoot! Should we take evasive action, Captain?" the XO called from the bridge.

"Negative, negative, it's too late," Young growled. "All ahead flank. Steer directly for the contact," he instructed. He waited for the XO to pass the orders along and then explained, "Ivan is not going to have time to remove the safeties on his fish, not if we can close the distance. We're going to run right over the sucker, tear his sail off. He doesn't have anywhere to go in this shallow water. Stand by to sound the collision warning."

****

Mirov's plan at first seemed to be working perfectly. His two Akulas had flushed the quail and now it was heading straight for him. However, he had anticipated the carrier would take evasive action, not try to run him down. Even as he considered his own options, he appreciated the brilliance of his opponent's move. The sonar operator disrupted his thoughts.

"Conn, sonar, the target is increasing speed and headed straight toward us."

"Sonar, conn, aye. Go active. I want to know his precise speed, bearing, and distance." He turned to the fire control party. "We've made our point. Fire Control, close outer doors and secure the torpedoes."

"Aye, aye, Captain. Closing outer doors and securing torpedoes."

A glance at the chart told him everything he needed to know. Even if he dove to the bottom, in this shallow water the pressure wave created by the supercarrier going over him at that speed could smash his submarine against the seafloor. The captain of the carrier had seized the initiative and was forcing him to take evasive action. It was time to bring the confrontation to an end, if it could be done safely.

"Helmsman, steer course one-nine-zero. Planesman, stand by for an emergency surface."

"Conn, sonar. Target bearing is one-zero-five, speed thirty-five knots, range twenty-five hundred meters. Doppler shows target is still accelerating. Closing rapidly."

"Very well, sonar. Secure from pinging," Mirov said calmly. He turned to the helmsman, "All ahead flank." He silently counted off thirty seconds and then barked to the planesman, "Emergency surface, now!"

****

Young climbed the ladder from the CIC level to the bridge, then stood looking at the Soviet Victor III submarine cruising five hundred yards off the port beam. The *K-264* had come about after surfacing and was paralleling the *Vinson*'s course. The two Akulas had also surfaced briefly, turned to the east and then submerged again, apparently returning to base. The Sea Kings were monitoring them just to make sure.

Suddenly a semaphore lamp began blinking out Morse code from the *K-264*'s sail, where several officers could be seen watching the carrier through binoculars.

"The Soviet is signaling, sir," reported the quartermaster of the watch. "He says, 'Enjoy the rest of your voyage, Captain Young.'"

"I know what he said, son," Young muttered. "Nothing like adding insult to injury. Signal back, 'What captain?'"

The answer came back, "Mirov."

"I've read about him," Steve Mallory, the XO, commented. "Some say he's the best sub driver in the Soviet navy."

"Well, he was good enough to beat me today," Young admitted, as CAG Ross Morgan joined them.

"Ross, what say you harass those boys all the way back to Vladivostok?" Young said.

"My thoughts exactly. They're gonna get very tired of hearing active sonar pinging against the hull all the way home."

Chapter 10

Thursday, November 3, 1988

The vice president called the emergency meeting of the National Security Council to order and then invited Admiral Alfred Feldstein, current chairman of the joint chiefs, to give his briefing.

Feldstein was considered by his peers to be an unpretentious straight shooter, a man whose ascent to power and command had left the laconic midwesterner unchanged. Trim, bald, with a pair of penetrating blue eyes set in a wide forehead, Feldstein had an air of authority that clung to him like a well tailored suit, despite his five-foot-six-inch stature.

"Gentlemen, less than twenty-four hours ago the USS *Carl Vinson* was jumped by a trio of Soviet submarines: two Akulas and a Victor III. The Victor was able to close to within four thousand yards before being detected. That's less than two nautical miles, gentlemen. A Soviet Type 53 torpedo can cover that distance in under two and a half minutes. The Victor flooded his tubes and opened his outer doors. In other words he was all ready to take a shot. When an opponent behaves this way we have no way of knowing if it is a prelude to war or if he's just playing chicken. It's a dangerous breach of protocol between opposing forces during peacetime."

"Excuse me, Admiral," interrupted Donald Reinholder, the attorney general. Reinholder was a Harvard product, but had never served in the armed forces. "How do you know that the Soviet 'flooded his tubes and opened his outer doors,' as you say? Wouldn't you have to be on that submarine to know that information?" he asked.

"No, Mr. Attorney General," Feldstein said firmly. "The sounds those two actions create are called transients, and they are loud enough to be picked up by passive sonar. They are easily identified."

Feldstein continued his statement. "If Ivan had pulled the trigger we could very well be writing letters to over six thousand families explaining that their loved ones perished because we didn't respond appropriately to a clear, warlike provocation, one that normally presages an attack. We'd also be trying to explain to the American people how an eight-and-a-half-billion-dollar national asset wound up on the bottom of the ocean."

"How is this possible, Admiral? How could this submarine have gotten so close to our carrier? I was under the impression that Soviet submarines were years behind ours! There must have been some gross incompetence on the part of our people. Surely, the command staff of the carrier must be held responsible," said Nolan Beale, the vice president's chief of staff.

Feldstein frowned. Beale was a political animal of the first order. The man's first rule of politics was that when the stuff hit the fan make sure you weren't the guy holding the bag. His second rule was make sure that someone in a uniform *was* holding the bag. For Beale the main issue was assigning the blame. Correcting the situation was someone else's problem.

"Mr. Beale, I have to disagree," Feldstein responded. "A preliminary review of the actions of Admiral Waggoner, who commands Carrier Group Three, and Captain Young, in command of the *Vinson*, shows that those men acted in perfect accordance with Navy procedures. While the incident will be studied much more thoroughly, at this point there does not seem to be negligence, irresponsibility, or incompetence at any level of the chain of command.

"Rather, it appears that the Soviets concocted a brilliant ambush and pulled it off with consummate skill and élan— not to mention a heavy dose of luck. The officer commanding the trio of submarines that ambushed the *Vinson* is Captain First Rank Boris Sayanovich Mirov. Mirov is probably the most capable officer in the Soviet submarine corps. He's highly regarded in the USSR, as well as by our own people.

"In addition, Mr. Beale, your opinion about the capabilities of the Soviet submarine force is one that, until recently, was also shared by both naval intelligence and the CIA. However, it's become clear that as a result of technology transfers by the Walker spy ring and other traitors, the Soviets have advanced far more quickly than was anticipated. Add to that Ivan's acquisition of advanced propeller milling equipment from Toshiba, and we're looking at submarines that are nearly as quiet and advanced as our own. We have seriously underestimated our enemy—in both his equipment and his skill level—and it's put us in a dangerous position."

Mollified, Beale acknowledged Feldstein's statement with a slight nod.

Feldstein resumed, "This latest aggression is consistent with what we have observed of Soviet naval behavior in the western Pacific over the last several months. I'm not aware that we are seeing this sort of aggression in the other branches of their military."

Stanton Washburn, a four-star general and the chief of staff of the air force interjected, "Al, we've not seen any unusual aggressive behavior by their pilots. We've got the garden variety probes of our air defense system and the usual incursions of our airspace over Alaska, but this sort of thing has been ongoing for years. It's not registering as unusual."

"Ditto here," General Kendall Dabney offered. "We're not seeing anything unusual in West Germany or anywhere else along the Iron Curtain." Dabney was the chief of staff of the army.

"That's all I have, Mr. Vice President," Feldstein said as he returned to his seat.

"Paul?" The vice president looked at the Director of Central Intelligence (DCI) and raised his eyebrows. "What can you tell us?"

Paul West looked at his notes. "Mr. Vice President, as you know, Operation *Zephyr* was launched at our last meeting for the purpose of verifying Anatoly Geredin's claim that a dangerous conservative faction is rising in the USSR, a faction whose aim is to overthrow Gorbachev. Geredin claimed that this faction currently lacks adequate popular support in the military to accomplish their goal. They intend to remedy this weakness by uniting the Soviet military around its conservative, hard-line flag officers. This will be accomplished, Geredin warned us, by starting a limited shooting war with the USA.

"Right now we are working on a theory that at least some portion of the Soviet Pacific Fleet at the command level is controlled by this faction. I've asked Bill Jensen to put together a team to look into this. Bill, have you anything to report so far?"

"Yes, I do. In order to provide actionable credibility for Geredin's rather fantastic claims, two assertions must be confirmed: first, that the aggressiveness we're seeing in the Pacific Fleet is originating from the fleet command level, and second, that the aim of these confrontations ultimately concerns Soviet domestic politics rather than real military objectives. Operation *Zephyr* is investigating both assertions.

"We believe we have verified the first assertion. The NSA last week intercepted orders from the vice commander of the Pacific Fleet to rush three submarines to readiness—a radical change in their normal operational tempo. Those three submarines are the ones, we suspect, that ambushed the *Vinson*. If we are correct, the encounter with the *Vinson* was very likely their only mission on this deployment. We will be watching to see if they return directly to their berths.

"The second assertion is much harder to substantiate, given our lack of intelligence resources on the ground. We are examining every piece of data we can get our hands on, but so far there's not been anything that reveals their intentions."

The vice president nodded. "I will update the president on this matter. Walter, why don't you register a protest with the Soviet ambassador, and let him know in the strongest possible terms that this behavior could start a war none of us want."

"Actually, Mr. Vice President, may I make a suggestion?" Bill Jensen interjected. He was taking a risk of getting slapped down for speaking when not spoken to.

Bush looked at his watch and frowned. "What is it, Jensen?"

"Sir, if we register a protest with the ambassador the word will spread quickly to the Soviet fleet that their navy got the jump on our navy. If Geredin is correct in his concerns about this conservative faction trying to build popular support in the military by taking us on, our protest could play right into their hands. It's one thing for the Soviet navy to celebrate its victory somewhat quietly, but it becomes a different matter once word gets out that Soviet submarines went mano-à-mano with a US carrier group and won. What was a mostly unknown maritime incident will wind up getting airtime in the world news and we would be confirming it by our protest. National pride from the publicity, if nothing else, would draw their military together.

"My recommendation, sir, is that for the time being we pretend that nothing at all happened. If we don't react, sir, it could take the wind out of their sails—at least, temporarily."

"That's plausible," Bush admitted. "Opinions?" he asked, looking around the group.

"I think it's a good idea," Admiral Feldstein offered. "The coup plotters will undoubtedly expect us to protest. If we don't, it might cause them to wonder what we're up to."

When several heads nodded around the table, the vice president said, "Okay. We'll try it your way, Jensen."

The meeting continued for another ten minutes before breaking up. As the vice president was about to leave, Paul West cornered him.

"Sir, could we have a word with you—privately?"

Bush nodded and motioned West back to the conference table. As they waited for the others to leave, the vice president smiled at Jensen. "How does the harness fit, Bill? Are you getting used to being the man, now?"

Jensen laughed. "The harness pinches in places, sir, but I'm getting used to it."

West looked at Bush's chief of staff, Nolan Beale, who was hovering behind the vice president, and shook his head. "Mr. Vice President, what we have to talk about is for your ears only."

"Nolan, wait for me outside the door, please." When they were alone, the three men sat down at the table.

"This is your play, Bill. Have at it," West said, grinning with a you-asked-for-it expression.

Jensen placed his hands palms down on the table and swallowed before beginning. "Mr. Vice President, we don't have any assets in Vladivostok. I cannot assess the political currents developing in the Pacific Fleet without ears in the watering holes used by their sailors. Sailors are notorious gossips, sir, especially concerning their commanders."

"Are you telling me you can't do the job, Jensen?" Bush asked, eyes narrowed.

"No, sir, I am not telling you that. I'm telling you that I'd like to insert an agent into Vladivostok."

The vice president sat back. "You're not talking about recruiting a Russian—you're talking about sending an American. Someone with diplomatic cover, I assume?"

"No, sir. A diplomat would have minders all over him—he'd never be able to do the job. I'm talking about a covert insertion—someone posing as a Soviet citizen."

"That's pretty risky, Jensen."

"Yes, sir."

"You have someone in mind?"

"I do. I'd like to send Major Kelly back in. He speaks Russian like a native and he's spent enough time there to know how to fit in with the culture. I believe he can pull off the Soviet citizen act with no difficulty."

"Jensen, the cold war is just beginning to thaw. If we send a covert in and he's discovered, it could set relations with the Soviet Union back ten years."

"Yes, sir. With all due respect, if rogue elements in the Soviet navy continue this aggressive behavior and we don't get it figured out first, we won't be looking at a cold war, sir, we'll be looking at a hot one—possibly World War Three."

"Good point." Bush folded his hands and shut his eyes, considering the matter. After a moment he said, "Okay, I'm going to bump this up to the president. But I will support your idea. I'll get back to you later today."

"Thank you, sir. One more request, if I may. I'd like this to be a black op, with no one but you, the president, and Director West in the loop. We can't risk compromising Kelly—we can't risk a leak."

"Agreed."

By the end of the day, Jensen had the president's approval

for a covert insertion. The very next morning Jensen was on a flight to Ogden, Utah.

****

Kelly pulled open the squeaky file drawer on the drab green filing cabinet and picked through the tabs until he found the right one. He slipped the readiness report he'd just completed for the *Rude Rams*, the 34th Fighter Squadron, into the file folder. *My squadron*, he sighed to himself. *Back when I was a pilot. Now I'm nothing more than a cipher.* He pushed the drawer shut, and it closed with a reluctant squeal.

When he turned around, Bill Jensen was standing in his doorway, smiling.

"Major Jacob Kelly! How are you doing? I haven't seen you since your wedding," the DDO said enthusiastically.

"Bill! Great to see you! Been expecting you, although I didn't know what time your flight arrived. Come into my—office," he said, rolling his eyes. "Care for a paper clip? I've got plenty."

Jensen picked up on the young man's sadness. "Not like your old office, is it?" he said.

"No. I've traded an ejection seat for an office chair. Doesn't give you quite the same feeling."

"Well, I can't get you back into the cockpit, but I think I can get you back in the thick of things," Jensen said mysteriously.

"What are you talking about?"

Jensen looked around. "Care to take a little walk? Maybe where there aren't as many ears?"

Falcon grinned. "I should have known your visit was a little more than catching up on old times. Once a spook, always a spook."

Jensen spread his hands and shrugged his shoulders. "Guilty as charged."

As the two men walked around the base in the Utah sunshine, Jensen revealed the reason for his visit. "Jake, what I am about to tell you is highly classified sensitive compartmented information—a matter of national security. I have to remind you that all the confidentiality agreements you signed when you were vetted for the *Hydra* project are still in effect—which means that if you share any of this it is a violation of federal law. Because your top secret security classification is still current and because this concerns you, I've been cleared by Director West to share this matter with you."

Kelly blinked. "Wow. This sounds serious. Okay, you have my word—my lips are sealed."

"That includes Galina. You can't tell her either."

"Of course not. You don't have to remind me—I know the rules."

Jensen nodded. "Okay, here we go: a little more than a month ago I had a surprise meeting with an old acquaintance of yours."

"Really? Who?"

"Geredin."

"Anatoly Geredin, the head spy of the KGB? Were you visiting the embassy in Moscow?"

"No, I was sitting on a park bench in Great Falls, Maryland. I had no idea he was in the country—none of our people detected his entry," Jensen confessed, shaking his head. "And no one detected him leaving, either—I only know he is back in Moscow because I saw him yesterday on the news standing in the background during Gorbachev's speech to the *Duma*."

"Ouch! Ivan two, CIA zero," chuckled Kelly.

"Tell me about it," Jensen admitted wryly. "Geredin is a wily old bear. He's probably the best the USSR has ever produced. I'm not surprised he got past the gatekeepers, he's a master of fieldcraft."

Falcon stopped and turned to his friend. "Mr. Geredin puzzles me, Bill. He's the head of the KGB, so there must be buckets of blood on his hands. But he also seems to have a soul. I've found him strangely gentle, sentimental even, when it comes to Galina and me. He could have arrested me at the Moscow airport, interrogated me and then dumped my corpse in an unmarked grave, and no one would have been the wiser.

Instead he let me leave the country—with my weapon—and then later shows up at my wedding."

"Do not mistake his intentions, Jake. Geredin is not your friend—he's your enemy, and he'd be the first one to tell you that. I've followed the man's career for years and read everything the intelligence services have on him. He is undoubtedly the most dangerous man in the Soviet Union. He's a man of uncompromising loyalty to his country. He's considered by those who know him to be utterly incorruptible.

"Anatoly Geredin is not a wanton butcher, by any means. He never uses unnecessary violence, but neither does he shrink from bloodshed when he thinks that's the best way to serve his country. He let you go last January mostly because you no longer presented a threat to the Soviet Union. He also needed a reliable messenger to our government, and you were handy. And, he knew you were going to marry the apple of his eye—Galina Toporova. Were it not for those considerations, you'd be pushing up daisies somewhere in Russia right now, and he'd have thought nothing of pulling the trigger himself.

"Geredin has one love: Mother Russia. He will do anything to promote her cause—including endangering himself by secretly coming to meet with me. Think about it: his enemies in the Politburo would accuse him of treason, of selling out, if they knew he was here. It was a gutsy move."

"So why did he come?"

Jensen proceeded to describe his meeting with Geredin at Great Falls, and the new aggression of the Soviet Pacific Fleet. He related Geredin's concerns that the coup plotters intended to initiate a hot conflict in order to create greater political unity in the Soviet military—unity that would then be used to support a conservative overthrow of Gorbachev.

"It is critical that we verify his information," Jensen continued. "That's my job. Unfortunately, the limited intelligence intercepts I have access to are not adequate to the task. Consequently, I've been given *verbal* authority to insert a covert agent into Vladivostok."

"It sounded like you just stressed the *verbal* qualifier. *Verbal authority*, you said. Is there a reason for stressing that?"

"Yes. This will be a black operation, known to fewer than ten people—with no written record or authorization."

"Isn't that rather dangerous for your agent?" Kelly asked. "What if he's caught?"

"It *is* dangerous for the agent," the DDO agreed. "If a covert agent is caught, normally the Agency would disavow any knowledge of his activities. The agent would be on his own, at the mercy of his captors. That doesn't mean he wouldn't eventually be returned to the US through an agent swap. We catch one of theirs, they catch one of ours, and we trade."

"*Normally*, you said. But this is somehow not normal?"

"Correct."

"How so?"

"Because of your work in Operation *Thunderbird* last year, we have some leverage with the Soviets. If they catch the agent, we can threaten to expose what they did with all those scientists they captured."

"Ah. Yes, I can see that. You indicated this insertion was verbally authorized. By whom?"

"I'm not at liberty to say, other than to assure you that all the necessary legal boxes have been checked. Now here's what I'm looking for: the agent to be inserted must be indistinguishable from a run-of-the-mill Soviet citizen. They must speak the language like a native and be comfortable in the cultural setting. I want them to frequent the harbor bars in Vladivostok—watering holes where the Soviet navy's sailors go. I need them listen to conversations and report on the political machinations and leanings of the fleet—particularly the fleet commanders."

Jensen stopped walking again and turned to face Kelly. "In a word, Jacob, I need you."

"Me? You want me to be a spy?"

"Yes."

"You're asking me to work for the CIA?"

"Yes. It would be a temporary duty assignment. You'd still be in the air force, but under the temporary command of the

CIA."

"Whoa. I doubt Galina will go for this."

"You can't tell Galina."

"I can't tell her anything about the mission, but I could tell her I'm on temporary duty with the CIA, and that it would involve some overseas activity."

"Well, yes," conceded the DDO, "you can tell her that much."

"And she won't go for it. And if she says no, I'm saying no. My marriage is worth more than my career."

Jensen stared at his friend. "I really hope she doesn't say no, because you are just the man I need. I don't have anyone else that fits the mission profile like you do, Jake. I really need you."

"If this came up before Galina and I married, I'd say yes in an instant. You know that, Bill. But now I can't make decisions unilaterally as though her opinion doesn't count."

Jensen sighed and nodded. "I'm glad to hear you say that —that's how it should be. But I'm going to pray that she says yes.

"Look, I've got to make some arrangements with your commanding officer just in case she does agree to it. You need to get back to your office. I'll see you guys at your place this evening."

****

Jake was grilling steaks in the backyard and Galina was putting finishing touches on the salad when Jensen knocked on the front door.

"Galina, it's wonderful to see you!" He gave the young woman an affectionate hug. "It's been awhile since the wedding. How are you feeling? You're due in, what, April?"

"I am well, Mr. Jensen. And yes, the big day will be in April. It's great to see you, sir."

"Is Jake around?"

"He's in the backyard—I'll take you to him. So what brings you to Utah, Mr Jensen?"

"Oh please, Galina—call me Bill. *Mr. Jensen* makes me feel like a fossil. It's both business and pleasure that brings me to Utah. You two are the biggest reason for my trip."

Galina didn't respond. Jacob had told her all about his friendship with Jensen—how the man had become a family friend, how Bill and Susan Jensen had supported Jake when his parents died. She also knew that Jensen was now the Deputy Director for Operations, CIA, and she suspected that his visit had to do with something more than friendship. It worried her.

"Welcome, Bill!" Kelly put down his spatula and gave his friend and mentor a bear hug. "Your timing is perfect—the steaks are almost ready."

Galina left the two men in the backyard and returned to her preparations in the house. She fought down a feeling of panic and told herself that she would give Jensen a fair hearing—whatever he might have to say.

The conversation over the meal was confined to catching up with each other. The DDO asked extensively about Galina's upbringing in the Soviet Union, and questioned her closely about Anatoly Geredin's relationship with her deceased father. He was particularly fascinated by her account of the logging operation she and her late brother Boris had started. Jensen also wanted to hear more about Jake's escape from Siberia.

Finally, Jensen put his wine glass on the table and looked at Galina. "Galina, my friendship with Jacob, and now with you also, is why I am here. But there is another reason as well. I want Jacob to work for me on a particular assignment. He is the most qualified person I know, and his particular skill set and training are exactly what I need for this job."

"You want Jacob to work for the CIA? As an agent?" she asked, her fears realized.

"That's right," Jensen affirmed. "Just temporarily."

"How long would this assignment last?" asked Galina.

"Three months. Maybe four. I envision him being home before your baby is born."

She stared at Jensen, fighting down the anger she felt

growing inside. "And is it a dangerous assignment?"

He looked down at his wine glass and ran his finger around the rim before answering. "Yes, it is. I must be honest with you."

"I don't like it. I don't like it at all," she declared firmly. "Just two years ago he was kidnapped by the Soviets and faced execution—he would have surely been killed if he had not escaped. He ran for his life across Siberia, chased by thousands of Red Army soldiers. He barely survived the ordeal that landed him back in Alaska, not to speak of the military operation last December to free the other captives—and now you're asking him to do something dangerous again? How can you?" Her body trembled with anger. "He's done his part. Can't you just leave him alone?"

Jensen gazed at her, his eyes full of compassion. He understood her fear, indeed, knew himself to be responsible for some of it. The young woman had already been through a great deal of emotional pain, having lost Jake twice. She lost him when he fled the logging operation in Sidima, trying to stay one step ahead of the oncoming Soviet army. For a full year she had no idea whether he was dead or alive. Briefly reunited with him in the fall of 1987, she lost him a second time when the CIA faked his death in a bid to end the GRU assassination contract on Kelly. In order to make Kelly's 'death' look real, Jensen had let Galina believe he was dead. Her grief had touched Jensen to the core.

"Galina," he said gently, "I don't know what to say. I need Jacob's help. There's a situation that might soon put many lives in danger. We need to stop it before it gets out of hand. I'm not at liberty to say any more."

"But why Jake?" she asked, her voice breaking. "Why can't you ask someone else?" She reached for a tissue and dabbed the tears streaming down her face.

Jensen glanced at Jacob, and then looked back at Galina. "Because I don't have anyone else as qualified for this mission. Your husband is the only person I know that can help me put a stop to the danger that is developing as we speak. He's the right man for the job—a critically important job."

She nodded and with trembling hands reached for another tissue. No one spoke for a few minutes, then Kelly looked at his watch. "It's late, Bill. Let us sleep on this and we can pick up the discussion in the morning. I'll show you to our guest room."

****

"You were a CIA agent during the Vietnam war, weren't you? Jacob told me you were operating out of Cambodia and Thailand," Galina said, sitting across the kitchen table from Jensen. She was wearing a flannel shirt, jeans, and hiking boots. The three were planning a day of hiking and exploring in the Unita-Wasatch-Cache National Forest.

"That's right," Jensen admitted. "Even to this day I'm not allowed to say much about it—but yes, you are correct."

Kelly was at the stove, frying bacon. The sizzle and smell created a pleasant atmosphere in the kitchen. Outside the sun was coming up, peering over the Wasatch Range to the east, announcing another beautiful, cloudless Saturday.

"Was it a dangerous assignment?" she pressed.

He stirred his coffee before answering, then looked at Galina. "Yes, it was. Very dangerous."

"Did your wife know what you were doing?"

"Only partially. Susan knew I was in the CIA and that I was embedded somewhere in the war zone, but everything else was classified."

"How did she deal with it—the fear that you might never come back and that she might never know why?"

"We both lived with fear, Galina, both Susan and I," he admitted. He chuckled without humor. "She was afraid of what might happen to me, and I was afraid of what might happen to her and the girls if something did happen to me. And—I must admit—I was also afraid for myself. I had a whole list of fears—such as the possibility I would be betrayed, caught and tortured, get shot in a firefight, or die in an airplane that was trying to land or take off from a rough, secret jungle airstrip that was just too short.

"In the situations I encountered—practically daily—I was living on adrenaline—always on the edge. It was alternately invigorating and exhausting."

Jacob placed the bacon in a glass dish and put it in the oven to keep it warm. He started breaking eggs for the omelet he was making. As he whisked the eggs, he looked back at Jensen. "That's pretty much how I felt when I was on the run in Siberia."

Galina shook her head. "But how did Susan live with that fear? I don't think I can do that."

"Some people live with fear by burying it, denying it, or bottling it up. Others cope by leaning on alcohol or drugs. For many people, Galina, the fears resurface later as post-traumatic stress disorder, or PTSD.

"Susan and I both countered our fear with faith. We were both Christians and we had confidence in the goodness of the sovereign God who was in control of our lives. The root of much fear is anxiety about death and suffering. For the Christian, God has addressed both of those problems. Jesus Christ is the pioneer who blazed the trail of suffering. Because He suffered more than anyone else, He knows what human suffering is like and He is able to comfort those who suffer. And because He died on the cross and was raised from the dead, He destroyed the ability of death to hold Christians captive to fear."

"Hold on, Bill. I don't get it. How on earth can the death of a Jewish guy, what, some two thousand years ago, have anything to do with me or with fear?" Kelly asked, irritation creeping into his voice.

"It's really quite simple, Jacob. Every person has an intuitive knowledge of God and their accountability to Him. They know in their heart of hearts that when they die they will face the judgment. The Bible says this in Romans 1:18-19: *For the wrath of God is revealed from heaven against all ungodliness and unrighteousness of men who suppress the truth in unrighteousness, because that which is known about God is evident within them; for God made it evident to them.*

"Certainly part of the fear of death is the natural fear of

the unknown—something all people wrestle with, Christian or not. But the much larger part of the fear of death has to do with the intuitive expectation of judgment after death."

"And you're saying Christians don't fear that judgment?" Galina suggested.

"Correct."

"Why not? Like I said, how can somebody else's death have anything to do with how I face my own death?" Jake said. He'd stopped his omelet preparations and was glaring at Jensen.

"The Bible says, Jacob, that the ultimate cause of death is God's judgment against sin. Paul says in Romans 6 that the wages of sin is death. In other words, our sins create a moral obligation to God—a debt, if you will. A debt for which the only end can be judgment.

"But what if a substitute—someone who has no sin and therefore no debt of His own—steps in and pays the debt in your place? What if He takes the judgment due you? He dies, and you go free."

When Jensen said that, something clicked in Kelly's mind. Suddenly all the attempts people had made to tell him about Christ coalesced in his mind, from Oswald Simmons—with whom he'd escaped from the Soviet interrogation facility—to one of the men he held in highest esteem, General James T. Franks, to the man he loved as a son loves a father—Bill Jensen. The realization hit him with such force he was unable to answer.

"You mean, Jesus Christ," Galina offered softly, enmeshed in her own thoughts.

"Yes, I do. Wait a minute," the CIA man said. He went back to the guest room and retrieved his Bible. When he returned, he opened it to Isaiah 53. "Listen to what Isaiah the prophet wrote 700 years before Christ: *He was despised and forsaken of men, a man of sorrows and acquainted with grief; And like one from whom men hide their face He was despised, and we did not esteem Him. Surely our griefs He Himself bore, and our sorrows He carried; Yet we ourselves esteemed Him stricken, smitten of God, and afflicted. But He was pierced through for our transgressions, He was crushed for our iniquities; The chastening for our well-being fell upon Him, and by His scourging we are healed. All of us like sheep have gone astray, each of us has turned to his own way; But the LORD has caused the iniquity of us all to fall on Him."*

Kelly was experiencing something he'd never felt before. There was an immense tugging in his heart to believe what his friend was saying, countered by a stubborn refusal to have anything to do with it. Even though he could now see the light, he fought against it. "You only believe those things because you live in a western culture trained to believe such things, Bill. It's an American thing, kind of like baseball, mom, and apple pie."

"No, Sokolov, you are wrong," Galina interjected. "This is the exact same message I heard in the church I attended in China. It is the exact same message I heard in the Chinese Presbyterian church in San Francisco. It's the same message that Janet Lancaster, the wife of your squadron leader, shared with me. And besides, the prophet Isaiah was part of the ancient Jewish culture, long before the western culture even existed."

The conversation paused. Kelly turned back to the omelet he was making. But his mind was racing. *Can this be true? No it can't be, it's just another religious myth people use as a crutch! But why do I know that it's not a myth? Why do I know it's true?*

Finally Bill continued. "Anyway, Galina, that's how Susan and I dealt with our fears. We both have faith in a sovereign God who loves us so much He put His own Son on the cross to pay for our sins, so we wouldn't have to pay for them. Three days after He died, Jesus rose from the dead proving that our sins have been paid and that He is who He claimed to be—God Himself. He now sits on the throne of heaven ruling the entire cosmos. Because of what He did for me, when I die I'll live forever with Him in a new heaven and new earth. With a God like that, whom should I fear?"

"If this is true at all," Galina observed, "then it must be true for everyone. That's just the nature of true truth—it's objective, not subjective." Galina's degree was in mathematics—she understood that the philosophical divide was not between *spiritual truth* versus *empirically-verifiable truth*, but between *what-is-true* and *what-is-not-true*. She knew that the notion of *relative* truth was a pleasant fiction, but not *true* in any meaningful sense of the word.

Jensen nodded. "That's right. But there is something else involved, too. Everyone, no matter what they believe or what culture they are from, will stand before God to give an account for their lives. But the redemption that Christ secured and that God offers is not given to everyone. Though it is true that Christ offered Himself as a sin offering, only a few receive the benefit of what He did. The work He did on the cross is not enjoyed by everyone."

"What? Why not?" Jacob asked. This was not what he was expecting to hear.

"God's salvation is only granted to those who repent of their sins and place their faith in what Jesus accomplished on the cross. The apostle Paul says in Ephesians 2 that *by grace you have been saved through faith; and that not of yourselves, it is the gift of God; not as a result of works, so that no one may boast.* In Romans 10 he says this: *that if you confess with your mouth Jesus as Lord, and believe in your heart that God raised Him from the dead, you will be saved; for with the heart a person believes, resulting in righteousness, and with the mouth he confesses, resulting in salvation. . . for whoever will call on the name of the lord will be saved.* The writer of Hebrews tells us in chapter 11, *without faith it is impossible to please Him, for he who comes to God must believe that He is and that He is a rewarder of those who seek Him.*"

"What are you saying, Bill?"

"I'm saying what the Scripture says, Jacob. Salvation is not automatic simply because Christ died. You must intentionally receive it. It's offered only to those who repent of their sins and place their faith in Christ. Those who refuse to do so will face the judgment of God. Jesus commanded us in Mark chapter 1, *repent and believe the gospel.* I believe He actually meant what He said."

****

The three friends spent a strenuous day on the Thurston Peak loop trail, a twelve-mile circuit offering a five-thousand-foot gain in elevation and beautiful views from the top. It was very late in the year for the hike, and as they neared the summit it began to snow lightly. Even though the weather had closed in, limiting the view, they spent a half hour on the summit taking photographs before heading down. The descent into Adams Canyon was difficult, as the trail was poorly marked and they kept losing it amid the scrub oak.

By the time they returned to the Kelly's home the sun was setting. The DDO was secretly disappointed with his failure to recruit Kelly—he was no closer to finding an agent for Operation *Zephyr* than he was two days ago. Jensen took a quick shower, packed his bag and had just enough time for a cup of coffee before heading to the airport to catch his red-eye flight back to DC.

"It has been a great visit. Thanks for your hospitality, Jacob, Galina—I really enjoyed spending the day with you. Next summer, why don't you guys join Susan and me on the Snake River for a week? I know you'll have your baby by then, Galina, but our cabin is warm and comfortable with plenty of room."

Jake looked at his wife, who smiled and nodded. "We'll plan on it. Let's put our calendars together later this spring and get it on the agenda."

"Sounds good." Jensen checked his watch. "Got to run. Let me pray for you guys and I'll be on my way." They held hands and Jensen asked God to protect his friends, to grant Galina a full term and safe delivery, and most importantly, to open their eyes to the love of Christ.

As he turned to leave, Galina put a hand on his arm and stopped him. "Bill, wait." She turned to her husband, her voice quavering. "Do you want to serve on the mission Bill was talking about?"

Jake wrapped his arms around his wife. "I do, sweetie. But not without your full support."

She hugged him tightly and said softly, "Then you have it. I will support you, even though I am afraid."

                                                C. H. Cobb

Bill looked at the woman with admiration. "Galina, you're made of some pretty strong steel. We'll do our best to bring him home safely. You have my word on that." He shook Kelly's hand. "Gotta go. Jacob, I'll contact your commanding officer to let him know. General Franks has already cleared the path—I talked to him about that before I flew out, just in case you said yes. I'll see you in my office at 0800, day after tomorrow. You won't need any gear—we'll have what you need."

****

As they lay in bed that night, Jacob asked Galina, "What made you change your mind, Galya? About the mission, I mean. I thought you were dead set against it."

"I was."

"So—what happened? Why the change?"

She rolled over and faced him, propping her head up on her elbow. "I realized I'd finally come to the end of my project."

"And what project would that be?"

"My study of religions, Jacob. In all my exploration of religion, it was Christianity that was most consistent with the facts of history. And the message of bible-believing Christianity that I heard across cultures that were as inherently opposite as China and San Francisco was also consistent. I suppose you could also include the love I have experienced at the hands of genuine Christians. It all adds up to the same thing. I realized today—it was during the hike—that Christianity really is true. I've decided to place my faith in Jesus, Jacob. And at the same time I realized, if I can trust Him to save me, I can also trust Him to do what's right concerning you."

Chapter 11

November, 1988

Rick Freeman put a small sat phone in Jacob Kelly's hands. Freeman was the CIA station chief in Embassy Moscow. "This phone is not available commercially. It was developed by the technical services arm of Mossad and communicates with one of their birds. We added our own encryption chip to it. You won't need to use any code words—the encryption purports to be unhackable. Not even the Israelis will know what you're saying. The signal will go through their satellite but on a frequency the Russians use. I've tinkered with the digital packet headers—it will appear to anyone snooping to be an encrypted Soviet military transmission. As long as the Sovs don't suspect a security breach, they'll probably ignore the signal, thinking it's one of their own. The phone travels inside this shaving cream can. The can will actually dispense a small amount of shaving cream, but don't use it because there's just enough in it to fool an inspector.

"When you call you'll hear a series of three tones on the other end. Punch in the six-digit code I'm going to give you and then leave your report. It will be recorded, so it doesn't matter when you call. When you're finished, press the star key. If anyone has left a message for you, it will play. You can only listen to it twice before it deletes itself, so pay attention.

"These are your documents: your internal passport, your military veteran's travel pass, and a form letter from the office of the Admiral of the Fleet asking that you be considered for employment on the naval base at Vladivostok. Your reason for travel is that you are returning home after serving in the military. When you arrive in Vlad you'll have to register with the local *militsiya* to receive your *propiska*, which is sort of a combination work and residency permit. With these credentials you'll have no difficulty registering.

"You'll need to spend the rest of the day memorizing your cover story. Your name is Andrei Petrovich Borodin. Your background is Soviet navy, but 'further details are classified'—you're not allowed to say anything about it. These are your military discharge papers. Your official status as a discharged veteran, according to the Soviet government, is 'ex-service personnel, who served in the Limited Contingent of the Soviet Forces and had been temporarily stationed in the Democratic Republic of Afghanistan.' I know it's a mouthful, but that's their label for your status. But be careful—being a veteran of Afghanistan is no longer a badge of honor to the typical Soviet citizen. The Soviet population is tired of the war and nobody's going to buy you a cup of coffee because you fought in it—you might even get some disrespect.

"As you can see, due to the fact that your background is 'classified' there's very little other information on your documents. Most Soviet personnel people—military or civilian—won't bother to run a check on you because they already know it will come up empty, since it's classified. I also gave you a current security clearance which will help you get work in the secured areas of the base."

"Why was I discharged?" Kelly asked, studying the material.

"You developed heart trouble and were dismissed from the service. You're very bitter and cynical about it. You've taken a low-stress occupation—you're a custodian. By the way, you're going to spend the rest of today being trained by our custodial staff here at the embassy so you'll know at least something about custodial work."

"I'm a janitor?" Kelly smirked. "How far the mighty have fallen."

"What do you mean?"

"Well, a couple of months ago I was flying F-16s—now I'm scrubbing toilets."

"Whatever. You do what you gotta do. Anyway, the reason I made you a janitor is because it's traditionally difficult to staff Soviet custodial positions, which means they're always looking for workers. This will practically guarantee that you get a position on the naval base."

Freeman put several sheets of paper in Kelly's hands and continued the briefing. "As an only child whose parents died when you were young, you have no family. This paper contains a précis of where you lived from birth until you left home—memorize it.

"Here are two Soviet navy duffel bags containing your clothes and personal effects. The clothes all show signs of wear—nothing in these bags is new. When I'm done with you I want you to unpack them and repack them several times so you know exactly what you've got. Average temps in Vladivostok right now hover between the low thirties and the mid-twenties, so I've provided some warm clothes for you. Sewn into the lining of your overcoat is a generous supply of rubles. You're not going to run out of money. Just don't flash it around, because people in your position don't have lots of money."

Kelly shook his head. "How on earth did you come up with all these documents? Are they real?"

"No, of course not—they're forgeries, only they are very good forgeries. We know a guy who knows a guy who knows a guy in the Ukrainian mafia. He's very well paid and very motivated not to betray us. If he were to compromise us to the Sovs he can expect his mafia buddies to do some rather unpleasant things to him—and they specialize in pretty creative unpleasant things. For them, it's one of those *don't kill the golden goose* arrangements."

"So even though these documents look great, they're not really on any Soviet database," Kelly said.

"Correct. If anyone starts looking too closely into Andrei Petrovich Borodin, you are toast," Freemen admitted unapologetically.

"What a comforting thought," Kelly said sarcastically.

"Hey, we did everything we could on short notice, guy," Freeman snapped.

"Relax, man, I'm just practicing my cynicism and bitterness."

Freeman stared at him for a minute, not sure how to take him. "Whatever. Tomorrow morning you're booked on Aeroflot through to Khabarovsk. For some reason we couldn't get a direct airline ticket from Moscow to Vladivostok, or from Khab to Vladivostok. I'm not sure why. So you'll land in Khab and travel overland the rest of the way."

"What's my ride into Vladivostok?"

"That's your problem. You're a Soviet citizen, remember? I recommend the train, but that will be your choice."

"What about weapons?"

"You don't get any weapons. Custodians aren't usually packing a Makarov."

"What about backup?"

"You don't have any."

"Extraction plan?"

"None that I am aware of. Spy swap in ten years or so, probably. Just don't get caught."

****

"Comrade Geredin, Colonel Dobrynin is in the outer office, waiting to see you."

"*Spasibo*. Please send him in."

Geredin got out of his chair and painfully limped over to his credenza. Opening the fine-cut crystal doors, he withdrew two beautiful porcelain teacups rimmed with gold leaf. The St. Andrew's ensign—symbol of the Imperial navy—was etched in gold on the outside of each cup. He poured the tea from his samovar as the office door opened behind him.

"Come in, Vladimir Leonidovich," Geredin said, not bothering to turn around. "Have a seat. Tea?

"Please."

Geredin handed one of the cups to Dobrynin. The chief of the KGB's Third Directorate was Geredin's deputy, but also his best friend and most trusted confidant. As Geredin settled into his chair he motioned to the fragile teacup. "Do you know where this china came from, Vlad?"

Dobrynin shook his head. "*Nyet.*"

"These cups are part of the original set of china used by the officers of the Imperial battleship *Petropavlovsk*, the only dreadnought the Bolsheviks possessed shortly after the October Revolution. They remind me that some things—the *rodina* in particular—are worth fighting for. So what are you fighting for today, my friend?"

Dobrynin smiled grimly. "An orderly transfer of power, as opposed to a *putsch*, I suppose."

"*Da.* It's a good fight, an important fight. What do you have for me?"

"The security detail I put on Admiral Zelenko reports that there has been no attempt or suspicious activity that threatens the admiral's safety. If Shukshin is going to make a move against him, it hasn't happened yet."

Geredin sighed heavily. "Good. I'd rather that it never did happen. Perhaps Shukshin is just blustering?"

"That's not likely. In my opinion he hasn't finished consolidating his power. Churkin is reporting that Shukshin continues to strengthen his position in the Pacific Fleet, transferring the officers who are Gorbachev loyalists to the Northern Fleet, or to desk jobs where they have very little influence on the enlisted men." Dobrynin paused to sip his tea.

"And Zelenko is just letting this happen?" Geredin asked.

"Scuttlebutt has it that he's actually pretty far removed from managing the Pacific Fleet. I've been communicating with some of the political officers, just sort of casually keeping track of things. They all see what is happening and most of them are in favor of Shukshin's moves. I doubt Admiral Zelenko is aware of Shukshin's nefarious actions. Sooner or later, though, he'll find out and he'll attempt to rein the man in—although by then it might be too late.

"One notable exception to the purge is Captain Mirov, who is known to support Gorbachev. Mirov is very popular in the fleet. He's trained a significant portion of the Pacific Fleet's officer corps and they are quite loyal to him."

"That's odd. With the political clout he's got as a Gorbachev loyalist, why wouldn't Shukshin want him out of the way?" Geredin asked, pulling on his lip.

"It is very odd, but it could be that Captain Mirov is actually an unwitting part of Shukshin's plot. Mirov is the best sub driver they've got. There are rumors that Shukshin is keeping him around for a delicate mission—one that requires Mirov's skill—but so far I don't have any intelligence about what that mission might be."

Geredin nodded. "*Da.* If he's keeping the most skilled submarine captain close at hand, despite his political views, then it must have something to do with Mirov's naval abilities. Keep working on this angle, Vlad. Anything else to report?"

"Yes, sir. Major Jacob Kelly, of former *Yakov Sokolov* fame, showed up in the American embassy yesterday. Flew in on his own passport."

"That's rather audacious."

"I agree, sir. He's not hiding the fact that he's here—it's almost as though he wants us to know. Our source says that he's quartered in the secured portion of the embassy compound."

"You're assuming that he's up to something. He might just be visiting. Maybe he's serving as a courier for sensitive information."

"I disagree, Anatoly. Think about it. Given his recent background and the ordeal the GRU put him through, would you send him back in for any reason short of a major mission?"

Geredin shook his head. "*Nyet.* I would not—good point. Nonetheless, he is here. So, why is he here? What's he up to?" Geredin had an idea but kept his thoughts to himself.

"I don't know," Dobrynin admitted, "but I've posted a surveillance detail to keep an eye on him."

Geredin chuckled. "Good luck with that. One hundred rubles says that he leaves the embassy and gets past your surveillance team. I know this young man, Vlad. He's good."

Dobrynin smiled. "So is my team. I'll match your one hundred and make it two hundred. He's not getting past my men."

Two days later Dobrynin left a pair of hundred-ruble notes on Geredin's desk.

****

"Documents, please."

Falcon handed his identification documents and his military veteran's travel pass to the bored woman at the Aeroflot counter. She gave them a perfunctory glance and handed them back.

"Why are you traveling to Khabarovsk?" she asked, as she keyed in his name.

"I've been discharged from the military. I'm returning home." As he said this, it struck Kelly that his own life situation was similar—he'd been removed from the flight line for medical reasons. It would not be difficult, he decided, to play the part of a bitter, cynical veteran.

"What is your occupation?"

"I'm a janitor."

The lady shrugged and resumed typing. The printer clattered to life and she tore off his ticket, stamped it, and pushed it across the counter to him.

"How many bags are you checking?"

"Two," Falcon replied, handing over his duffels. He knew they would be searched, but there was nothing in them incriminating, unless they figured out how to open the shaving cream can.

She grabbed the bags and tagged them and handed him the claim checks. After hoisting them onto an already-too-full baggage cart, she called brusquely, "NEXT," and looked past him impatiently as though he'd just entered the realm of nonexistence.

The flight was a nine-hour, cramped-leg, chilly ordeal. The friendliness and attentiveness of the flight attendants mirrored that of the comrade at the Aeroflot ticket counter. The best he could say for the experience was that the pilot was excellent, greasing the plane down onto the centerline at Khabarovsk in strong crosswinds with not so much as a bump. *Obviously former military*, Falcon thought to himself.

The train station in Khabarovsk was three miles from the airport. Walking gave him a good opportunity to detect a tail. There was none. After purchasing a ticket for the 0200 train to Vladivostok he convinced the local *militsiya* patrol to allow him to spend the evening on a bench in the train station.

The careful interrogation at the hands of the train ticket agent was nothing like the perfunctory questioning he'd received from Aeroflot. In years past, foreigners were not allowed to travel to Vladivostok, and even Soviet citizens were carefully interrogated before being provided with the necessary travel permissions. Though the restriction had loosened up considerably in the Gorbachev era, both the GRU and the KGB kept close tabs on traffic into and out of the port city. The reason for the security had everything to do with the fact that Vladivostok hosted the headquarters of the Pacific Fleet and was the major naval base in the region. Included in its many berths were the pride of the nation: the USSR's Pacific-based ballistic missile submarines.

Two years prior he'd nearly been captured by Soviet troops who spotted him in this very station. He smiled remembering the utterly improbable chain of events that began with his near-capture. After clobbering a trio of officers who had identified him as the fugitive sought by the GRU, he'd fled the station, breaking his arm in the process and then hijacking a car which enabled him to make good his getaway. Looking back on the experience, it staggered his imagination to think that the beautiful young woman who'd been in the driver's seat of the hijacked automobile in Khabarovsk was now his wife expecting their first child, back in the states. *I expect Bill Jensen would call that 'providential.' And I can't argue with him.*

The following day in Vladivostok, Falcon registered with the local authorities. His forged documents passed muster, so registration was uneventful and consisted mostly of standing in lines, waiting for the bored officials on the other side of the counter to put their requisite stamps on his internal passport. *This is worse than waiting for a license renewal at the Division of Motor Vehicles back in the States*, he thought. *Which is quite a feat.*

The personnel office at the Vladivostok naval base was delighted to gain a custodian with a naval background and a mid-level security clearance. The job made him eligible for housing in a tiny one-room flat in an apartment building owned by the base. His assigned duties involved cleaning the enlisted men's center, a facility on the base that included a gymnasium, cafeteria, canteen, bathrooms, and political indoctrination classrooms.

****

Jensen picked up the phone. "Sam, come up to my office, please."

A few minutes later Bergman stood in his door. "What's up, Bill?"

"Follow me down to the SCIF." The Sensitive Compartmented Information Facility was a part of Langley where the most critical secrets could be discussed without fear of compromise or interception.

After passing through several layers of badge and biometric security, Jensen picked one of the unoccupied cubicles and shut the door.

"Sit down, Sam. This won't take long. One of Israel's satellites is collecting data from a source named *Blackbird*. I need you to walk Evelyn Stinson through the process of accessing the data. It's going to come down as an encrypted file—neither she nor you will be able to look at it. All I can tell you is that it is related to Operation *Zephyr*. Since you are both already seconded to *Zephyr* I've decided to give you this task—besides, I need Stinson's NSA network to get to that satellite. The satellite is storing the information—it has to be specifically interrogated in order to download it. I'll provide you with the necessary security protocols to access it.

"Stinson is to check the bird several times a day to see if *Blackbird* has communicated."

"Who will check it in off-hours?"

"No one. We are expecting critical information from *Blackbird*, but it's not so time-sensitive that we need someone checking twenty-four seven. I will need her to check it once a day on Saturdays and Sundays, however. This part of the operation shouldn't take more than thirty days to complete, so it's not going to dislocate her personal schedule for more than a month. At least, that's what we anticipate. If things heat up we may have to pull another NSA employee into the loop to check the satellite more frequently, but I really don't want to do that unless we have to.

"Sorry, Sam, but I'm asking you to be a courier in addition to your analysis work. This is a black project and we're playing it very close to the vest. I don't want any more hands than absolutely necessary on the information from *Blackbird*."

Bergman shrugged. "I understand. It's not a problem, Bill. It's a beautiful drive to Fort Meade, and I—I kind of like going over there anyway."

"Um-hmm. I understand that the drive is not the only beauty that attracts you on those trips."

Sam blushed. "Yeah, well, no comment."

Jensen continued. "You will bring the downloaded files to me immediately. I have the decryption algorithm that will untangle them."

"Look, Bill, you've given me the analysis job for *Zephyr*—how can I analyze the data if I don't know what *Blackbird* is saying?"

"Sorry, Sam, but we are keeping the people with knowledge of *Blackbird* to an absolute minimum. The fact that the source even exists is top secret SCI. With the permission of the vice president, I am involving you and Evelyn Stinson because you're already working on *Zephyr*, and I need Stinson's NSA hardware to get *Blackbird's* reports. Don't worry—I'll keep you in the loop—but all of *Blackbird's* reports will be filtered through me before it gets to you. Stinson is not to have any access at all to decrypted information from *Blackbird*."

"It sounds like *Blackbird* must be a newbie, someone who's not been trained what not to include in a report, lest they compromise themselves," Bergman mused.

Jensen frowned at him. "You know better than to try to ferret out that sort of information," he said sternly. "Do not conjecture about *Blackbird's* identity!"

"Of course not—I was just thinking aloud. My mistake," the analyst admitted.

The two men exited the SCIF, Jensen heading for his office and Bergman heading for Fort Meade.

****

The door to Evelyn's office was shut. Sam Bergman stood in the hallway, intimidated by the closed door. He did not look forward to knocking on it and experiencing her chilly reception when she opened it and saw that it was him.

He raised his hand to knock, but faltered, uncertain as to what to do. His NSA escort eyed him curiously. "Sir, you were looking for Evelyn Stinson's office? Well, this is her office."

Bergman nodded. "I, um, is it—is it okay to interrupt her? Her door is shut, I—is there maybe someone in there with her?"

The escort frowned and swept his hand around the hall. "See, sir? They're all shut. It has to do with the nature of the work. You know, classified, right?"

"Of course." Bergman stood for another moment staring at the door as if he could glean some information from the bare wood.

"Sir?" the minder asked again.

"Ah, yes. Um, would, would you mind knocking?"

The young man rolled his eyes, sighed, and then rapped heartily on the door and walked off, leaving Bergman standing there alone. Sam had been hoping the fellow would stay long enough for her to open the door, under the theory that her angry reaction would be muted with a third party present. No such luck.

****

Falcon unlocked the door of his tiny flat. He was on the ninth floor of a ten-story concrete monstrosity, a drab apartment building in which the heat worked sometimes, the electricity was on occasionally, and the hot water might be warm between two and four in the morning, but icy at all other times. At least the elevator was consistent—it worked as long as the electricity was on.

On the positive side, there were no bedbugs and his windows weren't broken out. That pretty much summed up the positive side.

He put his packages down on the cheap table. He'd bought food and three extra blankets. It was getting toward dusk and he wanted to file his first report. He'd have to hurry.

Falcon put the shaving cream can and a few of the other

items into a net bag he'd purchased for the purpose. If he was stopped, he wanted a plausible explanation for carrying around a can of shaving cream—it was just part of his purchases.

Trotting down nine flights of stairs and exiting the building, he turned to his right and started down the sidewalk. The street was lined with a half mile of identical apartment buildings on both sides, before terminating at a decrepit waterfront consisting of a rotting wharf that hadn't seen a boat tied up since World War II. Rusted rails for cranes scored the concrete quay, disappearing into a cluster of abandoned warehouses, some of which were in various stages of collapse.

The two apartment buildings closest to the waterfront were unfinished. Looted piles of decaying construction materials were hiding among the hip-high weeds that had overtaken the building site. It was a depressing sight.

He was sitting on a stack of empty pallets when three toughs came around the corner of the nearest warehouse and approached him. One of the men was carrying a baseball bat over his shoulder.

"Look at him, Dmitri, he acts like he owns the place. Just strolls down to our turf, sits on our pallets, and doesn't even ask permission. So what should we do with him?"

"Maybe I should take his boots, Sergei."

"I'll take the coat," the third said, laughing.

The man called Sergei walked up to Falcon, a sardonic smile creasing his lips. "Listen, comrade. Today we'll go easy on you. No beating, okay? But we have to collect a toll— you're on our turf and you didn't ask permission. Nobody comes down here unless we say so."

Falcon spread his hands apologetically. "Hey, comrade, I'm sorry. I'm new here—I didn't know. I'll just leave."

"*Da.* You will leave—but it's going to cost your boots, coat, and whatever is in your bag."

"Look, I don't want to cause any trouble," Kelly said. He couldn't afford to give up his sat phone, nor have any contact with the local *militsiya*. His mission would be over before it started.

"Maybe we *do* want to cause trouble. I figured you were new, so we'll spare you the beating. But your coat, boots, and bag—hand them over and we'll let you leave."

"What the devil, Sergei? You are going too easy on him! Take his wallet, too."

"And give his money to the poor?" Sergei asked, grinning at his companions.

"Of course! We're the poor, Sergei."

The three men laughed.

Falcon sighed. He realized the only way out of the situation was to bluff—and if they called his bluff he'd have to put all three of them down. He was confident he could do it—he just hoped it wouldn't be necessary.

"My fine comrades, before you begin distributing my goods you must take them from me first," Falcon said, setting his bag down behind him.

"To be sure. We were planning on it," said the third man unpleasantly.

"Okay," Falcon replied, nodding agreeably. Then he held up his hand. "But wait, before we get started, where do you want me to take the bodies?"

"What bodies? What are you talking about?" Sergei asked.

"Your bodies. After I kill you, where do you want me to take your bodies? Or should I just dump them in the bay? That would be much easier for me, and you won't care—you'll be dead."

Dmitri smirked. "I think this hooligan needs a beating after all, Sergei."

"*Da*, Dmitri, *pravda*. If I'm not mistaken, he just threatened us."

"Boys, boys, we don't have to do this. I'm willing to let you just turn around and crawl back into whatever hole you came out of, and I won't tell anyone. Your secret will be safe with me."

Something about Falcon's easy confidence gave the trio pause. This wasn't going as expected. They looked around, wondering if he had some backup they hadn't spotted.

"Look," Falcon said, "I've got things to do, so can we

please get this over with? I'll give you a quick taste of what you're in for, and then you can decide what you want to do." He beckoned to the man with the baseball bat. "You with the bat, you're Sergei, right? Closer—come on, don't be afraid. Well, actually, you should be afraid but never mind that. Now go ahead, take your best shot."

As the thug drew the bat back, preparing to swing, Falcon held up his hands again. "Wait, stop. I need to know this before you swing: which knee do you want broken? The right or the left?"

The man lowered the bat and was silent for a moment, studying his opponent. Something about the man rattled him. Instead of begging for mercy, the intruder exuded supreme confidence. He decided he didn't want to find out why. Not taking his eyes off Falcon, he said to the other two, "You know, I think we can let him be, as long as he doesn't cause any trouble."

Falcon grinned and spread his hands wide. "Wise choice, Sergei. I'm good with that. You don't cause me trouble, I won't cause you trouble. Deal?"

Sergei stared at him for a moment, then nodded. "*Da*, comrade, *dogovorilis'*."

"Now, I'm going to come down here pretty often because sometimes I just want to be by myself. I promise I won't bring anyone else here, and I won't go wandering around or sticking my head into any of these buildings. I will respect your turf. If anybody asks me, I didn't see anything. In return, you and your people will leave me alone."

The three men shrugged and walked away, wondering if they'd just narrowly missed an appointment with death. And that was that.

Kelly waited ten minutes, then retrieved the sat phone. He powered it up and keyed in the numbers. In a few seconds he heard the promised three tones.

He whispered in Russian, "Hey, Willy, this is John Smith. I'm in Norfolk at the base, working on the enlisted side. Things are going well—I think this job will work for me just fine, my employer seems quite pleased with my work. I'll try to check in again, once I learn anything. Talk to you later."

There were no messages for him. It was getting dark, so he put the sat phone away and returned to his flat.

****

Stinson opened her door and was surprised to see Sam Bergman. For a moment she just stared at him. Suddenly she was angry again—even though she knew the break in communication had been due to her own mistake. *He should not have assumed I wanted to break it off. It's his fault. He could have come to see me!*

"Sa—Mr. Bergman, hello. What do you want?"

Bergman blinked. She was clearly hostile—he'd not expected that. He'd hoped that after receiving his card she'd at least be civil. To hide his own hurt he shifted into professional mode.

"Miss Stinson, as you know, you've been seconded to the DDO CIA to work on Operation *Zephyr*. Mr. Jensen sent me to show you how to access a new source, called *Blackbird*, from the store-and-forward facility of a satellite owned by the Mossad."

She didn't answer but merely waved him into her office.

"Please shut the door, Miss Stinson. The information I have for you is top secret SCI. Your colleagues are not cleared for this information." He spent the next ten minutes passing along the protocols, passwords and codes needed to access the satellite.

"Let's try it now," he urged.

"Mr. Bergman, this is my work, my career. I don't need you sitting here looking over my shoulder to make sure I'm doing it right. I don't need your help."

"Evelyn—excuse me, I mean Miss Stinson—I have always considered you one of the most competent persons I know and perhaps the best at what you do. I was not suggesting that you need my help in the slightest. The DDO wanted you to check to see if there was any communication from *Blackbird* before I returned to the Agency—that's all."

She didn't reply but swiveled around in her chair. Tapping on her keyboard, she closed the programs that were open and then launched the software that would communicate with the Israeli satellite. The computer beeped.

"What do you know?" she said, half to herself. "There's data there." With a few more keystrokes she downloaded and saved it to a floppy disk, which she handed to Bergman. "What sort of data is it?"

"I don't know, and even if I did I don't think I'd be allowed to say. This is a black project—that's all I know. I don't even know if Blackbird is HUMINT, or some sort of ELINT, or something else entirely. Thank you," he said as he locked the floppy disk into a briefcase chained to his wrist.

"You're welcome," she said softly, not looking at him.

"Did—did you get my letter?" he asked hesitantly.

"I don't want to talk about it," she replied brusquely. Then she relented slightly. "Yes, I did. I read it."

"May I—can I have your real phone number?"

She was silent, her back to him as she pretended to study her computer's monitor. Finally she said, "No."

He nodded and exited the office, quietly shutting the door behind him.

After he left, she sat down heavily in her chair, trembling. *Why did I just treat him so badly? Why am I so angry? Am I mad at him—or myself?*

****

Bill Jensen sat in a cubicle in the SCIF. The computer on the desk was not connected to the Internet nor to the Agency's local area network. For security reasons, it was a completely isolated standalone. He inserted the floppy disc acquired from Evelyn Stinson and scanned it for viruses. After it came up clean, he inserted a second floppy containing the decrypting routine. The output was an audio file, which he played.

       HEY, WILLY, THIS IS JOHN SMITH.
       I'M IN NORFOLK AT THE BASE,

WORKING ON THE ENLISTED SIDE.
THINGS ARE GOING WELL—I THINK
THIS JOB WILL WORK FOR ME JUST
FINE, MY EMPLOYER SEEMS QUITE
PLEASED WITH MY WORK. I'LL TRY TO
CHECK IN AGAIN, ONCE I LEARN
ANYTHING. TALK TO YOU LATER.

Jensen replayed the message, which was in Russian. Evidently, he was meant to identify himself as *Willy*, and Kelly was *John Smith*. Bill chuckled, because Kelly used the name he'd assumed when getting trained as a Combat Controller for the air force. *Norfolk* was, of course, a reference to Vladivostok. Jensen surmised that Kelly had landed employment at the naval base in Vladivostok, in a position that might give him access to some of the information sought by Operation *Zephyr*. The base personnel people were pleased with Kelly.

Jensen launched a file-scrubbing program, overwriting the decrypted file with hexadecimal zeroes and purging the directory information. He retrieved both floppy discs—to be returned to the safe in his office. He sat back in the chair, thankful that the insertion had gone well. Finally, Operation *Zephyr* would begin to collect actionable data.

****

A week later Shukshin strolled down the quay in Sevastopol, admiring the thirty-eight-meter luxury yacht moored alongside. The name of the boat, *Sunrise*, was displayed in bright red letters on the bow and stern, contrasting tastefully with the gleaming white aluminum hull. He stopped at the foot of the gangway and called to Pushkaryov. "Permission to come aboard, Mr. Vice President?"

Pushkaryov, dressed in white and sporting a white yachting cap, responded crisply, "Granted, Admiral. Come aboard, comrade."

The two men walked together into the boat's enclosed saloon, where Valentin Aristov, the defense minister, Kirill Yegorov, chief of the army general staff, and Yulian Churkin, the interior minister, were seated, drinks in hand. A steward was busy serving *hors d'oeuvres,* baked salmon on thin crackers topped with a mild cheese sauce. The pleasant aroma of dinner being prepared wafted into the saloon from the five-star galley and reminded Shukshin that he'd not had breakfast or lunch.

Shukshin glanced at the steward then looked back at the vice president, eyebrows raised, an unspoken question.

"It's okay. They're my hand-picked men. Everyone aboard is mine."

Shukshin didn't care for the implications of Pushkaryov's last sentence, but he nodded and poured himself a drink.

"I am pleased with our progress so far," Pushkaryov said. "The preparations are nearly complete. Yulian, you have informed me that the leadership of the Moscow *militsiya* are loyal to you and will follow your lead, is that not so?"

"*Da*, comrade. When the time comes my *militsiya* will come down on the side of the *rodina*—I can guarantee it."

Shukshin thought he detected some subtle ironic ambiguity in the interior minister's response but then chided himself for being too suspicious.

"Our courageous General Kirill Ilyich Yegorov," Pushkaryov continued expansively, "tells me that the majority of the general officers in the Red Army are tired of the general secretary and his so-called liberalizing policies. Gorbachev has accomplished nothing other than to destroy the economy and provide a breeding ground for corruption."

Yegorov nodded vigorously. It occurred to Shukshin that the four other men must have arrived at the yacht somewhat earlier, for they all appeared to be deep in their cups.

"And finally, our noble defense minister, Valentin Valentinovich Aristov, has provided assurances that the military bureaucracy will support our planned leadership transition."

"Yes, indeed, Alexander Ivanovich," agreed the defense minister, as he held up his glass. The white-coated steward hurried over and topped it off with American whiskey.

"It would appear then, my dear Shukshin, that we are all waiting on you. Tell us how your work with the Pacific Fleet is faring."

"Certainly, Alexander Ivanovich. About one month ago three of my submarines penetrated the defenses of an American carrier group, coming within four kilometers of the USS *Carl Vinson*. Captain Mirov was in a position to sink the American ship. In all likelihood he could have done so and escaped unscathed himself. This has created immense pride among our submariners—the overall mission was a bold and brilliant success. I have but one disappointment—if the Americans had protested the incident we would have received much wider publicity. The effect on our officer corps would have been much greater. Still, it was an astounding success."

"Congratulations, Admiral!" Pushkaryov looked at Shukshin with new respect. "I was not aware this had happened. Are you telling us that the final piece is in place?"

"*Nyet*. The Soviet submarine officers and crews are distinct from the rest of the navy, indeed, from the rest of our armed forces. They are all volunteers—there are no conscripts among them. They are better educated and better informed about the wider world than the average Soviet military man. They are not as easily led."

"And your point is—"

"My point is that I have merely gotten their attention. I have earned their favor with these aggressive missions. It is building their national pride. But I do not yet have their total loyalty. If we want them to rally around my leadership, Mr. Vice President, we must implement the rest of my plan. We must get into a conflict with the United States."

Irritated, Pushkaryov got to his feet. "We must avoid that step at all costs."

"Then our revolution will not succeed, Alexander Ivanovich. You said we must avoid my plan at all costs. Failure is the cost; are you willing to pay? Gorbachev will go on with his plan. He will destroy the Soviet Union and we will be unable to stop him. All because you weren't willing to risk it all. In the final analysis, you, Mr. Vice President, are stopping short of what must be done. When we began meeting months ago, you pressed each of us, asking how far we were willing to go, what we were willing to do. But now we will fail because you aren't willing to do what must be done to ensure our success." He glared at the vice president, and set his glass down on the table a little too firmly.

The three other men stirred uncomfortably. After a moment of silence, Churkin offered, "I agree with Pushkaryov. I really don't think we should start something with the United States."

"And I agree with Admiral Shukshin," Yegorov affirmed. "It's the only way to wind up sitting in the Kremlin instead of standing in front of a firing squad."

"*Da*," said Aristov. "It's the only way," he repeated. "We must have firm control of the Pacific Fleet and its ballistic missile submarines."

Pushkaryov sensed that the momentum of influence was swinging to Shukshin, and it angered him. Hoping to put the arrogant man in his place, he snapped, "What have you done about Zelenko, your superior?"

"Nothing," Shukshin replied coolly.

"Nothing?" Pushkaryov roared. "You want us to approve military action against the United States, and you fear to eliminate one man?"

"I have done nothing about him because he has not interfered with my plans," Shukshin replied sharply. "If I am seeking the loyalty of the officers, it would be stupid of me to eliminate the most beloved and respected officer in the Pacific Fleet. If he begins to interfere, I will find a way to deal with him. Otherwise I will leave him alone."

"If you are to initiate a conflict, how soon can it begin? We will need time for logistics, stockpiling matériel, and preparing the troops for combat," Yegorov said.

"No, you won't," Shukshin answered confidently. "We are not attacking the US, and so we must not give any appearance that we are preparing to do so. We are going to bait the US into attacking us. And we do not intend to follow up on the initial skirmish, so no logistical preparation will be needed."

"And what if you cannot limit the conflict? What then?" Pushkaryov demanded.

Shukshin did not respond immediately. He needed Pushkaryov's support, at least at first. No one else in the cabal realized it, but Shukshin intended Pushkaryov to be his puppet—until he was no longer needed at all.

"Alexander Ivanovich, this whole thing was your idea. You are the one who brought us together, who pointed out Gorbachev's flaws, who told us what we needed to do to save the Soviet Union. Without you, we would not even be here discussing this," he said calmly, trying to stroke the man's ego. "You told us months ago that this involved risk, but that the risk was worth it because the *rodina* was worth it. I am essentially agreeing with you—the risk is worth it. I am just saying that sometimes risk calls for greater risk.

"The Americans have very little stomach for battle if they can handle a matter diplomatically. If we back off from the conflict, so will they. The UN will line up behind us—we will play the victim card—and they will censure the US for taking the first shot. Gorbachev will be gone, you'll be our new leader, and our stock on the world stage will rise.

"We can't do this without you, Mr. Vice President," he added obsequiously.

Pushkaryov nodded. He considered the matter, turning the arguments over in his head. Finally he sighed, "Very well, Konstantin Grigoriyevich, if you believe it to be absolutely necessary, we'll do it your way. How soon can you be ready?"

"I would like to propose a date, Mr. Vice President. On 20 January, the Americans will inaugurate their next president. As that ceremony begins, I propose that the conflict also begin. It will complicate their transfer of power and reduce their ability to respond definitively. I would recommend that the overthrow of Gorbachev happen four days later, on 24 January." No one thought to ask him how he could guarantee that the Americans would attack the Soviet navy at precisely that time. Shukshin shared his real plan with no one, but his intention was to bag a US aircraft carrier. Having failed to provoke the Americans into firing last month, he was planning to take the first shot.

****

On the same day of the meeting on Pushkaryov's yacht *Sunrise* the *Admiral Vinogradov* was racing south, her four Zorya-Mashproekt gas turbines effortlessly driving the ship at thirty knots through light seas. She was a brand new Udaloy-class destroyer, and her captain was methodically shepherding the ship and crew through her final sea trials. Her orders were to rendezvous with a pair of attack submarines in the southern portion of the Sea of Japan. The plan was to play cat and mouse while her sonar suite and its operators were put through their paces.

"Captain, there's an inbound chopper twenty minutes out, a Ka-27. It's carrying Admiral Zelenko, sir, and the pilot is asking permission to land."

"Granted." The captain turned to the OOD. "Sound flight operations. Prepare to receive a helicopter over the fantail. Helmsman," he added, "make revolutions for five knots."

Admiral Zelenko's personal chopper circled the destroyer twice before hovering over the landing pad on the ship's fantail. The Soviet Ka-27 (known to NATO as a Helix-A) is normally configured for antisubmarine warfare. However, the helicopter assigned to the commander of the Pacific Fleet was stripped of its dipping sonar, sonobuoys and weaponry. Instead, the internal weapons bay was configured with fuel tanks to provide extended flight range.

A few minutes later, the captain of the *Admiral Vinogradov* and his executive officer greeted Admiral Zelenko as he debarked from the Kamov.

"Permission to come aboard, Captain Zhiglov," a smiling Zelenko requested.

"Granted, comrade Admiral. Please, come aboard. You are most welcome, sir."

The sentiment was genuine. Zelenko was revered across the fleet by both officers and enlisted men. Equally skilled in handling ships or men, Zelenko was a sailor's sailor. Quick to correct and quick to praise, he demanded excellence and he got it. He left administrative matters to his second, Shukshin, but he himself practiced hands-on leadership and mentoring.

"*Spasibo.* I have come to observe your fine crew, Captain, as your ship completes its sea trials."

The officers took a tour of the ship. Zelenko wrote notes to himself regarding the electronics and equipment the shipyard had not yet installed, as well as the pieces requiring replacement. True in navies across the globe, logistical officers could be stingy with equipment and slow to respond to a ship's needs. Zhiglov knew that Zelenko would cut through the red tape when the *Admiral Vinogradov* returned to her berth. The needed items—which had been requisitioned months ago—would be installed within a week.

Four hours later Zelenko was in the officers' wardroom, eating supper with the off-duty officers of the sonar division. The admiral regaled the men with anecdotes of his storied career, and then began to ask them questions.

"Tell me about your sonar suite."

Senior Lieutenant Mikhail Vetrov, commanding officer of the ship's sonar division, smiled broadly. "We have the latest upgrade to the MGK-355 Polinom sonar. Hull mounted in the front, variable-depth towed array in the back. The electronics, Admiral, are the best I've ever used. If an American submariner has a cold, sir, we'll hear him blowing his nose."

"I read your report from last month's trials, Lieutenant. You were concerned about the amount of flow noise on the towed array. Has that been fixed?"

"Yes, sir. The software for the signal processor required an update. When it's working properly it is able to cancel out our own flow noise. It's much better now."

The conversation continued for several more minutes. When Zelenko stood to leave the wardroom, Vetrov spoke up again. "Admiral Zelenko, may we ask you a question?"

"Certainly, comrade"

"Did one of our submarines really ambush an American aircraft carrier and threaten to launch his torpedoes?"

Zelenko stiffened. He'd been hearing rumors of strangely aggressive behavior in the submarine services, but he'd always discounted it as mere sailor's gossip. But he hadn't heard *this* bit of gossip. If true, his submarines were clearly stepping over the line into very dangerous and provocative behavior.

He smiled mysteriously, not wanting to give away the fact that this was new news to him. "Tell me what you've heard, Lieutenant."

"Only that one of our submarines managed to get within four klicks of an American aircraft carrier and threatened to launch its torpedoes. Supposedly there were three of our submarines involved in the action. I've heard that Captain Mirov was appointed commodore and led the mission."

Zelenko, the smile frozen on his face, shrugged and said, "Lieutenant, you know I can't comment on that."

"So it happened?"

"No comment."

But the gossip was all over the ship. In the next four hours he was asked about the incident six more times. His concern grew, and finally he cut short his visit and helicoptered back to headquarters, anxious to look into the matter further.

Chapter 12

Tuesday, December 6, 1988

After working with the first shift cleaning crew for a week during his brief orientation, Falcon was assigned the shift no one else wanted: the graveyard shift—midnight to 0800. Except for the duty officer and a skeleton staff, the enlisted men's facility was empty during those hours.

Kelly walked from his flat to the naval base, a two-mile hike through drizzle and a darkened town. The guard at the base entrance requested Kelly's newly issued base identification card.

"Where are you going, Borodin?" the guard demanded, studying the ID badge.

"Enlisted men's facility. I'm on the graveyard shift cleaning crew."

"Wait here."

The guard entered the guard post and checked the ID against a list. Satisfied, he emerged and returned the badge. "Sign in," he instructed, and handed Kelly a clipboard. Kelly signed *A. P. Borodin*, checked the guard post clock, and recorded the time, *2345*.

The guard waved him through the gate with a friendly comment, "Stay dry!"

Borodin smiled at him. "You too, comrade."

After checking in with the duty officer he went to the custodial store room and examined the chalk board for his evening duties. His first task was to clean and mop the heads. *Oh, joy*, he thought.

During his break several hours later, he drank a cup of coffee while chatting with the duty officer.

"What are some of the, uh, places in town that the sailors go to?" he asked, flicking a finger on his neck, the Russian gesture for drinking. "I'm new to this area, and haven't found my way around yet."

"You probably better stay clear of the navy watering holes, Borodin," the officer said. "They don't appreciate civvies invading their turf."

"They object to naval veterans?"

"No, vets are welcome. You're a veteran? Well, that's different. Here, I'll draw you a map to the most popular place." He ripped a page off a notepad and drew a map showing the location of the speakeasy. "Officially, of course, this place doesn't exist. But everyone on base knows about it. The *militsiya* take a cut of the profits every month to pretend it's not there. The place is run by a former sailor who was cast ashore for insubordination. It's actually pretty decent."

The final task on Kelly's job list was setting up chairs in the facility gymnasium for a political lecture scheduled at 0900. He did a double take when he saw the topic on the schedule: *"Glasnost and Perestroika: the Next Step, or Betrayal?"* The lecture was unusual, in that the chief political officer of the Main Political Directorate of the Red Banner Pacific Fleet would be delivering it, rather than the unit's own political officer. When his supervisor arrived at 0730 to inspect his work, Kelly secured permission to sit in the back of the meeting.

****

"Find the patrol reports for orders seventy-seven through seventy-nine, and bring them to me," Admiral Zelenko barked at his aide. The admiral was irritated and worried. As he reflected on the last several months, he began to see that his deputy, Admiral Shukshin, had initiated the transfers of top command officers prematurely—before their tour at Vladivostok would normally expire. While he did not have enough information at hand to detect a pattern, it was clear that something beyond, or even contrary to, the demands of the service was going on.

The admiral had spent the first hour of his morning examining the master order log, trying to discover what might have occurred. Three sheets of the numbered master order book were missing. After searching fruitlessly for the missing sheets, it occurred to him that perhaps the patrol reports for those three missing orders had been filed.

The second hour of Zelenko's day did nothing to help his

attitude. After reading the requested patrol reports, he was livid. Purple with rage, he jumped out of his chair, threw open his office door, and shouted at his aide, "I WANT TO SEE CAPTAIN MIROV IMMEDIATELY! I DON'T CARE WHAT HE IS DOING—I WANT HIM IN MY OFFICE RIGHT *NOW!*"

Captain Third Rank Abramov stared at his superior, shocked. He'd never seen the admiral in such a state of agitation. He jumped to attention. "Admiral, sir, *chto sluchilos?* What happened?"

Zelenko dropped his head and struggled to control himself. "Forgive me, Nikolay Nikolayevich. I should not treat you so—you are an excellent and faithful officer. Please locate Captain Mirov and bring him to me immediately." He returned to his office, shutting the door gently, leaving the surprised Abramov to wonder what had disturbed his admiral.

Thirty minutes later Mirov was ushered into Admiral Zelenko's office. "You wished to see me, Admiral?"

Zelenko's rage had passed, and he responded gravely, "Please sit down, Captain. I read your most recent patrol report, associated with an operation called *East Wind*. Please explain to me why you felt possessed to brace an American aircraft carrier as you did. Your actions seem to me to be foolhardy and reckless, endangering both your vessel and your crew. Choose your words wisely, Captain, as it is in my mind to convene a court martial to examine your actions."

Mirov swallowed, surprised by Zelenko's words. But his conscience was clear and he felt fully able to justify his actions. "May I speak freely, comrade Admiral?"

"Please."

"My actions were taken in perfect accord with the orders issued by this office, sir. I objected to those orders, expressing my concerns almost exactly as you yourself just said: *foolhardy and reckless*. Admiral Shukshin overrode my objections and directed me to carry out the orders as written. I had no choice but to do as I was commanded. Therefore, despite my concerns, I executed the mission to the best of my ability. Captains Gromyko and Fetisov likewise performed their duties with excellence, despite the fact that they shared my concerns."

"You are claiming that you acted as ordered in this incident?"

"That is correct, sir."

"May I see your orders, please?"

"I did not bring my copy, sir, not knowing what this meeting would be about. If you wish, I will fetch mine immediately, although a copy should exist in the master order logbook in this office, sir."

"Three orders are missing from that book—the orders associated with your patrol report as well as Gromyko's and Fetisov's. Would you have any idea as to why those orders are not in the master logbook?"

"None, sir. I do have my copy, however. Shall I fetch it?"

"*Da.*"

****

Rear Admiral Stavin from the Main Political Directorate concluded his lecture. "Finally, you must judge for yourself. Do the policies of the general secretary—*perestroika* and *glasnost*—advance the great evolutionary doctrines of Marx and Lenin, or will they throw us backward, restoring the evil power of the bourgeoisie over the worker? I say they are a step backward.

"Do not misunderstand me, comrades. I do not advocate the murderous policies of Stalin. I reject and disavow them. I credit the general secretary with his compassion for those who've been unjustly detained by the *rodina's* security organs. And I credit the general secretary with his desire to improve our economy and productivity. Mikhail Sergeyevich Gorbachev is not our enemy—he is our brother and comrade. But his policies must not be allowed to stand. The pure doctrines of Marx and Lenin must be restored."

As the enlisted men filed out, Falcon grabbed his coat and walked out with them. One of the men looked at him and said, "Say, you're the night custodian for our facility, aren't you? I pulled the late watch several nights ago and saw you cleaning here."

Falcon smiled. "*Da*. That was me."

The sailor held out his hand. "Victor Padorin. What's your name?"

"Andrei Borodin."

"Since you've been on the cleaning crew, I've never seen the facility look better. My comrades and I appreciate that. The last cleaning guy did a terrible job—the heads were really gross.

"So, what are you doing in this lecture? You're a civilian, aren't you?" Padorin was not unfriendly, just curious.

"I'm a veteran. Navy."

"What unit?"

"Sorry, can't tell. I'll just say that it was one of those units you're not allowed to talk about."

"Really? Why'd you get out?"

"Not my choice. I was pushed out. Medical," Falcon said, tapping his chest. "Unreliable ticker. The doc said I needed a low-stress job, so here I am, scrubbing toilets."

"Sorry to hear that," Padorin said. "So, didn't you get enough political indoctrination during your time in the service? I can't imagine anyone coming to these speeches voluntarily."

"Oh, I don't know," Falcon replied. "With all the changes in the country under Gorbachev, I'm just curious as to where it's all going. I guess I'm just trying to keep my finger on the pulse."

Padorin nodded. "Makes sense. My buddies and I get together occasionally and debate the changes. Some are on one side, some on the other. Sometimes it feels like we're headed toward a crisis of some sort."

Falcon nodded. "Yeah, I think so, too. Anyway, I'm just trying to learn as much about it as I can."

When Falcon arrived back at his flat, he put together his customary sack of items, including the shaving cream can, and headed for the decaying wharf at the end of the street. He'd not observed the thugs again since his initial confrontation.

"Hey, Willy. It's Smitty again. I've been talking to guys around the naval base here at Norfolk, and it's clear we've got both Republicans and Democrats. The Republicans are all for keeping the old ways. The Dems want change.

"Listened to an important lecture today by a high-ranking politician. He was clearly a Republican. Seems to be influencing a lot of the street-level party workers. Things are definitely in flux, and the two opposing parties are speaking very openly. Probably going to come to a head.

"My initial thoughts are that the Republican party platform on which you were informed is quite accurate. By the way, I'm going to be checking out the bars in Norfolk—I hear that there are some really good ones."

****

Sam Bergman knocked on Evelyn Stinson's door. Bergman was a gentleman's gentleman in the best sense of the word. Though the man was an accomplished analyst—at the top of his craft—he was shy and unassuming with women and was particularly intimidated by beautiful ones. He was especially careful to avoid any appearance of innuendo or macho power plays. All of which added up to the fact that whenever he knocked on Stinson's door, he was very nervous, made more so by her cold reception of the past few weeks.

When she opened the door, he said, "Good afternoon, Miss Stinson. I understand that you have another file from *Blackbird.*"

"I do indeed, Mr. Bergman. Please come in," she said in a pleasant voice.

He entered and shut the door behind him. When he turned around, she was studying him. It rattled him, even though he didn't see the hard lines in her face present in previous visits.

After an uncomfortable pause, she nodded. "Checked the bird this morning and discovered the file. It seems a little longer than the last several messages, judging by the file size." She handed him a floppy disc, which he placed in his briefcase. He locked the case and stood up, the chain rattling faintly on his wrist.

Grateful that the atmosphere seemed a little warmer, he smiled at her. "Thank you kindly, Miss Stinson," he said as he turned to leave.

"You're welcome, Sam."

She used his first name! He stopped and decided to gamble. Turning back to her, he asked, "You—you got my flowers?"

"I did. They're beautiful."

"And you didn't throw them away?"

"Oh, goodness no! I'm enjoying them. Thank you for sending them."

He hesitated, uncertain of what to say. He wanted to prolong the contact but was fearful of pushing too far. He nodded, "Good. I'm so glad you like them, Miss Stinson," he said, clumsily. He turned back to the door.

"Wait, Sam." She looked down at the floor. "I'm so sorry," she said softly. "I guess I made two mistakes, not just one."

"Two mistakes? I don't understand."

"The first was accidentally giving you the wrong phone number last year. The second was blaming you for my mistake after you pointed it out. I was just too—proud, I suppose. I've spent the last nine months hating you for leading me on and then dropping me, only to discover that it was my fault all along. It was a tough pill to swallow, and I've treated you horribly. I'm so sorry."

He smiled at her and shook his head. "All is forgiven, Miss Stinson. Please, don't let it trouble you any longer."

She looked at him and blinked away a tear. "Please, Sam—my name is Evelyn."

He nodded, "Thank you, Evelyn. The formality felt so, so —distant." He cleared his throat and thought to himself, *I've got to know if there is any possibility at all of a future here.* Fearful of rejection but determined to know, he asked, "Hypothetically now: if some guy from the CIA called a girl from the NSA and asked her to dinner, would she even consider it? Hypothetically?"

"Wait a minute," she said, raising her eyebrows. "Didn't you use that line last year?"

He laughed nervously and shrugged. "Might have, I don't know."

"You did," she insisted with mock severity. "The answer is: it depends on who is making the phone call. I'm sure it would have to be the right guy. But," she said, a faint smile tracing across her lips, "I'll bet she'd hope he would at least give it a shot."

He grinned at her, relieved. "Well, how can he give it a shot if she won't give him her phone number?"

She frowned. "If he works for the CIA, I wouldn't imagine that getting her phone number would be too difficult."

"Oh, it isn't. But what if he wants to do it the right way, not the CIA way?"

"Tell you what: I'll give you her number. See that your hypothetical friend gets it, would you?" She scribbled her phone number down on a piece of greenbar paper and gave it to him.

"Umm, are you *sure* this is the right number?" he asked mischievously.

She punched him playfully in the shoulder. "Oh, go away. I've got work to do."

He folded the paper, put it in his pocket and winked at her. "I'll see that he gets it."

****

Zelenko studied the order and then reread Mirov's patrol report, his concern growing as he read it. "You surfaced. What happened next?"

"That was the end of it. Once I was on the surface the Americans must have figured I was no longer a threat. But it was clear they were very unhappy. They pursued us with their ASW aircraft almost all the way back to port, dropping sonobuoys on us the whole way. We were under constant surveillance by active sonar, even after we were hundreds of kilometers away from the carrier group. I believe the harassment was retaliation for getting so close to the American ship."

"Probably so, Captain, probably so." The admiral folded the order carefully and put it in his breast pocket. "I'll return this to you, Captain Mirov, after I make a copy of it."

"Certainly, sir. Will that be all?"

"No." Zelenko rose from his chair and walked over to his window. It was a sunny but bitterly cold afternoon, with a stiff north wind raising whitecaps in the anchorage visible from his office. One of the harbor's pilot boats was knifing through the chop, undoubtedly carrying a pilot to meet an incoming ship. Navigating Vladivostok's crowded maritime waters was no easy task. Military vessels of all sizes, commercial freighters, fishermen, buy boats, dredges, tugboats, sometimes icebreakers, and the occasional irresponsibly operated pleasure craft belonging to a member of the *nomenklatura*, all plied the black waters. The traffic volume, combined with the treacherous currents and underwater hazards of the harbor, made it necessary for vessels arriving and leaving to employ skilled pilots who were expert at handling ships and knew the waterway perfectly.

"What is he doing, Boris Sayanovich?"

"Sir?"

Admiral Zelenko walked back to his desk and sat down. He fixed the captain with a steely gaze. "What is Admiral Shukshin up to?"

Captain Mirov hesitated. Finally he answered carefully, "I don't *know* that he is up to anything, Admiral, other than pursuing the objectives of this command."

The admiral pulled the folded order out of his pocket and waved it at the other man. "These do not reflect the objectives of this command, Captain," he said heatedly.

Mirov did not respond.

"You give yourself away, Captain Mirov. A moment ago you hesitated to answer me. I think you were trying to decide what *not* to say. You know, or suspect, much more than you are admitting, Boris Sayanovich.

"You are a sharp and observant officer, Captain. You are the best submariner we have. You did not attain this excellence by blindly following orders, seeing nothing, hearing nothing. You are a thinking man, and I must know your thoughts. What can you tell me about Admiral Shukshin?"

"It is not my place to talk about my superior officers, sir."

Zelenko jumped up and slammed his hand down on his desk. "STOP THIS!" Mirov flinched. "I know what constitutes proper and professional conduct among my officers!" the admiral barked. "But my second-in-command is violating important headquarters regulations by removing orders from the master order book. He is issuing orders in my name that are reckless and irresponsible. He's been transferring officers before their postings have expired, and I MUST KNOW WHAT IS GOING ON!"

Admiral Zelenko sank into his chair, holding his head in his hands. After a moment he said quietly but firmly, "Captain First Rank Boris Sayanovich Mirov, I am the commander of the Pacific Fleet. I am ordering you to tell me what you know, what you think you know, and what you suspect about Admiral Shukshin's actions. I am ordering you," he repeated, "for the good of the Pacific Fleet and for the good of the *rodina*."

Mirov looked at the floor and took a deep breath. "Sir, I am sharing my thoughts about Admiral Shukshin with you very reluctantly, only because you have ordered me to do so. It goes against my training as an officer in the Soviet navy to speak ill of any superior. I haven't shared my thoughts about the admiral with anyone else—not even my wife."

Zelenko nodded gravely. "Very well. I understand. Go on."

"When I came off my combat service deployment last January, Admiral Shukshin visited me in my quarters aboard the *K-263* before I turned the boat over to the port crew. He was very frank, right in front of my political officer, in fact, saying that Gorbachev must go. He complained against the general secretary's policies of *glasnost* and *perestroika*. He said that Gorbachev's policies were destroying the country. His exact words were these, sir: 'and destroy it he will, if comrades of good character do not unite to stop him.'"

Zelenko frowned. "How did your *zampolit* react to that?"

"He said he was in perfect agreement with Admiral Shukshin. The admiral asked me if I agreed. I responded that I was not interested in a revolution if that's what he meant. I told him I believed that we need to give Gorbachev more time—perhaps his policies will work after all. The admiral was not happy with that.

"I've thought about that conversation many times over the last eleven months as I've watched other strange things happen. For example, many of my brother officers have been reassigned before their tours here were up. Can you guess, Admiral Zelenko, what their political persuasion was, vis-à-vis the general secretary?"

"They were supportive of Gorbachev?"

"*Da*. Every last one."

"But if this is what was behind Admiral Shukshin transferring them, as you apparently believe, why weren't you transferred, Captain Mirov?"

"Because he had other plans for me. I'm not sure how this works into his thinking, but I am convinced he intended for me to die on Operation *East Wind*. He gave me an older boat and actually explained to me that if anything happened, he could not afford to lose a newer submarine."

"So what does all this conjecture lead you to conclude?"

"Admiral, I believe that Admiral Shukshin might be mixed up in some attempt to overthrow Gorbachev. Somehow *East Wind*, under my command, was to be a trigger to make it happen."

Zelenko sat back in his chair and stared at Captain Mirov. "Those are very serious charges, Captain," he said icily.

"No, sir. They are not charges at all. They are precisely what you asked me for—my thoughts, my opinions, my suspicions—and they would have remained mine alone had you not ordered me to share them with you."

Zelenko didn't answer. He fixed his eyes on Mirov and stared intensely at him—eye-to-eye contact. He wanted to see if the officer would crack. He didn't. Mirov stared back at his superior without flinching.

Finally the admiral relented. *Good*, Zelenko thought, *he has the courage of his convictions*. He asked. "Is there anything else I should know?"

"Are you familiar with Standing Order 17, sir?"

"No, I haven't seen any reference to it anywhere."

"That's because it was not written down—for obvious reasons, in my opinion. It was verbal only. Admiral Shukshin addressed Standing Order 17 to every commander of every attack submarine in the Pacific Fleet. It urges us to take an increasingly aggressive posture against all ships of the US navy, including stalking them, drawing dangerously close, then flooding our torpedo tubes. It stops short of commanding us to do what *East Wind* directed me to do—opening my outer doors—but it is a very aggressive order nonetheless."

"Indeed it is," the admiral agreed. "One miscalculation and somebody's going to launch a weapon; who can tell where that will end?" He stood up, signaling that the interview was over. "Thank you, Captain Mirov, for your frankness. I needed to hear what you had to say. But you are to speak of this interview to no one. That's a direct order."

"Certainly, Admiral. I serve the Soviet Union."

Mirov kept his word, but in the end it would not matter, because in a dank, dark corner of the basement of the headquarters building, an electronic device was recording every word spoken in Zelenko's office. Months ago, Shukshin had turned the security team that swept Zelenko's office for listening devices every morning. The sweep always came up clean—regardless of the listening device implanted there.

****

"It's not one of ours, sir." The senior *michman* on the Ilyushin IL-20 ELINT aircraft pointed to the digital message header on his screen. He'd just detected a burst transmission on a satellite frequency used by Soviet military communications. The fact that he'd even seen it was pure chance; the equipment should have been turned off hours ago when they completed their mission. It was still running simply because it gave him and his crew something to do on the long, boring flight home.

"Are you sure?" asked the officer in charge of the electronic intelligence crew aboard the aircraft. Both men were wearing headphones, it was the only way to communicate over the whining roar of the four Ivchenko AI-20 turboprop engines. The lumbering Ilyushin was just entering the pattern to land in Vladivostok.

"*Da*, comrade. The header looks like one of ours, and the frequency is ours, but the encryption algorithm isn't."

"Maybe it's a new encryption scheme?"

The *michman* shook his head. "No, sir. We're the electronics intelligence group. We always get the latest stuff first."

"Perhaps someone is testing a new encryption protocol, and it's not yet been released to production."

It had been a long and tiring flight for a simple and straight forward mission of spying on a minor joint exercise between the Australian and American navies. It had been something of an endurance contest, and the pilot-in-command had wondered aloud if they'd set a record for time-on-station. The big Ilyushin had been refueled multiple times, and the nine-man flight crew and the twenty-man intelligence complement were all exhausted. Multiple reels of data tapes containing valuable electronic intelligence were safely stored in a crash-proof locker aboard the aircraft. All the ELINT officer wanted to do was land, write up his report, turn over the tapes, and go to bed for sixteen hours. He was definitely not looking forward to what almost always turned out to be a lengthy and semi-hostile interrogation if his crew turned up anything unusual.

"I'd bet a month's pay that's not the case, sir. It was a brief burst transmission, too short to serve as a test."

The officer sighed. "Okay. Was it recorded?"

"Yes, sir. I'd mounted a scratch tape to give the young guys more experience working with the data and the equipment. The burst should be on it."

"Alright, as of right now that's no longer a scratch tape. Label the tape, dismount it, and put it with the others in the locker. What was the bearing of the transmission?"

"That's the odd thing, sir. There's ten degrees of separation between the bearing at the beginning of the transmission and the one at the end of it. That means we're practically right on top of it."

The *michman* wrote down the two bearings, the exact time the burst occurred, as well as its duration in milliseconds, and gave the paper to his officer. The officer moved to the navigation station, and began triangulating the location of the transmitter. He was just finishing his calculations as the big aircraft touched down.

That's funny, he thought to himself. *The transmission came from a rundown part of the harbor area here in Vladivostok. There aren't any military facilities there. Not good. I'd better report this one.*

Chapter 13

Friday, December 9, 1988

The large auditorium in the Pacific Fleet headquarters building buzzed with several dozen conversations going on simultaneously. With the exception of Admiral Shukshin, who was on leave, all the officers of the fleet not on deployment were present, from first lieutenants up.

Admiral Zelenko stood off to the side, quietly conferring with his aide, Captain Third Rank Nikolay Nikolayevich Abramov. Standing at the back of the room was the fleet intelligence officer, Captain Third Rank Stefan Stefanovich Udom.

A cluster of officers walked in, laughing loudly. Zelenko looked up and noted the arrival of the fleet political officers —men who were securely in Shukshin's pocket.

Zelenko had spent the last two days reviewing all of Shukshin's orders and administrative decisions of the past eighteen months. The pattern was clear, validating the concerns Mirov shared two days prior—Shukshin did appear to be grooming the command officers of the Pacific Fleet to support a putsch. It had also occurred to the senior admiral that if Shukshin was intent on toppling the general secretary of the Communist party, he might not have qualms about trying to topple his boss. When Zelenko left his house this morning, he carried a concealed side-arm.

Despite the seriousness of the situation, Zelenko had decided to deal with Shukshin privately. Publicly, Shukshin would retain his role as vice commander of the Pacific Fleet, at least until Zelenko figured out how to handle him without creating a backlash in the officer corps. He didn't want to create a new *Storozhevoy* affair. Until that time he hoped to maintain a facade of normalcy.

Zelenko checked his watch. It was time. He strode up to the lectern on the platform and began the meeting. The first thirty minutes dealt with the myriad mundane updates, notices, bulletins, and announcements that were part and parcel of any large organization. There were also personal updates, congratulations to Captain so-and-so for the new addition to their family—*momma and baby are doing fine, thank you*, and so forth. Recognition was given to junior officers for passing qualification exams for the command of new equipment or new shipboard duties.

Finally Zelenko got to the main piece of business. "Comrades, you will remember that Admiral Shukshin issued Standing Order 17 back in September, calling for aggressive exercises against the American navy. This was a necessary order at the time. The American imperialists had lost respect for our heroic men and mighty ships. We decided to give them a dose of their own medicine, yes?"

There was a rumble of approval from the men.

"What's good for the goose is good for the gander, am I right?"

Another rumble.

"Our submarines have thoroughly humiliated their carrier groups. Our valiant captains have piloted their deadly vessels to within a few kilometers of American aircraft carriers, stopping just short of launching a killing strike."

At this the men stood and cheered. The political officers began to sing the state anthem of the Soviet Union, and soon all the officers were singing. Zelenko joined in and briefly directed a stanza before holding up his hands to quiet his enthusiastic officers.

"You have done well, comrades. We have made our point and proven how vulnerable to our superior submarines are the Americans' vaunted carrier battle groups. But we don't want to reveal all of our capabilities to our witless adversary. It is now time to resume normal operations. As of immediately, I am rescinding Standing Order 17. There are to be no further provocations against the American navy at the present time. All submarines and surface vessels currently on patrol will be notified that Standing Order 17 has been rescinded. Thank you, comrades. You are dismissed."

This was greeted with stunned silence. Zelenko watched as the fleet intelligence officer, Captain Udom, his face red and angry, turned and stalked out of the auditorium. The section of political officers stood silently, as if on command, and walked out stiffly, their body language telegraphing hostility and disgust.

As Zelenko stepped off the dais, Captain Abramov murmured, "I believe we have problems, sir."

Zelenko turned to him and shot back, "*Nyet!* It is Admiral Shukshin who has problems, Nikolay Nikolayevich!"

****

Udom picked up the phone and dialed the number Shukshin left with him when the admiral flew to the Black Sea for a visit with Pushkaryov.

"Admiral, not an hour ago Zelenko rescinded Standing Order 17 and ordered the fleet to stop all provocative actions against the American navy."

"He knows about Standing Order 17?" Shukshin asked, brow furrowed. Zelenko hadn't been aware of daily operational details for ages. Close to retirement, he'd shown little interest in commanding the fleet, leaving all operational matters to Shukshin and taking over the training aspects himself—a reversal of the normal roles of a fleet commander and his deputy.

"*Da.* And that's not all. He also knows about *Vostochnyy Veter*. He grilled Mirov for several hours two days ago."

Shukshin swore. "What's going on? I know Admiral Zelenko! The man has not looked at the master order log for at least a year. He's not been running the fleet, *I* have! He's completely out of touch. Besides, I pulled the orders for Operation *East Wind* out of the log. How could he have found out?"

"He located the patrol reports, Admiral."

Shukshin swore again. He'd gambled on the likelihood that if the orders did not appear in the master order log, it would be assumed that there were no corresponding patrol reports.

"Then we're going to have to do something about Admiral Zelenko," Shukshin said curtly. He sighed and told himself, *Ah, well, there was no way this could stay secret forever. But now I have to deal with Zelenko. I was hoping it would not be necessary. I cannot al-*

low my personal favorites to stand in the way of saving my country.

"Yes, sir," Udom responded. He paused and then asked, "Are you suggesting what I think you are suggesting?"

"I am."

"Okay. It might take several days. You should remain out of contact until it is done, sir. While listening to the recordings from the bug in his office, I heard him tell Mirov that he's going to recall you and confront you. It would be far better for all if that confrontation never happened."

"*Soglasno*, agreed. You have seventy-two hours. Do not disappoint me, Captain Udom."

****

Kelly threw off the thick woolen blanket and sat up, swinging his feet to the floor. It was 1800 hours local. On most nights he'd be headed into work in several hours, but not tonight. It was his one night a week off from his custodial duties at the base. Tonight he was planning on finding the speakeasy and gathering what intelligence he could from the conversations of the sailors.

He sat for a moment, shivering—the massive heating plant that provided steam and hot water for the whole block of high-rise apartment buildings was down again. He grimaced—*that means the shower will be ice cold too*, he thought, *just like it was yesterday, and the day before, and the day before that, and the day before that.* He grabbed a towel and walked over to the corner of the room that served as the combination bathroom and shower. A small round hole in the bare concrete floor served as both the toilet and the drain for the shower and the sink. When not in use, it was covered by a thin rubber mat that kept the noisome sewer gases at bay.

The shower and sink each had hot and cold water knobs, but it was the rare day that the hot water was any warmer than the cold. It certainly hadn't happened since he'd been staying in the flat. After a bone-chilling shower, he dressed quickly.

Shortly after 2000 hours, he located the place. It was a nondescript concrete building that looked like it might have been a mid-sized warehouse at one time. There was no sign and nothing to indicate which door was the entrance. He hung back in the shadows, watching. After a few moments a noisy knot of sailors came walking down the street. One man from the group rapped on a rusty steel door in a certain pattern: two knocks, one knock, a pause, and then three. The door opened and the group entered.

Falcon remained in the shadows for another few minutes and then approached the door. He rapped out the same pattern, and the door opened. A big, burly man whose biceps were the size of Kelly's thighs opened the door. He looked suspiciously at the newcomer and then shrugged and waved him in.

Cigarette smoke as dense as fog hung in the too warm air. Electronica-technica music blared from somewhere, and Falcon observed twenty to thirty men, most sitting at tables, some at a makeshift bar, and a few playing pool on a well worn pool table. Several heavyset barmaids were bustling about with trays full of shot glasses and mugs of beer. Falcon didn't know the drill, so he found an empty table and sat down to watch.

The barmaids ignored him. Everyone else pretended to ignore him, but he knew he was being scrutinized. After a few minutes, a smiling man whose expression would have looked more appropriate on a shark, sat down opposite him.

"What's your name, comrade?"

"Borodin. Yours?"

"Chekhov. I don't see any insignia on your jacket. What ship?"

"No ship."

"Well then, my friend, we have a small problem. This fine establishment is a private club dedicated to the sons of the motherland who go to sea aboard our warships. I will buy you a drink, but when you are finished you must go."

Kelly nodded and spread his hands. "Sorry. I was told you admitted veterans. I don't mean to cause trouble—I'll leave."

Chekhov's eyes narrowed. "You're a vet? What service?"

"Navy."

"Really? Where did you serve?"

"I apologize, but I'm not allowed to tell you. I was in one of those units that does not exist, if you know what I mean."

Chekhov nodded slowly. "So why did you get out?" he asked, his eyes showing new respect.

"Not my choice. Medical discharge."

Chekhov motioned to a barmaid, then turned back to Kelly. "Let me see your internal passport."

Kelly pushed it across the table. Chekhov studied it for a moment, then passed it back. He smiled again and this time it was genuine. "You're good—you can stay. You're welcome here anytime, Borodin. And I'll still buy you a drink." Chekhov stood up and bellowed to the room at large, "He's new, but he's one of us, comrades. A navy veteran. Welcome him!"

The men surrounded him with warmth and interest that surprised him. It was the same sort of camaraderie that he'd experienced back home with his air force unit. They fired curious questions at him about home, family, and service. Kelly quickly realized he had to get out of the spotlight before he got tripped up. And then one of the men recognized him as the night shift custodian for the enlisted men's facility, and told the group how much cleaner the facility was since Borodin had been there. That triggered a new round of back-slapping and drinks.

The last thing Falcon, aka Borodin, wanted was to be turned into some sort of mini-celebrity. It would become very dangerous if anyone started asking too many questions or looked into his backstory. When several men came in the door and all heads turned briefly to greet them he managed to fill his shot glass from the bottle of mineral water on the table. He stood and cried, "*Dovol'no*, enough, good comrades! Allow me to stand the room a round and offer one last toast, and then you must let me sit at my table in peace and quiet so I may enjoy the music and this fine establishment." He paused for effect and raised his glass. "To the mighty Soviet navy, may it always stay on the right side of the waves!" That produced a raucous cheer as everyone knocked back their drinks. Finally,

Kelly was able to sit at his table and just watch the activity around him.

The place was loud and boisterous—he didn't have to eavesdrop. The challenge was trying to focus on just one conversation at a time. As he anticipated, alcohol had loosened both inhibition and tongue, and politics was everyone's favorite topic. Some of the talk became heated and more than once those with cooler heads had to separate inebriated sailors who took exception to the fact that their fellows did not agree with them.

Taking the mix of patrons in the bar for his sample, Falcon decided that talk was running about seventy percent in favor of Gorbachev's policies—not a surprising thing since the *proletariat* had none of the advantages of the *nomenklatura*. The enlisted men occupied the bottom of the greased pole of Soviet economic status.

Kelly overheard several of the non-coms claim that the officer corps was being purged of Gorbachev loyalists and being replaced by communist hardliners. One man who served as a driver for a senior captain in the submarine fleet hinted that something big was in store for the American navy in January. An angry whisper from his sober companion shut the man up, and he refused to say any more.

A trio of young men sauntered in the door. Falcon could tell by the insignia on the shoulder of their work shirts that all three were submariners. After making the rounds, greeting colleagues and friends, they settled at the table right in front of Falcon. At first their conversation was standard fare, complaining about the slowness of shipyard workers, complaining about the food on their last deployment, complaining about the recently increased operational tempo. At the mention of that, Falcon began paying attention.

Speaking in low tones, the stockiest of the three leaned in and said, "Say, have you guys heard about Mirov's latest?"

"I heard that Mirov got chewed out by the Old Man," replied one of the others, chuckling. This fellow was short, with a prominent hooked nose.

"That's not what I'm talking about. Mirov braced one of

Uncle Sam's flattops," Stocky said, looking around to make sure no one was listening. Falcon was pretending to be engrossed in an arm-wrestling match several tables over.

"Just what do you mean, *braced*? We got within fifteen kilometers of one just three weeks ago. I thought the political officer was going to pee his pants, the wuss," replied the third man, who was totally bald and had an anchor tattoo on the back of his head.

"Yeah, well, did your captain order that the torpedo tubes be flooded and the outer doors be opened?" Stocky asked, grinning.

"What do you think, moron? Of course not! That's inviting the Americans to launch a weapon!" Baldy rejoined.

"Mirov did."

"What?" the other two cried in unison. Heads around the room turned and looked their way.

"Hold it down, guys!" Stocky growled under his breath. "You're going to get me in trouble. I'm not supposed to be talking about this. Wait a minute," he said, jerking his head to indicate the would-be eavesdroppers in the room.

Both men nodded and waited for everyone else to turn back to their own conversations.

"Okay, shut up and listen. Back in the beginning of November, I was the helmsman on Mirov's boat, the *K-264*. We crept up on the *Carl Vinson*, one of the Americans' supercarriers—got within four kilometers before we were detected. Could have blown her out of the water. So what does Mirov do? After it's obvious that they've got us on sonar, sonobuoys dropping everywhere, Mirov orders the tubes flooded and the outer doors opened. I think everyone in the control room peed their pants."

Hook Nose leaned forward. "What happened next?" he asked.

"We had him dead to rights, so the American captain took the only option open—he increased speed and tried to ram us. At that point he was so close we'd have to take the safeties off the torps if we were really going to shoot. Mirov ordered evasive action and an emergency blow and we surfaced. Everyone stood down. But they harassed us all the way home."

Baldy shook his head. "The man is nuts. If we ever get in a war, I hope I'm not on his boat."

Stocky grinned. "I hope I am. He's one cagey son of a gun. If anyone can get us out of a scrape and keep the sea on the outside and the air on the inside, he's the man."

"You're nuts, too. You're all crazy," Baldy said seriously.

"If you're not a little nuts, then why did you volunteer for submarine duty?" They all chuckled, and then Stocky continued. "Anyway, there's something big going down late in January. We're going out again, and my buddy in the weapons division said that we're going out with a full weapons complement."

"Practice weapons?" asked Hook Nose.

"*Nyet*. Live ammo."

****

A cold, moist wind was blowing out of the south as Falcon sat atop a stack of old skids and watched the night lights over the water. At least a dozen anchor lights dotted the harbor. The superstructures of several commercial ships were brightly illuminated. Somewhere in the distance a bell buoy clanged discordantly. He listened to the hypnotic *lap, lap, lap* of perpetual wavelets caressing some hidden portion of the decaying wharf beneath his feet, and savored the breeze-borne aroma of sea and diesel fuel and creosote.

Jake's head was still buzzing from too much vodka at the speakeasy, but the cold night air was helping to clear it. He was trying to compose something clever about the Norfolk Naval Base in order to pass along the information he'd learned, but no matter how he phrased things it was too obscure and too open to the wrong interpretation. *Oh, well,* he thought to himself, *Rick Freeman said code language isn't necessary since the encryption on this phone is so good. I guess I'll just say directly what I've learned tonight.*

He was about to send his report when he heard a car approaching. *That's odd. I've never seen any traffic this far down the road.*

The car was too close for him to escape the area without being seen. He put the sat phone away and crouched behind several rusty fifty-five gallon drums.

Whoever was in the vehicle obviously did not wish to be seen, because they were driving without headlights or running lights. The car pulled around behind one of the old warehouses, not thirty feet from where Kelly was hiding. When the driver got out, the cabin light briefly exposed his face. It was Captain Udom! Kelly had seen the fleet intelligence officer at the base several times.

Why would Captain Udom be here this time of night, and why would he be driving without headlights? Who is he going to meet, and why? It was a cross between curiosity and intuition that drove Kelly's next move. Udom disappeared into the warehouse door. Kelly did a quick scan of the area and spotted no guards. He examined the exterior of the building and spotted an outside stairway leading to a door on the second floor. Kelly ran over to it and decided that, despite the rust and corrosion, it could probably still hold his weight. He crept cautiously up the stairs—holding his breath lest they collapse under him. At the top was a door with a glass window which had been broken out.

He silently opened the door into an office that had obviously been ransacked years before. Another door on the opposite side of the room led out to a hallway. Quietly he eased the door open. A murmur of voices floated down the hallway, and he could see a faint light down at the end of it. Treading carefully to avoid the broken glass and other detritus littering the floor, Falcon advanced down the hall. It opened onto a mezzanine looking down on the warehouse floor, where he saw Udom talking with four men, one of whom held an electric lantern. Carefully Falcon lay down on the floor and peered over the edge to watch.

"It must look like an accident, and it must happen soon. Within two days, tops," Udom was saying.

"What kind of accident?"

"I don't care. A fatal one. I just don't want anyone to trace it back to me."

"Accidents are expensive nowadays, very expensive."

"How expensive?"

"Twenty thousand rubles expensive."

"Ten. I'll give you ten."

"Perhaps you should be talking to someone else, Captain Udom." The man looked at his companions and said, "Let's go." They turned and began walking to the other side of the warehouse.

Udom cried out, "Wait!"

When they turned around, Kelly recognized one of the faces: it was Sergei, the thug who had challenged him several weeks earlier.

"What, Captain?" Sergei sighed, communicating disinterest and exasperation.

"Okay, twenty. But it's ten now, and ten after the job is complete—*if* the coroner records it as an accident, not a homicide."

"*Nyet.* It's thirty now. Thirty or we walk."

"Thirty? Why? A moment ago you said twenty thousand rubles, and I agreed to it. Twenty, and stop playing games with me."

"We don't play games, Captain. We are very serious. I could wave my finger right now, and you'd be a dead man."

With a shock, Falcon wondered whether there were other men hidden in the shadows. He studied the cavernous space carefully before realizing Sergei was bluffing—but Udom surely did not know that.

The intelligence officer swallowed nervously. "Twenty," he said weakly, without conviction.

"Captain Udom, let me explain this to you. You don't think we're going to make this hit on Admiral Zelenko ourselves, do you? Of course not! We're going to hire an independent contractor, who might himself hire someone else. Why? Because the hit must not be traceable back to us and through us to you. That extra ten thousand rubles is buying you protection, comrade. Protection for you, your wife, your children. Do you understand, Captain?"

Udom perceived the veiled threat and paled. He managed

to croak, "Yes, I understand. Thirty thousand rubles. I'll have half of it here tomorrow night."

"Then we have a deal, comrade. A pleasure doing business with you. And, by the way, if it ever comes into your mind to double cross me or my organization, we know how to find you."

****

Falcon waited in place until everyone left, and then he lingered twenty minutes more. He realized he'd just seen the Russian mafia in action, and it chilled his blood. Apparently the only reason they had accepted a truce with him several weeks earlier was not out of fear, but a business-like reluctance to do something that might bring official scrutiny on their operations.

Kelly returned to the wharf, broke out his sat phone, and made the call.

"I can now confirm the intelligence given to us by Geredin. The Soviet navy is intentionally goading the US to launch a weapon. There appears to be a concerted effort to purge the Pacific Fleet officer corps of Gorbachev loyalists, especially in the submarine service. The majority of enlisted men appear to support Gorbachev, but after talking with a number of them I am convinced that if push comes to shove, they will line up behind their officers, political inclinations notwithstanding.

"There have been repeated hints of something significant happening in late January that will impact the US navy. I don't know what it is because the men I've been listening to don't know either—they just know it is big. A least one submarine and possibly more will be sailing in January carrying a full complement of live weaponry. Apparently that is unusual for the submarine service in the Pacific Fleet.

"As a side note: by chance this evening I observed a contract put out on Admiral Zelenko, the commanding officer of the Pacific Fleet. The man who is arranging the hit is a Captain Udom, the fleet intelligence officer. I don't know his first name or patronymic. Thirty thousand rubles have been placed on Zelenko's head, and the hit is to be made very soon—within forty-eight hours. It will look like an accident. I do not know if this is related to the political situation."

****

"There it is, sir! Same frequency and same encryption as the last one, but a longer burst this time."

"Did we get a vector?"

"Affirmative, sir."

The ELINT officer nodded and then pressed the transmit button on his mic. "*Momma Bear*, this is *Baby Bear*. Did you pick up that last burst? We have it as an X-band transmission, 8.175 gigahertz, duration 2408 milliseconds."

The detection of the unaccounted-for satellite phone transmission picked up by the Ilyushin IL-20 four days prior had kicked over a hornet's nest within the Vladivostok naval base's security and intelligence apparatus. The decision was made to keep two aircraft aloft, one south of the base and one east of it, to see if there were any further transmissions and to enable a more accurate triangulation of the source, if in fact it happened again.

After a few seconds the response came back. "Affirmative, *Baby Bear*. We copied the same burst, and have a solid vector on the origination point."

The ELINT officer grinned at the *michman* manning the console. "Got him!"

****

Admiral Zelenko was quartered in a large *dacha* on top of a hill at the end of a remote macadam road, overlooking *bukhta Gornostay*, Ermine Bay. Luxurious by Soviet standards, the home befitted the admiral's rank and illustrious career. His wife had died years earlier and the union had produced no children. Committed to the memory of his deceased wife and in love with the sea and naval service, Zelenko had never re-married. He considered the fleet his family and its enlisted men his sons. He lived alone, but he was content.

Zelenko's driver arrived at 0700 hours and picked him up for the thirty-minute ride to the base. As he turned onto the main road at the bottom of the hill, a truck bearing the logo of the municipal telephone service turned onto Zelenko's street.

The truck parked on the street opposite Zelenko's house. After a few minutes, a man emerged from the truck and climbed the telephone pole. He patched into the line and used a service handset to dial Zelenko's house. There was no an-swer.

The "repairman" walked around to the back door and re-moved his shoes and put booties on his feet and surgical gloves on his hands. After picking the lock, the man located Zelenko's bathroom and opened the medicine cabinet, finding the expected bottle of digitalis. Zelenko's heart trouble was well known on the base, a piece of information Udom had passed along with the initial payment for the hit. The man poured its contents into a baggie, which he pocketed, and then added two capsules that looked exactly like the admiral's prescription pills, two of which were to be taken with water every evening.

On the back of the shelf, hidden behind the other medicines, he placed a small bottle of cyanide capsules, with a skull and crossbones logo on the label. The bottle's label listed the quantity as four pills. In fact it contained only two.

****

Sam fixed himself a beer and poured a bunch of chips into a big bowl. Digging around in his refrigerator he located the jar of salsa. Placing it all onto a tray, the CIA analyst carried it into his living room, tuned the television to Monday Night Football, and settled onto his couch ready to enjoy a relaxing evening. The Cleveland Browns were traveling to Joe Robbie Stadium to take on the Miami Dolphins, and it was a matchup

Bergman wanted to see.

Ten minutes into the game his phone rang. "Bergman," he said tersely, not trying to hide his irritation at the interruption.

"Sam, this is Evelyn. I'm sorry to bother you at home."

When he heard her voice his attitude changed. "Evelyn, there's no one I'd rather be bothered by than you. I'm glad you called. What's up?"

"Sam, I just downloaded a new, rather lengthy transmission from the source." She didn't want to use the code name *Blackbird* over an unsecured line.

"Evelyn, it's after nine. Why are you still at the office?"

"The source's satellite was down today. Communication was not reestablished until half an hour ago. For some reason I can't explain, Sam, I felt like I had to stick around until I could check to see if the source had transmitted. And I'm glad I did, because while I was waiting on the satellite this evening some significant intelligence intercepts from other channels landed on my desk. You need to see what I've received."

"Tonight?"

"Yes, as soon as possible. I have a feeling it's critical. I can't say any more on an unsecured line."

"Of course. Okay, I'll leave right away. See you in a few."

Thirty minutes later he was tapping on her office door, secure briefcase in hand.

"Hi, Sam, thanks for coming out so late. Here's the *Blackbird* transmission," she said, handing him a floppy containing the encrypted download. "The file is about three times the size of what we usually receive from *Blackbird*, and I can only imagine that it's important."

Sam thanked her, dropped the disc in his briefcase, and started to close it when she put her hand on his arm. "Not yet. I have more to give you. It's been a bumper crop of an evening. The project manager of TRANSIENT knows I'm vacuuming up all the intel I can get my hands on pertaining to the Pacific Fleet and the naval base at Vladivostok. Well, a *Vortex* satellite passing over the Siberian far east late Thursday —Friday, Vladivostok time—snagged a phone conversation originating from somewhere on the naval base at Vladivostok.

                                    C. H. Cobb

ECHELON flagged it, and two hours ago it finally wound up on my desk. The conversation was in the open—it was neither scrambled nor encrypted. I finished translating it just before I called you." She put a sheet of paper in his hand and sat down as he read it silently.

> *"Admiral, not an hour ago Zelenko rescinded Standing Order 17 and ordered the fleet to stop all provocative actions against the American navy."*
>
> *"He knows about Standing Order 17?"*
>
> *"Yes. And that's not all. He also knows about East Wind. He grilled Mirov for several hours two days ago."*
>
> *"What's going on? I know Admiral Zelenko! The man has not looked at the master order log for at least a year. He's not been running the fleet, I have! He's completely out of touch. Besides, I pulled the orders for Operation East Wind out of the log. How could he have found out?"*
>
> *"He located the patrol reports, Admiral."*
>
> *"Then we're going to have to do something about Admiral Zelenko."*
>
> *"Yes, sir. Are you suggesting what I think you are suggesting?"*
>
> *"I am."*
>
> *"Okay. It might take several days. You should remain out of contact until it is done, sir. While listening to the recordings from the bug in his office, I heard him tell Mirov that he's going to recall you and confront you. It would be far better for all if that confrontation never happened."*
>
> *"Agreed. You have seventy-two hours. Do not disappoint me, Captain Udom."*

"Whoa!" Sam exclaimed, as he sank into the chair next to her desk, contemplating the implications of what he'd read.

"I know who Zelenko is," Evelyn said, "but who is Captain Udom, and who is he talking to?" Evelyn asked, her curiosity getting the best of her. "ECHELON did not have enough metadata from the call to make the identifications."

"Udom is the fleet intelligence officer for the Red Banner Pacific Fleet," Sam murmured, scratching his chin, "but who is he talking to? Good question."

He studied the transcript. "Udom's being very deferential. He's obviously talking to an admiral—that narrows it down. And," he snapped his fingers, "the other guy is claiming to have run the fleet. That's got to be Admiral Konstantin Grigoriyevich Shukshin, Zelenko's deputy. And if I read this right, it looks like Zelenko is in the crosshairs."

"That was the same conclusion I came to, though I didn't know who is who. Which is one reason why I wanted to see you immediately. It appears that Admiral Zelenko's days are numbered."

"It would seem so. Too bad there's nothing we can do. Zelenko is supposed to be a moderate in their system, a level-headed guy. Shukshin has a reputation as a bomb thrower."

"You're not going to warn them? You're just going to let them kill Zelenko?"

"Of course. We have no choice. We'd compromise our intelligence gathering if we tried to warn someone. You know that as well as I do, Evelyn."

"Yeah, I guess I do. It rattles me, though. In my work I usually just translate SIGINT—I never get caught up in the implications, until now. Ugh. I don't like it—I'd rather not know. Hard on the conscience."

"You said that was *one* of the reasons you called. Was there something else?"

"Yes." She put another transcript in his hands. "This also hit my desk late today. On Saturday—that would be Sunday in Vlad—another one of our spy satellites picked up communications between two Ilyushin IL-20s. They were using a fairly standard routine to encrypt the conversation. It was one that the NSA cracked about six months ago. Anyway, the gist of the transcript is that these two flying listening posts were working together to triangulate the location of a sat phone transmission."

"Okay, that's not surprising. So why are you concerned about it?"

"Because they were saying that the signal is not Soviet—it's not theirs—and the location they identified is a short walk from the naval base in Vlad. Somebody is about to get bagged and tagged—perhaps already has been—and given that you are neck-deep in this project, I thought you ought to know ASAP."

****

It was 2200 hours when Bergman pulled into the mostly empty Agency parking lot. The DDO's parking spot was occupied, however. *Good*, he thought. *Jensen is just the man I need to see—and right now.*

When he got off the elevator he went straight to the DDO's door and knocked. He heard Jensen say "Enter," and he opened the door.

Bill Jensen swiveled in his seat to glance at the intruder. CNN was blaring from his TV monitor. "Oh, good, Sam, it's you. You've got to see this. CNN picked up a feed from the Soviet Union—the TASS news office in Vladivostok is reporting that Admiral Zelenko is dead—an apparent suicide."

"Oh, no! Already?" Sam sighed, sinking into one of the leather chairs.

"*Already?*" Jensen turned back to the analyst. "What do you mean, 'already?' Were you expecting this? If you were expecting this, how come I wasn't expecting this?"

"Wait, Bill. I just got back from the NSA, just now. Evelyn Stinson received several pieces of SIGINT this evening that suggested something like this. It's fresh intelligence—literally breaking news. I just didn't think it would happen quite this fast. It's not a suicide, by the way, it's a murder designed to look like a suicide."

"How can you know that?" the DDO demanded.

Sam opened his secure briefcase, and wordlessly pushed the transcripts across the desk to Jensen. Jensen read the first one twice and simply said "Shukshin."

"Yep. And Udom arranged the hit."

Jensen nodded, rereading the transcript.

"Bill, you need to read the second one, too. For both personal and professional reasons."

The DDO's eyebrows went up, and he tilted his head. "Personal reasons?"

Sam rubbed his face. "Look, I know I wasn't supposed to figure this out, but I think I know who *Blackbird* is. It's just too obvious, given his background and recent history. Anyway, read the transcript. You might have to act soon. Real soon."

Jensen studied the transcript and paled. He set it down on his desk. "Sam, was there a new file from *Blackbird*?" he asked carefully.

"Yes, sir." He pushed the floppy across the desk and stood up. "I know you've got to run down to SCIF to listen to that. I'll be in my office for the next thirty minutes if you need me."

Chapter 14

"*Abort, abort, abort!* Return to Moscow station immediately if possible. Alternate extraction plans being considered. Sat phone compromised, use only in extreme emergency." Jensen's voice on the recording sounded tense but controlled.

Abort? Extraction? Falcon quickly shut down the sat phone. In the distance he could hear a chopper approaching. His mind was racing. *Okay, think! The sat phone has been compromised. That probably does not mean the encryption has been cracked, at least if Rick Freeman knows his stuff. And Jensen didn't say that I have been compromised—just the phone. So they must know where the transmissions are coming from—but they probably haven't connected the transmissions to Borodin. At least, not yet. As long as I'm quick about it, I should be able to get back to my flat and grab my alternate identity papers before they connect the dots.*

He jumped to his feet and began trotting up the empty street, heading for his apartment. But before he'd gotten far, he was stopped by the bright searchlight of a helicopter penetrating the shadows and dark places where he might hide. He dove into the open entrance of one of the abandoned, unfinished apartment buildings a scant second before the light played across the entrance. Withdrawing deep within the shadows of the room, Falcon watched as the helicopter hovered over the wharf and a squad of six troops fast-roped to the deck. They spread out and began searching the waterfront area as the helicopter resumed its search from the air.

Jake's heart sank as he heard a second chopper approaching. He groaned. *This is not going to end well.*

His conversation with Bill Jensen immediately before flying to Moscow came to mind. "Jacob, if you are compromised and under threat of capture, remember this: the situation is different from last year. Then, you were being held illegally and the Sovs were fair game. They were going to kill you if they caught you. So if you killed someone while escaping, you were justified and it did not complicate your situation. That is not the case on your mission today. You will be in their country illegally. If they capture you, we can negotiate for your release. If you injure some of their people in an attempt to escape, that might complicate things a bit but we can probably still negotiate. However, if you kill someone while attempting to escape or evade capture, you will be subject to Soviet law and Soviet penalties. They will probably execute you. We won't be able to reel you in through negotiation—you'll be on your own."

For the moment all the search activity was happening on the street side and at the waterfront around the abandoned warehouses. He felt his way through the darkened apartment building until he reached the back side. The construction project had been abandoned before doors and windows were installed, leaving rectangular openings in the concrete. Looking from a window opening, he plotted a possible course through the weeds and stacks of decaying construction supplies, a route that might enable him to leave the area unseen.

He was on the verge of making a dash for it when one of the helicopters circled, splaying its searchlight on his escape route. The backwash from its rotors raised dust and litter into a swirling maelstrom. He withdrew further into the building again and then heard barked commands coming from the street side, behind him. The search had caught up with him. He turned to greet the threat.

****

"Thank you, Mr. Vice President, for calling this emergency meeting of the National Security Council on such short notice." Jensen paused and looked at his notes as a few latecomers entered and took their seats.

"Gentlemen, Operation *Zephyr* has achieved its objectives. I will summarize what we now know. As you are aware, back in September Anatoly Geredin, head of the Soviet KGB, personally informed me of his concerns about a hard-line conservative faction developing in opposition to General Secretary Gorbachev. This faction is suspected of planning a coup to sweep Gorbachev aside and take control of the organs of power in the Soviet government. Geredin's contention was that the coup plotters intended to unite the military around the putsch by fomenting a limited conflict with the United States. The idea was that, in the midst of a widespread patriotic fervor brought on by combat, the military would fall in line with the coup and carry it through to success.

"The genius of the plot, according to Geredin, was that the Sovs would bait us into taking the first shots in the conflict by the extremely aggressive actions of their naval units. They would attempt to place our naval vessels into situations of extreme peril, hoping we would fire, so that in the international media we would be cast as the belligerents and themselves as innocent victims. Thus they would gain three advantages—a successful coup while simultaneously damaging our reputation before the world and enhancing their own.

"We have seen these aggressive actions slowly mounting in frequency and intensity over the past six months. But we still needed to verify Geredin's information before deciding on a course of action. The possibility existed that Geredin himself was part of the coup plotters, and that he was trying to maneuver our navy into a posture that would allow the Sovs to take a free shot at us.

"Operation *Zephyr* is our intelligence effort to confirm or falsify Geredin's claim. I can now report that it has been verified. Information provided by a source code-named *Blackbird* gave us three pieces of the puzzle. First, that officers sympathetic to Gorbachev have been purged from the Pacific Fleet. Second, that fleet officers have in fact been ordered to take these aggressive actions as a matter of the standing operational policy of the fleet. Third, that the recently reported suicide of Admiral Pyotr Stefanovich Zelenko, commanding officer of the Red Banner Pacific Fleet, was not a suicide at all. It was, rather, an assassination ordered by Admiral Konstantin Grigoriyevich Shukshin, Zelenko's deputy commander."

This last piece of information was greeted with momentary stunned silence, then everyone began talking at once. "Order, order, please!" demanded the vice president, slapping his hand on the table.

"I have a question, Mr. Vice President," said the secretary of state, Walter Atkins, when the hubbub diminished.

"I'm sure we all have questions, Wally, but go ahead."

"Dr. Jensen, I've been tracking the growing political split in the Soviet Union through our daily intelligence briefings. I know that as their economy tanks and basic goods are disappearing from the shelves, tempers are growing hot, factions are spreading, and Gorbachev's opponents can smell blood in the water," Atkins said. "But what you're telling us is several orders of magnitude beyond that. The assassination of a top Soviet flag officer—Zelenko is a highly decorated Hero of the Soviet Union—is tantamount to starting an armed revolution. You've said that this information has been verified, but I have to ask: you are *absolutely* sure this was a murder and not a suicide, as TASS reported?"

"I am, sir. But remember: the Sovs don't see this as the 'shot fired around the world,' Mr. Secretary. The Sovs actually believe Zelenko killed himself. All indications say that even their intelligence services have bought the suicide narrative. I'd go so far as to say, sir, that the *only* parties who know the true nature of Zelenko's death, besides us, are the men who put out the contract on Zelenko and those who did the job."

"Assuming you are correct, Dr. Jensen," continued Atkins, "I have my own ideas about what Shukshin was after by bumping off his boss, but I want to hear your theory."

Jensen nodded. "As you are aware, Admiral Zelenko was known to be a moderate on the current spectrum of Soviet politics and a supporter of the general secretary. Shukshin, on the other hand, is an outspoken communist hardliner, bitterly opposed to Gorbachev's policies. With Zelenko's 'suicide,' Shukshin is next in line to assume command of the Pacific Fleet. By getting Zelenko out of the way without bringing any suspicion on himself, Shukshin positions himself to continue remaking the political direction of the fleet in his own image. This, of course, will support the coup plans."

The secretary of state nodded. "That aligns with my thinking as well, Dr. Jensen."

"Does all this really matter to us?" the vice president's

chief of staff interjected, looking around the room. "Why do we care how the chips fall in their political system?"

"From an isolationist, purely political standpoint we really don't care, Beale," replied Admiral Alfred Feldstein, chairman of the joint chiefs. "But that isn't all that's in play. What we do care about is keeping tabs on the guy who controls their nukes, particularly their boomers, and that's what this is really all about. Gorbachev is a liberalizing influence. He's not a sword-rattler. Recently he's opened the Soviet military to several very interesting interactions with our own military. It is in our interest to make sure that the US takes no unnecessary action that could lend support to those seeking to overthrow the general secretary.

"Peter the Great once said, 'Any ruler that has but ground troops has one hand, but one that has also a navy has both.' We don't want to supply the coup plotters with both hands, so to speak."

Beale cleared his throat and looked at Jensen. "Who or what is this source you're relying on? I believe you referred to it as *Blackbird*. And how do you know that information from this source is trustworthy?"

The vice president's chief of staff irritated Jensen. The man was a self-important political drone who always had an eye on his own ambitious political future. Beale was the sort who would climb over people to get to the top of the heap, or to get to the nearest lifeboat in a disaster. Jensen swallowed his disdain and managed a forced, frosty smile. "As to your second question, the source is highly reliable. As to the first, I'm afraid that information is on a need-to-know basis, and most of the participants in this room don't need to know."

"But if we're going to trust the word—"

"Let's move on," the vice president said, interrupting Beale. Nolan Beale had been imposed on the vice president by a campaign donor, and the man had been a liability ever since. "Dr. Jensen, what is your recommendation?"

"Mr. Vice President, I am willing to stake my reputation on the trustworthiness of these facts: that the groundwork is being laid for a coup; that Mr. Gorbachev is the target; that the

Pacific Fleet is being groomed to support the coup; that Admiral Shukshin is one of the principal plotters; and that a limited military conflict with the United States is part of the planning—a conflict that we are supposed to start.

"But to go further and advise the navy on a response is something I cannot and will not do—it simply is not my area of expertise. I believe the safety of our sailors and ships is paramount. I would not want to put them in danger by recommending that they take no self-defensive action when threatened by an adversary. With all due respect, sir, I must defer to the judgment of our military officers."

The vice president scrutinized Jensen's face. "That's a good answer, Dr. Jensen. This government needs more honest men who know their limits and are not blinded by ambition or the lure of power," he said, casting a brief glance at Beale.

He turned to Paul West, the director of central intelligence. "Paul, what do you say? Do you concur that *Blackbird* is reliable, and that Dr. Jensen's information is actionable?"

"I do, Mr. Vice President. I believe Geredin's information has been confirmed, and all that remains is for a decision to be made as to what action in particular we will take."

The vice president nodded. He turned to the chairman of the joint chiefs. Admiral Alfred Feldstein was his personal friend and years before had been his air group commander on the USS *San Jacinto*, CVL-30. "Al, I need to take something to the president. What do you recommend?"

Feldstein pursed his lips and looked down at the table, rotating his empty coffee cup, thinking. "Mr. Vice President, I know you need a recommendation from us, and soon. Can you give me three days, sir? I'd like a chance to share this with my fleet commanders. If we respond aggressively, we could start a war. If we don't respond, we could be allowing them to take a pot shot at our ships. Either way, there's a good chance for loss of life and assets. I'd like to get the pulse from my commanders before I make a recommendation."

"How about it, Dr. Jensen?" the vice president asked. "Can Admiral Feldstein share with his officers what you shared with us today? Do we run the risk of compromising our sources?"

"No, sir. He can share it."

"Very well. Al, I want options in three days—no more."

****

Falcon could hear booted feet crunching on the dirt and grit that covered the concrete floor. He crept down a darkened hall, further into the building. A soldier wearing a headlamp appeared at the far end, luckily looking the other way. Kelly ducked into the nearest door as the soldier approached, sweeping his light and weapon from side to side.

The room was pitch-black. Kelly put his hands on the wall as he padded deeper into the room. He didn't have to follow the wall far before he realized he'd hidden in a room with no exits. He was trapped! He moved back toward the door as the soldier drew near. *I can take him out as long as I don't kill him*, he rationalized, although the outcome of violent action was often impossible to control.

The light moved closer. Kelly was gathering himself to spring when suddenly the staccato rattle of automatic weapons fire pierced the night. Immediately there was an answering burst. Within seconds he could hear the sounds of a widespread firefight. The soldier turned on his heel and raced out of the building to support his comrades against whatever threat had developed. Kelly could also hear that the choppers overhead had moved toward the waterfront where the gunfire was happening.

Thankful for the unknown diversion, Jake raced out of the back of the building along the path he'd picked out earlier. Staying on the water side of the apartment high-rise, opposite the street side, he sprinted to his building. Easing around the corner, he could see that there were no cars parked in front of the building—evidently the local intelligence organizations had not yet tied Borodin to the rogue transmissions. But it would not be long before they did. As Kelly raced up the stairwell, he speculated that the soldiers must have inadvertently surprised Sergei and his henchmen in the warehouses while searching for the source of the transmission. *I'll bet the Russian mafia is now missing more than a few of its men. If Sergei started that action against elite Soviet troops, he's dumb as a post. Maybe he didn't have a choice, but it sure saved my bacon.*

Kelly began to gather his clothing, his alternate internal passports, all of his cash, and the sat phone. He stuffed everything into his duffel bag, and looked around the room to check if he'd missed anything. Suddenly there was a knock at his door. He pushed the duffel bag under the bed, and answered the door. He was greeted by two men in dark suits.

"Mr. Borodin, KGB. Would you accompany us please?"

Kelly shrugged his shoulders. "Sure. Can you tell me what this is about?"

"We just want to ask you a few questions down at the office. Shouldn't take long. Please turn around and put your hands on the wall. Don't worry, comrade, this is just standard procedure."

The second man frisked him while the first agent watched. "He's clean," said the second agent.

"Very well. Come with us, please, comrade."

Kelly shut his door, and the men moved with him toward the elevator.

"Um, do you mind if we take the stairs?" Kelly asked. "The elevator works coming up, but it's been getting stuck going down. It's only nine flights."

"*Da.*" The men turned and guided Kelly toward the stairwell.

That's your second mistake, gentlemen, Kelly thought, smiling to himself. *The first was failing to handcuff me.*

When the stairway door shut behind them, Kelly strained his ears to detect anyone else in the stairwell. Someone was coming up. After a moment he heard a door opening then shutting several floors below. He listened carefully as he and his KGB minders descended. After a brief moment he assured himself that the stairwell was empty. *Showtime.*

Falcon pretended to stumble about halfway down the flight and grabbed the arm of one of the agents for balance, but then flung the man down the stairs. The other agent reached in his coat to draw his firearm, but Kelly was quicker, smashing the man in the stomach and following with a vicious uppercut to the jaw. The man collapsed in a heap and tumbled down the steps to the landing, where the first agent was trying to collect his wits after running headlong into the concrete wall. Falcon leapt the remaining steps to the landing, and snap-kicked him in the head, knocking him out.

Rifling through their pockets, Kelly helped himself to their KGB credentials and the keys to their car. One carried a radio which Kelly smashed with his heel. Using their own cuffs he handcuffed them both to the stair rail and pocketed the keys. *Not enough time to gag 'em, but someone's going to discover them soon enough anyway.* Leaving the two unconscious men, he ran back up to his flat, retrieved his duffel, and then took the fully operational and reliable elevator down.

As he exited the building he spotted the agents' vehicle, a black GAZ-24 station wagon with government tags. He tossed the duffel bag on the back seat and started the car. Without so much as a stutter, the V8 roared to life. The fuel gauge indicated a full tank. *That's convenient*, he thought. He turned the car around and headed for the center of the city. When Jensen had recruited him for this assignment, he'd memorized a map of the major thoroughfares in Vladivostok.

Falcon weighed his situation. His ability to communicate with the satellite was intact, but the Sovs would be monitoring the frequency closely. He could expect helicopter-borne troops to be on top of him a mere minutes after the signal was detected and the location triangulated. So using the sat phone was out. Within three hours most major modes of transportation would be closed to him—the ticket agents would all have a picture of him. His forged documents had been sufficient to get him through the checkpoints and into the city, but now compromised they would not get him out of the city in the middle of a manhunt in which he had the starring role. Perhaps the KGB credentials would do the trick. He turned on the overhead light as he drove, and examined the ID cards he'd taken from the two agents. One of the pictures vaguely resembled him, as long as it was seen in low light and not studied closely. *Okay, for the next several hours, anyway, I am*

Vitaly Rodchenko.

As he drove he made a few mental calculations. *It will take those two ten minutes to wake up, and another five to get someone's attention. I've got the key to their cuffs, so they're not going anywhere anytime soon. All told, I might have as much as thirty minutes before they put out the Soviet equivalent of an APB on me. If I can get out of the city before that happens, I might have a chance. This car is an asset of value for a limited time only. I'd best work at putting distance between me and Vladivostok.* He thought for another moment, and decided he'd make for Khabarovsk. It was a city he knew fairly well from his previous experience in Siberia, and it was sufficiently far away to allow him to arrive and settle before the search extended there. The turn for the highway that would take him north to Khabarovsk, the M60, was coming up. He turned onto it and headed out of the city.

****

The real Vitaly Rodchenko groaned. As he slowly came to, he became aware of two things. First, his head felt like it was split wide open, throbbing with pain. Second, he was lying on his back with his hands stretched up over his head. He tried to pull them down, wanting desperately to hold his aching head —but something was restraining them. He mulled on that, trying to figure out how he'd come to be in this situation. Finally he coaxed his eyes open. He was lying on the cold concrete floor of a stairwell with his hands cuffed to the stair rail. *What—?*

Something kicked his leg. Gingerly he turned his head. The action caused stars to explode in his vision. There was another man, lying partially on top of him, whose hands were also handcuffed to the stair rail. He looked at the man stupidly for a second, before he realized it was his partner, Filipp Kulik.

"Filipp! Get off me! Oh, my head!" Pain shot through his skull as he spoke.

"Huh? Oh, my head, my head," Kulik echoed groggily. Like Vitaly had tried a moment ago, he attempted unsuccessfully to get his hands to his head.

Slowly it came back to Rodchenko what had happened. They'd come to bring Andrei Petrovich Borodin into the office for questioning. The man had attacked them in the stairwell and locked them up with their own handcuffs.

"Wake up, Filipp! And get off me, you clown. Borodin got away!"

"What? Huh? Oh, man, what happened to me?" Kulik moaned. He stirred himself and maneuvered his legs off his partner. He struggled to a sitting position, his back against the wall, his hands still extended about his head.

Rodchenko sat up, nearly crying out from the pain in his head. "That's got to be a concussion, maybe a skull fracture," he said, mostly to himself. His vision slowly cleared. "We've got to get back to the office, put out an alert."

Kulik groaned again. He nodded. "You know this is not going to end well for us, don't you? We should have handcuffed the man before we left his flat."

"I know. My fault. He seemed so cooperative I didn't think it would be necessary. Well, first things first—we need some help." He looked at the smashed remains of his radio and cursed.

"HELP! Oh, oh, it hurts to shout. HEY! Oh!"

The two men began calling out, but it was past midnight in an apartment building where loud parties, loud arguments, and loud talking was the norm. Nobody paid attention to their shouts. It wasn't until past four in the morning when a resident found them.

****

Kelly approached the checkpoint leading out of the city. There were three cars in line ahead of him. The officers at the roadblock appeared to be relaxed, and the checks they were doing seemed random and perfunctory. They inspected the trunk of only one of the cars and otherwise peered briefly through the windows with their flashlights. Soon it was his turn.

"Name and identification," the officer barked as Kelly

pulled up to the barrier.

Kelly held up his stolen ID in a lazy fashion and looked directly into the flashlight. "Vitaly Rodchenko, KGB."

As the other guards walked around his car, shining flashlights through the windows, the officer glanced at the ID, then asked, "Why are you leaving the city, and what is your destination, comrade Rodchenko?"

"Headed for Nakhodka, following up a hot tip on a case. It couldn't wait until morning."

One of the guards called out the letters on the license tag, and the officer wrote them down on his clipboard. "Very well. Proceed, comrade," he said. The barrier rose up out of the way and Kelly drove through.

The M60 was mostly empty in the early hours, and Kelly observed the official eighty-kilometer-per-hour speed limit though he felt like punching the accelerator.

Five hours later he was approaching the outskirts of Dalnerechensk. He looked at the gas gauge—it was getting close to a quarter of a tank. Seeing a gas station, he pulled off the highway. He drove up to the self-serve pump, put the nozzle into the fill hole, and squeezed the handle. Nothing happened.

"You have to pay first, comrade!"

Kelly turned and saw an old woman in the tiny attendant's booth. He walked over to the booth and slid a fifty ruble note over the counter. "I need seventy-five liters," he said.

"I need to see your gas coupons," she said, shaking her head and pushing the money back. "We don't take cash here, only coupons."

"I'm sorry, I seem to have left my coupons at home. All I've got is cash."

"And all I take is coupons. You're out of luck. You'll have to go home and get your coupons."

He pulled out the ID badge and waved it at her. "I'm with the KGB. I need the gas and I need it now."

"I don't care if you work for the *tsar*. I need your gas coupons and I need them now," she replied tartly.

Kelly stared at her. She crossed her arms, raised her eyebrows and stared back.

"Two hundred rubles says you'll take my cash," he said, finally, sliding two hundred ruble notes over to her.

She looked down at the money, paused, then nodded. "*Da.* That's what I heard it saying, too." She scooped up the cash, turned on the pump and said, "Have at it, comrade."

The truck traffic became heavy once he passed Dalnerechensk. At 1000 hours he was approaching the outskirts of Khabarovsk. It was a cold, gray morning, spitting snow. He wasn't looking forward to ditching the warm vehicle, but it was time. If the Sovs located it, they would know where he went.

The terrain was still heavily wooded. He saw a turnoff ahead leading to a gravel road that went east, into the Sikhote-Alin mountains. He turned on to the road and drove several miles back into a heavily forested area. A smaller dirt trail took off north, plunging deeper into the forest. There were no tire tracks, it didn't appear that anyone had taken the road in several years. Tiny saplings were growing up in it, but it was passable. He turned onto the trail and drove until he could no longer see the main gravel road. Parking the car, he turned it off and left the keys in the ignition. Falcon wiped it down carefully, removing his fingerprints.

Kelly shouldered his duffel bag, walked back to the M60, and hitchhiked the rest of the way into Khabarovsk.

****

The intercom on Yulian Semyonovich Churkin's desk buzzed. "Yes, Anika, what is it?"

"You're playing handball with your son, sir, in twenty minutes. You asked me to remind you."

"Ah, thank you. I'd forgotten. Would you call my—"

"Already done, sir. Your car will be here in ten minutes."

"*Spasibo.* What would I do without you, Anika?" Churkin chuckled.

"Probably miss all your appointments, get fired, and spend the rest of your days in some cold place in Siberia, sir."

"*Pravda.* And then the Politburo would make you interior

minister."

"Don't say that, sir. It might tempt me," his secretary responded, laughing.

Churkin picked up his gym bag, shut down his computer, and walked down to the waiting car.

"Are we secure?" he asked, after climbing into the back seat of the Zil.

"Swept it five minutes ago. It's clean. We're secure. What is the latest?" the driver asked.

"The death of Zelenko is either a very fortuitous circumstance for Admiral Shukshin, or Shukshin just raised the stakes significantly. Pushkaryov has been pushing hard on Shukshin to deal with Zelenko. Tell Geredin that I think Shukshin's hands are dirty in this unfortunate occurrence."

The driver nodded without turning around. He served as Churkin's secret communication conduit to Geredin. "What else?"

"Shukshin's plan was finally approved by Pushkaryov. The plan is to incite the US navy to fire on our ships on 20 January, the day of the inauguration of the new American president. The coup will be carried out four days later. I've assured Pushkaryov that the Moscow *militsiya* are all loyal to me. And they are, but not in the way Pushkaryov is counting on. Those units that might support the coup attempt I will send out of the *krai*, ostensibly for training—so they won't be anywhere near Moscow when the coup attempt happens.

"As an interesting side note, I've learned that Vice President Pushkaryov and our courageous defense minister, Valentin Valentinovich Aristov, are both preparing alibis for plausible deniability in case the attempt is unsuccessful. They've privately advised me to do the same, just in case. Both Shukshin and Yegorov are unaware of this and are being set up to take the fall, if necessary.

"As far as Shukshin's own preparations, he has assured us that all the remaining captains of the Pacific Fleet will support the coup, except Mirov."

"What's with Mirov?"

"Shukshin left the man in place because of his popularity

with the officer corps as well as his unique skills. It was a political calculation on the admiral's part. But Mirov is scheduled to be a casualty on 20 January. Shukshin is convinced his boat will be destroyed in the opening action. Mirov's death at the hands of the Americans is intended to add fuel to the patriotic fervor Shukshin is trying to ignite."

"And the coup commences on 24 January?"

"*Da.* Shukshin believes that will be enough time for the effects of the military action to sway the entire nation."

"Anything else?"

"*Da.* I get the distinct sense that both Pushkaryov and Shukshin each believe they will be at the top of the heap when the dust settles—if the coup is successful. I would not put it past either of them to have made secret plans to that effect, but I am not privy to such plans, if they exist."

****

Mikhail Gorbachev emerged from his office in the Kremlin and took his seat at the head of the table in the appropriately named Walnut Room. The other men, the inner circle of the Politburo, were already gathered and seated around the round table. To the general secretary's left was Alexander Ivanovich Pushkaryov, the vice president of the Soviet Union. Next was Nikolai Kosygin, premier, and Valerian Voznesensky, the first deputy premier. Seated directly across from the general secretary was Valentin Valentinovich Aristov, the defense minister, and Kirill Yegorov, chief of the general staff of the Soviet armed forces. To Gorbachev's right was Anatoly Geredin, director of the KGB, and Yulian Semyonovich Churkin, interior minister.

"Comrades, we have lost a Hero of the Soviet Union with the untimely death of Admiral Pyotr Stefanovich Zelenko. It has been reported as a suicide. I find that most unusual for such an accomplished and decorated man. Has any more information about his death been forthcoming?" Gorbachev asked.

Aristov opened his mouth to answer, but Geredin, his eyes

fixed on Aristov, cut him off. "The KGB is looking into it, Mikhail Sergeyevich. We wish to see if there were any . . . irregularities associated with his death."

Aristov said, "Comrade Gorbachev, perhaps the man was depressed. His whole life was wrapped around the navy, and it is common knowledge that he was well beyond retirement age. It might be that he was simply unwilling to face a future in which he was not in command." Aristov glared at Geredin.

Geredin shrugged his shoulders dismissively. "Perhaps the defense minister is right. Be that as it may, we will look into Admiral Zelenko's untimely death closely. Very closely," he repeated, raising his eyebrows as he returned Aristov's glare.

"Please keep me informed, Anatoly Romanovich. In any case the first order of business is the funeral. It should be a state funeral, with Zelenko lying in state in the House of Unions. General Yegorov, I expect you will see to the details and planning," Gorbachev said.

"Me?" Yegorov asked, surprised.

"Certainly. Zelenko was a high-ranking military officer, and you are the chief of the general staff of our Soviet armed forces. It is appropriate, is it not, that you arrange the funeral?"

"Yes, of course, Mr. General Secretary. I—I am honored. Of course I will take care of it."

"*Spasibo.* The next order of business is also military. We need to appoint an acting commander of the Red Banner Pacific Fleet, especially since the fleet seems to be frequently tangling itself up in the American navy. That needs to stop immediately."

Geredin noted that Pushkaryov shot an almost imperceptible glance at Yegorov. Aristov was staring at the table, as though afraid he'd give something away if he looked his compatriots in the eye.

"Ah, yes," General Yegorov, said. "After examining possible candidates, Mr. General Secretary, I am recommending to this body that Admiral Konstantin Grigoriyevich Shukshin be given that command. He has been Zelenko's deputy for the past four years and has distinguished himself in both military affairs and ideological loyalty to the revolution."

"Valentin, are you comfortable with this appointment?" Gorbachev asked the defense minister.

"I am, comrade General Secretary. I think it's a good choice."

"Any further comments?" Gorbachev asked, looking around the table.

"Perhaps Admiral Shukshin could be made *acting* commander, providing both good direction to the fleet and time for us to vet him more closely," Geredin suggested.

"I don't see why that is necessary," Pushkaryov objected. "He's proven his military acumen, and he's proven his loyalty to the revolution. What could we possibly learn about him that we don't know already?"

"That is the question, isn't it, comrade?" Geredin replied, his hard eyes glittering.

"I don't think the tentativeness of a title like 'acting commander' will stand us in good stead in this time of uncertainty. I am comfortable giving the command of the Pacific Fleet to Admiral Shukshin. Are there any further objections? No? It is done then." Gorbachev looked at his watch and stood. "Comrades, thank you. I'm expecting a call from the head of the party in Ukraine and must return to my office. Good day."

****

"How about a wintertime tour of Gettysburg on Saturday? I know the leaves have long since fallen, but the ghosts are still there," Sam Bergman said. He heard a chuckle on the other end of the phone.

"As it happens, this weekend actually works. A coworker has been assigned to keep an eye on any transmissions from *Blackbird*, so I have the day free. But having looked at the weather forecast this morning, wouldn't a visit to Valley Forge be more appropriate, given the wind chills expected on Saturday? Why don't we skip the tour and you can just take me out to your favorite restaurant in DC?" Evelyn suggested.

"What if my favorite restaurant is in Gettysburg?" Sam

wanted the date to last longer than just a meal, but he didn't want to come out and say it. The drive up to the battlefield in Pennsylvania would offer more time for conversation.

"Works for me," she said.

"How 'bout I pick you up at, oh, one-thirty? That will give us time to drive around the battlefield before dinner, even if we don't get out of the car."

"I'll be ready!"

Chapter 15

Thursday, December 15, 1988

Jacob Kelly shouldered his duffel bag and walked out of the alley. It had been a miserable, cold night sleeping on the ground, hidden behind a mound of stinking trash, but at least it had been dry. For the moment he knew he was safe—but that would not last long. His picture was bound to be in every police station and ticket office and on every television channel within hours—if it wasn't already. He had to find someplace to hide out, where he'd also be sheltered from the weather.

He still had a good supply of rubles—but he couldn't spend them on lodging. Though he had several alternate IDs, he had no narrative, no story. Making one up was simple enough, but in the USSR there was always paperwork backing up your story. The first thing any hotel, hostel, or shelter would ask to see would be his paperwork and internal pass-port legitimizing his presence in Khabarovsk. That he did not have, apart from his Borodin identity, and it would be foolish to continue using those credentials when the KGB was pulling out all the stops to locate Andrei Petrovich Borodin.

He walked through the city looking for abandoned con-struction projects, deserted properties, or some other situation that would get him out of the weather and out of public view. Six hours later he was no closer to a solution. His wandering through the city had brought him to an urban neighborhood of dingy gray high-rise apartment buildings towering over both sides of the street. One side of the farthest eight-story building was windowless and contained a huge, bright red and black mural depicting the New Soviet Man and the hammer and sickle of the Soviet flag.

A smaller building in the center of the block on the south side of the street sported four active smoke stacks. Large insu-lated steam pipes snaked from it to the two apartment build-ings on either side. Two sets of elevated pipes crossed the street above the traffic, connecting to the pair of high-rises on the other side. Falcon realized that the small building was a central heating plant, doubtless containing a steam boiler providing heat and hot water to the four apartment buildings.

Hoping to find someplace warm where he could sit and eat a bit of the black bread and cheese he'd purchased for lunch, Kelly circled behind the heating plant and came upon a massive pile of coal. Next to the pile was a wheelbarrow that had overturned, spilling its load of coal. An old man lay on the ground by the wheelbarrow, groaning, his face contorted in pain.

Kelly ran to the man's side. "What happened, comrade? Are you hurt?"

"Oh, my back, my back!" the man cried. "It went out on me. Had to let go of the wheelbarrow."

"How can I help you, comrade? What can I do?" Kelly asked, concerned. The man appeared to be in agony.

"Help me stand up."

Kelly crouched behind the fellow, grasped his arms, and slowly helped him to his feet.

The fellow tottered slightly, standing hunched over. "*Spasibo*, my friend. It hurts too much to stand up straight. Could you help me into my office, so I can get out of this cold wind?"

"*Da, absolyutno.*"

Kelly helped the man hobble into the back of the heating plant. Welcome warmth washed over him. Kelly looked around the room. Four large steam boilers were mounted over four steel fireboxes, each fed by its own crank-operated conveyor belt. On the near end of the conveyor belt, opposite the boiler, was a feed bin. Each boiler had a large, red pressure gauge accompanied by a confusing assortment of pumps, valves, pipes, gauges, and cranks. To the left was a small, dirty office with glass windows looking into the boiler room. The whole place was filthy with fine black coal dust.

"Oh, thank you, comrade. No, not the chair. Help me sit on the edge of my desk—it's easier on my back."

Kelly glanced around again—he saw no one else in the building. "Sir, would you allow me to sit in here while I eat my lunch? It's a lot warmer in here than it is out there."

"*Da.* You want to use my chair? You're welcome to it. I

can't really sit there anymore—hurts too much. What is your name, young man?"

Falcon thought quickly, picking one of his alternate credentials. "Ilya Ilyich Maslov, Grandfather. And yours?"

"Stanislav Fyodoryevich Usilov."

"What do you do here, comrade? Is this your office?"

"*Da.* I shovel coal into these boilers. I live in the apartment building east of here in return for monitoring the boilers. The feed bins will each hold up to eight hours of coal. I make sure they don't run out."

"How do you—I mean, with your bad back—how do you manage?"

"It's hard work, but it's not been a problem until yesterday. I slipped on the ice and wrenched my back. I've been in a lot of pain since.

"What about you, son? What do you do?"

Falcon looked down at his hands. "I'm just a laborer. I've been a custodian. Right now, I'm doing nothing. I'm in between jobs. I'm kind of in between places, too. Trying to find work, trying to find a place to stay."

Usilov studied him. "Where are your papers?"

"I have no papers, other than my internal passport."

"It's going to be very difficult, if not impossible, Ilya Ilyich, to find work or lodging without papers, as you know. Are you trying to stay out of the *militsiya's* sight?"

Kelly hesitated, unsure of how to answer. Something about the old man made up his mind, and he decided to gamble. "*Da.*"

"Are you on the run?"

"I'd just rather not cross paths with the police," Kelly answered somewhat evasively.

The old man chuckled. "*Da,* I think that is true of every Soviet citizen. Have you hurt someone, Maslov, or stolen something?"

"*Nyet.* I am not a hooligan, I am a hard worker. I just want to be left alone."

Usilov thought for a moment and nodded to himself, as though he'd come to some sort of decision. "Can you shovel coal?" he asked.

"All day long, Grandfather. Why?"

"If I don't keep these boilers going, I will lose my job and my flat. What if I let you stay with me as long as you do my job? You'd have to sleep on the floor, but you'd be plenty warm. If you can shovel coal, I can cook."

Kelly looked at the man suspiciously. "You don't even know me—why would you do this for me?"

Usilov laughed. "I have two reasons, young man, and one of them is very selfish. Until my back heals—if ever—I can no longer do this job. I am trading you lodging for work. The second reason is more important, though. I am a believer in the God of the Bible, and He tells me to help the helpless. Right now, that would be you."

"What if I told you I am not a believer? I don't know what I believe anymore."

"Makes no difference to me. God makes His sun rise on the righteous and the wicked, Jesus says. Paul says in Galatians that I am to do good to all men. I figure that includes you."

"If I accept your very kind offer, does this mean you're going to preach at me?"

"Probably," Usilov chuckled. "What's the matter—you scared of a little preaching, son? Can your fragile unbelief handle it? The Bible is a *very* dangerous book, you know. That's why our government frowns upon it."

Kelly smiled. "Yes, sir. Where's the shovel, Grandfather? I'd better get started."

****

"Enter," the head of the KGB called in response to a knock on his door, knowing already who would be entering. The only person who could get past his secretary, Victor, without being first announced on the intercom, was Colonel Vladimir Leonidovich Dobrynin, chief of the KGB's Third Directorate. Dobrynin was one of the few men Anatoly Geredin counted as a friend, and one of the fewer he trusted. Geredin was grooming Dobrynin, in hopes that the Politburo would name the younger man as the new KGB director when he retired. Like Geredin himself, Dobrynin was untouched by either scandal or corruption at a time when most of the *nomenklatura* were busy feathering their own nests with the formerly state-owned properties and industries being privatized through *perestroika.*

Colonel Dobrynin stuck his head through the door. "Got a minute, Anatoly?"

"Yes, but I'm only interested in good news today. I've got a splitting headache and I'm feeling very grouchy."

"Sorry, comrade, but the news isn't good, and you've got to hear it."

"Oh, come in, Vlad," Geredin sighed. "Have a seat and tell me your woes, or rather, *my* woes."

"As you know, our people in Vladivostok are investigating Admiral Zelenko's suicide, and they've come up with some irregularities. They located a bottle of cyanide capsules in Zelenko's medicine cabinet—but Zelenko's fingerprints are not on the bottle or cap, which is very unusual. It's like he never touched the bottle. In fact, the bottle is completely clean, no fingerprints at all, as though no one ever touched it."

"Or—as though it's been wiped," muttered Geredin.

Dobrynin nodded. "Those are my thoughts, too. Second, the pharmacy that's been filling his digitalis prescription for the last two years says that Zelenko takes the medication religiously, always the exact amount, never misses a day. According to them he should have had a two-week supply left in the bottle—but the digitalis pill bottle was empty."

Geredin popped two aspirin in his mouth and washed them down with a glass of water before replying. "Sounds like a classic bait-and-switch. If that is the case, someone had to get into his house to switch the medications. I assume all of his neighbors have been interviewed, and no one saw anything."

"Zelenko's *dacha* is on a remote section of road. There were no neighbors. There's no sign of forced entry. Freshly fallen snow combined with the thoughtless trampling of the scene by the investigators has wiped out all tracks, so we have no footprints. The Vladivostok office has been pretty thorough in its investigation, sir, other than that."

"If it was an assassination, eventually someone will get drunk and talk too much. A professional hit on someone like Zelenko involves more than one person. Sooner or later, someone will slip up."

"*Da.* In the meantime I'm beginning to think that Churkin's gut feeling about this was correct. Churkin told his contact that, in his opinion, Shukshin's hands were dirty in Zelenko's death. Shukshin would have had a motive: he was the most likely candidate to be promoted to fleet commander if something happened to Zelenko—as we've already seen. When you add that to their political differences, Zelenko's death seems mighty convenient for the coup plotters. It eliminates their principal obstacle to gaining control of the Pacific Fleet," said Dobrynin.

The KGB director sighed again. "And we have neither the proof nor the political capital to stop these hooligans outright. There are enough men on the Politburo opposed to the general secretary's policies that if we make an overt move, it could precipitate the coup. And if it looked like the coup was going to be successful, all the men who have their political fingers to the wind will align themselves with Pushkaryov, and it will be a *fait accompli.* So for the moment, we watch and wait."

"We could meet fire with fire, Anatoly. They assassinated Zelenko. We take out Shukshin. Or Pushkaryov."

"*Nyet.* Once we start pulling the trigger on high ranking officials, where does it stop? It quickly becomes convenient to govern by eliminating one's political opponents. And once it becomes convenient, it becomes a habit. Suddenly, those you had not previously thought of as threats or opponents begin to look like enemies. Soon there are even more bodies. And once governing by murder becomes a habit, we are right back to the purges of Stalin. *Perestroika* and *glasnost* may damage the country—a return to Stalin will destroy it.

"I have no qualms about ordering the sanction of someone who is demonstrably an enemy of the state, and I don't need to wait for a trial, Vladimir Leonidovich. I can pull the trigger myself and sleep like a baby. But until we have firm proof that Shukshin was involved in a hit on Zelenko, or until Pushkaryov does more than blow hot air, I cannot terminate them."

Dobrynin shrugged and nodded. "There is another matter, sir, you should know about. Several illegal sat phone transmissions from an unknown source were detected around the Vladivostok Naval Base. Concerned that their security might have been breached, the base intelligence office began combing through the backgrounds of all recent hires at the base. They hit upon one Andrei Petrovich Borodin. He claimed to be a naval veteran, formerly in a secret special operations group, discharged for medical reasons. Working with the local KGB office, they sent a team of agents to pick him up for routine questioning. Borodin trashed both agents and escaped in their vehicle.

"Since then, they've done a more thorough investigation into his background."

"I imagine so," Geredin interjected dryly.

"He is a complete fiction. No such character exists in any service records. Now they are trying to ascertain what sort of information he might have had access to, as they assess the damage he might have caused."

"What area of the base was he working in?"

"He was basically a toilet-scrubber in the enlisted men's facility. As such he would not have had access to any classified information. Consequently, the initial assessment is that he could not have caused much damage. It may be that he was hoping to be assigned the headquarters building."

"So what is the current status of the search for Borodin?"

"We know he left Vladivostok in the early morning hours of Wednesday, posing as a KGB officer, using credentials he stole from the officers he trashed. When the officers manning the checkpoint were interrogated, they recognized his picture. Other than that, we have no idea where he is."

"You have a picture?"

"Yes, sir. The office in Vlad sent it a few minutes ago. And you're going to be really unhappy about this." Dobrynin handed the picture to his boss.

"Oh, no! Not you again!" Geredin sighed, looking at a picture of Major Jacob Kelly.

"You remember the bet we had when Kelly appeared in the American embassy back in mid-November?" Dobrynin asked, shaking his head.

"*Da.* You said your boys could keep track of him, and I put money on the probability that you could not. And I won."

"And you won. So, I guess we know where he went when he left the embassy."

"I guess so. But we don't know why he went there, or where he is now." Geredin stood up from his desk and hobbled over to the window. From his third-floor office he had a good view of Lubyanka Square. The statue of Felix Dzerzhinsky, founder of the *Cheka,* the Soviet Union's first secret police, was being covered by falling snow. Traffic was moving slowly in the snowpacked street under the leaden sky. Geredin turned back toward his friend. "They're not going to catch him, not the local boys in Vladivostok. He's way too good. We'll have to send a crack team to hunt him down and bring him in. I assume he was spying on the fleet. We've got to interrogate him to find out how bad the breach was at Vladivostok and what he's been sending his handlers in the States. And then maybe we can use him as a bargaining chip with the Americans.

"And, Colonel Dobrynin, we have to find him before the GRU does. Sooner or later they'll hear he's in country and on the run again. They've got a score to settle with him. When he escaped their custody two years ago, he made them look like incompetent fools. Some very high-ranking heads rolled. They have not forgotten that, and they certainly haven't forgiven it. If the GRU finds him, they'll kill him. That's going to add to our problems.

"If the GRU kills Kelly, the US will go public with the GRU's crazy scientist-kidnapping scheme from two years ago. If that idiotic scheme becomes widely known, we won't be able to buy a friend on the international scene. The damage to the *rodina* will be incalculable. Our current problems would seem insignificant, compared to that. We've got to find Kelly first."

****

The next morning the phone on Major Roman Romanovich Nikitin's desk rang. He tossed the morning edition of *Pravda* on his desk, set his coffee down, and picked up the jangling nuisance. "This is Nikitin. Speak."

Major Nikitin had served in the elite *Spetsnaz* in Afghanistan. When his commanding officer, mentor, and patron—Colonel Nikolai Pavlovich Chernikov—was recruited into the GRU and promoted to major general, he brought Nikitin along with him as his staff officer. Now Nikitin commanded a semi-independent special investigations unit within the operations structure of the GRU's Fifth Directorate. That directorate was responsible for, among other things, fleet intelligence. He was stationed in the Far Eastern Military District Headquarters in Khabarovsk.

"Major, the KGB office here in Vladivostok lost a suspect on Tuesday night. The two officers dispatched to apprehend the man were beaten and locked to a stair rail with their own handcuffs. The suspect escaped in their vehicle and got past the city checkpoint using credentials belonging to one of the officers. It sounds like a comedy of errors, sir." Captain Grigoriy Yegorovich Yunge served under Nikitin and ran the GRU office in Vladivostok. Their main job was counterintelligence, as well as spying on the Soviet submariners themselves, to ensure that the men who controlled the USSR's seaborne nuclear deterrent were loyal and dependable communists.

"Indeed. And why do I need to know about this?" Nikitin asked imperiously.

"The suspect was believed to be spying on the submarine base, Major, and was thought to be communicating with his handlers via an encrypted sat phone. This is a military intelligence matter directly within our purview, sir. Shouldn't the KGB have gotten us involved, or at least briefed us? I only found out about it through our informant in the Vladivostok

KGB office."

"Yes, Captain, they certainly should have informed us—but they didn't. Which explains why we have an informant in their office in the first place. Those incompetent fools don't tell us anything. I should think you would know that by now, Captain."

"Yes, sir."

"Well, do we have a name, Captain?"

"Oh, um, yes. Andrei Petrovich Borodin. Navy veteran, apparently a special operator. Medical discharge. On 24 November he was hired as a custodian. He was put to work cleaning the enlisted men's facility on the base."

Nikitin sighed. "Okay, Grigoriy, let's find this elusive suspect. Send me a complete description of Borodin and every piece of information we have on him. I want the vehicle description. I want a timeline of events. If you can, interrogate the two KGB officers he beat up, although I seriously doubt the KGB will give us access to them.

"And find out who was on duty at that checkpoint and interrogate them. I want them reassigned, preferably to some unit in the far, far, north."

"Will do, sir."

"Anything else?"

"Yes, sir. I just faxed a picture of Borodin to you, Major. You should have it by now. I have the strangest sense that I've seen this man before, I just can't remember where, or when."

That piqued Nikitin's curiosity. "Let me put you on hold, Grigoriy, I'll go check the fax machine." He put the phone down and stepped into the outer office and asked his secretary, "Has anything come through on the fax?"

"We are receiving something right now, sir. Shall I bring it to you when it's done?"

"*Da, spasibo.*" The major returned to his office and took a sip of coffee before picking up the phone. "It's just now coming through, Grigoriy. While I'm waiting, do you have any information on the status of the KGB's search for Borodin?"

"Only that they have not yet found the car he took. Today they widened their search radius to one hundred kilometers

and are distributing bulletins with Borodin's picture to all police stations, train and bus stations, and airports within that
area."

"Hang on," the major said as his secretary laid the fax on
his desk. He lifted the cover page and gazed at the picture underneath. It was a perfectly clear photograph of Major Jacob
Kelly, Nikitin's arch nemesis. "Oh, no. Not you again!" he
groaned, shaking his head in disbelief.

"Sir?"

"Captain, do you remember the manhunt I was leading
about two years ago for that soldier who raped and murdered
a fellow soldier's wife?" Nikitin grimaced. The gruesome story
about Yakov Sokolov, as Kelly was known, was a lie invented
by General Chernikov to motivate the troops to search harder
for the fugitive. To this day only a handful of people, Nikitin
being one of them, knew the true details of the entire affair
and the actual identity of Sokolov.

Major General Chernikov was the mastermind behind the
scientist-kidnapping plot that unraveled when Kelly escaped
their custody two and a half years ago. The pilot's escape
eventuated in the largest manhunt in Soviet military history,
employing thousands of troops in an effort that finally failed.
After the US destroyed the interrogation facility in a surprise
raid, Chernikov was disgraced—and the GRU with him—and
relieved of his command. The general perished in a suspicious
fire that consumed his *dacha* last January. An autopsy confirmed that Chernikov actually died from a bullet in his head,
before the fire started. Major Nikitin couldn't prove it, but he
would go to his grave believing that the bullet that killed
Chernikov was fired by a KGB sniper.

"Yes, sir. I was leading the company that almost caught
him in the train station in Khabarovsk. His name was Yakov
Sokolov." The captain paused. "Oh! That's why this guy looks
familiar. He looks just like Sokolov."

"Actually," Nikitin observed, "I think it *is* Sokolov. And if I
am right, the KGB needs to expand their search radius to one
thousand kilometers, and probably more. When Sokolov has
an asset of any kind, he squeezes every advantage out of it.

He's going to put as much distance between him and Vladivostok as possible and probably in a direction we don't anticipate. When he catches a break—such as the car—he's got a sixth sense about how long he can use it before he has to abandon it.

"This changes everything, Captain. Put all your other investigations on hold and concentrate on Sokolov, or Borodin, or whatever his name is. I want your entire office working on this. Set the initial radius to five hundred kilometers. Sooner or later Borodin would have had to stop for gas, so assign some men to take his picture to all the gas stations on the major roads leaving Vladivostok within the search radius. I want updates from you twice a day.

"And for crying out loud, put the fear of God into that snitch in the KGB office! I want to know everything those fools are doing and every lead they get, and I want to know about it right away!

"Listen to me, Captain, and take it to heart. I spent a year trying to corral this guy. He's not just good—he's the best. And he's as dangerous a man as you'll ever meet. I'd prefer we take him alive, but if your men have a bead on him and he's getting away, tell them to shoot to kill."

****

Vice President Bush called the meeting of the National Security Council to order. "Gentlemen, we've got to keep this meeting brief because there's a lot on my schedule today. What I want from you, Admiral, is a recommendation to take to the president regarding the navy's posture and response to the provocative actions of the Soviet Pacific Fleet. And what I want from the rest of you is a brief discussion on Admiral Feldstein's proposal."

"As you know from your own military experience, Mr. Vice President, what you are asking for is a new set of Rules of Engagement, or ROE, for our naval forces in the Pacific," said Admiral Alfred Feldstein, chairman of the joint chiefs of staff (CJCS). "Our current ROE allow our naval commanders to respond to any hostile attack without going up the chain of command. Were one of these Soviet submarines to fire a weapon at our ships, the commander on the scene already knows that he may defend his command with lethal force. This was a more or less unwritten position of the United States navy until the chief of naval operations delivered written standards in '81.'"

"I concur with the admiral, Mr. Vice President," said attorney general Donald Reinholder. "It is a time-honored rule of the sea that a military commander always has the right of self-defense, even in peacetime, although he is obligated to use the minimum amount of force necessary to avert the threat. This is clearly recognized in international law; for instance, Article 51 of the United Nations Charter."

Feldstein nodded. "Mr. Vice President, as you are aware, formulating ROE that will accomplish the objectives of the National Command Authority must include considerations in three distinct arenas. The military interests in peacetime would include the protection of our naval forces, keeping the sea lanes open, and providing a deterrent to bad actors through our naval presence. The legal interests would include ensuring that our commanders do not run afoul of international laws or treaties, or encroach upon another country's territorial waters. The political concerns revolve around advancing the various interests of the United States, not least of which is avoiding unnecessary wars."

"Admiral, I am well aware of the basic theories of ROE. You don't need to review them for my benefit," said the vice president impatiently.

"Yes, sir. You'll understand when I'm through why I have reviewed them. I've also done it for the benefit of the members of this council who may not be as familiar with the details. And as you know, sir, the devil is in the details. If you will indulge me?"

"If you insist. Please continue."

"Where the naval situation gets very sticky in a time of peace is in the definition of self-defense—and it's a definition that can change, depending on how the ROE are written. Everyone knows they can defend themselves, but what exactly does that mean? It can actually mean two different things. *Reactive* self-defense is in play when a commander under hostile threat is not allowed to fire unless first fired upon. *Anticipatory* self-defense is when he perceives hostile intent and fires before the adversary can launch a weapon. The trick is in knowing whether an opponent who is engaging in provocative behavior is actually going to launch a weapon, or simply wave his sword around."

"But how could anyone know in advance what the enemy is going to do?"asked Nolan Beale, the vice president's chief of staff. "After all, isn't the concept of surprise one of the most valuable advantages in conflict?"

"Congratulations, Mr. Beale. You've managed to put your finger on the precise problem. Perhaps I can illustrate using submarines as an example. The lowest level of hostile intent for a submerged vessel stalking another vessel would involve flooding the torpedo tubes—a necessary step prior to launching a weapon, and one that the intended victim is likely to hear via passive sonar. The situation becomes yet more dangerous if the aggressor then uses active sonar to refine a firing solution. This, too, the intended victim will hear quite clearly. The final escalation would be opening the outer doors of the torpedo tubes, a transient sound that the targeted vessel's sonar will likely also hear. At this point the aggressor is ready to fire, his finger is on the trigger, and the targeted commander will likely be aware of the danger he is in. But will the aggressor take that final step? In peacetime, the commander of the targeted vessel does not know—cannot know—with any certainty, as Mr. Beale has observed."

He continued. "When you consider that, in a situation with modern weapons, the fellow who fires first usually wins, then suddenly the definition of self-defense gets very important. There's a great deal at stake for the targeted commander, including the potential loss of his vessel and all souls aboard. If a clearly hostile and provocative posture is taken by the aggressor, does the universally recognized right of self-defense mean responding with lethal force prior to the aggressor's weapon being launched, or must the commander wait to be attacked before a response is justified?

"This, gentlemen, is where clearly defined ROE are helpful, especially in peacetime. If the rules are written for anticipatory self-defense, the targeted commander is probably going to take lethal, defensive action and fire at the aggressor when he hears the active sonar—but certainly no later than when hearing the outer doors open. If he is instead under the obligation of reactive self-defense, he cannot fire until he hears the aggressor launch the weapon. The advantage, in that case, swings decisively to the aggressor." Admiral Feldstein paused and adjusted his glasses.

"In other words, we are right back to the situation with the USS *Stark* last year," Walter Atkins, the secretary of state, observed.

"Correct," replied the CJCS. "The USS *Stark* was on a peacekeeping mission during peacetime in what was thought to be a relatively benign environment. The commander of the *Stark* interpreted the ROE with the most restrictive idea of hostile intent—in other words, as mandating reactive self-defense. The result was that his ship was attacked by an Iraqi fighter, with the loss of thirty-seven lives.

"Following that incident, the National Command Authority decided that the domestic political price of the restrictive ROE was too high and loosened them. Now, instead of reactive self-defense, commanders were told to engage in anticipatory self-defense. But this led to the USS *Vincennes* incident some five months ago, in which an Iranian civilian airliner was on a flight path that appeared to be threatening the ship. The airliner either did not possess or was not using the IFF gear that would have identified it as a civilian aircraft. The *Vincennes* commander was already under aggressive attack from Iranian gunboats. Thinking that the incoming bogey was an Iranian F-14 fighter on an attack run, the commander followed the updated ROE. Under the specified anticipatory self-defense principle, he launched a SAM and shot the bogey down. But it wasn't a bogey—it turned out to be a civilian airliner, and we killed two hundred ninety innocent people."

The facts of both incidents were well known to the major players sitting around the table. To have both affairs reduced to the on-scene commander's interpretation of the Rules of Engagement underscored the seriousness of the recommendation the vice president was asking for. No one said anything for a moment.

Admiral Feldstein finally continued. "Complicating matters for the man on the scene, especially with these two incidents in our recent history, is the knowledge that whatever decision he makes to respond to a threat could result in the death of many on either side and even the potential loss of his vessel. His decision will assuredly affect his career. If he miscalculates he will face a Board of Inquiry—that is, if he himself even survives the incident."

"I appreciate the difficulty, Al," admitted the vice president. "We are living in an age where there are no easy answers. Our citizens are largely unaware of the complexity that our commanders face on the high seas, and the media doesn't seem to have the patience or interest to educate them. Journalists seem more interested in the 'gotcha!' aspect of reporting and of assigning blame when people die. It's unfair, but it is what it is. That's why we only promote the best to command level," said the vice president. "That said, I still need your recommendation. POTUS and SECDEF will make the final decision."

"Yes, sir, I understand. It is my judgment, though, that of the three factors which contribute to effective ROE, in this case the preeminent one is the political."

The vice president chuckled grimly. "Ah. This is why you wanted to give us all a little lesson on the rules of engagement, right?"

Feldstein nodded. "Yes, sir. But I'm not trying to pass the buck or engage in butt-covering. I will make the recommendation you are asking for, and I will stand behind it when it all hits the fan. But you must convey this reality to the president: when unpleasant international incidents have involved the navy, our after-action postmortems show that, worse even than the fog of war, uncertainty surrounding the political objectives of the National Command Authority have resulted in poor decisions being made by the on-scene commanders. In order to give our commanders the best guidance possible, peacetime ROE need to include clear political priorities and objectives, because those priorities will often clash with and even trump combat objectives in the midst of a crisis."

"There is a question behind this, isn't there, Al?"

"Yes, sir, there is. I must know this: is the president willing to risk entering into an accidental war with the Soviet Union?"

"He is not."

"How badly does the president want to avoid an accidental war with the USSR?"

"At all costs."

"All costs?"

"That's what I said."

"Very well. Thank you, sir." Feldstein turned to Paul West, the DCI. "Paul, last chance. Do you consider the intelligence Dr. Jensen has provided to be credible to the point of being actionable?"

West looked at Jensen, who was seated in the second row of chairs. Jensen nodded. The DCI turned back to the chairman. "I do. And I would remind this council that so far the repeated Soviet pattern has been one of apparently dangerous hostile intent that, in the end, has always fallen short of firing a weapon. This is precisely what KGB Director Geredin warned Dr. Jensen to expect and what our source *Blackbird* has also confirmed."

Admiral Feldstein nodded. "Thank you, Paul." He turned back to the vice president. "There is your answer, Mr. Vice President. I am recommending that under no circumstances do our Pacific commanders exercise anticipatory self-defense —they must not fire unless first fired upon. If they are fired upon, they should immediately respond with as much lethal force as is necessary to eliminate the immediate threat, but no more than that. I have a formal written recommendation to this effect that I can give you to deliver to the president.

"I must add this warning, however. These ROE could conceivably result in the loss of US lives or naval assets, as we will effectively be allowing the Soviets to have first-strike privileges before our forces are permitted to respond in self-defense."

The vice president nodded. "I understand, Admiral, and I will convey that concern to the president as well your written recommendation." He looked at the secretary of state, Walter Atkins, "Wally, are you on board with this recommendation?"

"I am, sir. I think it is the best we can do."

"How about you, Don?"

"Yes, sir."

"Mel?" he asked Melvin Smithson, the secretary of defense.

"Honestly, Mr. Vice President, I don't see what else we can do. If we initiate a scrap with the Sovs, it will strengthen the hand of Gorbachev's enemies. If the coup is then successful, we could wind up with a Soviet Union far more dangerous than the present one, with hawkish hardliners running the Kremlin. I don't doubt we can win any straightforward military conflict with them—it's just that getting into such a conflict in the first place would be very expensive in lives and equipment. And who knows where it would end? No, sir, I support the recommendation of the CJCS. No anticipatory self-defense."

In the end the recommendation received unanimous support. The president and the secretary of defense, acting in their joint capacity as the National Command Authority, approved the recommendation. Within six hours it was communicated to every ship, group, and fleet operating between the west coast of the US and the east coast of Africa.

****

"Grandfather, I need to write a letter and send it airmail to a friend of mine in the United States." Kelly, aka Ilya Ilyich Maslov, was black with the coal dust that stuck to his sweaty body. It was the second full day of work under his arrangement with Usilov. He leaned on his shovel as he stood in the door of Usilov's small office.

"Okay, fine, Ilya. Is there something you need from me?"

Usilov asked, frowning.

"*Da.* If I give you the money, while I am watching the coal bins and the boilers, do you feel up to going out and purchasing a sheet of paper, an envelope, and sufficient postage?"

"Certainly. Walking is good for my back, as long as I'm not carrying anything too heavy."

"*Spasibo.* I will give you five rubles for making the purchases and another five for mailing the letter."

Usilov chuckled. "Do you think me a mercenary, Ilya? You don't need to pay me to do these things. Just give me enough money to buy them—that's all I need."

Kelly smiled. "You are a good man, Stanislav Fyodoryevich, and I thank you. Here—twenty rubles. Purchase what I need for the letter, and then buy us food with whatever is left."

****

Captain Kira Aleksandrova Fukina, Senior Lieutenant Aleksei Bok, and Lieutenant Stefan Pankiv walked into the Vladivostok KGB office, weary after the long flight from Moscow. They set their bags against the wall, and Fukina said crisply to the duty officer at the desk, "Tell Major Chekhov we're here."

"I'm sorry, but the major is on his tea break and is not to be disturbed. Who are you, anyway?"

She was in no mood for officious behavior. She looked at the duty officer and without a word walked around the desk. Pushing him out of the way, she picked up the handset and demanded, "Which button is his office?"

The shocked officer moved to push her back, and before he knew it he was flat on his back on the floor, not quite certain how it happened.

"Which button did you say?"

He groaned and rolled to his knees. "The first."

She punched the button. When Major Chekhov picked up, without waiting for him to speak she said, "This is Captain Kira Fukina, from KGB headquarters in Moscow. I'm in command of the special investigative unit. I'm taking over the search for the fugitive Borodin. Your drone out here evidently didn't know we were coming. Am I correct in assuming that the Lubyanka has at least informed you we would be coming?" She mouthed the words to the disconcerted duty officer who was dusting himself off, *that's who I am.*

She heard a click as Chekhov hung up the phone and then opened his office door. He emerged from his office with an angry expression, which changed to delight as soon as he appraised the woman standing in front of him. Major Oleg Timurov Chekhov was fifty-five, and his best years in the KGB were a distant memory. Short, overweight and fundamentally lazy, he owed his rank to powerful patrons in the Kremlin. He was a man entirely too fond of his vodka. He was viewed in the Lubyanka as an incompetent, and both he and KGB headquarters were just marking time until he retired.

"Come in, come in, Captain. I am Major Chekhov. Welcome." His eyes greedily devoured her lithe form. He wondered if she might be willing to trade favors for the next step up the rung of command. As she walked past him into his office, he managed to brush against her hip.

She noticed and it irritated her. She was also irritated by the heavy smell of vodka on his breath. *Tea break, my foot*, she thought with disgust.

"Well, well, well, Captain, please be seated. It is not every day that Moscow sends me such a beautiful assistant, and—"

"I'm not your assistant, Major. I'm taking command of the search for Borodin."

His eyes narrowed and he decided to pull rank. "I don't tolerate disrespect in my command, Captain. I am in command of all KGB assets and activities in the southern part of this military district, which means I am in command of the search. While I welcome your assistance, Captain, I take great exception to your attitude! I would hate to have to report it. Perhaps I might be persuaded to overlook it this time."

"How many agents do you have working out of this office, Major?"

"What?" he asked, irritated that she had not crumbled before his threat.

"How many agents are under your command in this office?" she asked impatiently.

His brow furrowed. This was not going the way he thought it would. "Ten in this office. I have more in the district, but ten in this office."

She stood up. "I am taking eight of them. You may conduct your other business with two. I expect my eight to be in your meeting room by 0700 tomorrow morning, with bags packed and ready to travel. Please see to it."

He slammed his hand down on his desk and shouted, "I AM IN COMMAND HERE! YOU WILL NOT TALK TO ME THAT WAY!"

"Yes, Major, you are in command of two officers in this office and over all the KGB activities in the region other than my search. I am now in command of eight of your officers and the search for Borodin. Stay out of my way. I expect to have full use of all the assets of your command, including vehicles, weapons, and communications gear."

His face glowered with rage but before he could open his mouth again, she asked him, "Do you know who General Anatoly Romanovich Geredin is, Major?"

"What does that have to do with anything?" he spluttered. "Yes, of course I know who he is, Captain. He's the director of the KGB."

"Correct. I was sitting in his office when he called you and ordered you to cooperate with me and to place all of your assets at my command. I know what he said to you, because I was there. I would hate to have to report your attitude, Major. Perhaps I might be persuaded to overlook it this time," she said dryly. She walked to the door and turned around. "I want to see my eight agents in your meeting room, packed and ready to roll, at 0700 hours."

****

Captain Kira Fukina looked at the eager, ambitious eyes of

the eight KGB officers seated in front of her. *Like dogs seeking a treat from the hand of their master*, she thought with disgust. *What has Chekhov done to these men to turn them into such sycophants?* She wondered, not for the first time, how was it that the Vladivostok office of the KGB could be commanded by such an incompetent? Especially when one took into account the proximity of prime espionage targets like the sensitive military installations in the area. She shrugged her shoulders, *whatever.* Her two lieutenants were standing in the back of the room, leaning against the wall, watching. She knew they were making their own initial evaluations of the officers they'd been given. Bok nodded at her, and she started the briefing.

"Your quarry is an American air force officer who has probably been seconded to the CIA. He speaks Russian like he was born here and is sufficiently familiar with our country to blend right in to the woodwork. He penetrated the naval base under the name Andrei Petrovich Borodin, but he is almost assuredly no longer using that name. This is not the first time we have encountered this man. He was once known to our country as Yakov Sokolov. His real name is Major Jacob Kelly.

"The man is very resourceful and skilled. He is able to fly just about anything that's airworthy: helicopters, commercial or military jets, civilian aircraft. He is equally comfortable in the remote wilderness or the city.

"We do not believe he is armed, but you are to consider him extremely dangerous nonetheless. He has demonstrated in the past that he does not require a weapon in order to be lethal. Remember this in any confrontation with him: unless your weapon is well handled, it is liable to wind up in his possession.

"When we locate him, do not attempt to apprehend him unless there are at least three of you. The third man should stand back and hold him under gunpoint, but well out of range of his hands and feet. Cuff him as quickly as possible, making sure you don't get between Kelly and your comrade with the gun.

"Under no circumstances are you to kill him—you will not

be rewarded for such an act, quite the opposite in fact. If you must shoot him, aim for his feet or hands. We have been given strict orders to apprehend him alive."

She passed out pictures. "This is what he looked like several weeks ago. Doubtless he has taken steps now to disguise his appearance.

"We are greatly expanding the search radius. Kelly is known to travel far and fast. Are there any questions?"

Captain Fukina divided her agents into two teams, one led by Bok and the other by Pankiv. Pankiv's team headed toward Nakhodka, while Bok took his team north. Six hours later the gas station attendant at Dalnerechensk gave a positive identification of the man in the photograph as one who had gotten gas in the early morning hours of 14 December. She described the vehicle, and that clinched it. Kelly had fled north from Vladivostok. Captain Fukina studied the map and concluded that he must have been heading for Khabarovsk. She checked in with the KGB duty officer in Vladivostok then contacted her southern team, and they all headed north.

Three hours later, thanks to the stooge in the KGB office in Vladivostok, Major Nikitin was assembling a GRU team to begin searching Khabarovsk and the surrounding metro area. The race was on.

****

While Captain Fukina was briefing her team early Sunday morning (fifteen hours ahead of Eastern Standard time), Sam Bergman and Evelyn Stinson were touring Gettysburg on Saturday afternoon. They sat in Bergman's car in the parking lot at the Angle, looking over what had been a great field of slaughter on the day of Pickett's Charge, 3 July, 1863.

"I cannot come to this place without feeling an intense sadness," Evelyn said. She scrutinized the three-quarters-of-a-mile expanse over which more than twelve thousand Confederate soldiers had marched, in route step, under a murderous cannonade from Union artillery. "I am thankful the North won the battle, but what a senseless slaughter. I believe General Longstreet knew what was coming. So many good men died on this killing field, and it's as though I can feel their horror, grief, and sadness, even to this very day."

"Are you familiar, then, with Pickett's Charge?" Sam asked. The empty meadow before him was brown and dry under a gray winter sky. On the far side of the field he could see several batteries of artillery among the many monuments.

Gazing across the meadow, she was silent a full minute. "I am," she finally said, nodding. "Here, right where we are parked, was Brigadier General Alexander Webb's Second Brigade. He had four regiments of Pennsylvania boys defending the wall at the Angle, along with the brigades of Harrow, Hall, and Gates. They were all Hancock's men, Second Army Corps, Second Division under General John Gibbon. The South had invaded and for one of the very few times in the war, the Union soldiers were defending their own turf—their own homeland.

"They faced some of the South's best, most battle-hardened troops. This one, small point—the Angle—was the objective of some forty-seven Rebel regiments. They were going to split the Union line right here. The Union army would break and flee, and the road to Washington would be open."

She looked around as though seeing the disposition of the troops. "Webb's 69th Pennsylvania regiment acquitted itself very well, but soon found itself in hand-to-hand combat with the men in gray. Several of Webb's other regiments broke and retreated. But in the end the line held, and the South was finished. The butcher bill would come to thousands more of combatants and non-combatants alike before the war ended. But after Gettysburg, it was really only a matter of time—the final outcome of the war was certain."

"Wow," Bergman said, "impressive! You really do know your Civil War history."

She looked at him and smiled. "Gettysburg, anyway. When I was a teen, my dad and mom used to bring me here on Saturdays during the summer. They'd drop me off in the morning on Little Round Top with a daypack, a bag lunch, several bottles of water and a sketch pad. I'd wander all over the battlefield on foot making my own maps of the action, recording the inscriptions on the monuments in a notebook. They'd pick me up in the late afternoon, and no matter how late it was, I would complain that I was not ready to go.

"It was then that I began to feel the deep, deep sadness of this place."

Sam gazed at her, enjoying the opportunity to know her. "So, General Stinson, how do you evaluate General Lee's plan of attack on the third day of Gettysburg?" Bergman asked, curious as to what she would say.

"It's obvious, Sam. It is an attack that never should have been launched, for there was never any real hope of its succeeding—except in the mind of Robert E. Lee."

"Perhaps it's obvious to us today, Evelyn, in retrospect. We can look back, knowing what happened," Sam objected. "But isn't that judgment a little unfair to Lee?"

"No, Sam. It should have been obvious on the morning of 3 July before spilling buckets of blood. Lee was the most brilliant general the South possessed, perhaps among the most brilliant warfighters West Point has ever produced, but he misread the entire engagement. He misread the North's troop disposition and morale, he misread the effect of the Union cannonade on Pickett's advance, and the ability of his own guns to knock out Meade's artillery. He did not take into account the knowledge he had of the tangled mess of his own supply lines, particularly the artillery caissons. They hadn't brought up enough ammunition for his guns to support the assault after the initial cannonade.

"Worst of all, Sam, he misread the times: the technology of war in 1863 had rendered his plan of assault worthless. Longstreet was right—it was nothing more than a matter of mathematics and all the equations were to the North's benefit. Lee executed a stand-up-straight Napoleonic frontal assault against men hiding behind this stone wall, men in good cover who had the high ground and who were supported by dozens and dozens of artillery pieces loaded with canister. Lee's men were cut to ribbons. Of all the field-grade officers in Pickett's entire division, only one returned to the Confederate lines that day. All the others were casualties or prisoners. Twenty Confederate regimental battle flags lay in front of this blood-soaked wall. The South lost nearly nine thousand of its best men in that one assault—men it could ill afford to lose. The North lost but fifteen hundred, and there were thousands to replace them."

Evelyn looked at Sam with a sad smile. "After Gettysburg, the Army of Northern Virginia was never again able to launch a major offensive campaign. From that point forward, it was just a waiting game, a delaying action until Appomattox Courthouse."

"You seem very sad about that."

"I'm glad the South lost the war. And I'm glad slavery was abolished. But I am very sad that thousands of men were just thrown away on such an ill-advised attack. Husbands, fathers, sons, brothers, uncles, grandfathers, grandsons—what a terrible, terrible waste. And what a weight on their commanders' consciences—knowing that the orders they issued were responsible for so many deaths in such an entirely futile endeavor. How could they ever live with that?

"To this day I feel a weight of sorrow when I visit this place, as though the very trees and fields are still weeping. As though the ghosts of the dead are still here, mourning what might have been—marriages they might have made, families they might have had, opportunities for life they never enjoyed —instead of the horrific deaths they experienced."

Sam stared at her, seeing how deeply affected she was. "I'm so sorry, Evelyn," he said quietly. "I—I should have chosen some other place to take you."

"Oh, no, Sam! It's very special sharing it with you." She turned to him and touched his hand before looking across the meadow again. "I love it here. Even though it makes me sad, Gettysburg still draws me like a magnet. I can't explain it," she said.

Sam turned the car on so he could run the heater as she pointed out her favorite spots on the battlefield. Intermittent flurries kept a bit of light snow blowing in the wind. The conversation eventually turned to their families and their backgrounds. The more time Sam spent in Evelyn's presence, the more impressed he was with this intelligent and attractive woman. And the more comfortable he felt around her.

"Are you ready for dinner?" he asked as dusk fell over the battlefield.

"Am I boring you?" she laughed. "I don't think I've talked this much in ages."

"Not at all. I'm afraid I might have bored you."

"No," she said with an affectionate sparkle in her eyes. "So where are we going for dinner?"

"How about the Dobbin House Tavern?"

She laughed again. "I was hoping you'd say that."

"Evelyn, can we talk about work for just a minute before we head to supper? There's something I have to tell you."

She raised her eyebrows. "Is this bad news?"

"It's not good news. Bill Jensen, the DDO, has given me permission to share information about source *Blackbird* with you. There's never been a concern about the level of your security clearance—it's quite adequate. But *Blackbird* has always been in the *need to know* category, and up until now you've not needed to know. Now you do."

She frowned and her eyes narrowed. "Go on."

"On Tuesday you gave me a transcript that indicated the Soviets had picked up an unauthorized sat phone transmission. As I recall, your concern was that someone was about to get *bagged and tagged*. I think you realized at the time it was probably source *Blackbird*. Well, you were correct.

"*Blackbird* is Major Jacob Kelly, USAF. He has been temporarily assigned to the CIA and was sent into the Soviet Union, Vladivostok specifically, to gather some critical intelligence. We believe he has been compromised and possibly captured. At this point, we have no way of knowing."

"Kelly, . . . Jacob Kelly," she murmured, trying to jog her memory. "Oh! Wasn't that the man connected with the case you and I were working on last year? The man who'd been stranded in the Soviet Union and managed to escape to the States?"

Bergman nodded. "Yes, that's him. I need you to be on the

lookout for any intercepts that mention Major Jacob Kelly, or Andrei Petrovich Borodin, or Ilya Ilyich Maslov. The CIA station chief in the Moscow Embassy will be sending you several more aliases under which Kelly might be operating. We've got to find him and extract him before the Soviets grab him, if they haven't already."

"What will happen to him if they catch him?"

"Depends on who catches him. If it is the KGB, we can probably negotiate his release. If it is the GRU they won't even tell us they've caught him. They'll just execute him immediately."

"I don't understand. Don't the KGB and GRU work together?"

Sam laughed. "Not likely. They hate each other."

"What? You're kidding!"

"No, I'm not kidding. Look, you know that every branch of government has its own bureaucratic turf warriors. It's certainly true here in America. The CIA is not best of buds with the FBI, for instance. We work together when we have to, but it's not like we celebrate each other's birthdays. We are rivals when it comes to gathering intelligence or apprehending bad guys, and we are *really* rivals when it comes to presenting budgets before Congress.

"It's a thousand times worse in the Soviet Union. The two premier Soviet intelligence services, the KGB and the GRU, are practically mortal enemies. Let me see if I can explain it. First, what do you know about the KGB?"

She shrugged. "The *Komitet Gosudarstvennoi Bezopasnosti*, or KGB, is generally responsible for State security. This includes matters like counterintelligence, domestic and foreign intelligence gathering, as well as quelling internal resistance to the Communist Party. They run the secret police and are generally hated and feared by the citizenry. The KGB's primary overlord is the Council of Ministers. I believe I read in a recent briefing that, at its high-water mark, the KGB employed more than a half million people."

"Good. Now what do you know about the GRU?"

Evelyn paused for a minute, collecting her thoughts. "The

Glavnoye Razvedyvatelnoye Upravleniye, or GRU, is the Soviets' super-secret military intelligence arm. It is under the control of the Soviet military General Staff. Most Soviet citizens don't even know it exists. The GRU is divided into multiple directorates, and underneath the directorates are administrative or operational units known as *directions*. The feared *Spetznaz* special operators, for instance, are controlled by the Third Direction of the Second Directorate. The various directorates of the GRU comprise a massive, comprehensive intelligence network."

She stopped and looked at him, shaking her head. "Frankly, Sam, the responsibilities of both organizations have so much overlap, it's hard for me to see why they need both. Seems to me they'd be tripping over each other constantly."

He nodded. "I think I can explain why both are necessary. The thing the Politburo fears most of all is neither nuclear nor conventional war with the United States. What they fear most of all is a counterrevolution." He paused for a moment as he backed out of his parking spot and started toward the restaurant.

"Think about it, Evelyn. Any government installed by violent revolution and maintained by deadly purges must of necessity have a great fear of being overthrown itself through the same mechanisms. This is foremost in the minds of nearly all top Soviet politicians—a concern that is warranted, as Stalin himself demonstrated. This is where having two separate intelligence agencies becomes useful.

"The political masters of the GRU and the KGB play the two organizations off each other, under the theory that if one organization is co-opted by counterrevolutionaries, the other will find out about it and squeal. So the KGB and GRU are kept at odds with each other while they also perform their intelligence functions, so that neither can be part of a plot to upend the Politburo. It is a Machiavellian solution, but it keeps things in an odd, perverse sort of balance."

She nodded. "That explains a lot—it makes sense. So, why will they treat Kelly differently? How does that factor in?"

"Because Kelly is the one who exposed the scientist-kidnapping scheme. He thoroughly humiliated the GRU. Several very important heads rolled. If they catch him, it's payback time. The KGB, on the other hand, came out of that scheme smelling like roses. They have no vendetta driving them. They realize it is in the USSR's best interest to treat Kelly gently. If they are too rough, then the CIA will leak a full account of the kidnapping scheme to the *New York Times*. The Politburo, and therefore the KGB, will do almost anything to keep that entire episode under wraps."

Sam pulled into the Dobbin House parking lot. "The lobster and filet here are absolutely wonderful. So is their roast duck. Hungry?"

"Oh, yeah!"

Chapter 16

Sunday, December 18, 1988

"I am Ilya Ilyich Maslov, Ilya Ilyich Maslov, Ilya Ilyich Maslov," Kelly muttered to himself. Earlier in the day when Usilov had called "Ilya!" it had not registered immediately with Kelly that he was being addressed. He'd not created a narrative for Maslov and had not practiced the identity, and Usilov caught him off guard. The old man had looked at him oddly, but made nothing of it. *That cannot happen again*, Kelly told himself as he trundled the empty wheelbarrow out to the pile of coal.

Rain overnight followed by a plunge in the temperature had turned the pile of coal into a frozen concrete-like mass. The coal shovel was ineffective; thankfully the old man also had a sturdy pick. Kelly swung the pick hard, putting his back and shoulders into it, and frozen chunks of coal started coming loose from the icy pile. He tossed chunks into the wheelbarrow until it was full, and wheeled the load inside. The heat in the building would soon melt the ice before the large coal chunks could jam the conveyor belt. He filled feed bin number three and went back out to the pile. It took about seven trips to fill an empty bin. The boilers would run for about eight hours before he had to refill the bins, although he needed to monitor the pressure gauges every thirty minutes. When the pressure in a boiler fell below a green line on the gauge, he'd turn the handcrank on the conveyor to refill the firebox with coal.

Thirty minutes later he was sitting at the desk in the little office. He wiped the coal dust off the surface with a rag he found in a metal tool locker. Yesterday Usilov had purchased writing materials. Jake pulled them out of a paper sack and began to compose his letter. An hour later, as the old man shuffled into the office with lunch, Kelly was sealing and stamping the envelope.

Usilov took two plastic plates and two bottles of water from his basket, and put them on the desk. These were followed by thick slices of a coarse black bread, goat cheese, and two thick slices of *kolbasa*, one for each.

"Thanks to you, Ilya, we are eating like *tsars* today. I've not been able to afford sausage for quite some time."

"Enjoy it while you can, Grandfather. Sooner or later my small supply of rubles will be exhausted, and then we'll be living on your income. Perhaps by then I will have another job."

"If you would like to continue living here once you find a job, it's fine with me, Ilya. Perhaps by combining our incomes we can continue to eat like this," the old man chuckled.

Kelly made a sandwich for himself and was about to bite into it when Usilov touched his hand. "Wait, Ilya. Let me thank the Lord and ask Him to bless our meal."

Kelly shrugged. "Looks to me like it's already blessed, Grandfather."

"All the more reason to give thanks, my son," Usilov said with a kind smile, before praying.

The two ate in silence for a few minutes, then the old man noticed the letter. "Is it ready to be mailed?"

"*Da.*"

"Good. I'll take it this afternoon."

"*Spasibo.*"

Usilov examined the address. "Clinton, Utah? Do you mind me asking who you know in the USA, Ilya?"

"Not at all—I enjoy talking about her, even though our relationship is over. It is a girl, Grandfather, a very beautiful girl. Her name is Galina Toporova."

"But the letter is addressed to Susan Bates."

"Oh, that. When we started dating, her father did not approve of me so we had to communicate secretly. We made a game of it, creating American-sounding names for each other. I am Roger Carson and she is Susan Bates. Her father eventually began to like me, but we still write to each other with our secret identities. It's sort of a private joke."

"How did you meet her?"

"I met her at a logging operation, over near Sidima. I worked there for several years some time ago."

"Logging operation, Sidima . . . now why does this sound familiar?" The old man chewed thoughtfully, looking off in the distance. "Oh! I heard about an illegal logging cooperative near Sidima. The authorities shut it down several years ago. There were several arrests, if I remember correctly."

"*Da*, that's the one. It happened after I was no longer working there. Galina was one of those arrested. The KGB exiled her to China, and somehow she managed to go from there to the United States. I received two letters from her after she got to the United States, but now the letters have stopped coming."

Usilov glanced at the envelope. "Why did you mark your return address as the Intourist Hotel, Ilya? Don't you want her to write back?"

"*Nyet*. It's not a letter that requires a response. We had sort of a romance going, but I'm writing her to tell her I'm moving on. She's in the US, I am here. It's very unlikely we'll ever see each other again. I expect she's already moved on, but in case she hasn't—well, I wanted her to know. Besides, I did not want the letter traced back here—to you—if the censors decide they want to ask questions."

The old man nodded and placed the envelope in his pocket. "I'll see that it gets mailed."

****

Admiral Konstantin Grigoriyevich Shukshin, recently appointed commander of the Soviet Red Banner Pacific Fleet, opened the folder marked with a red "Top Secret" tag. His intelligence officer, Captain Third Rank Stefan Stefanovich Udom, was sitting across the desk from him.

"We received the last piece of intelligence about two hours ago. I prepared this report as fast as I could, sir."

Shukshin nodded, but said nothing. He flipped through the pages detailing the anticipated movement and composition of two US carrier battle groups. "How certain are you, Captain Udom, of the reliability of this information?"

"Certain enough to give it to you, sir, knowing what you have in mind. We have sources in Yokosuka and Pearl, and both sources independently verified it."

"Both sources?"

"Yes, sir."

"Give me the short story, Captain," Shukshin said, taking a sip of his coffee.

"Your interest, sir, is in where the carriers will be at noon on 20 January, Washington DC time, or 0200 on 21 January, our time. Am I right?"

"Correct."

"Very good, sir. The USS *Midway*, CV-41, will be in the Philippine Sea, approximately 1,570 kilometers south southwest of Yokosuka, returning from a joint exercise with the Philippine and Australian navies. She will be headed for her home port of Yokosuka.

"On the same day, the USS *Nimitz*, CVN-68, will be in the South China Sea, returning from a deployment in the Arabian Sea. She will be nearing the Luzon Strait."

"How about their combat-capable consorts? What ships will be sailing in company with the flattops?" Shukshin asked, studying the folder.

"It is quite likely that both carriers will be accompanied by one, possibly two *Los Angeles*-class SSNs, sir. As you know, American submarines are not deployed by the same fleet command structure that controls their surface ships. We have no sources in COMSUBPAC at Pearl. In my opinion, sir, the *Midway* will be escorted by one SSN, and the *Nimitz* by two.

"Intelligence indicates that the *Midway* will be accompanied by one cruiser, the USS *Bunker Hill*, CG-52, a Ticonderoga-class ship, and two *Spruance*-class destroyers, the USS *Kinkaid*, DD-965, and the USS *Cushing*, DD-985. She'll also have a fleet oiler and other fleet supply ships with her.

"The *Nimitz* will be sailing with a Ticonderoga-class cruiser, two *Spruance*-class destroyers, and two *Oliver Hazard Perry*-class frigates. The names of the vessels are in your folder, sir."

"Thank you, Captain Udom. You may return to your duties."

Udom stood up to leave then turned back to the admiral. "Sir, there's one more thing you should know. Apparently the

Midway has some stability problems. In October she nearly turned turtle during Typhoon Unsang, or Typhoon Ruby, as the Americans called it. According to reports, she rolled twenty-six degrees. Wasn't supposed to survive a roll of more than twenty-four."

"Hmm. That's good to know. Can't say that I'm surprised, however. The Americans have updated her twice, to the point where she has an almost *Forrestal*-class flight deck perched on a *Midway*-class hull. She's bound to be top heavy."

"Perhaps she does not handle well when executing high-speed evasive maneuvers?" Udom suggested. "Just a thought, sir."

"Good point, Captain. Excellent work."

The wall opposite his windows had a huge map of the Pacific and Indian oceans. He studied the map, noting the estimated positions of the two carriers on the given day. *Which one do I pick?* He pondered. *The* Nimitz *is a nuke—it would be a lot more impressive to bag it than the conventional and aging* Midway. *But Udom is probably correct, I'll bet they have two submarines escorting* Nimitz.

On the other hand, sinking the Nimitz *might provoke a much more aggressive response from the Americans, causing a conflict they might not want to abandon before getting their pound of flesh. And she has more escorts, making the approach more difficult. Add to that the fact that the commercial ship traffic in the South China Sea will be heavier than in the Philippine Sea, further complicating matters. And if Udom is right in his speculation about the* Midway's *poor handling under evasive action . . .*

He stared at the map for a few more minutes, making a few measurements and rough calculations. Finally he stepped back. "The *Midway* it is," he muttered aloud, making a notation in the folder.

****

Natasha Zherdeva examined the last three pieces of mail from her first bag of the morning. The envelopes were cheap, the destination and return addresses were well formed and not belonging to locations known for political dissent. Neither the addressee nor sender were on her watch list. There was no need to open them and inspect their contents. Besides, she was already running behind on her quota, so she "processed" them straight to the Outgoing mail cart. The cart would be taken onto the sorting floor so that the contents could be sent on their way.

Though she'd only processed one bag, she marked two on her quota sheet. Zherdeva stood up from her worktable and stretched, then ambled into the break room where she would stay until the floor supervisor noticed she wasn't working and herded her back to the floor. Which today took about thirty wonderful minutes, because her supervisor was in a meeting of some sort.

When she was finally sent back to her table, she picked another canvas bag out of the Waiting-For-Processing mail cart and began working her way through the contents. Natasha Zherdeva was a low-level KGB clerk assigned to the mail censorship department of the main sorting facility of the Khabarovskiy Krai. She liked the pay and she liked the idea of reading other people's mail, but she did not like her pushy supervisor who was constantly demanding faster work from all the clerks. It was a poorly kept secret that sometimes entire canvas bags of Waiting-For-Processing mail would be dumped, without any inspection at all, into the Outgoing cart. This usually happened at the end of the month, on the day before the floor supervisors were required to turn in their monthly productivity reports.

Zherdeva pulled a letter from the bag and began to inspect the outside of the envelope. The first thing that caught her attention is that it was marked *AVIAPOCHTA*, or airmail. She looked at the address and smiled—in carefully handwritten Cyrillic letters it was addressed to a Susan Bates—spelled phonetically—in Clinton, Utah, USA. *This should be interesting*, she thought.

The sender was a Roger Carson, with the return address in Russian: Room 36, the Intourist Hotel, Khabarovsk. The American name was spelled phonetically with Cyrillic letters.

She checked her watch list and neither Carson, nor Bates, nor the address in the US were on it. She was about to toss the letter into the Outgoing mail cart but then decided perhaps she should check the Intourist guest lists, just to be sure. The clerk walked over to a table containing binders filled with daily reports of the guest registrations of all the hotels in the *krai*. Zherdeva located the Intourist binder and started flipping through the pages. There was no record of a Roger Carson staying at the Intourist Hotel going back three months. That was a definite red flag—now her curiosity was piqued.

Returning to her table, she carefully steamed the envelope open and extracted the letter. It was written in Russian, in the same careful handwriting as the addresses on the envelope.

> *My Dearest Susan,*
> *Having a wonderful time in Khabarovsk. I am staying at the Intourist Hotel. It seems that is the best location for finding people and places you wish to see, although it's not worked out so well for me. I'm here on business for Georgia-Pacific, hoping to follow up and confirm a potential deal but my counterparts never showed up. Apparently the logging industry near Sidima isn't all that healthy. I'm going to try to return home in January if I can get tickets. I don't want to be here when weather conditions get really bad later in January.*
> *My friend from the logging cooperative had promised to take me to a soccer match—which I was really looking forward to. Our meeting kept getting pushed back, due to various business issues, and to my disappointment I find it is no longer soccer season. As you know, Susan, I love sports. One of my fondest memories in football is "The Catch" from Montana to Clark back in '82. I had hoped to see some amazing football play here—I've heard that the team in Khab is really good. Of course, when you mention football in the USSR, you really aren't talk-*

ing about American-style football!
I look forward to seeing you and the baby when I return. Please be sure to give my regards to my dear friend Bill.
All my love,
Roger

Natasha sat back in her chair, staring at the correspondence in her hand, thinking. On the one hand, it appeared to be a perfectly normal letter from an American to his girlfriend. But why was it written in Russian? Why were both the destination and return addresses in Russian? And why did the writer claim to be at the Intourist Hotel, when he clearly was not? *Perhaps,* she thought, *Roger is cheating on Susan. Maybe Susan likes the Russian language, I don't know.* After a moment, she changed her mind. *No, there is something fishy about this. I'd better escalate it to the next level.*

She walked over to the department copier and copied the envelope and both sides of the letter. Returning the original to its envelope, she resealed it with a thin swipe of fresh glue, and pitched it into the Outgoing mail cart.

Natasha Zherdeva entered both the destination and return addresses into the department log with a brief summary of her suspicions. She then used the department typewriter to compose an account of her examination of the letter and why she escalated it to the next level. Zherdeva placed her report and the copies of Bates' letter into a manila envelope and tossed it into the stack of suspicious correspondence that would be more closely examined by the next higher layer of KGB officers. Having done that, she decided to reward herself with another trip to the break room.

****

"Checkmate, Ilya."

Kelly shook his head. It was the third time he'd lost to the old man. "How do you do it, Grandfather? I thought I was pretty good at chess before I played you."

Usilov chuckled. "Chess is always about thinking four or five moves ahead, Ilya. The further ahead you think, the more you can anticipate your opponent's moves and the easier it is to deny him the initiative. You force him to play your game, not his. Thinking ahead also makes it easier to bait him into taking the initiative in an unwise direction, like the boxer who leaves his chin open, enticing his opponent to take an ill-advised swing at him."

"Well, I guess I took a couple of foolish pokes at you in this game, didn't I?" Kelly chuckled.

Usilov shrugged humbly. "Maybe a few. Your gambit to capture my queen was your undoing."

The old man was silent as he carefully put the ebonywood chess pieces into the black velvet bag where they were stored. The wooden chessboard was beautiful, crafted out of Italian Briarwood Elm root. It was the only valuable possession Usilov owned.

"Where did you get this set? It's beautiful," Kelly said, admiring the pieces.

"My great grandfather received it as a gift from the *tsar*—he was captain of the *tsar's* personal bodyguard. It has been passed down in our family now for several generations. My only regret is that I now have no son or daughter to give it to. My wife died early in our marriage, before we had children. I could never bring myself to remarry."

"I'm sorry," Kelly said quietly. In the week that he'd roomed with Usilov, he'd grown to care for the old man.

Usilov smiled sadly, "So am I." He put the chess set away and stepped into the small kitchen. "Tea?"

"Please."

As the kettle boiled, Usilov spoke about his life. "We lived in Leningrad. Six months after Anna and I were wed, the Great Patriotic War began and I was conscripted into the army. In '41 I served in the Bryansk Front in a rifle division. For the next two years, amid bloody fighting, our unit was reformed multiple times until I finally found myself in the 37th Guards Rifle Regiment of the 12th Guards Rifle Division,

61st Army. I was fighting along the Dniepr River when I received word that Anna had died in the siege of Leningrad. She starved to death."

Usilov turned toward the stove, hiding the lone tear that rolled down his cheek. He waited until he could trust his voice and then said simply, "Never remarried. Just couldn't."

"That, Stas, is exactly why I don't believe in God," Kelly interjected, using Usilov's familiar name. "You two were perfectly happy, and God ruined it."

The old man carried two mugs of tea to the table with a couple of slices of black bread and a small pat of butter, and sat down opposite Kelly. "Really? How do you figure that?" he asked, eyebrows raised.

"What?"

"That God ruined it. Last time I checked, it was the Nazis."

"Well, yes, but God is supposed to be in control, isn't He? Isn't that what Christians believe?"

Usilov buttered a piece of bread, then pushed the plate and butter over to Kelly. "Certainly. God is in control of all things. That's what true Christians believe, anyway."

Kelly shrugged. "Then He could have stopped the Nazis." He took a piece of the bread and smeared butter on it.

"Of course."

"Well, there you have it. He's supposed to be in control and He's supposed to be good, and yet He allows all this evil and heartache. That's not a God I want anything to do with," he said.

"I see. And does man have any role in all this evil, or is it all on God?"

"He could prevent it," Kelly mumbled, speaking around a mouthful of the delicious black bread.

"Yes, if it was His will to do so. But what about man—does he have any responsibility in this problem of evil?"

"Maybe we're just robots, cogs in the cosmic wheel. If God is in control of all things, perhaps we are just puppets on a string."

Usilov laughed. "It's not likely you'd be making an argument against God if you were just a cog in His deterministic cosmic wheel."

Kelly grinned sheepishly. "Okay, I suppose not. Touché." He wiped his mouth on the sleeve of his work shirt.

"So what do you believe about God, Ilya? Do you really believe He is some sort of diabolical monster who gets His pleasure by ruining people's lives?"

"At one time I did feel that way, but now—now I don't know what I believe, Stas. I've been very happy being an agnostic and never even thinking about God, until my wi—." He caught himself just in time. He'd been about to say *until my wife became a Christian.*

"Until what?" Usilov asked, eyes narrowed.

"Until," Kelly coughed, buying time, his mind racing as he tried to think of what he could say to cover his near gaffe. "Until my *life* settled down and my wild days came to an end."

"What wild days?"

"Oh, you know how it is," Kelly said carelessly. "When you're young you think you're invincible, doing foolish, dangerous things, holding the world by the tail."

"Actually, I don't know anything about that. When I was young and foolish I was in a shooting war for the survival of my country, trying to stay alive and scared out of my wits."

Kelly shook his head and waved his hands apologetically. "Sorry. I guess I was pretty irresponsible. I never went through what you experienced."

They sat in silence drinking their tea, until Usilov asked, "So, now that your wild days are over, Ilya, what exactly do you believe about God?"

"That's just it: I don't know. Don't even know if He exists at all. Part of me hopes He does exist, part of me is terrified that He might. I don't even know if I'm talking about an actual person, a real being who has independent existence, or just some religious person's idea. Did God create us, or did we create Him? I don't know." He carried his and Usilov's dishes to the sink and washed them off.

The old man rotated his empty mug in circles on the table. "Would you permit me to tell you what I believe?"

"Oh, boy!" chuckled Kelly. "I was wondering how long it would take before the preaching started. Sure, go ahead, Stas. In all honesty, your kindness to me has earned a fair hearing."

Usilov stared at his cup, thinking. Finally he said, "The Bible, Ilya, is God's self-revelation. He tells us exactly what He is like in those sixty-six books that make up the Old and New Testaments."

"Wait a minute! Men wrote the Bible, not God."

"Indeed they did. But God moved them to write what they wrote."

"How can you be sure?"

"Because that's exactly what the Bible says in 2 Peter 1:20-21. But just step back and take a look at it, Ilya. How ludicrous would it be to believe, on the one hand, in an all-powerful, creator God who desires to reveal Himself to mankind—a God who calls Himself *The Word*, no less—and yet on the other hand think that this God is incapable of causing imperfect men to write a perfect Bible? No offense, but frankly, that's a ridiculous position to hold."

Kelly stared at him for a moment, thinking it over. "Okay, that actually makes sense. I'm not saying I buy it, but for the sake of argument, I'll accept it for the moment. So what does this Bible tell you about God?"

"It tells me that He is indeed in control. That He is loving, kind and good. While He does not approve of evil, He uses the evil of evil men to accomplish His good purposes for His people. He is personal, living, and eternal. He is perfect in every way. He is faithful to His promises, and has unlimited power to keep them. He always acts in complete accord with His character. He is holy, meaning there is no moral pollution or corruption in Him.

"It says in Isaiah 46:9 that there is no one like God. Verse 5 says there is no one to whom we may compare Him. That's helpful to know, because He reveals Himself as a triune being: one God eternally manifest in three equal persons: Father, Son, and Holy Spirit. Each person in the Godhead is fully God, yet there is just one God. It is a mystery we cannot fathom, nonetheless it is how He has revealed Himself in the

Bible. There is nothing in the natural world to compare to Him.

"That's the God of the Bible, Ilya. That's the God I believe in." Usilov checked his watch. "Time to refill the feed bins, my young friend."

****

"We might be doing this the hard way," Captain Fukina said to her two lieutenants. The trio were having an early morning cup of coffee together to plan the day's search activities. In half an hour the borrowed officers from the Vladivostok KGB office were scheduled to join them.

"What do you mean, Kira? We are covering the search grid very methodically. In another four days we'll have checked the entire Khab metro area," said Aleksei Bok. They'd been showing Borodin's picture to anyone who had any kind of contact with the public, grid by grid. One team circulated from 0600 hours to 1800 and the other covered the same grid from 1800 to 0600, on the theory that there were two different segments of society out and about in those different time frames.

Fukina preferred a cordial informality with her top two team members, over the cold professional etiquette she demanded from all others. If anyone else addressed her as Bok did they could expect a stinging rebuke, if not an official reprimand in their file.

"Yes, but we might be missing the low-hanging fruit. If Borodin is working with a foreign intelligence service, he's going to try to leave the country. He's going to need to communicate with his handlers to set up an extraction. He's not going to use his sat phone because it's been compromised. One of the most likely ways to communicate is to try to pass a message by someone in a foreign tour group staying at the Intourist Hotel."

"*Pravda*," said Bok, nodding. "I should have thought of that."

Captain Fukina came to a decision. "Pankiv, your team comes off the night shift in half an hour, and Bok, your team will hit the streets on the new grid. We'll continue the grid-by-grid, but meanwhile I'm going to jump ahead of everyone and cover a four-block by four-block square with Intourist at the center. Perhaps one of the tour guides, or someone else who frequents that area will have seen Borodin.

"Oh, and Pankiv, before you turn in, pay a visit to the postal censors for the Khab region, see if they've picked up anything odd in the last week."

Lieutenant Stefan Pankiv nodded. "Will do. I'll call you if I find anything."

****

Captains Mirov, Gromyko, and Fetisov filed into Admiral Shukshin's new office, the office formerly occupied by the late Admiral Pyotr Stefanovich Zelenko.

"Please be seated, comrades. Captain Mirov, shut the door, please," Shukshin said over his shoulder. His back was to them, as he gazed out at the anchorage. The sun was shining and the day was cloudless but frigid. There was enough of a breeze to raise whitecaps out in the bay. He watched a harbor tug nudging a recent arrival, an Udaloy-class destroyer, into its berth.

The three captains looked at each other, and waited.

Finally the admiral turned around and sat at his desk. "You three worked together in Operation *Vostochnyy Veter*. Your co-ordination and performance on such a highly dangerous mission was a credit to the submarine service and to the entire fleet. You demonstrated that our submarines can penetrate the ASW security perimeter surrounding an American aircraft carrier. Had we been at war, you would have sunk the *Nimitz*."

Mirov frowned. *Had we been at war the* Nimitz *ASW screen would have been a lot more aggressive, they would not have been operating in shallow water without SSN escort, and the three of us would have been sunk long before we could have launched a weapon*, he thought. He had the good sense, however, to keep his thoughts to himself.

"The *rodina* now calls upon you to go into harm's way

again, comrades. This time the target is CV-41, the USS *Midway*. She will be returning from a deployment south of the Philippines. In addition to several supply ships, two *Spruance*-class destroyers and a Ticonderoga-class cruiser will be sailing with her. On 20 January, gentlemen, she'll be in the Philippine Sea, right about here." He stood, and pointed to the map. "Approximately twenty-one degrees, fifty-six seconds north, and one hundred thirty-three degrees, eighteen seconds east. Captain Mirov, you are to penetrate her ASW screen and attempt to get within eight kilometers of her, closer if possible. Captains Gromyko and Fetisov, you are to draw off the battle group's main ASW assets to enable Captain Mirov to close on the carrier.

"All three of you will sail with a full weapons complement just in case the Americans decide to engage you. Make sure you are also carrying a full wartime complement of 9K38 Igla SAMs. Should shooting begin, you may consider yourselves free to defend your vessel with utmost lethality. That will be explicitly stated in your written orders.

"You will communicate with fleet headquarters six hours before commencing your final approach to the battle group in order to verify the *Midway*'s updated position and to access the latest intelligence."

"Will she have an SSN escort, Admiral?" asked Captain Mirov.

Shukshin continued to stare at the map. Then he turned and faced his officers, shaking his head. "That is a piece of intelligence we do not have. We must assume she does, and that they will be ranging ahead of the carrier several hundred miles. Captain Udom is predicting that she will have a single *Los Angeles*-class escort, but I would advise you to plan on encountering two escort submarines. Avoid them at all costs. Do not engage or provoke them, unless of course the Americans start shooting. If the Americans should for any reason launch weapons, remember that your survival will largely depend on sinking their submarines before they sink you."

Mirov stirred in his chair. "Admiral Shukshin, one of Admiral Zelenko's last acts was to rescind Standing Order 17. His concern was that we do not want to reveal too many of our capabilities to the imperialists. Are you now reinstating it, sir?"

Shukshin's eyes flashed and his face reddened. With difficulty he resisted the impulse to respond with umbrage to the question, which he interpreted as casting doubt on his authority. He paused to get his breathing under control, and then said, "No, Captain Mirov, I have not reinstated it. I agree with Admiral Zelenko's concern, and the Pacific Fleet will no longer engage in unnecessary provocations. This operation I am giving you command of, Operation *Tikhookeanskaya Groza*, is intended to reveal any operational changes the Americans have instituted since the success of Operation *Vostochnyy Veter*."

"Understood, sir. I did not intend to offend, Admiral," responded Mirov.

Shukshin nodded. "Apology accepted, Captain. You, Mirov, will be in command of the operation once again. You will have the most difficult part. I'm giving you the most silent submarine we have, *B-445*. As you know, she was commissioned last January and has all the latest upgraded technology. Bring her back in one piece, Captain."

Mirov nodded, pleased. The diesel-electric Kilo-class submarines were not intended to be blue-water vessels, being much better suited to littoral conditions. But as long as they weren't caught snorkeling, they were the quietest submarine of any navy, virtually undetectable by passive sonar when doing under three knots. Several years before Operation *East Wind*, Mirov had conned a Kilo-class to within six thousand meters of an American carrier. It was the first time such a feat had been attempted, and Mirov was outstandingly successful. His reputation spread through the entire Soviet submarine community, and billets on his boats were now highly sought after. It also produced an inevitable jealousy among his superior officers, which was the primary reason Mirov was still *Captain* Mirov. "Thank you, sir. I'll do my best."

"Captain Gromyko, you'll have the *K-284* again, and Fetisov, you'll take the *K-263*, as you did before." Both boats were highly capable *Projekt* 971 submarines, known to NATO as

Akula-class submarines.

"Comrades, have your submarines fully provisioned, fully crewed, and ready to sail in eight days. One of the essential requirements of this operation is that you arrive at your area of operations undetected, well ahead of the carrier battle group. I will be sending two SSBNs into the Philippine Sea ahead of you. Hopefully any American submarines in your AO will detect the boomers and tail them. If successful, the SSBNs will lead them out of your AO, sweeping it clean of American subs not attached to the carrier group.

"Your orders will be delivered to the safe in your quarters aboard your submarines. You may open them and read them during provisioning, in the presence of your *zampolit*. They are not to be shared with any of your officers or crew, however, until you are underway and submerged.

"Captain Mirov, I have left the tactical disposition of Captain Gromyko and Captain Fetisov to your judgment. I am anticipating that you will arrange them in such a way that they will be within ten kilometers of the *Midway* before disengaging."

The officers discussed the plans for Operation *Pacific Threat (Tikhookeanskaya Groza)* for half an hour before Shukshin dismissed them.

****

Shukshin owned the Pacific Fleet's political officers, lock, stock, and barrel. For the last eighteen months he had been very visibly involved in the recommendations for promotion of the political officers based in Vladivostok. He had seen that they obtained sought-after billets and had worked tirelessly to upgrade the base housing designated to both married and single political officers. Whereas many commanders tolerated their *zampolity* as a necessary but unwelcome evil, Shukshin treated them with great respect and deference wherever possible. His efforts paid off in spades, and he had the full loyalty of the fleet's political cohort. This was also partly due to the fact that he had arranged to transfer out of the fleet any political officers who had voiced support for Gorbachev, or who had refused to eat out of Shukshin's hand.

Between their loyalty to him and to the conservative Marxist-Leninist dogma that had been drilled into them for years, Shukshin was confident they would perform as expected at the right time. He was about to test that confidence with the three men who would serve as the political officers in Operation *Tikhookeanskaya Groza*.

"You three men have a vitally important role in Operation *Pacific Threat*. The submarines to which you are assigned will be aggressively prosecuting the *Midway* and her battle group. It is vital that you keep the morale and confidence of your crews at a peak performance level. They must be fully convinced of the superiority of our weapons systems, our sonar, our submarines and the men who command them. You are to constantly remind them that they are to perform their duties without fear and to have complete confidence in all the orders that come from this office."

Captain Second Rank Zakhar Rurikovich Khorkov stirred in his chair, a quizzical expression on his face. Khorkov was Captain Fetisov's political officer, on the Akula-class *K-263*.

"Yes, what is it, Captain Khorkov?"

"Sir, you said *aggressively prosecute* a moment ago. You did not mean by that expression that we will be launching weapons, did you?"

The expressions on the faces of the other two officers showed that they had been wondering the same thing. Shukshin put on his most fatherly, paternal expression and did not answer but merely stared at Khorkov until the man looked down at the floor with something like shame written on his face.

Always the master manipulator, Shukshin rose from his desk and walked around it, then sat on the edge nearest the three officers, projecting an image of intimacy. "Comrade Khorkov," he said gently, "Roshchin, Leonev: you must trust me and do exactly as ordered no matter what you fear may be the consequence. For the good of the *rodina*—always for the good of the *rodina*.

"When you are at sea and drawing near to the American battle group, each submarine will receive new orders from Fleet—from me. It is your responsibility to see that those orders are carried out exactly as written. Do you understand me?"

The three looked at him with troubled expressions and nodded.

"Each of you must take measures to see that the orders are obeyed—even if it means arresting your captain and confining him to his quarters. If then the XO refuses to carry out my orders in the captain's absence, you must have him arrested, too. At that point you will take command of the submarine and follow my orders precisely as written. Do you understand?" he asked again.

"Captain Roshchin, I do not believe that Gromyko will falter in his responsibilities, but you need to be prepared to act immediately in case he does." Captain Second Rank Terenti Marlenovich Roshchin would be sailing aboard Captain Gromyko's K-284, also an Akula-class vessel.

"Khorkov, although you need to be likewise prepared, I am confident that Captain Fetisov will faithfully carry out my orders.

"But you, Captain Leonev, as you will be on Mirov's *B-445*, you will have trouble on your hands. I am convinced that Mirov will buck my authority and refuse to carry out my orders. You must be in the control room when the new orders come through, and you must act immediately if Mirov refuses to obey me. You will be closest to the carrier and the Americans will pounce on you immediately. You'll have to act at the first sign of hesitation by Captain Mirov.

"I have given you, Leonev, an ally. I did not allow Mirov to pick his XO—I picked him. He's my man and he knows there might be trouble. He will back you up, but because you are the ranking officer, the first move to replace Mirov must be yours."

"But, sir, why don't you put the XO in command now and leave Mirov ashore?" Leonev objected.

"Because I am convinced that Captain Mirov is the only

commander in the fleet who can conn a submarine that close to an American carrier without being detected. The man has consummate skill. I hope he will obey the new orders he receives at sea, because he also has the skill to bring the boat safely home."

Shukshin allowed the officers to absorb what he was saying. He could see each man wrestling with his private thoughts. This was the only meeting on the topic he would have, and he wanted to make sure his intentions were clear, even if not stated openly. The cabal was approaching the time when any mistakes or leaks would be disastrous. It was crucial that all happened according to plan. They had one shot at a successful coup, and it was winner-take-all. If it failed, the lives of the coup plotters would be forfeit. Everything depended on the men in his office right now.

"So will there be weapons launched, sir?" Leonev asked.

Shukshin did not answer, but looked at the officer with a sad, grandfatherly smile.

When his silence made clear that no answer would be forthcoming, he said, "Know this, comrades: the orders for Operation *Pacific Threat* were conceived and approved by the Central Committee of the Communist Party—both sets of orders, the initial ones and the ones to be sent when you are in your AO." But Shukshin was lying. In actual fact he was the only person who knew what was in either set of orders, and they had no one's approval except his own.

"Now, you men must speak of this to no one. I know I need not say this—but if you speak to anyone, any person at all, of any rank or position, about what I have told you, you will be stripped of your rank and shot, and your family shipped to the Siberian northlands. Do I make myself clear? . . . Very well. Dismissed."

As the three political officers exited Shukshin's office, they felt the tremendous weight and responsibility of what the admiral was commanding them to do. They also had a sense for the great honor of the task set before them, for the *rodina*. It was as though a father was committing the future of the world to the hands of his sons. *Terrifying exhilaration* is how they later described the feeling to each other when the three were alone. Shukshin's command authority seemed magnetic, almost supernaturally compelling. None of the three had the slightest inclination to disobey him, despite their fears.

****

"Has the NSA picked up anything, any word at all?" Jensen asked Sam Bergman.

The analyst shook his head. "I'm checking with Miss Stinson several times a day—"

"For business reasons, of course," Jensen smiled.

"Purely business, Bill," Bergman responded defensively.

"You liar!"

"What? What do you mean?" Bergman demanded.

"You can't even admit it to yourself. You are head over heels for that gal. And you don't need to call her 'Miss Stinson' for my benefit, Sam. She's Evelyn, for crying out loud," the DDO said, chuckling.

Bergman sat for a moment, trying to be angry, but it just wasn't there. He grinned sheepishly. "Busted. Is it that obvious?"

"Uh-huh, it is. I hear the secretary in your office has started humming the *Wedding March* whenever you walk by. Now, back to business, what has Evelyn heard?"

"I am sorry to say this—but, nothing. She hasn't picked up a peep. The only thing that could even conceivably be related is an increase in encrypted sat phone traffic around Khabarovsk, on channels known to be used by the KGB. But that's four hundred some odd miles north of Vladivostok, Bill."

"I know, but Kelly can travel when he has a mind to. Could it be a search?"

"I suppose it could be, or it could be nothing more than a bunch of agents betting on a soccer match. We simply don't have any hard data."

Jensen grimaced. "Have her keep looking. What's the latest from the NRO? Are they seeing any unusual activity at the naval base in Vladivostok?"

"No, not at all. The provisioning docks are empty—no vessels tied up at them."

"Hmm. Perhaps the Sovs are standing down? Maybe picking up that rogue sat phone transmission has got them a little nervous about who is watching."

"Could be, Bill. Naval intelligence has not reported any new confrontations in the last two weeks, either."

"What about the political scene?"

"Things are heating up there. Pushkaryov gave a major speech in the *Duma* attacking Gorbachev's policies. The speech was shown on their domestic television stations, and the camera caught defense minister Aristov, interior minister Churkin, and General Yegorov, who is more or less their CJCS, all standing and applauding. The political fractures are deepening and widening, and it's going to be very difficult to put these cats back in the bag."

****

Captain Fukina had covered almost half of the sixteen blocks she'd marked out with no luck. No one had reported seeing the man in her picture—or at least, they had not admitted to seeing him. Fukina knew she was acting at a disadvantage—the Soviet citizenry wanted nothing to do with the KGB. They knew that if they admitted seeing the fugitive they could be hauled into the KGB office for interrogation. As a consequence, no one had seen him. Even if they had.

She approached a line of taxi drivers across the street from the Intourist Hotel. Going from cab to cab, it was the same question, the same answer.

"Have you seen this man?"

"*Nyet*, sorry."

When she leaned down and asked the fourth driver in the line, his faced betrayed him. His eyes widened and he looked away quickly, twisting his hands on the steering wheel.

"*Nyet*, never."

She knew he was lying, but she also knew it would be

counterproductive to make a scene.

"*Spasibo*. Sorry to bother you."

As Captain Fukina stood, she noted the number on the cab and memorized it. If they didn't get any better leads, they would track the man down and interrogate him.

After going through the line of cabs, she noticed an Intourist tour director shepherding a bunch of foreign nationals onto a tour bus. On a hunch she walked over, knowing that the tour directors were KGB employees.

She showed her credentials to the woman. "KGB Captain Kira Fukina. I'm sorry to bother you, comrade, but I am conducting a search. Have you seen this man?" She showed the woman the picture of Borodin.

"*Da*, as a matter of fact, I have. Just yesterday. He was sitting over on that bench, watching the hotel. I approached him to shoo him away, because sometimes the citizens will try to talk to one of the foreigners, and, you know, pass them a message or something. We don't allow unmonitored interaction with the foreigners. He got up and left in a hurry, before I could speak to him."

"Have you seen him before yesterday?"

"*Nyet*, just yesterday."

"And you are positive it was him?"

"*Da*. Very positive."

"What is your name, please? I wish to put a commendation in your file."

Later that afternoon she met with both teams at the KGB lodging and shared her news. "We're going to reset the search around the Intourist Hotel, and expand out from there. If he's been watching the hotel, he's probably not moving at the moment. We stand a good chance of spotting him in the immediate locale.

"Stefan, did you have any luck at the censors?"

"Hard to say, Kira. There was one odd letter that was mailed a couple of days ago. The letter and the addresses are in Russian, but the names are American, and the destination address is in the USA. It was mailed using the Intourist Hotel as the return address, but the censor says no one by that name has stayed at the hotel. Here, I secured a copy of both the envelope and the letter."

Fukina scanned the letter. "It may be nothing, but it is the best clue we've got, and it matches with his sighting at the hotel. I'm going to bump this upstairs."

After the brief meeting, she walked over to the KGB office building. "Got an an empty office with a phone I can use?"

The duty officer showed her to an office and returned to his desk. She shut the door then dialed the Lubyanka and waited as she heard half a dozen relays clicking as her call was routed through the local telephone network, then up to a satellite, another satellite, and then back down to Moscow.

"Speak."

"Go secure, encryption code 557," Kira instructed. There was a brief whistling noise as the sending and receiving devices synchronized.

"Affirmative, encryption enabled." The digitally mediated voice sounded slightly hollow, as if speaking from the bottom of a well.

"This is the Mongoose. I need to speak to the Fox with a priority-one message," she said, using code names.

"Please hold."

After five minutes, Geredin came on the line. "Fox here. Report, Mongoose."

"Two things. First, we've got a report of a positive sighting of the fugitive across the street from the Intourist Hotel in Khab. He was seen yesterday. We are shifting the search to the immediate area around the hotel. Second, a letter mailed on the 18th of this month in a mailbox near the hotel was snagged by the regional postal censor. She thought it looked suspicious, and I think she's right. The return address was the hotel, but the guest register does not show anyone by that name. The letter was addressed to someone in Clinton, Utah, USA. There are just enough odd circumstances about this piece of mail that I wonder if it is connected to the fugitive. I'd like to fax it to you for examination."

"Excellent. Yes, I'll take a look at the letter. Send it to the fax in my office. You've got the number?"

"Yes, sir."

"By the way, have you reported any of this to the Vlad office?"

"Not yet."

"Well, don't."

"May I ask why, sir?"

"There's a GRU snitch in that office. I'd rather keep the GRU in the dark."

"Ah. Of course. I won't make any more reports to them, then."

"Good. I would not be surprised if the head honcho himself is the snitch. Whatever. Keep up the good work, Mongoose. I'll look forward to seeing that letter."

"It's on its way, Fox."

****

Falcon checked the pressure in all four boilers, cranked a fresh load of coal into the fireboxes and then refilled all four feed bins. He pushed the empty wheelbarrow into the corner and stepped into the office, where Usilov sat reading *Pravda*.

Usilov put the paper down. "Thanks, Ilya. My back is doing much better now, I think I can start to help with the coal duties again."

"Not yet, Grandfather. I don't mind the work, and besides, I love your cooking. I'm getting the best part of this bargain. One of these days I will be moving on, and I will remember your kindness."

"My kindness toward you, Ilya, is really God's kindness toward you."

Kelly brushed the coal dust off an old, slightly rusty folding chair and sat down. "I don't mean to offend, Grandfather, but does your kindness earn points with your God? Is all of this just a way of storing up some kind of good credit, so you can go to heaven?"

Usilov laughed. "Oh, goodness no, Ilya. I am already going to heaven, nothing can change that. No, I want to serve people with kindness because God has treated me with kindness, and this is how I can show Him my gratitude."

"Isn't it sort of presumptuous to claim that you're going to heaven and 'nothing can change that'?"

"Not at all. It's simple faith in what Jesus very explicitly promised. But let me turn the question toward you. I know you are not ready to believe in God, so maybe it is doubtful whether you even believe there is a heaven or a hell. But for the sake of discussion, if there is a heaven, how would you imagine that people would go there? What would convince God to open the pearly gates, as it were, to let someone in?"

"Well, they'd have to be really good, I imagine."

"How good?"

"I don't know. Better than the average Boris, I suppose."

"Yes, there are many religious people who believe that. Every religion that confesses belief in a supreme being teaches that you have to be good to go to heaven. But that's not what Christianity teaches. Christianity teaches that you must be perfect for a perfectly holy God to admit you to His presence. Matthew 5:48 says *Therefore you are to be perfect, as your heavenly Father is perfect.* Even one single sin will condemn you, no matter what it is. Paul says in Romans 6:23 that *the wages of sin is death.* Ezekiel 18:4 says *the soul that sins will die.*"

Kelly raised his eyebrows. "Wait a minute. You actually believe you are perfect?"

"Not at all. I'm sinner. Wrestle with sin every day. I hate my own sins, but I sin nonetheless."

"Then if the requirement is perfection, how can you possibly think you're going to heaven? That makes no sense at all."

"It's actually a lot easier for me to explain than it is for you to believe it. Let me try.

"The grocer down the street where I buy my groceries, Ivan Dubrovsky, allows me to keep a credit line. We've known each other for years. I can't always pay on time, but he knows I'll always pay off my account at some point.

"Anyway, let's say that I run up a big bill at Ivan's, and I can't pay. So he threatens to bring me before the judge and have me thrown in jail if I don't pay what I owe. Let's say the bill is much bigger than I could ever hope to pay. So, assuming he follows through on his threat, what's going to happen to me?"

"You're going to jail."

"Right. But what if at the last minute, you stepped in and paid my bill, all of it, to the very last kopek? What would happen to me then?"

"You'd be free."

"Right again. And that's what Jesus Christ did for all who trust in Him. All sin, any sin, creates a debt—a moral obligation to God. Because God is perfectly holy and infinitely righteous, that moral debt is one we cannot hope to pay—it is an infinite debt. Someone has once said, 'It is not the importance of the thing but the majesty of the Lawgiver, that is to be the standard of obedience.'

"What the Bible teaches is that God's Son, Jesus Christ, by His death on the cross—remember, *the wages of sin is death*—took the punishment for my sins in my place as my substitute. He paid the moral obligation I owed God—the debt I could never pay. He was raised from the dead three days later, proving that His payment for my sins satisfied all the demands of God's holy law.

"But that is only half of what He did. Jesus had lived a perfect life, never sinning, always obeying His heavenly Father. In other words, He lived a life of perfect righteousness. When I placed my faith in Him for the forgiveness of my sins, God credited my record with Jesus' own righteousness. Now when God looks at the books, so to speak, under my name He does not see all my sins. What He sees instead is what His own Son has done—perfect obedience—and He counts that as though I did it. To put it in terms of our fictional grocery debt, He 'credits it to my account.' Paul records this amazing transaction in 2 Corinthians 5:21: *God has made Jesus to be sin for us, that we might be made the righteousness of God in Him*."

"So, if I'm hearing you right, what you're saying is that the perfection God requires has been given to you by God Himself," Kelly mused thoughtfully.

"Yes. What God requires, God Himself provides for those

who place their faith in Jesus' death, burial, and resurrection for their sins. God does it all. I don't do anything, Ilya, to merit heaven. I could never merit heaven. Eternal life is a gift to those of faith—not a wage. Paul says in Romans 6:23, *for the wages of sin is death, but the free gift of God is eternal life through Jesus Christ our Lord.* But this gift is not automatic—it's only for those who respond in faith. John says in his gospel, *But as many as received Him, to them He gave the right to become children of God, even to those who believe in His name.*

"And you know that perfection we were talking about a few minutes ago? Hebrews 10:14 says, *for by one offering He has perfected for all time those who are sanctified.* That's where my perfection comes from, Ilya. It comes from the offering of the Son of God on the cross as the sacrifice for my sins.

"I am a bad man, Ilya. But I have a very good Savior."

Kelly sat deep in thought. *What God requires, God Himself provides. Never heard that before. Never knew that.* Usilov's simple explanation of the gospel went against what he'd always thought about Christianity.

Usilov stood up. "I have a *borsch* recipe that's to die for. How about *borsch* tonight?"

Kelly smiled. "Sounds wonderful. I still have a few rubles in my pocket, do you need any supplies for it?"

"You want to splurge?"

"Why not?" Kelly grinned.

"I need fresh beets, some beef, and some sour cream."

Kelly gave the old man a few bills. "Can't wait for supper," he said, smiling.

****

Victor Timuryevich Smolin stood in the outer office and knocked on his boss's door, fax in hand.

"Enter," came Geredin's reply through the door.

"This just came in for you, General Geredin. I thought you might want to see it right away."

"*Spasibo,* Victor. By the way, how is that new baby?"

"Cries all night, sleeps all day, sir. My wife is wondering

whether this first should be our last," Geredin's secretary chuckled as he put the fax on the desk. "Can I get you some tea, sir?"

"Thank you, but no."

After his secretary left the room, Geredin examined the fax. It was a copy of the suspect letter that Captain Fukina had spoken of. The name Susan Bates meant nothing to him, nor did the destination address in Utah. However, he did recognize the name of the ostensible sender, Roger Carson. Carson was known to the KGB and probably half a dozen other foreign intelligence services as a bad actor, a CIA field operative who specialized in paramilitary operations and covert direct action. The KGB analysts who'd tried to chase down more information on Carson, plus the few agents who'd tangled with him in the field and lived to talk about it, believed that Carson's earlier career was as a military special forces operator, perhaps SEALs or Delta Force.

Geredin picked up the telephone and dialed the chief of the First Directorate, which dealt with foreign operations and intelligence gathering. "Vasily, Anatoly here. Listen, the censors snagged a US-bound letter as suspicious. I think it might contain information for a case being investigated in Khabarovsk. I need your people to research it and get back to me. There are some names and an address in Utah that should be checked out. I want to know the identities and current whereabouts of the named individuals, as well as where they have been over the last fourteen days. There are also some sports references to be researched. I must have answers within forty-eight hours, sooner if possible. Have you got some assets available to work on it? Good! *Spasibo.* I'll have Victor bring it to your department."

Chapter 17

Light snow was falling when Sam and Evelyn emerged from the taxi on Constitution Avenue. Just north of them across the Ellipse, the beautifully decorated National Christmas Tree illuminated the dark. Little knots of merrymakers were wandering the Capitol Grounds, moving from one light display to another. Sam could hear carolers in the distance. The pair stopped at a street vendor and purchased hot chocolate in plastic commemorative travel mugs.

"I'm glad we dressed warmly, Sam. It's a chilly evening," Evelyn said, sipping her hot chocolate as they strolled toward the lofty Christmas tree.

"Is it too cold?" Sam asked anxiously. "Would you rather find a coffee shop and go inside?" He was still trying to find his footing with this woman he'd fallen in love with. She rattled him and entranced him all at the same time.

"No, no. I love this—I'm so glad we came. When I was a little girl, we had a family tradition of bundling up and going around the neighborhood, enjoying the Christmas lights, and believe me, it was much colder in Chambersburg," she said laughing. "Tonight reminds me of that."

"I love this time of year," confessed Sam. "There is a magic to it that I've never gotten over and hope I never do. My parents loved Christmas and Hanukkah both. They were non-observant Jews, as I am, and so we enjoyed both holidays to the fullest."

"So what do you think about the Christmas Story, Sam? You know, the God who became man, the baby in the manger, the wise men and shepherds. Do you think any of it is true?"

He didn't answer immediately, and they strolled along in silence enjoying the sights and the silence and the time together. Finally he sighed. "I ask myself that same question every Christmas. I've never come to an answer I'm satisfied with. I don't know if it's true, Evelyn, but I hope so. What a great story—and even greater if it were true. What about you?"

"Same as you. I don't know. The gospel story just seems too good to be true, and too bad to be true, simultaneously. If Jesus did all the things the stories say, why on earth would anyone hang Him on a cross? But if the stories are just myth, how in the world could Christianity rewrite the history of the western world—as it most certainly has?"

The snow picked up as they walked around the White House, enjoying the decorations. They began heading south again, toward the Washington Monument. Sam spotted a bench, brushed off the snow, and they sat.

"Merry Christmas," he said, handing her a tiny, gift-wrapped box.

"Oh, Sam—you didn't have to," she protested. "I haven't gotten anything for you."

"Just being with you is enough, Evelyn. Open it."

She carefully unwrapped the gift and opened the box. It was a pair of silver pendant earrings, each bearing a tiny green emerald, cut in a teardrop.

'Oh, they're beautiful!" She removed her earrings and put the new ones on.

"They match your eyes," he said simply.

She smiled and hugged him. "Thank you, Sam. I love them. You have great taste."

"In more ways than one," he said quietly, his heart full. He stood up and held out his hand. "Are you up for a longer walk?"

She took his hand. "Certainly. Where to?"

"Let's go see how they decorated the Capitol Building."

They had just passed the Natural History Museum on the Mall when Sam's pager went off. He looked at the message and rolled his eyes.

"I'm so sorry, Evelyn. That was the Firm. They're calling me in—on Christmas Eve, no less."

She squeezed his hand and smiled. "Hey, buster, we both work in the intelligence business, and I know the price of admission as well as you do—interruptions go with the territory. It's not a problem. Go get 'em, Sam."

"Why the world can't arrange to have its crises between

nine and five Eastern is beyond me," Sam lamented. "Let me call you a cab."

****

The snow had picked up significantly by the time Bergman pulled into the CIA parking lot. After passing through security, he took the elevator to his floor and checked in with the Soviet Desk duty officer. "Got paged twenty minutes ago. What's up, Marty?"

"NRO called, wanted to talk to you immediately. Call them back on this number."

Sam nodded and stuck the note in his pocket. He noticed the duty officer's mug full of steaming coffee. "Java any good tonight, Marty?"

"You betcha. I just made a fresh pot. And some of Santa's elves passed through earlier this evening bearing fresh donuts for those of us stuck here on Christmas Eve. They're down in the canteen—the donuts, not the elves—and they're delicious. Almost makes it worth being here."

Bergman unlocked his office and grabbed his mug. After getting coffee and grabbing two donuts, he returned to his desk. He picked up the secure phone and dialed the duty officer's desk in the National Reconnaissance Office.

"This is Sam Bergman, CIA. Somebody there wanted me. I hope it's worth being dragged in to the office on Christmas Eve."

"Please hold." The duty officer located Bergman's name in the Intelligence Officers' Roster, and studied the basic identity verification passphrases associated with Bergman.

"Please verify your identity, Mr. Bergman."

Bergman quoted the first two lines of one of J. R. R. Tolkien's poems, "All that is gold does not glitter, not all those who wander are lost."

"Identity verified, thank you. Connecting your call."

A moment later a satellite reconnaissance technician picked up the phone. "Sam, this is Al Mercer, NRO. Thanks for getting back to me. You wanted me to contact you if the KH-11 picked up movement in the submarine pens in Vladivostok. Well, on the latest pass it did. Two boomers have been moved to the provisioning dock, and a pair of Akula-class nukes are heating the kettle. I thought you'd want to know."

"You're right. I do. Can you identify the specific hulls?"

"No, not yet, only the class. Sun was not at the right angle. Perhaps in another pass or two—if they're still tied up—I'll have a little more detail."

"How does this seem to fit with the Pacific Fleet optempo, Al?"

"It doesn't. Been watching these bad boys for a long, long time, Sam. Neither of these moves are coming at the right time. If they were two months down the road, maybe. Right now? No, it does not fit Ivan's operational pattern. I have no idea if the heat blooms coming off the SSN power plants are related to the provisioning of the boomers. Could be getting ready to escort 'em, I suppose.

"But there's something that's odd. The boomers are a couple of old Hotel II-class boats, probably among the noisiest vessels in their submarine fleet. These two have been tied up so long I actually wondered if they'd been decommissioned. Apparently not. But they're floating a little high, which makes me think their *Serbs* have been pulled."

"Come again?"

"Their D4 missile launch system, controlling a trio of *SS-N-5 Serb* missiles. It's pretty old stuff, but I imagine it could still ruin your day. The two boats are floating high—makes me wonder if their nukes have been removed."

"Ah. Gotcha. Is it possible they've sold the boats and are preparing to deliver them to the buyer?"

"Could be, Sam, but that's your end of intelligence, not mine. But that could explain why the nukes aren't there. Otherwise, I'm not sure what the point is of sending out a nuclear missile submarine on patrol, with no nuclear missiles."

"Yeah. Well, send me the photos, including whatever you have of the surrounding area. And include a set from mid-summer, too, to serve as a bench mark."

"You got it. By the way, how's Evelyn over at NSA?"

"Oh, good grief! Not you, too!" Bergman groaned. "Besides, that's sensitive compartmented information, on a need-to-know basis only. And guess what?"

"Yeah, yeah, I get it—I don't *need to know*. It's just that when the most eligible female super-model spook starts hanging around with a loser like you, tongues wag. I'll warn you, Bergman, your little dalliance is known throughout the intelligence community. You're probably already being followed around by the Sovs, the Norks, the ChiComs, the paparazzi and probably her mom as well."

Sam rolled his eyes. "Okay, Al, we're done. Send me those photos." He hung up before the NRO man could continue his light-hearted torment.

****

"So what do you want Grandfather Frost to bring you for *Novyy God*, Anatoly?" asked the head of the KGB's First Directorate, Vasily Vasilyevich Orlov, chuckling.

"I want a troublesome American spy, gift-wrapped in shackles from head to toe. Actually Grandfather Frost already brought me a bottle of vodka and promised me another if I was good. So I am trying to be good. Not having much success, though. How about you?" answered Geredin. He was sitting in his office in the Lubyanka, a roaring fire in the fireplace, holding the phone in one hand while adding a dollop of vodka to his tea with the other. It was 26 December, and the sun was shining in a clear, cold sky. The glare reflecting off the snow was so bright that he'd had to close his curtains.

"I know what I'm getting because my wife already gave it to me. She was so excited about it she could not wait for the holiday. She gave me an American laptop computer, a Dell. I have no idea how she got it out of their country, or more importantly, into ours. She refuses to say. Makes me wonder if she's smuggling anything else. I'm sure all sorts of laws were broken getting it here, but I'm looking the other way. In any case it's an amazing device, Anatoly. Do you have a laptop computer?"

"*Nyet*! Abominable devices! I refuse to touch them. I don't even have a computer on my desk, thank you."

"How can you run the world's largest intelligence organization without a computer, my friend?"

"Simple, Vasily. I run the *organization*. I have people working for me who run the *computers*. People like you."

Vasily laughed. "You're a living fossil, Anatoly. Your gravestone will read, *He stood athwart progress, shouting STOP!*"

Geredin chuckled. "Perhaps so. But I've never had to reboot my pencil, and my pen has never crashed. Now, I assume you did not call to tease me about my Luddite eccentricities—what's up?"

"I've got the information you asked for. As you already knew, Roger Carson is indeed a CIA operative specializing in direct action. He's been in northern Virginia for the last two weeks, on the basis of multiple sightings reported by his neighbors as well as several credit card transactions. He could not have been your letter writer.

"We got nowhere on the name Susan Bates. It seems there are just over four thousand people with that name, scattered all over the USA. I guess all I can say is that she is a woman."

"*Da*. I figured that out myself, Vasily."

"The address in Utah happens to be the residence of a Jacob and Galina Kelly—"

"Who did you say?" Geredin asked, hoping he'd not heard correctly.

"Jacob and Galina Kelly. The wife is there—my agent actually saw her—she's been home continuously for the past fourteen days according to neighbors. However, no one reported seeing the husband for weeks. Apparently he's out of town."

"Apparently so," Geredin said ironically. He shook his head angrily. The finding served to verify that the odd letter was some sort of coded communication, and that it was definitely tied in with Jacob Kelly's clandestine presence in the USSR. But this created immense problems for the old spy. Geredin was caught between his sincere well-wishes to Jacob Kelly's wife, a young woman who was practically his goddaughter—and expecting a child, no less—and his duty to his country. He slammed his open palm down on the desk. *Why did you have to do this to me, Jacob, you young fool?* he thought furiously.

"Sir?"

"Ah, nothing, Vasily, sorry. I was smashing a spider on my desk. Any headway on the letter itself?"

"We have examined the letter carefully, operating from the assumption that it contains some sort of coded information. Obviously if the original contained a microdot, we have no access to that. But I seriously doubt that was the case. The letter is too clumsy to have been written by a professional spy.

"It appears that he is trying to set up a meeting of some sort near the Intourist Hotel. It may be that the lumber refer- ence identifies a specific location of a dead drop somewhere around the hotel—perhaps we should be looking for some sort of wooden structure. The Georgia-Pacific reference rein- forces that idea. The actual company Georgia-Pacific denies having any salesman by the name of Roger Carson, and fur- thermore is not even licensed for import/export to our coun- try. So the reference must somehow refine the intended loca- tion, perhaps for a meeting, a dead drop, or something else."

"Could the location be in Sidima?" asked Geredin, remem- bering that the letter mentioned the town.

"We don't think so—our experts believe that is simply a fiction the writer created to communicate the idea that his mission was somehow unsuccessful, at least to some degree," Vasily said.

"Might the intent of the letter be to request an agent ex- traction?" Geredin queried. That was what he had concluded from his own study of the document.

"*Da*, that is high on our list of possibilities. And if that is the case, the writer would like to be extracted before the end of January, as he mentions at the end of the first paragraph, *I don't want to be here when weather conditions get really bad later in Jan- uary.*

"However, Anatoly, we almost discarded it as being too obvious. But then, if the letter writer is not a professional spy, he might have told us exactly what we need to know without intending to do so."

"When in January is the extraction to take place?" asked Geredin, confident now that Kelly was seeking help to escape the country.

"Don't know. A date does not seem to be included—or if it is, we haven't seen it yet."

"What about the sports reference?"

"*Da.* My researchers discovered that the reference to *The Catch* points to a play in an American football game between the Dallas Cowboys and the San Francisco 49ers in January of 1982. The quarterback, Joe Montana, threw the football to a man named Dwight Clark. Apparently there was something remarkable about the catch or the throw that makes the play stand out."

"Is it significant?"

"We think it is, because the writer seems to indicate in the last line of the paragraph that he's not really talking about football. Again, that's another sign that the writer is a novice —no professional would be that obvious. In any case, we've been studying the stadium, the two individuals named, and everything else connected with the game, and as of yet we've come up with nothing. The reference is clearly important—we just don't know why."

After hanging up the phone, Geredin stood and hobbled around his office, making several circuits around his desk, ignoring his pain in a burst of angry energy. He concluded that Jacob Kelly had been spying in his country at one of its most sensitive installations, the home port of the Pacific Fleet, in one of its most secretive cities, Vladivostok. Even Soviet citizens were prohibited from entering that city without first being thoroughly vetted—but somehow Kelly had gotten in. And now that the young man had been compromised and almost captured, he was desperately seeking to get back to the US. Geredin also assumed Kelly's operation had to do with the CIA's need to verify the information he had passed to Jensen in September. Nonetheless, Kelly's actions could not be overlooked.

Normally the action of a foreign intelligence agent in his country would fill the old spy with grim determination to eliminate the intruder, but it had never produced the fury he was now feeling. *Get ahold of yourself, Anatoly. Angry people make mistakes, and you can afford no mistakes on this matter!* He knew that his agitation came from the difficult spot Kelly had placed him in—caught between his love for Galina, the promise he'd made to the girl's dying father, and his love for the *rodina*. He leaned heavily against the mahogany mantle of the fireplace and shut his eyes, shaking his head. The *rodina* would win in this contest of loyalties. It always had. It always would.

****

Major Roman Romanovich Nikitin slammed the telephone down on his desk. The fool in the KGB office had no information whatsoever about the status of the KGB search for the fugitive. Nikitin wondered if the man had developed second thoughts about snitching for the GRU. If so, he would soon find out that a relationship with the GRU worked in one direction only: you got in by invitation, but once you were in you never got out. Unless, of course, it was in a two-meter pine box.

He sat at his desk, calming himself, then buzzed his secretary on the intercom.

"Sir?"

"Get Captain Oborin on the phone for me." Oborin was the GRU officer running the search for Borodin.

A few minutes later his phone rang. "Nikitin. Speak."

"This is Captain Oborin, sir. You wanted to speak to me?"

"*Da*. Report."

"So far we have come up with nothing, sir. One of my teams has checked all the groceries, gas stations and transportation facilities north, south, and east of the city to a distance of fifty kilometers. No one has seen the man. That team will be shifting to the western sector today. My other teams are working inside the city and have canvassed about fifty percent of it. Again, no hits.

"What does the KGB office in Vlad report to you, sir?" Oborin asked.

"Nothing. It has gone dark. Either the KGB search team isn't talking to the office in Vlad anymore, or my informant in that office has been turned and he's not talking to us. Is the KGB team still working here in Khab?"

"Yes, sir. Occasionally our people run into them on the streets."

"Okay. I want you to reassign several of your teams. Have them put the KGB search teams under both audio and visual surveillance. If the KGB goons turn up anything, we can move in and grab Borodin before they do."

****

Galina backed out of her driveway and headed for Janet Lancaster's house. Lancaster was the wife of the group commander of the 34th Fighter Squadron, and had invited Galina and several other women to a holiday get-together.

Galina was lonely, worried, depressed and somewhat angry. There had been no word from Jake or from Bill Jensen. She desperately missed her husband, a longing made more acute by the holidays. Her emotional funk colored everything and was making even the normal tasks of life feel insurmountable.

The work of setting up the baby's room had become overwhelming, given her bleak mood. It should have been a joyous thing shared with her husband, but now it was all on her shoulders. And though she was excited about the birth of her first child, now just four months away, she'd begun to wonder if it would be an experience she would face alone: no husband, no mother, no family member with whom to share this joy—no one to give her courage through her fears.

The party invitation had come as a life preserver on a stormy sea, and she grabbed it eagerly. She'd been looking forward to the event ever since the invitation arrived. Galina hoped the gathering would help shake off her gloom and get her mind off her worries.

Janet greeted her at the door. "Come in, come in, Galina. Let me take your coat. Ooo, you're showing already, even though there's, what, four months plus change to go?"

Galina smiled. "Thank you. Yes, my baby is due in April."

"How are you feeling?"

"I'm okay. The morning sickness has stopped, but now I'm ravenous. I feel like I'm eating all the time."

Janet stepped back and swept her eyes over Galina's lithe frame. "Well, honey, I wouldn't worry about it. You don't seem to be putting on any weight. Come on back, the girls are in the den."

"Where's Colonel Lancaster?"

Janet laughed. "I've banished him from the house for the evening. This is a girls only affair. I think Brent is probably catching up on his paperwork at the base."

****

"Okay, she's gone. Move in."

Four figures crept around to the back side of the Kelly house, shielded by the dark, overcast evening. They were each wearing mottled black and white camo, and melded into the shadows cast by the streetlight against the snow. One picked the backdoor lock while the others stood watch, then they all silently entered the house. Once inside, each put on a pair of booties to prevent snow from being tracked through the residence.

"We're in. How are we doing?" the leader asked over his throat mic.

"Fine," replied a man parked a block down from the Lancaster's house. "She just arrived and went inside. You're good. I'll let you know if she leaves."

The team inside the house planted a bug in the telephone and several listening devices around the house. Tiny video cameras were installed in the kitchen's ceiling light, as well as in a heating duct in the living room.

"Vitaly, how's it look?" the leader asked.

An agent in a van parked down the street responded, "The signal from both cameras is clear, but adjust the kitchen cam. I've got too much of the refrigerator, and not enough of the table and sink . . . a little more . . . a little more. Yeah, that's good. Now give me a sound check."

Ten minutes later the men exited the house, and the last man brushed out their tracks in the snow.

****

As the party drew to a close, one by one the other ladies left until only Janet and Galina remained. "Have you heard anything from Jacob?" Janet asked. She had avoided the subject all evening and had steered the conversation elsewhere when any of the other women swerved close to the topic of Jake's whereabouts. All Janet knew was that Jake was on a special top secret assignment that involved a significant amount of danger—she didn't know where he was or who he was working for.

"Nothing. Nothing at all. I guess one side benefit is that I'm learning to pray a lot more readily than I otherwise would have," she responded, trying to put a positive face on the situation.

"Okay, honey. Everyone is gone—it's just you and me. How are you really?"

Galina burst into tears. Janet set a box of tissues next to the distraught woman, then put her arms around her and hugged her until Galina's sobs subsided. When she could finally speak again, Galina dabbed her eyes and dropped the wet tissue on the growing pile at her feet.

"I'm afraid. I'm lonely. I'm worried that something bad has happened to Jake, or might happen. I'm falling apart and I'm embarrassed. And when you add the fact I've got a baby coming, well, it's just too much. I thought Christians were supposed to be strong, and right now I'm not very strong."

Janet smiled, "Oh, honey, you got it all wrong. We're not strong—we're weak. We just throw ourselves on Christ's strength. Paul says in 2 Corinthians 12 that His strength is perfected on our weakness."

The two women talked for an hour, and by the time Galina was ready to leave she felt much better. Just before she got up to get her coat, Janet asked, "How's your Bible reading doing?"

"Okay, I guess. I'm reading four or five chapters every day, but I'm not really getting a whole lot out of it. It's just sort of going over my head."

"What are you reading?"

"I'm in the book of Numbers right now."

"Oh, mercy sakes, honey! That's not what you need to be reading at the moment, especially considering all you are going through. The Old Testament is wonderful, Christ is on every page, but when you're just starting out you're going to miss it simply because you don't have a good handle on the New Testament. You've already read the Gospels, right?"

"Yes, several times. I loved them."

"Okay, here's what I want you to do. Read through the rest of the New Testament, starting in Acts. But every day, I also want you to read three or four of the Psalms. You'll find very quickly that the psalmists had rough days just like you. You can even pray the Psalms back to God, because you'll frequently find that's what your heart wants to say anyway. You'll soon discover that God strengthens your heart through His Word.

"I'll call you several times each week, and we can talk about what you're reading, and you can ask questions about things you don't understand. How does that sound, Galina?"

"Wonderful. Thanks so much, Janet—I think I really needed to tell someone what's really going on inside." She hugged the older woman. "I feel a lot better now. I'll look forward to your calls."

****

"What's the latest?" the driver asked, never taking his eyes off the road. He was wearing sunglasses though the morning was dark and overcast.

Interior Minister Yulian Churkin tried to examine the man through the rearview mirror, but it must have been bumped out of alignment because all he could see was the driver's knees. Churkin shrugged and began his report. "Everything is in motion, it's happening soon. Pushkaryov has scheduled a major speech to the *Duma* at 3:00 PM on 20 January. He's circulated a draft of his speech among the members of the *putsch*. I've read it. He'll be accusing Gorbachev of letting the Americans get away with the harassment of Soviet naval vessels on the high seas *in the service of his irresponsible dream of glasnost*. Those are his exact words. Five hours later, during the inauguration of the new American president, the provocation with the US navy will happen, and Pushkaryov will look like a prophet while Gorbachev looks like a traitorous fool."

"And the actual coup attempt?"

"Still scheduled for 24 January. Everything then will be focused on Moscow. The nation will be experiencing outrage over the 'unprovoked attack' by the US battle group on our submarines. Shukshin and Pushkaryov both believe those four days of outrage will secure most if not all of the military to their side. No one will be in the mood to defend Gorbachev by then. He'll be a man completely alone."

"Which carrier battle group will be provoked?"

"I don't know. In the name of operational security, Shukshin refuses to tell anyone. Not even Pushkaryov knows that."

"Will we fire first, or will they?"

"Admiral Shukshin is being very coy about that, too. The official plan is that we provoke them to launch the first weapon. But so far that has never happened. The Americans have remained very cool-headed about our past provocations."

"So what does your gut tell you?"

"You want my opinion?"

"*Da.* I believe that's what I just asked for."

Churkin hesitated, then came to a decision. "Okay, listen: I haven't mentioned this to anyone because I have no hard evidence to back it up. In my opinion Admiral Shukshin is a dangerous loose cannon. I think his submarines will be ordered to fire if the Americans don't take the bait. I believe Shukshin wants to bag an aircraft carrier, and I think he'll wind up getting us into a major war. It's just my opinion, but I've been around Shukshin enough to get a hint of his insane dreams.

So please be sure you pass that along to Geredin.

"And as long as you want my opinion, tell Geredin that the last man standing is not going to be Pushkaryov—I think it will be Shukshin. Again, I have no hard data to support this, but I'm convinced that Shukshin has his own plans for Pushkaryov. Shukshin sees himself on the top of the pile—Pushkaryov is nothing more than his ticket to get there."

The driver raised his eyebrows in surprise. This was a vital piece of information he had not expected.

Churkin asked, "Is there anything else you need to know?"

The driver shook his head. "*Nyet*, but I have a piece of intelligence for you. It's in my coat pocket, let me get it." He slowed down and pulled over to the side of the road.

The driver removed his sunglasses, turned around, and shoved a silenced semi-automatic in Churkin's face. "You might want to make sure your driver really works for the KGB before you open your mouth, you pathetic rat." He fired twice, and Churkin's lifeless body slowly slid sideways down the seat.

The driver drove downstream of the city along the Moskva River, then turned onto a dirt road that led to the river in a heavily wooded area. There was a rowboat tied up to a tree. He pulled the body out of the car and attached lead weights to the hands and feet. Wiping the weapon clean, he unscrewed the silencer and threw it into the river, then placed the pistol in the corpse's coat pocket. He rowed out into the river fifty meters or so and dropped the body overboard. "Long live the *rodina*. Death to rats and imperialist traitors," he muttered as he rowed back to the bank.

****

It was New Year's Eve and Galina still had no word from Jake or Bill Jensen. But her conversations with Janet Lancaster and reading the Psalms had helped. She was still lonely and worried, but the frustrated anger was gone along with the depression.

The grocery store was crowded with people purchasing

last-minute staples and snacks, and it took her twice as long as usual to make her weekly purchases. Finally she got through the long checkout line.

Galina wrestled the bags of groceries into Jake's red Chevy Silverado, cleared the snow off as much of the windshield as she could reach, then brushed the snow off her jeans and slid behind the wheel. Normally she would be teaching advanced math in the Ogden City school district, but the schools were closed for the holidays. Even if they hadn't been closed because of Christmas and New Year's, they would have been closed because of the early winter storm that had already put down six inches of snow, with much more to come. The forecasters were predicting a brief midday lull followed by blizzard conditions with a two-inch-per-hour snowfall that would continue into the next morning.

She reached down to verify that the truck was in four-wheel drive and then carefully drove through the crowded parking lot and turned onto Washington Boulevard. If the grocery store was crowded, the roads were not—traffic was very light. Light enough that when she turned off the boulevard into her subdivision, she noticed a black Suburban following her into the neighborhood. Yesterday she'd observed a strange black van parked half a block down the street from her home, but had thought nothing of it. Now, however, the hair on the back of her neck stood up. After having lived most of her life in the Soviet Union, the consummate surveillance state, she'd developed a sixth sense for it. Somebody was watching her.

"Well, buster, let's see what you do with this," she muttered.

She pulled into her driveway, and the Suburban pulled over a half-block down. Putting the truck in reverse, she backed out of her driveway and then continued forward down the street. The Suburban pulled out and followed her. She took a three-mile tour through north Ogden, and the tail stuck with her all the way.

"Aren't you people a little obvious, whoever you are?" she spoke aloud to herself.

She was clearly under surveillance, but she didn't know who was watching her or why. Multiple scenarios raced through her mind, none of them good. Though she kept a steely grip on her nerves, Galina felt herself edging toward panic. She drove back to her home and pulled in the driveway. The Suburban resumed its station half a block down. Quickly she grabbed her groceries, retrieved the day's mail from the mailbox, and retreated into the house.

Galina locked the door and set the groceries on the kitchen table. Running to the bedroom she retrieved Jake's pump-action twelve-gauge and loaded the magazine with five rounds of magnum double-aught buckshot. She carried it into the kitchen and hid it in the broom closet. Returning to the bedroom, she pulled the Smith and Wesson Model 60 out of her nightstand. She spun the cylinder and checked the loads. Satisfied, she safetied the weapon, stuck it in her waistband at her back and pulled her sweatshirt over it.

After rechecking that all the doors and windows were locked, she sat at the kitchen table and wondered what she should do. Trying to stay calm, she made herself a cup of coffee and a sandwich. The wind outside rose to a howl, and she could hear snowflakes pelting the kitchen window.

****

"Churkin is missing."

"Well, find him! He was supposed to report this morning, and things are heating up. He met with the cabal two days ago, and we must know what he knows," snapped Geredin. He immediately regretted it. "Vladimir, I'm sorry," he admitted to the chief of the Third Directorate. "My headaches have gotten worse, and my arthritis is so painful today I can hardly endure it. I had no cause to be short with you."

"No offense taken, Anatoly. How much longer do you think you can do this? Why don't you retire? I can see the pain in your face--you're white as a sheet. It's time to buy a *dacha* on the Black Sea, my friend, and enjoy the rest of your days. You don't need this," Dobrynin said. His concern was genuine.

Geredin was his friend and mentor and though the man was ruthless, he was also honest and loyal to his friends, so long as they were loyal to the *rodina*.

"Just, just let me see us through this crisis, and then I will step down. You should know this, Vlad—I'm going to be recommending your name to the Politburo as my replacement. I have full confidence that you can lead this organization as it requires."

"I am honored, comrade."

"Yes, well, locate Churkin before you start redecorating my office, will you?"

"I'm afraid you don't understand, Anatoly. Churkin's contact, his driver, was found dead and stuffed in a trashcan this morning. Churkin's office confirms that he was picked up by his car just after 9:00 AM. He hasn't been seen since."

Geredin sat down heavily, his head in his hands. "Then they know that we know. The coup plotters, I mean."

"*Da.* Somewhere along the way Churkin must have slipped up, or perhaps their surveillance on him was better than we thought."

"*Da.* The watchers watch the watchers, who are watching others, who are, in their turn, watching still others," Geredin sighed. "That's the problem in this country—you never know when there's going to be a new revolution—always have to be looking over your shoulder. It's exhausting.

"Get me some tea, will you, Vlad? It hurts too much to walk over to the samovar to get it myself." Geredin paused, thinking. "Has there ever been even a hint that the GRU is involved in this coup plot?"

"No, sir. Neither Churkin nor our intelligence from other sources has ever implicated the GRU—not in this, anyway."

"Good. At least there's not that complication. Okay, alert the *militsiya* that the interior minister is missing. Tell them to begin an aggressive search to locate him—or his body, if it has come to that."

****

"Dr. Jensen, you have a call on the secure line from Admiral Blackstone."

"Very well. Put him through, Marge."

Jensen picked up his secure telephone. "Jensen here."

"Dr. Jensen, this is Wally Blackstone, Office of Naval Intelligence."

"Congratulations on your appointment, Admiral. I've read some of the classified briefings on your exploits with the SEALs before you landed at ONI. Very impressive."

"Thanks, Dr. Jensen. You're no slouch yourself. You probably don't remember this, but it was my boys securing your landing sites when you were visiting all the places in Southeast Asia where we weren't supposed to be during 'Nam."

"Was it your guys in Cambodia, sir? Thirty or forty clicks east of Kampong Thom? As I remember, that was a particularly, ah, exciting landing. One that I was glad to walk away from."

"Oh, Jensen—let's not talk about Cambodia, please! What a headache. There weren't supposed to be any hostiles in that area, according to intelligence. I believe it was that mission in which I realized that 'naval intelligence' was a contradiction of terms. The irony is that now I'm heading up that contradiction."

Jensen laughed. "We both survived, Admiral. Now, what can I do for you?"

"I'm sure you've seen the latest NRO images of the sub pens at Vladivostok. Wondering what you make of it."

"Yes, I have. On Christmas Eve there were a couple of boomers tied up at the provisioning wharf. Yesterday's pass showed those vessels in the anchorage—which is unusual for a submarine—and two *Akulas* and a *Kilo* at the provisioning docks. The satellite tech at NRO who's been riding herd on the Vlad sub pens for several years says that these movements do not align with the Pacific Fleet's normal operational tempo.

"More worrisome than that, Admiral, is the weaponry they are taking on. The best analysis of the Keyhole images indicates that the SSNs and the *Kilo* are being provisioned with a full weapons loadout. That's definitely abnormal. Due to maintenance problems and parts shortages, Ivan's SSNs usually sail with only a fifty-percent weapons loadout.

"Something is definitely in play and whatever it is, it isn't good. We've received HUMINT that there are some nasty things planned for later January, but we have no details as to what."

"You've got boots on the ground in Vlad? How'd you manage that, Jensen?"

"Admiral, you know I can't comment on that."

"Of course. My bad. Does this change any of the recommendations you made at the last NSC meeting?"

"No, sir, because I was told that the president wants to avoid a potential war at all costs. That little phrase, *at all costs*, is rather crucial."

"Indeed it is."

"Admiral, if I were in your position, I would be strongly encouraging the brass over at Seventh Fleet to let their flat-tops know that we're expecting something nasty from the Sovs later in January. Maybe we can't use anticipatory self-defense, but we can sure sail with eyes wide open. No vessel operating between the east coast of Africa and the west coast of the USA should be treating those waters as peacetime waters. Not in January, anyway."

****

The wind howled, the snow swirled, and the day got even darker. Picking up her coffee, Galina walked to the front window. Though it was midafternoon, the thick, blowing snow had reduced visibility to almost nighttime levels, and she could no longer see whether the Suburban was still there. The snow was falling in nearly horizontal lines.

She returned to the kitchen and suddenly remembered the mail. There was a life insurance advertisement, a gutter-guard sales piece, two credit card offers, and an envelope bearing Cyrillic characters. She threw the junk mail away and sat down at the table, examining the strange envelope. Though the destination address was hers, the addressee was Susan Bates. Susan was a dear friend and had comforted her the year before, when she thought Jake was dead. *I wonder if it's been misdirected? No, that can't be, it's my address. Is it to her, or to me? Should I open it?*

Then Galina noticed the sender—Roger Carson, somehow in Khabarovsk. She knew Carson—he was with the CIA and had provided security at her wedding. *What is he doing there? Why would he risk his cover by sending a letter here? Surely he knows about the censors?*

Thirty years in the USSR had equipped her with skills possessed by most alert Soviet citizens. She stared at the envelope for a moment and then examined it more closely. Sure enough, it had been opened and then resealed. She tore open the envelope and read the letter.

> *My Dearest Susan,*
>
> *Having a wonderful time in Khabarovsk. I am staying at the Intourist Hotel. It seems that is the best location for finding people and places you wish to see, although it's not worked out so well for me. I'm here on business for Georgia-Pacific, hoping to follow up and confirm a potential deal but my counterparts never showed up. Apparently the logging industry near Sidima isn't all that healthy. I'm going to try to return home in January if I can get tickets. I don't want to be here when weather conditions get really bad later in January.*
>
> *My friend from the logging cooperative had promised to take me to a soccer match—which I was really looking forward to. Our meeting kept getting pushed back, due to various business issues, and to my disappointment I find it is no longer soccer season. As you know, Susan, I love sports. One of my fondest memories in football is "The Catch" from Montana to Clark back in '82. I had hoped to see some amazing football play here—I've heard that the team in Khab is really good. Of course, when you*

> *mention football in the USSR, you really aren't talk-*
> *ing about American-style football!*
> *I look forward to seeing you and the baby when I*
> *return. Please be sure to give my regards to my dear*
> *friend Bill.*
> *All my love,*
> *Roger*

It was complete nonsense. She doubted it was written by Carson, and she was confident it was not written to Susan Bates. And yet it referenced some things she was familiar with, particularly the logging operation near Sidima. And then it dawned on her: the carefully written Cyrillic was in Jacob's own handwriting. Her hand went to her mouth and her heart skipped a beat. The only reason Jake would write such non-sense, yet referencing things Galina was familiar with, was if he was in deep trouble and needed to communicate but knew the censors would open the letter. Apparently there was some-thing she was supposed to figure out, but she couldn't make heads or tails from the letter. And then her eyes rested on the last line: *Please be sure to give my regards to my dear friend Bill.*

Bill Jensen! She raced to the bedroom and retrieved her purse. The day Jensen recruited Jacob he had given her the phone number of a direct line to his office at the CIA.

Her hands were shaking and she was holding back tears as she dumped the contents of her purse on the bed and franti-cally sorted through them, looking for the slip of paper. *Ah, there!* She grabbed it and ran to the telephone. Her hands were shaking so badly she had to try three times before she was able to dial the whole number correctly.

"This is Dr. Bill Jensen's number. I'm sorry, I'm not at my desk. If this is an emergency, please press star-one-nine, and you'll be connected to someone who can find me."

The reels on the tape recorder in the black van three blocks down the street began to turn.

She fumbled with the handset but finally was able to punch in the number.

"Soviet Desk Duty Officer. Who are you trying to reach?"

She tried to say Bill Jensen but it came out as a sob.

"I'm sorry, could you repeat that?"

"Give me a minute," she managed to squeak, trying to control her breathing.

"Take your time, miss."

When she was able to control her voice, she said, "Bill Jensen, please. This is an extreme emergency."

"What number can he reach you at?" She provided her phone number, and the voice on the other end assured her, "I will contact him immediately. Please hang up and wait for his call."

She hung up the phone and sat at the table wondering how long it would take Jensen to return the call. She got up and walked to the front window. The wind was beating against the living room window so powerfully she could see the pane of glass flexing. Snow was hitting the window and sticking to it. *Soon*, she thought, *I won't even be able to see outside.*

Suddenly the lights went out. She ran to the phone and picked it up. The line was dead.

"It's—it's just the storm," she said aloud to the empty house. She hurried over to the broom closet and retrieved the shotgun, then sat down at the kitchen table to wait. Then she realized that Jensen would not be able to contact her since the phone line was down, and she began to cry again.

****

"He says to move in," said the first man, snapping his sat phone off.

"Now? In this?" replied the second of three. They were sitting in a black Suburban half a block down from the Kelly residence.

"That's what he said. And he cautioned us that she's probably armed."

The driver started the car and picked his way through the blizzard. It was hard to see the road and virtually impossible to tell where the driveway was located. He made his best guess and turned in but the vehicle lurched violently as it bumped over the curb.

"Good enough. Turn it off and let's go."

Chapter 18

"Come on, come on, come ON!" Jensen muttered as the phone continued to ring. He'd been trying Galina Kelly's number repeatedly for the last ten minutes, but there was no answer, and he was worried about what that might mean. When the duty officer gave him the message, he had mentioned that the woman was so distraught she could hardly speak.

All kinds of heartbreaking possibilities occurred to Jensen: was there a problem with the pregnancy? Had she lost the baby? Had she been in an accident? He was on the verge of calling his wife Susan and having her return the call, woman to woman, when a troubling possibility occurred to him—what if the Soviets had captured Kelly and somehow they were putting pressure on Galina?

His secure line rang, startling him. He snatched it up. "This is Dr. Jensen."

"Dr. Jensen, this is Al Mercer, NRO. The bird just passed over the sub pens at Vlad. The submarines have sailed—all five of them. Not a trace of them. Just thought you'd want to know."

****

"Stop it! Stop it! Get ahold of yourself, Galya! You can't fall apart now!" Galina shouted at herself. Gritting her teeth, she wiped the tears from her eyes, blew her nose and went in search of a flashlight, toting the shotgun with her. Not only was dusk coming on, but the fierceness of the blizzard had reduced the light to practically nighttime conditions.

As she walked through the living room headed for the bedroom, she saw a dark form pass by the living room window. Her heart skipped a beat and she dropped behind the couch. Her brain told her that it was darker inside than outside, that the window was almost opaque with encrusted snow, and whoever was out there could not have possibly seen her.

Someone began banging on her front door. Taking cover

behind the couch, she raised the shotgun. Anyone coming through that door was going to earn a bellyful of buckshot. She clicked the safety off.

"WHO IS IT?" she shouted, trying to raise her voice above the clamor of the storm.

She couldn't hear a reply and the banging continued. She got up from behind the couch and crept to the front door to look out, but the peephole was blocked by snow.

Moving off to the side of the door, she shouted, "WHO'S THERE?"

The banging stopped and a garbled shout gave the reply.

"WHO? I CAN'T UNDERSTAND YOU!"

"Mrs. Kelly?" a voice behind her inquired.

She screamed and whirled around, shotgun at her hip, ready to defend herself.

"WHOA, WHOA, MA'AM!" shouted the snow-covered man, empty hands above his head. "DON'T SHOOT! Please, for mercy sake, don't shoot!"

"WHO ARE YOU? WHAT ARE YOU DOING IN MY HOUSE?" she screamed, tears of terror running down her face.

"CIA, ma'am. Bill Jensen sent us. I'm part of the security detail Dr. Jensen dispatched to protect you."

"What? How could—Oh, my, I need to sit down before I fall down."

"Can I get you a chair, Mrs. Kelly?"

"DON'T MOVE!" she shouted, the shotgun coming up again.

"Whoa, hey, I'm not moving, I'm not moving."

She slowly sank to the floor, shotgun still at the ready, trying to catch her breath. She looked up at the man. "I don't believe you. I just called Dr. Jensen. No way you could already be here."

"No, of course not. Dr. Jensen decided yesterday that there should be a protective detail keeping an eye on you. We arrived early this morning, ma'am. I know you spotted us earlier today. Dr. Jensen tried to return your call a few minutes ago. When he couldn't get through he became worried about you and ordered us to make contact with you."

"How do I know you're not lying? How do I know you're not KGB?"

The man started to lower his hands.

"HANDS ABOVE YOUR HEAD!"

"Oh, sorry. Yes ma'am." He thought for a minute. "Last time Dr. Jensen was here, you asked him about his CIA career in Vietnam, and you asked him how his wife Susan dealt with her fear for his safety. He told you that they both dealt with their fear through their faith in Jesus Christ. Later that day, you, Major Kelly and Dr. Jensen hiked the Thurston Peak loop trail."

"How could you know that?" she asked, surprised.

"Jensen told us. He also told us that you would probably welcome us at gunpoint, and that we would need to prove our bona fides to you. Did I pass the test?"

She nodded.

"Can I put my hands down?"

She nodded again, lowered the shotgun, and fainted.

When she came to, she was lying on the couch covered by a blanket, and there were four men seated around her kitchen table drinking coffee. She got up and walked into the kitchen. They all jumped to their feet. Two of them she recognized from the security detail at her wedding.

"I've seen you before," she said, pointing at the man who seemed to be their leader, "you were at my wedding."

"Roger Carson, at your service, ma'am. This big tall galoot is Paul, he was at your wedding, too. That guy over there who's built like a Sherman tank, that's Murphy. And the young fellow there who picked the lock on your back door, well, that's Jimmy."

"I've seen you before, Mr. Carson, why didn't *you* come in the back door? At least I would have recognized you. Jimmy scared me to death; I nearly killed him."

"Well see, ma'am, that's the very reason I didn't come in myself. I figured you might pull the trigger on your scattergun, and I didn't want that thing pointed at me when you did. So I sent our most expendable guy. We wouldn't lose much if we lost him. He's kind of like our sacrificial lamb, ma'am, if you know what I mean."

He said it without smiling. Galina studied his face, trying to discern if he was joking.

"It's true, ma'am. I always get the dirty work," affirmed Jimmy gravely. He looked around at the other men. "Let's see, how many times have I been shot, now? Five? Six? I'm losing count."

The corners of Murphy's mouth twitched and he coughed, trying to cover the grin on his face with a handkerchief.

Galina shook her head and rolled her eyes.

Carson chuckled, took out a sat phone and started dialing. "You'll be wanting to speak to Jensen, and I expect he's dying to talk to you. He was worried sick about you."

****

Jensen's secure line buzzed. "This is Dr. Jensen."

"It's Carson, sir. I have a young lady here who wants to speak to you. She's a little calmer than she was a few minutes ago."

"Oh, praise the Lord. Put her on, please."

"Mr. Jensen, this is Galina. I am so relieved to speak with you."

"Are you well? Is everything okay? The message I received said you were distraught."

"Yes, I was—or, I am. I received a letter today from Khabarovsk. It is addressed to Susan Bates at my address, and the sender on the envelope is Roger Carson. I don't know what to make of it."

"What? Carson? Impossible—he's standing right next to you. He's not been out of the country in at least a month." Jensen thought for a moment and decided to level with her. "Galina, are you sitting down?"

She turned around and gestured for a chair. One of the men brought her one and she sank into it gratefully.

"Yes, sir. Is this about Jacob?" she asked, fearing the worst.

"Yes."

****

One of the men in the black van shook his head as the reel on the tape recorder continued to turn. He removed his headphones and looked at his partner. "They must be using a sat phone. We're only getting one half of the conversation."

"But is the audio distinct? Can you tell what they are saying?"

"*Da.*"

****

"Is Jacob okay?" Galina asked, trembling.

"We don't know. I can't tell you where he is or what he's been doing, but we know he's been compromised."

The secrecy irritated her. This was her husband Jensen was talking about, and America was her country now. *Does he really think I'm a security risk?* she asked herself angrily. "Well, then, Dr. Jensen," she replied icily, "let me tell you where he is and what he is doing. He's in Khabarovsk and he's asking for help —he's trying to come home."

There was silence on the line for a moment and then Jensen asked carefully, "Galina, how can you possibly know that?"

"Because that letter is from him—it's in his handwriting. It's written in some sort of code, but I know it's from him."

"Are you positive?"

"Of course," she snapped. "I know my husband's handwriting. And although it's hard to figure out what he is saying, it is clear he is trying to get home."

"Give it to one of my men—he'll see that I receive it."

"Dr. Jensen, I know that you are Jacob's friend. But I'm not about to part with this letter—especially after your protective team lied to me. How do I know you won't just bury this letter and Jacob becomes just another casualty in the spy game between America and the USSR? How can I trust you?"

"Lied to you? How did Carson lie to you?"

"He said they just arrived this morning—but I spotted them yesterday."

"What do you mean?"

"I spotted a black van down the street yesterday. It had followed me through town, just like earlier today. They've been watching my house."

There was silence on the line for a moment. "Put Carson on."

She handed the phone to Roger Carson. "Yeah, boss?"

"Did you spot any other surveillance?"

"No, sir. But we arrived in a blizzard and you honestly can't see more than thirty feet at most."

"Have you swept her house?"

"No, not yet. I thought you'd want to hear from her immediately."

"Hang up now and sweep it. Then call me back."

****

Vitaly cursed and ripped off his headphones. He reached over and stopped the reel-to-reel recorder. He spoke into his throat mic to the other half of his team. "Pack it up. They're going to sweep the house. They'll find our stuff, and they'll come looking for us. We need to leave town now. If we get separated for any reason, head for the consulate in San Fran. Besides—the weather's better there anyway."

Two hours later Geredin received a message:

```
COVER BLOWN. ABORTING MISSION,
RETURNING TO SAN FRAN CONSULATE.
TARGET HAS CIA PROTECTION DETAIL
LED BY ROGER CARSON, ARRIVED
TODAY. "CARSON LETTER" ALSO
ARRIVED TODAY. CONFIRMED KELLY IS
IN KHAB, SEEKING EXTRACTION. NO
FURTHER DETAILS AVAILABLE.
```

****

"Yeah, it was dirty. Two video cams and a handful of bugs, including one in her phone."

"So they would have heard there is a letter," Jensen observed, shaking his head.

"It's no loss, though, Bill. Mrs. Kelly says they already have the letter. She knows it was opened by the censors."

"Okay. Well, have Jimmy fly back with the letter so the lab can examine it. You and the rest of your team stay in Utah to keep an eye on Mrs. Kelly."

"Sir, with all due respect you're probably going to need Mrs. Kelly to interpret the letter. Falcon might have included some personal allusions only she would recognize. Besides, it will be safer for her in DC."

Jensen thought for a moment, seeing the wisdom in Carson's suggestion. "Okay, another change of plans. Grab the first flight you can and fly back with Mrs. Kelly. Bring your whole team, except leave Jimmy to keep an eye on the place. Have Jimmy open the mail each day, in case Kelly tries to contact us with another letter. Susan and I will put Galina up at our house—she'll be safe there, and she can help us parse the letter. Have her phone calls forwarded to my house."

"Got it."

****

It was Tuesday morning, 3 January, 1989. The headline story in the *Washington Post* was a piece citing unnamed sources in the State Department claiming that the political battle in the Soviet Union was heating up between conservative anti-Gorbachev forces and the more liberal faction supporting *glasnost* and *perestroika*. One source had questioned whether interior minister Churkin's unexplained disappearance might be related to the conflict. Sam Bergman read the article carefully twice, looking for evidence that anyone in the intelligence community was leaking information. He breathed a sigh of relief, concluding that the basis for the story had come from Foggy Bottom, not the Firm.

Bergman glanced at his watch and downed the rest of his

coffee in a gulp, then headed for the office. He arrived just as Bill Jensen was escorting Galina Kelly into the building.

"Keep this with you at all times," Jensen said, handing Galina a lanyard with her photo ID. It was her temporary "visitor" credentials that would allow her on the elevators, in the cafeteria, canteen, and the halls of the Agency, but not in any secured areas without a properly credentialed escort.

"Sam, this is Galina Kelly, Jacob's wife. Galina, Sam Bergman, the CIA's top Soviet analyst." As the doors opened and the three boarded the elevator, he turned to Bergman. "Meet me in my office in ten minutes, please. I need your help with something."

****

"Come on in, Sam, and take a seat," said Bill Jensen. "I need to enlist the assistance of both you and Mrs. Kelly in a matter, but before we get started let me lay out the ground rules. Recent circumstances have made it necessary for me to brief Mrs. Kelly on very limited aspects of highly classified matters. I have received written permission from the DCI for both you and me to discuss these things with her. The DCI went all the way to the top to get that permission. Here is your copy," he said, sliding a piece of paper across the desk to Bergman. Bergman picked it up, scanned it briefly, then folded it and placed it in his coat pocket.

"Therefore I am informing you," continued Jensen, "that you are free to speak of the following matters in her presence, though she has no security classification. She is aware that her husband is in the Soviet Union on a CIA operation, and she knows that Major Kelly has been compromised. That's it. She is not aware of his code name nor is she cognizant of the nature of his mission or the name of the operation, nor any of the extended circumstances associated with it. It is not my intention to divulge any of that information to her. Do you understand?"

"I understand, sir," Bergman said, nodding. It was a serious federal offense to disclose classified information. Bergman was thankful that Jensen was toeing the line by getting explicit authorization in writing.

"Now that we have covered the legal necessities, can you both agree with me to drop the Mr, Mrs, Major, Dr, and so forth? It will make our conversation much less clumsy if we can just be Sam, Galina, and Bill. Everyone okay with that? . . . Good, let's get started.

"The reason I need you two in this room is to help me decipher a letter Galina received from Jake."

"What?" Sam asked, surprised. "A letter? How on earth? Are you sure it's really from him?"

"Positive, Sam," Galina replied. She pulled the letter out of her purse and handed it to Bergman. "It's in his handwriting."

Bergman scanned it. "Russian. Hmm. Maybe we ought to get Evelyn Stinson to help with this," he suggested, looking at Jensen. "Her Russian is much better than mine."

Galina cleared her throat. "Excuse me, Sam, but I was born in the USSR and lived there for thirty years. I can translate it just fine."

Bergman slapped his forehead with the palm of his hand. "Oh—right. Of course, forgive me Galina." He handed the letter back to her. "Please read it to us."

After she read the letter aloud twice, the DDO said, "What we need to do, then, is to figure out exactly what Jake is communicating to us. Clearly, at the time he wrote this, he was still free."

"Yes," agreed Bergman. The analyst thought for a moment and then said, "I think there are several things that pop out to me at once. First, he is somewhere close to the Intourist Hotel in Khabarovsk, and he's telling us that's where to find him. Not at the hotel, of course, but close to it. Second, he wants to leave this month—January. His statement about the weather conditions probably has to do with wanting to leave before the search for him intensifies. So I'd say he's asking for an extraction sometime in January and that he can be found somewhere close to the Intourist Hotel."

Both Galina and Bill nodded in agreement. "Galina and I discussed that much on the way over. It's helpful to have another set of eyes concur."

"What about the references to logging industry and Sidima?" Sam asked.

"I think that Jacob was mentioning those because I know about them. I think he was putting them in the letter as another way of signaling to me that the letter is coming from him."

"It would also be a piece of accurate information, combined with the Georgia-Pacific reference, that might fool the censors into thinking it was a completely innocent letter," suggested Jensen.

"True," nodded Sam. "If that is the case then we probably don't need to look for any other hidden information in the logging references. Read the letter again, Galina, would you?"

After she did, the analyst commented, "Based on the last couple of sentences, he knows you are pregnant—that's another confirmation that the letter is from your husband. And he clearly wants Bill to get ahold of the letter. But why would he sign it as Roger Carson? Why not John Doe, or John Smith?"

After a few moments' thought, Jensen replied, "Because he knows Roger. He'll recognize Roger. Given that the KGB is searching for him, Jake will probably be in disguise or remain in hiding until the last minute so he is exposed as briefly as possible. Our people won't see him, and he won't know our people unless I send someone he will recognize. So he wants me to send Roger."

"That makes sense. It's good thinking on Kelly's part," Sam acknowledged.

"What about the soccer reference?" asked Galina. "He's never paid the slightest bit of attention to soccer. As far as Jake is concerned, American-style football is the only football there is."

"Read that paragraph again," asked Jensen.

Galina reread the paragraph:

> *My friend from the logging cooperative had*
> *promised to take me to a soccer match—which I was*

really looking forward to. Our meeting kept getting pushed back, due to various business issues, and to my disappointment I find it is no longer soccer season. As you know, Susan, I love sports. One of my fondest memories in football is "The Catch" from Montana to Clark back in '82. I had hoped to see some amazing football play here—I've heard that the team in Khab is really good. Of course, when you mention football in the USSR, you really aren't talking about American-style football!

"The soccer references are not about soccer," Jensen suggested. "They are a way of getting football—American football—into the letter. I don't think the reference to his friend is significant, either. It's all about giving a credible intro to a statement about football."

"Which would mean there's something important buried in the reference to *The Catch*," observed the analyst.

"Yes," Jensen agreed, nodding.

"But he says he is not talking about American-style football," objected Galina.

"No, he says *when you're in the Soviet Union* you're not talking about football. There must be some sort of clue buried in that reference."

The three sat thinking and batting around ideas but nothing seemed plausible. After half an hour of this, Jensen picked up the phone. "Marge, place a call for me to the *Pro Football Hall of Fame* in Canton, Ohio."

"Smart move," Sam muttered. "Why didn't we do this earlier?"

Jensen's phone buzzed and he picked it up. "They're on line three, sir," said Marge.

"Thanks, Marge." He punched line three. "Hello, is this the Hall of Fame? Great. Listen, my name is Bill Jensen and I have a question about a specific game from 1982. Do you have a historian there? No? A curator? Yes, can you connect me to him, or her?" After a moment Jensen continued, "Thanks for speaking with me, sir. I understand that there was a famous football play in 1982 known as *The Catch*. . . Yes! That's the one—Montana to Clark. What can you tell me about that game?" Jensen scribbled furiously for the next few minutes. "Okay—that's just what I needed. Thank you so much."

He hung up the phone and clapped his hands excitedly. "Of course! It makes perfect sense. We know the letter is from Jake. We know he wants an extraction. We know that we'll find him somewhere around the Intourist Hotel in Khabarovsk. But what are we still missing?"

Galina looked confused, but Sam Bergman said slowly, "We don't know *when*. Jake cannot continuously expose himself in public when the KGB is looking for him, so he's got to tell us when he'll show up. I'm guessing it needs to be a pretty brief window."

"Exactly!" exclaimed Jensen. "We don't know when he wants the extraction—at least we didn't, not until that phone call. The game was the NFC Championship game played on January 10, 1982, and the game time was 4:30 PM."

"He's looking for Roger Carson to lead an extraction on January 10 at 4:30 PM, somewhere close to the Intourist Hotel in Khabarovsk," said Bergman, looking at Jensen. "That's just seven days from today."

"Yes. And he's given me just barely enough time to set it up."

****

"Come in, Roger."

Roger Carson entered the DDO's office and took a seat. "What's up, boss?"

"How would you like to perform in a little Kabuki theater, Rog?" asked Jensen, grinning.

"As long as you don't make me wear a muumuu. What's on your mind?"

"Major Kelly has gotten himself into a bit of hot water, and we need to get him out of the USSR. I've made an extraction plan, and you are at the center of it."

"Sounds like fun, but you do know the KGB and I are practically on a first-name basis, right? I can't get on a flight at Dulles without everyone in the whole Soviet security apparatus knowing about it."

"Actually, that's what I'm counting on."

Carson's eyebrows shot up. "Oh, really? This should be interesting."

"I'm sending you in under a diplomatic passport as an economic attaché. Your cover story is that you're investigating economic opportunities for US companies to invest in logging operations in the Khabarovskiy Krai."

"Yeah, but as long as it's my mug on the passport, that's not going to fool anybody."

"I know, Roger. Kelly asked for you specifically, and I understand why he did. But this extraction isn't going to look like anything you've ever done before."

For the next fifteen minutes Bill Jensen outlined the plan. Carson was still chuckling when he left his boss's office.

****

"Anatoly, I've got it! I know the date when Major Kelly wants to be extracted." The voice on the phone was that of the head of the KGB's First Directorate, Vasily Vasilyevich Orlov.

"Come up to my office, then, Vasily. And bring Dobrynin with you."

A few minutes later the heads of the First and Third Directorates were sitting in Geredin's office. "Help yourself to tea, comrades. And if one of you would pour me a cup, I'd appreciate it. I find that I'm having trouble moving about today."

Dobrynin poured his boss a cup of tea and brought it to him.

"*Spasibo.*"

The head of the Third Directorate pointed to a wheelchair in the corner. "Is that why—"

"*Da,*" snapped Geredin, cutting him off. "Don't ask. Ignore it. Pretend it isn't there."

When all three were seated again, the director of the KGB said, "Share your news with us, Vasily. What have you learned?"

"The American football game mentioned in the letter the censor intercepted took place on January 10, 1982. I believe the reference was placed in the letter to tell the Americans when their spy would be looking for the extraction."

Geredin pinched his lip, thinking. He reread the copy of the letter which had been sitting on the top of his desk ever since he had received it. Finally he nodded. "*Da.* That makes good sense. Well done, Vasily. Do you have any indication that the Americans are preparing for an extraction?"

"I do, sir. The American embassy has submitted a request for travel approval to Khabarovsk on 9 January for an economic attaché traveling on a diplomatic passport. They are asking for reservations at Intourist, Khab. And sir, you simply will not believe me when I tell you who that attaché is."

"I'm not up to guessing games today, Vasily. Just tell me who it is."

"Roger Carson."

"No!"

"Yes."

"Carson? The only American better known in this country is the president. Are you sure it's the CIA's Carson and not some different Carson?"

"Positive: the embassy has already submitted his name, a photograph, and a faxed copy of his passport in order to get travel permits."

"Wait a minute," said Dobrynin. "Carson has a reputation for direct action. He's a lethal operator. Aren't they risking a lot exposing him in this way?"

"*Nyet,*" mused Geredin. "We've known what he looks like for a long time—and what's more, the American DDO, Dr. William Jensen, knows that we know. The thing about Carson is that you never see him coming. He's the consummate clandestine operator. That's what makes this so odd.

"When they send him out for this operation, there's no risk

to him as long as he keeps his nose clean—especially not when traveling on a diplomatic passport. Vladimir, make sure your people are on him like red on the flag. Pick him up if he steps over the line even in something minor.

"No, . . . this is a chess move worthy of a grand master. Jensen is up to something—I just don't know what. It seems a classic ploy of distracting your mark with the left hand while you pick his pocket with the right. Except for one thing."

"What?"

"It's too obvious even for that, and my opponent, Dr. Jensen, is far more subtle. Which bothers me."

Later that afternoon Geredin called Captain Kira Fukina, who was handling the KGB search in Khab.

"Kira, report."

"We've not spotted him, sir, but we know he's in this area somewhere. I now have six confirmed sightings of him from various citizens, but my team has not spotted him once. He's like a ghost, sir, a specter."

"How about the GRU search teams?"

"They are watching us, and we are watching them watching us. Their teams have been beefed up, sir. They outnumber me and they don't seem to mind that we've spotted them. In fact, I'd say they are flaunting their presence. If I had to guess, Director, they're going to try to take him away from us if we nab him."

"*Da*, that sounds like the GRU. Okay, listen Kira, that letter has paid off handsomely. The Americans are sending Roger Carson to handle the extraction, and it's going to take place in three days on the tenth, at or near the Intourist Hotel."

"Carson? They're sending him?"

"*Da*, and get this: he is coming as himself, no less, and on a diplomatic passport. Which makes me think he is not the real extraction team. Be aware that some sort of trick is probably in play by the Americans. We just haven't figured it out yet."

"What do you want me to do about the GRU?"

"I'm sending you twenty more agents, Kira. They will arrive tomorrow. Analyze the tactical situation and deploy them as you see fit. Just don't lose our prize."

"I'll do my best, comrade Director."

"Kira, I have full confidence in you—that's why I sent you and not someone else. I know you can do this. Make me proud of you."

****

January 10 dawned clear, dry, and cold. With a frigid wind blowing out of the north, the breeze brought the two-degree temperature down to a wind chill of minus ten. As the clock advanced toward the late afternoon, Kelly filled all four coal bins, then cranked a fresh load of coal into the fireboxes, and refilled the bins once again.

He leaned the shovel against the wall in the little office, walked back to Usilov's flat and showered, then gathered a few personal items. He shrugged on his coat and then dropped all that remained of his rubles on the kitchen table. He turned to face his friend.

"Stas, I have to leave you now, and I won't be back. I don't know how to thank you for all your kindness and generosity to me. You'll never know how badly I needed it. You've had more of an impact on my life than you can imagine. You said something several days ago that I cannot get out of my mind: *what God requires, God provides*. That is an entirely new thought to me, and I've been chewing on it ever since. I will continue to think about it, Grandfather, for a long time."

The old man hugged him and then stepped back, his hand on the younger man's shoulder. "You may refuse to accept it, but you, Maslov, were an answer to my prayers. God brought you along at just the right time. My back is fine now, but I could not have tended the boilers the last two weeks. I would have lost my position and probably my flat. *Spasibo*, dear friend."

Kelly turned to go, and Usilov said, "God go with you, Yakov Kelly."

Kelly stiffened and slowly turned around. Usilov was smiling at him. "Did you know that you talk in your sleep, Yakov? In English?"

Kelly blinked. "How long have you known?"

"Oh, a week at least. No worries, Yakov. Your secret is safe with me. I'll be praying for you to get home safely, my friend, to your beloved Galina. *Do svidaniya.*"

****

Roger Carson sat in the lobby of the Intourist Hotel reading the English-language edition of *Pravda* and glancing at the clock every now and again. He knew that all the employees of Intourist were KGB employees, but he'd spotted two in particular that were keeping him under surveillance. In addition, a pretty waitress at the hotel's small bar was very attentive—too attentive, actually—to the point of flirting with him. But Carson knew a KGB come-on when he saw it. He played along, acting flattered by her attentions and projecting the image of a naive American government employee.

At precisely 4:30 he stood and wrapped his coat around him, keeping the collar away from his face so he'd be easily recognized. He walked out of the front entrance clutching a tourist brochure and map. Carson stood uncertainly on the sidewalk examining the map, as though trying to get his bearings. Fifty yards down the street he saw an old man sitting on a bench, bundled up against the cold, an *ushanka* covering most of the man's face, the flaps over his ears.

Carson started toward the man. Two men crossed the street next to the fellow and stood on the curb as though waiting for a cab. *KGB*, thought Carson. *This isn't going to go down well.* He continued walking and then a bearded old man in a coat and hood with a cane hobbled out of an alley to his right, nearly bumping into him.

"Roger," the old man whispered.

At that instant the street exploded into chaos, agents coming out of cars, taxis, the doors of the businesses along the street, and at least five men racing out of the entrance of the Intourist Hotel.

A trio of burly plainclothes men pressed Carson face-first against the wall, shouting, "KGB, put your hands behind you! Now! Now!"

The old man with the cane evidently found a surprising surge of energy as he dropped the cane, straightened up, and dispatched three attackers in as many seconds, one with a snap-kick, another with a helicopter kick, and the third with a smashing blow to the face.

The old man down the street was dragged howling off the bench and stuffed in a car until someone evidently in charge ran down the street screaming, "*Nyet! Nyet!* He's the wrong guy!"

Kelly dropped three more KGB agents with ease. No one managed to lay a hand on him until finally six men surrounded and overwhelmed him. They wrestled him to the ground, handcuffing his hands behind him.

Carson did not resist, and was likewise handcuffed and forced into a car while loudly protesting his diplomatic immunity.

"SHUT UP AND SIT STILL!" snarled the man in the front seat.

Kelly was yanked to his feet and frog-marched to another waiting car when suddenly a dozen black-clad men descended on the scene from every direction, brandishing identification credentials. "GRU! GRU! HE IS OUR PRISONER!" shouted Major Roman Romanovich Nikitin.

"I don't think so," said Captain Kira Fukina calmly. She nodded to her confused agents. "Put him in the car. He's ours."

Nikitin gave a signal to his men and suddenly a new melee erupted. It was a blue-on-blue fight, KGB agents fighting hand to hand against the GRU officers. The GRU quickly gained the upper hand due to the fact that each was a highly trained *Spetsnaz* operator. Adding to the one-sided nature of the scrap was the fact that Fukina had not counted on Kelly taking six of her toughest operatives out of action all by himself. The KGB found itself seriously undermanned and in less than five minutes it was over. GRU officers pushed Kelly into a waiting Zil-117 sedan and drove away.

All of this without a weapon being drawn. Officers from both sides knew that fisticuffs were acceptable, but gunplay would ignite a murderous conflagration that would spread between the two organizations from one end of the USSR to the other—and no one wanted to risk that.

Fukina turned her back on the scene and spoke into a radio, "They're on their way."

The KGB men gingerly helped one another up. There were not a few broken bones between them, and multiple nasty gashes and bruises. After dispatching the injured to the local hospital, Fukina came over to the car holding Roger Carson.

"I've always wanted to meet the great Roger Carson," she said, enjoying her triumph. "But I'm a little disappointed. Your buddy put six of my men down. I didn't see you do any. You were like a lamb."

He chuckled sourly. "Orders from headquarters, lady. I was told not to lay a glove on anyone. And besides, the guy you just picked up and promptly lost? You're pretty lucky that he didn't put down your entire crew. Ask Geredin next time you see him.

"I believe I have the right to call my embassy, and you don't really have the right to hold me. I'm traveling under a diplomatic passport, and I did not resist arrest nor did I threaten any of your people."

She nodded. "You can call your embassy, but you are staying in handcuffs under my supervision until we drop you on the doorstep of your embassy."

"Fair enough."

She shook her head and rolled her eyes. "Economic attaché, my foot. By the way, that was the sorriest attempt at an agent extraction I have ever witnessed."

Carson just looked at her and grinned.

Chapter 19

The black Zil, followed by a second one, sped through Khabarovsk toward the headquarters of the Far Eastern Military District, which also housed the GRU headquarters and the district holding cells. It was exactly where Fukina thought they would go, on the off chance the GRU managed to steal the KGB's prize.

Suddenly a garbage truck darted out of an alleyway, and the Zil crashed into it. The second Zil barely missed rear-ending the first by swerving into oncoming traffic, which proved to be a mistake. It collided headlong with a taxi going the opposite direction. A swarm of ten KGB agents rapidly descended on the two vehicles while the occupants were still stunned. They yanked Kelly out of the car and just as quickly melted into the alleyways. They brought him to the local KGB headquarters where a strengthened perimeter guard of twenty-five agents took up positions, but the precaution was unnecessary. The contest was over and the KGB had won the second round.

Roger Carson was flown back to Moscow under guard and immediately expelled from the country.

****

Geredin cleared his desk, storing the papers he was working on in his safe. He extinguished his samovar and hobbled wearily to the door where his heavy overcoat hung on a coat tree. He sighed as he struggled to get into the overcoat, his shoulders painfully protesting the movement. Grabbing his briefcase, the old spy took the elevator to the street level, and exited the Lubyanka to *Lubyanskiy Proyezd*. As he made his way toward his waiting Zil-4104 limousine, a passerby bumped into him, nearly knocking Geredin over. Geredin's driver rushed over and pinned the man against the wall.

"Idiot! Watch where you are going!" he shouted.

"Forgive me, comrade, I did not see him!" cried the terrified man.

"It's okay, Boris, no harm done. Let the poor man go. Just help me get in the car," said Geredin, grimacing.

As the driver began to negotiate Moscow traffic, Geredin heard a phone ring. He looked around the seat and found no source of the sound. Suddenly he realized the sound was coming from the pocket of his heavy overcoat. He pulled out an unfamiliar American-made sat phone and then realized the accident outside the Lubyanka was actually a 'flash meeting,' or in CIA lingo, a 'brush pass.'

Confused, he flipped a switch to raise the soundproof barrier between him and the driver and then answered the call.

"Hello?"

"Now, don't get excited, Anatoly. Your boys can reverse engineer this phone all they want, but I have ensured that they'll find nothing that you haven't already stolen from us, including the encryption."

Geredin ignored the jibe. "I assume I have the pleasure of speaking to Dr. Bill Jensen."

"You do indeed."

"So why didn't you just contact me through normal channels, Dr. Jensen?"

"Well, I considered a bench in Gorky Park, but I don't expect you are jogging nowadays."

"Your intelligence is superb as always, Doctor," Geredin said sardonically.

"In truth, Director, we have matters to discuss that we both wish to remain private. I figured it might be useful to have a backchannel where we can be quite frank with one another. Now, speaking of things stolen, I believe you have something that belongs to me."

"I believe I do."

"I want it back."

"*Nyet.*"

"You'd better rethink that. You don't want the US government to make a speech before the U.N. General Assembly, laying out in glaring detail what your country did to us, to Britain, to France, to Israel—need I go on?"

Geredin didn't respond, but massaged his temples with his free hand. In addition to the pain of his arthritis, he now had a pounding headache.

Jensen continued, trying to sound conciliatory, "Listen, Anatoly, the entire reason Major Kelly was at Vladivostok was to verify the concerns you shared with me in September. You wanted me to do what I could to ensure that American naval vessels did not rise to the aggressive provocations of your Pacific Fleet. You were concerned that the conservative factions within your country might start a war in their attempts to overthrow General Secretary Gorbachev. You asked for my help to prevent a coup. That's why Kelly was in Vladivostok. We were not trying to steal Soviet secrets—we were trying to ascertain the accuracy of what you said. And we did verify it. I have helped you—now it's your turn to help me."

"Dr. Jensen—"

"Bill, please."

"*Dr. Jensen*," Geredin said emphatically, "please understand the position you have placed me in. Major Kelly's spying is known to the GRU, the KGB, and virtually the entire body of enlisted men and officers at Vladivostok. If I simply hand him back to you, that will ensure the success of the coup. I will be accused—and Secretary Gorbachev as well—of being in league with the American CIA. That will give the hooligans plotting this coup far more power and clout than if the US were to fire a couple of torpedoes in our direction. Surely you can see that? If you box me in, we will execute Major Kelly as a spy. You can go to your United Nations and say whatever. But I cannot do what you ask."

It was Jensen's turn to be silent. He had not anticipated the consequences to his counterpart. He had inadvertently placed Geredin into an impossible position. And now Jensen's ace in the hole was an unplayable card. The internal unrest that would be fomented by Kelly's release easily trumped the international outrage that would be raised by the exposure of the scientist-kidnapping scheme. It was high stakes poker, and Jensen's bluff had been called.

Jensen played his last card. "What if I sweeten the pot?"

"How? What do you mean?" asked Geredin.

"I know who killed Admiral Zelenko. I have firm, physical evidence that I can give you. I know who ordered the hit, I know who arranged for the hit, and I know who carried it out. This evidence would go a long way to solving the problem with your coup plotters—it would put them in a very bad light."

Geredin pulled at his lower lip, thinking. He had his suspicions, but he had no evidence. With evidence—if his suspicions proved true—he could probably sway much, if not most, of the wavering loyalty of the navy. Zelenko had been a very popular officer with both the enlisted and officer corps.

Ah, all of life is a gamble anyway, is it not? Who knows whether they will live or die, or how death will take them? Random chance rules. And is that not just as true with a nation as it is with an individual? thought Geredin. *I have gambled on trusting my adversary once, perhaps a second time will prove out as well. In my soul I hope it does—I could not bear the thought of breaking Galya's heart by executing Kelly. But I will if there is no other option.*

Geredin sighed. "Dr. Jensen, I will give you twenty-four hours to come up with a way in which both of our concerns are served—but no more. I am sitting on a powder keg and the fuse is burning."

"Thank you, Director. Can I give you a piece of critical advice for the next twenty-four hours?"

"And what would that be?"

"Even if it is false hope, give Major Kelly a reason to believe that we are working something out. Two years ago the GRU learned what Kelly can do when he feels he has nothing to lose. You don't want the KGB to learn the same lesson. I'll call you again this time tomorrow," promised Jensen.

****

The DDO burst out of his office, startling his secretary. "Marge, I hate to ask you this, but can you stay till midnight? I'll need you to make calls and do some research for me."

"That's no problem, Dr. Jensen. I'll call my husband and

let him know."

"Thanks so much. I have a list of phone calls for you. Have you got a pencil? . . . Good. First, call my wife and tell her I won't be home this evening—an emergency has come up. Then call Sam Bergman, tell him to meet me in my office in an hour, and to be prepared to stay overnight. As soon as Roger Carson lands—he's on a flight from Moscow which lands in thirty minutes—I want him in my office, too. Then call that Asian carryout in Fairfax—I forget the name of the place—and get dinner for, say, six people. Have it here by 7:00 PM, please, and make sure you order some of what you like."

Two hours later, Bergman and Carson were in Jensen's office. "We have twenty-two hours to come up with a plan—diplomacy, trickery or direct action—to secure Major Kelly's release," Jensen announced.

"Where is he being held at present?" Carson asked.

"The KGB facility in Khab, I presume," Jensen said.

"No, that can't be. The GRU snagged him. Snatched him right away from the Lubyanka boys," said Roger. "I watched it happen—it was quite a brawl."

"Yeah, well, the KGB picked the GRU's pocket a little later, Geredin informed me. He didn't elaborate, but Kelly is now in KGB custody."

Carson shrugged. "Good grief. Our fair-haired boy has had more partners than a pretty girl at a dance. What now?"

"What's the possibility of a rescue by force?" Bergman asked.

"Slim to none, and Slim's out of town," Carson quipped. "The KGB is probably loaded for bear right now, watching for a counterraid by the GRU. I watched the *Spetsnaz* guys pick them apart in hand to hand on the street. My guess is that Mr. Makarov will be calling the tune in the next showdown."

"So how can we get Kelly out of this mess? We need to give Geredin a good reason to hand him over," Jensen said.

"I expect the USS *Nimitz* could provide a pretty convincing argument," Carson muttered.

"Roger, you're not helping. Whatever solution we come up with must avoid inflaming the Soviet hard-line faction and strengthening their hand."

Several hours and an Asian carryout dinner later, they were still drawing blanks. It was beginning to look like a problem without a solution, and Jensen was steeling himself against a heartbreaking conversation with Galina Kelly.

"We actually have two problems," Carson said, wearily. "If the Sovs don't give him up willingly then we'll have to spring him from their custody, and then get him—and anyone else involved—safely out of the country. And in case anyone has forgotten, it was our inability to exfiltrate Kelly that got us into this mess in the first place."

Somehow that line about "getting him safely out of the country" triggered a vague memory gnawing at the edge of Jensen's consciousness. And it also brought an idea. "Sam, the Sovs have a terrorism problem, don't they?"

Bergman rubbed his bleary eyes and shook his head. "No, not really. They keep things pretty locked down. Why?"

Jensen persisted, "C'mon, Sam, with all the people the USSR has run over, surely they've got some organized opposition somewhere?"

"Well, if you put it that way, certainly," Bergman agreed. "I guess the Afghan mujahideen would qualify. They hate Ivan's guts."

"The mujahideen will have to do," Jensen said. "What if we enlist their help?"

****

"Marge, get me Rear Admiral John Bridger on the line. He's the CO of Navy Special Warfare Group One in Coronado, California. If anyone sandbags you, tell them it's an emergency. Once you get him on the line, Margaret, you can go home. It's nearly 1:00 AM. I just sent the other two home as well."

A few minutes later she buzzed Jensen's intercom. "He's on line one."

"Thanks, Marge. See you tomorrow." Jensen punched line one. "Admiral Bridger, thank you, sir, for taking my call. I've got something of an emergency here, and I need your help. You remember Major Jacob Kelly, I'm sure."

"Till my dying day, Bill. So, what's up?"

"Well, you'll never guess where Kelly is right now."

"You're kidding?"

"No, I am sorry to say, I am not. And I need a way of getting him home that has plausible deniability for everyone involved. Isn't it true that the first clue regarding Kelly's shootdown several years ago came from a friend of yours, a man operating, shall we say, on the slightly shady side of the law?"

"Why do you ask, Bill?" Bridger asked suspiciously. The last thing he wanted to do was get Ned Bascomb in trouble. Bascomb had been one of the best SEAL team leaders Bridger had ever mentored. The man was tough, intelligent, and decisive, and had never failed any mission he'd been given. But his family had grown and Bascomb had eventually retired from the SEALs, to the everlasting relief of his wife.

Bascomb now ran a general merchandise store in Nome, Alaska with two branches serving the Yup'ik Eskimos on Saint Lawrence Island, one in Gambell, and one in Savoonga. However, the close proximity of the eastern tip of Siberia was too tempting, and the former SEAL had set up a profitable smuggling arrangement with a retired Soviet Air Force officer, Georgi Sukharov, living in Provideniya.

It was Sukharov who had first heard of the illegal shootdown of Major Kelly's F-16 in the summer of 1986, and Sukharov who brought it to Bascomb's attention. In the end, it wound up being the principal clue that cleared Kelly of suspicion that his long stay in Siberia had been a defection rather than a high-tech kidnapping.

Bascomb and Sukharov never dealt in illegal drugs, weapons, or human trafficking, but be that as it may, their smuggling operation was still on the wrong side of the law—in both countries.

"I need Commander Bascomb's help getting Kelly out of the Soviet Union and back to the States."

"No can do, Bill. First, he doesn't deal in human traffic. Second, he doesn't want anyone looking too closely into his business. And he's told me the same goes for his Soviet counterpart. I'm sorry to waste your time. My heart goes out to Major Kelly, but I cannot help you."

Jensen had predicted Bridger's response and was ready for it. "Okay, would it change anything if I could get an affidavit guaranteeing that any goods Bascomb brings into the United States would be legal and duty-free for Bascomb's lifetime? This statement would be signed by the president and the attorney general, as well as Alaska's governor and the state attorney general. That would put Bascomb's operation on the right side of the law for the rest of his life."

Bridger thought for a moment. "Yes," he said slowly, "Ned might agree to that. But what about his Soviet partner?"

Jensen swallowed hard, because not only did he lack the authorization from US authorities (although he was certain he could get it), but he clearly had no pull on the Soviet side. Geredin would have to play ball if it was going to get done. *In for a penny, in for a pound*, he thought, *might as well go for broke.* "Yes, I think I could swing a similar deal for his Soviet partner."

"Then yes, I think that might change Ned's mind."

"Admiral, could you float it to him as a hypothetical and get his response? I don't have much time left to do this—hours, really."

"Is it that important, Jensen?"

"Admiral Bridger, I know you understand the intelligence business—I don't have to explain 'need to know' or 'sensitive compartmented information' to you. But Kelly has been involved in some crucial intelligence gathering at the risk of his own life. The critical intelligence that he has provided could result in saving navy lives and even entire navy vessels, both here and in the Soviet Union. Unfortunately, he was captured. I simply can't leave him there."

"If he's in custody, how do you expect to get him out? Can my SEALs help?"

"Not this time, Admiral, for reasons I can't get into. But I need a plan to exfiltrate him if we are able to spring him. And I am rapidly running out of time."

Two hours later, Jensen was sleeping on the couch in his office when he was awakened by the CIA's Soviet Department duty officer to take a phone call from Admiral Bridger. Bridger assured him that if he could get the necessary agreements signed, Bascomb was onboard.

****

Kelly lay on his cot with his hands behind his head, staring blankly at the ceiling and musing on his situation. *Some extraction. And Carson didn't help in the scuffle one bit. Okay, that's not exactly fair—he probably saw immediately that the situation was hopeless. Looks like the GRU and KGB are still in the midst of their catfight. What a goofy place. And wasn't I in a situation like this just two years ago? At least that sadistic maniac Chernikov is not involved—I can be thankful for that.* He sat up and swung his feet to the floor. *Well, I got myself out of the last scrape, maybe I can get out of this one, too. Sorry, Mr. Jensen—you've had your try. Now it's up to me, and it's liable to involve a lot of blood.*

He heard footsteps and then the rattle of keys. The iron door at the end of the hall swung open, and a uniformed woman walked to his cell and stood, looking him over. "Captain Kira Fukina, KGB," she said.

"Major Jacob Kelly, USAF," he responded, standing up and stepping over to the bars that separated them.

"Are all US pilots trained in mixed martial arts, Major? You did pretty well for yourself in our little scrap."

"Yeah, well, I was in a bad mood. I don't like it when people interfere with my extraction. Although the *Spetsnaz* boys had the upper hand, you somehow reeled me in anyway. Not bad."

"They're too predictable. I knew where they were taking you, so I had a second team in place—just in case. They weren't ready for it, and my people won the second round. By the way, you might find it interesting that the same GRU officer responsible for finding you on your last tour of Siberia, Major Roman Nikitin, was also heading up the GRU search for you this time. He failed again. You've beat him twice now

—not bad yourself, Major Kelly."

Kelly laughed dryly, "Yeah, with an unexpected assist from my KGB friends. So what's next, Captain?"

"Your government is negotiating for your release. Any violence on your part, any attempt to escape, will terminate those negotiations. So behave yourself and you just might find yourself on a flight home."

"What happened to my pal who was supposed to extract me?"

"Oddly enough, he violated no laws and he made no effort to resist arrest. We tried to bring some charge against him, but since he didn't approach you or even speak to you we couldn't really tie him to you. I watched the surveillance tapes after the scuffle because I found Carson's behavior curious. Carson's attention was focused on an old man on a bench down the street, so it appears he misidentified you. Since Carson was here on a diplomatic passport, Director Geredin ordered him released. So we sent him home. Knowing Roger Carson's reputation in the CIA, I was rather surprised at his docile behavior."

"You're not the only one. Some hero," Kelly scoffed. Since she seemed willing to talk and he had nothing else to do, Kelly asked, "So what happened to the old fellow on the bench? I saw your people dragging the poor guy into a car."

She smirked. "When Carson focused on him, some of our over-eager officers thought the old man must be you, so they grabbed him. After questioning the old fellow—Usilov was his name, I believe—they realized he was unrelated to the whole incident. He was released. Just happened to be in the wrong place at the wrong time." She shook her head. "Odd. Were it not for the old fellow distracting him, Carson would probably be occupying another cell down here."

Kelly smiled. *I believe Bill Jensen would call that divine providence. And I can't argue with him.*

"What? Why are you smiling?" Fukina asked.

"Do you believe in God, Captain?"

"Are you kidding? The notion of God is a crutch for weak people who are blind to reality. Why do you ask?"

"Like you, I have not believed in Him either. But I'm beginning to wonder if it is I who have been blind all this time."

****

"Director Geredin," said Jensen, "I might have an idea that will address both your needs as well as mine. I admit, it is very unusual, but it just might work. What if . . . ?" It took some explaining and convincing, but in the end Geredin was sold on the idea and even enthusiastic.

"Dr. Jensen, I will take care of all the arrangements on my end. It will take me two days to get a signed agreement for Major Sukharov, but I believe we should move ahead in the meantime with all the other preparations. Are we agreed to put the plan into action on the 17th?"

"Yes, Director Geredin. The tides, the moon and the weather are all forecast to be favorable on that day."

"Very well. In two days I will call you on this phone to verify that Major Sukharov has agreed. On the other matter, I must tell you that all the intelligence I have is pointing to some sort of showdown on 20 January. Can you confirm, Dr. Jensen, that your ships have been told not to fire first?"

"Anatoly, you know that I cannot and will not divulge operational information about the United States navy or its posture."

"Of course, Bill. I had to ask. I'm sure you understand."

"What I can tell you is that the intelligence you shared with me back in September has been confirmed to the best of our ability.

"And Anatoly, as soon as I learn that Major Kelly is back on US soil, I will divulge to you everything we know about the assassination of Admiral Zelenko. I think you'll find it interesting. You'll also find it quite actionable."

****

Retired Major Georgi Sukharov was underneath the deck

in the bilge on his fifty-foot work boat, replacing a faulty bilge pump. After installing the new pump, he clambered out of the bilge and walked over to the control console. He turned the bilge circuit breaker back on, flipped the bilge switch to manual and heard the reassuring *whoosh* of water coming out of the bilge thru-hull. He'd already tested the sender on the float that automatically activated the pump. Sukharov turned the bilge switch back to automatic, then dogged down the bilge access hatch and stood up. His coveralls were spotted with grease and his knees were soaking wet. The heater was on down in the galley, and he moved in that direction to put on dry clothes before his coveralls froze solid.

"Major Sukharov!"

He turned and spied a woman walking down the pier toward his boat. She was wearing the uniform of a KGB captain. His heart sank and he wondered if his smuggling days, as well as his freedom, were coming to an unpleasant end. He self-consciously looked down at his greasy coveralls and noticed that the knees were now frozen stiff.

"May I come aboard, Major Sukharov?" asked the woman.

"Please do, Captain. I'm sorry, but you have me at a disadvantage."

"Captain Fukina, KGB. I'd like to have a word with you."

"Of course. Please step into the galley. My wet clothes are already freezing, and I must get out of the wind."

He shut the hatch behind the woman and motioned to one of the seats. "Can I get you some coffee, Captain?"

"*Da*, please. *Spasibo*." She laughed and her face, which had exhibited a rather hard set to her jaw when up on the dock, now relaxed pleasantly. "This feels odd. You are the captain of this vessel, and yet you're calling me captain."

He chuckled. "Just trying to honor your rank, Captain. So what can I do for you?"

"Major, you are a man who understands the importance of secrets and the penalty in the Soviet Union for those who fail to keep secrets."

"Of course. As a major in the air force I was privy to many state secrets. Please continue, Captain Fukina."

"What I am about to tell you is one of those secrets. You may not repeat it to anyone, and if asked you are to deny all knowledge of it."

Sukharov nodded, "*Da*. Please continue."

"I have a mission to ask of you, a mission that comes straight from the General of the Army and head of the KGB. I refer, of course, to comrade Geredin. I am here as his representative.

"General Geredin is asking you to undertake this mission, but he is allowing you to choose, yea or nay, whether you will accept it. There will be no punishment nor recrimination if you decline."

"That is most unusual," Sukharov said. "And just what is the mission?"

"We want you to deliver a man to your American partner, Ned Bascomb."

"I'm sorry, but I don't understand. I have no 'partner,' as you put it. I do not know any Americans."

"You are a terrible liar, Major," Fukina said. "Comrade Geredin is fully aware of your smuggling activities, and we know whom you deal with."

Sukharov flinched.

"Relax, Major. Neither you nor your business is being threatened. We simply need you to make one delivery—and you will be amply rewarded for it."

"Rewarded how?"

"In addition to a monetary reward, a high-ranking official of the KGB will provide you with two formal documents on the same day your passenger is brought to you. The first is a blanket indemnity for all your prior smuggling activities. The second is a lifetime blanket permission to continue to engage in duty-free trade with your American partner. There will be, of course, a proviso that you may not transport illegal drugs, legitimate pharmaceuticals excepted, nor may you trade in weaponry of any kind, nor human trafficking.

"What we are saying, Major Sukharov, is that you may enjoy being a smuggler for the rest of your life—legally. No more worrying, no more looking over your shoulder."

"May I ask who this man is that you want me to transport?"

"You may not. All I will say is that he is an American. If he wishes to tell you more, that's his business. But whatever he tells you—this mission must remain a secret for the rest of your life, on penalty of death if you speak of it to anyone. You may inform your wife that your business is now officially approved by the State, but you may not tell her anything more about this mission."

"What if my American partner does not agree on his end?"

"He already has. He'll be looking for you just west of Gambell Shoal on the 17th."

"What about my crew?"

"Since your business is legal, their participation in it is also legal. Of course, you must never reveal to them our conversation."

"Yes, but I'll need a crew to make the trip."

"Fine, but again, you must not mention this conversation. They will, of course, know you are transporting someone, but they are to know nothing other than what they see with their own eyes."

"You realize this is a terrible time of year to make the trip."

"Your problem. Do you accept the mission or not?"

"I accept it."

****

"I don't understand. You never make this trip in the winter. You yourself told me—it's highly dangerous. The weather is bad and unpredictable." Karen Bascomb poured her husband a cup of coffee while he donned a thermal drysuit as the first of several layers of clothing.

"Karen, I'm just going to check on the stores at Savoonga and Gambell, and as long as I am making the trip I will bring them some extra supplies." It was true, but it wasn't the whole truth. Ned Bascomb was, after all, taking his sixty-foot aluminum Kingston to Saint Lawrence Island to resupply the stores the Yup'iks managed for him. He'd overnight in his Quonset hut at Gambell. What he didn't tell his wife is that tomorrow he'd make for the west side of Gambell Shoal to meet his trading partner and there pick up some mysterious person at the request of Admiral Bridger. Bascomb had decided to wait until his return to break the good news to his wife that his illegal smuggling business was now fully legal.

Through pure sweat equity and a piece of unfathomable luck—he purchased tech stocks before the boom—Bascomb had managed to purchase a brand new gleaming Kingston crew boat some years before. With the help of a local shipyard he'd removed the crew amenities and turned the boat into a small cargo vessel complete with a rotating boom containing a counterweight and traveling block. In good weather he could transfer six tons of goods to his similarly equipped Russian trading partner. Bascomb ran his two remote stores on Saint Lawrence Island at a loss, both as a humanitarian service to the Yup'iks as well as a means to launder his smuggling income. He also ran a legitimate general merchandise store in Nome.

"Okay, sailor, 'fess up," Karen demanded. "I know Admiral Bridger called you three days ago, and I also know you met him at the airport briefly yesterday. This is something he put you up to, isn't it?"

He grinned with the guilty expression of a child whose hand was caught in the cookie jar. "How on earth did you know I met Bridger?"

"I have my spies. Sally Parsons works the Alaska Airlines ticket counter, and she saw you two huddled together over coffee, thick as thieves. So spill the beans, Bascomb. And this time I want the truth—all of it."

Ned struggled with his neoprene drysuit for a moment and finally got both legs and arms into it. "This thing must be shrinking," he muttered.

"Actually, I think you're expanding a little around the middle," Karen snickered. "Don't change the subject, Ned," she warned.

Ned zipped the drysuit up, then sat at the kitchen table. He reached for his coffee and took a swallow before answering. "Okay, sweetheart, I wasn't going to tell you until I got back—but you already know too much to wait until then. Bridger contacted me with a task, a sort of mission. I can't say who's behind it, but you can use your imagination and you'll probably be right. I'm supposed to meet Georgi just west of Gambell Shoal tomorrow to pick up a special cargo. Unfortunately, I'm sworn to secrecy and cannot say what the cargo is. I know it's dangerous out there this time of year, but the mission is essential and time sensitive to those who are engaging me. And the payoff is—well, the payoff will solve your anxieties about my smuggling."

"What's the payoff?"

"In addition to our fees, both Georgi and I are getting signed affidavits stating that our trading business is now entirely legal and duty-free, for the rest of our lives."

She blinked. Worry that Ned would be caught someday, then convicted and jailed, had produced an almost permanent level of anxiety and churning in her gut. This could change all of that. "Seriously? Totally legal?"

"Totally legal. Georgi and I can continue our trading with no changes, except that now we are both on the right side of the law."

A few tears of joy trickled down her face. "I can't believe it. That is the best news I could imagine. And this one trip is all you have to do?"

Bascomb nodded.

"Oh, Ned, I am thrilled! But I'm scared, too. This is a terrible time of year to take the boat out."

"I know," he said simply. "I'll be careful. But remember—you cannot mention any of this to anyone. Period."

****

Bascomb took two of his regular crew with him. They were all wearing drysuits, multiple layers, and flotation devices. A southerly breeze of twenty-five knots produced chop and whitecaps in the tiny harbor as they left the mooring. Once beyond the breakwaters it got much worse for a few miles until the water depth went past seventy feet, and then the long, rhythmic ocean swells replaced the shallow water chop.

Bascomb kept his speed at fifteen knots, which would put him in Savoonga in about ten hours. Each man pulled a rotating duty at the helm, one hour on, two off. Halfway there the wind veered, and by the time they tied up at the Savoonga mooring buoy it was coming out of the north but had dropped to about twelve knots.

John White Bear met him at the landing. Bascomb had radioed ahead, asking the caretaker of his store to meet him.

"Look who's here. It's my fair-weather friend." White Bear teased Bascomb. "What brings you out in midwinter?"

"Surely it is my overwhelming love for you, John," Bascomb quipped, grinning.

The two men traded good-natured barbs for a moment, then Ned said, "Help me with these tubs, John. I have other reasons to be here, but thought as long as I'm coming, I'll rebuild your stock."

His crew remained on the boat as they wrestled heavy, sealed tubs into the skiff. Ned rowed them to the landing, and White Bear carried them up to his four-wheel-drive pickup. It took five drenching trips, but finally the tubs were safely stacked in the back of the truck.

"Can't stay, John. Want to get to Gambell before dark. Inventory the tubs, and we'll settle up this spring."

Three hours later Bascomb and his two men were in his chilly Quonset hut at Gambell. One man was firing up the coal stove, the other was cooking dinner, and Ned was studying the chart of the waters around Gambell Shoal. He was supposed to meet Georgi at N 64°00′00″ W171°06′00″ at 0900 hours tomorrow. Then it would be a long, cold run back to Nome.

****

"Put these on," the guard ordered. He threw a pair of

black jeans, a black sweatshirt, black thermal underwear, and black socks and boots through the bars.

"I think you've got the wrong guy," Kelly said, "aren't these for Johnny Cash?"

"Huh?" the guard asked, squinting at Kelly through the bars.

"You know—the man in black? Oh, never mind."

After Kelly had changed into the clothes, the guard thrust a black balaclava and black gloves at him. "These, too."

Falcon pulled the balaclava over his head. Only his eyes and nose were showing. He pulled on the gloves, wondering what was going on.

"Now back up to the bars. All the way. Good. Put your hands behind you." The guard reached through the bars and shackled Kelly's hands and feet, then unlocked and opened the door. "That way," he pointed.

Two other guards joined them as Kelly shuffled up steps, through a series of steel doors, and then out to a parking lot. It was early evening. The sun had already set, but it left a faint, fading glow in the west.

Kelly counted eleven figures in the dim light and noted that they were all carrying Kalashnikov assault rifles. He was pushed into the back seat of the middle vehicle of a three-car convoy and found himself sitting next to Captain Fukina, who was likewise armed with an assault weapon.

"You realize, Captain, you could have done me in with a twenty-two pistol down in my cell. Isn't this a waste of resources just to shoot one guy?"

"Certainly, but I've heard you are a very dangerous man, and one can't be too careful," she replied sardonically. "Besides, my men need target practice and you were rather handy." She spoke into a throat mic, "This is Night-star. All units report." Kelly noticed she was wearing an earbud. After a moment she spoke again. "Move out, Night-1."

For several minutes no one said anything as the convoy wound through Khabarovsk. After they had traveled several miles, Kelly could see the control tower of an airport in the distance. Then Fukina spoke again. "Night-1, this is Night-star. Pull over." The convoy pulled over to the side of the road. "Get out," she directed the two officers in the front seat. When they had exited the vehicle, she clicked off her radio and turned to Falcon.

"Listen to me very carefully. My government has approved your release, but it must not appear so. It must appear that you escaped. Do you understand?"

Kelly nodded.

"Good. In a few minutes we will pull onto the airport tarmac. Directly ahead of us will be a fully fueled Yak-40D. On board is a pilot and a high-ranking KGB official. This is the aircraft that is supposed to take you to prison in the Lubyanka, but the flight plan which has been filed makes a stop first in Provideniya, because the official has business there. You are going to hijack that aircraft. Sort of."

"Really? And how does that work? You've got eleven people armed to the teeth who are very motivated to not let me get away? And even if I do get away, how do I commandeer the aircraft? Threaten to choke 'em with my shackles?"

She looked at him and frowned. "Just shut up and listen. You will hijack the aircraft with this," she said, handing him a 5.45mm PSM semiautomatic. "Put it in your pocket until you need it. It is unloaded, of course. You won't actually need to hijack the aircraft, because the pilot knows the plan. The hijacking and the pistol is just a cover for them in case something goes wrong. They can make a plausible claim that you really were hijacking the airplane.

"When our convoy approaches the aircraft, we will be attacked by Afghan mujahideen terrorists. The airport will lose power momentarily—all the lights will go out. There will be a lot of gunfire, but do not worry—you will not be hit as long as you follow the plan precisely. My men will exit the automobiles and return fire. In the darkness and confusion you will escape. You will have no more than sixty seconds to sprint to the aircraft and board it before the lights come back on.

"The mujahideen will retreat—they are not your concern —and the lights will come on. My men will begin searching the perimeter of the airport for you. It will be believed that you are still in the area, which is why no one must see you board the aircraft. That is the most crucial part of the operation—everyone must believe you are still here. A new search for you will commence here in Khab.

"Once the danger of the assault has passed, the Yak will take off, following the flight plan to Provideniya. When you arrive there in about six hours, it will still be dark. You must exit the aircraft, dropping to the runway as soon as it completes its rollout, but before it taxis to the terminal. You will be met by a man who will issue the challenge, 'I believe you were here in August.' Your response is, '*Da*, the fishing was terrible.' He will respond with 'Let's go hunting next time.' From then on, follow his instructions precisely. He will return you to the United States."

"I don't get it. Why the drama?" Kelly asked.

She sighed. "It must not appear that the Soviet Union caved in to demands by the United States to release a spy who had penetrated our most sensitive installations. We cannot appear weak to our own people. Not in a time of such political conflict—it would be deadly to our nation. That is why you must 'escape,' and why you must be thought of as still here. In a month this will all blow over, you will reappear in the US, and the search here will be discontinued. It will be assumed by all that you escaped the country on your own—just as you did last time."

She reached down and turned her radio back on. "This is Night-star. It is time. Move out."

The agents reboarded the vehicle and the convoy entered the airport access road. They passed through two electrically operated gates and drove onto the tarmac. A Yak-40, its three Ivchenko AI-25 turbofan engines spinning at idle and its navigation lights blinking, sat on the apron about one hundred meters away. Boarding stairs were wheeled up to the cabin entrance.

Suddenly the sky was lit up with an explosion, and the airport lights went out. Automatic weapons fire erupted from a culvert to the right. The agents in all three cars spilled out, some taking up prone positions behind the vehicle wheels and others rolling into the culvert on the left.

Fukina unlocked Kelly's shackles and pushed him out of the vehicle. Kelly crawled to the left-hand culvert. It dawned on him that it was not until they'd all exited the vehicles safely that the windows were blown out, shattered from the gunfire, and rounds began hitting the side of the empty vehicles. He also saw that the agents in the culvert with him studiously ignored him.

Hunching low, he ran along the culvert until out of the line of fire, then raced directly for the Yak. He bounded up the stairs and entered the cabin seconds before the airport's emergency generators kicked in.

"Welcome, Major Kelly." A man in a business suit stood up and offered his hand. "I am Colonel Vladimir Leonidovich Dobrynin, KGB. I understand you are to be my fellow passenger to Provideniya. Would you care for a drink?"

****

Kelly heard and felt the wheels drop and lock into their landing position as the jet began its descent to the runway. Dobrynin turned to him and said, "There has been a slight change of plan from what Captain Fukina outlined. You will remain on the aircraft until we reach what passes for a terminal in this desolate place. The man who will transport you will board the aircraft momentarily, for I have some business with him. Then you and he will leave and I will return to Moscow. He will conduct you safely to where an American vessel will pick you up."

The spoilers and flaps on the wings deployed, and the pilot greased the Yak-40 down so gently that the contact with the runway was barely discernible. Dobrynin noticed how impressed Kelly was and commented, "He is a former air force pilot—among the best." The plane taxied to a darkened terminal, but evidently someone was there because a fuel truck sat idling and someone pushed the boarding stairs up to the cabin.

Dobrynin turned to Kelly as a man entered the cabin.

"Major, please put your balaclava back on and remain in your black clothes until you are at sea. I do not want to risk anyone seeing you."

"This is the man I am to meet?" Kelly asked.

"It is."

"Then please allow me to go first, Colonel." Kelly turned to the newcomer. The two men stared at each other until Kelly said, "Well?"

"Ah, forgive me. Um, I believe you were here in August."

"*Da*. The fishing was terrible."

"Let's go hunting next time."

Kelly nodded. "Thank you, Colonel. Please, proceed with your business."

Dobrynin passed over an envelope to the newcomer. "Major Sukharov, this envelope contains an affidavit from the general secretary of the Communist Party, as well as from the head of the KGB, certifying that your, ah, import/export business is now fully recognized as legal and is duty-free in perpetuity. There is a second document which indemnifies you from all past activities. A third document in the packet can be given to the local officials stating that they are not to interfere with your business, nor attempt to collect taxes from you. There is also some cash to cover your expenses for this mission."

Sukharov removed the papers from the envelope and examined them carefully. Finally his weathered face crinkled into a grin. "*Da*. All is in order. My thanks, Colonel Dobrynin."

"You realize, Sukharov, that the penalty for speaking of this mission to anyone will be death? What you are doing is considered a state secret of the highest order. Do you understand?"

"I do, sir. I would expect no less."

"Very well," said Dobrynin. "Good luck, comrade."

The two shook hands, and Sukharov turned to Kelly. "Follow me, please. I want to cast off before dawn."

****

A silent black shadow flitting through the depths, the *Los Angeles*-class submarine USS *Olympia*, SSN-717, prowled along the continental shelf separating the East China Sea from the Philippine Sea. Its mission was to compile data and statistics on the submarine traffic in the region and to survey likely areas for an extended Sound Surveillance System (SOSUS) network. SOSUS is a passive network of hydrophones designed to detect submarines at a distance, and is used by the US navy to facilitate tracking Soviet submarines in both the Atlantic and the Pacific.

The East China Sea ranges from a little less than one hundred feet deep as you approach the coast of China to around seven hundred feet at the edge of the Asian continental shelf. Once beyond the edge the depth falls to over three thousand feet. Travel another one hundred thirty nautical miles southeast from the initial drop off, and after briefly rising to a depth of two thousand feet, the ocean floor plunges to thirteen thousand feet and more.

If you draw a line connecting Kyushu, Japan to Taiwan, that five-hundred-fifty-mile line roughly describes the edge of the Asian continental shelf. It is a prime hunting ground for submarines. Chinese, Taiwanese, Philippine, and Russian submarines stalk their prey in the silent world under the surface of the ocean between those two points. The American *Los Angeles*-class attack submarines (also known as the 688 boats for the hull number of the prototype) attempt to detect, classify, and track them all.

The 688s were considered among the quietest nuclear fast attack subs deployed by any nation. However, by 1988 the Soviet Akula-class submarines (also known as the *Projekt* 971 boats) were providing stiff competition, thanks to honest improvements in Soviet domestic technology combined with some fortuitous foreign technology steals. The *Los Angeles*-class submarines still retained a significant edge, however, in passive sonar.

"Chief, I'm picking up weak intermittent tonals on the fifty hertz spectrum," Petty Officer Second Class Tim Emlet affirmed to the sonar supervisor, Chief Petty Officer Stan Lilly.

"Which sensor, Tim?"

"Spherical array, Chief, bearing three-three-one."

Lilly nodded. "Okay, let's see if we can get the TB-23 involved." An array of hydrophones towed several thousand feet behind the submarine, the TB-23 is particularly good at picking up low frequency sounds at long distances.

"Conn, sonar. Intermittent low frequency contact, bearing three-three-one. Probable submarine. Requesting a temporary course change to zero-six-zero to refine the contact."

"Sonar, conn, aye," said the Officer of the Deck, acknowledging the request. "Helm, come right to course zero-six-zero, ahead one third."

"Aye, aye, sir. Coming right to zero-six-zero, reducing speed to one third."

"Gotcha!" Emlet exclaimed ten minutes later. "Confirming submarine contact, now bearing three-two-seven. By triangulation, I'd say her range is approximately sixty thousand yards. She's a real egg beater, Chief, as noisy as they come. I'll bet next week's pay she's one of Ivan's old Hotel II-class boats."

"Conn, sonar. Confirming contact bearing three-two-seven, approximate range sixty thousand yards. Probable Soviet boomer, sir. Likely a Hotel II-class."

"Sonar, conn, aye. Designate the contact and send it to the tracking party."

"Designate Sierra-15, sending to tracking, aye, aye, conn. If you can give us another ten minutes on this heading sir, we can probably give tracking enough data for a TMA."

"You got it, Chief."

****

Captain Ben Mitchell, CO of the USS *Olympia*, SSN-717, came up the accommodation ladder from the wardroom and stepped into the control room. He watched in silent satisfaction for a moment, observing the control room crew perform their duties with quiet efficiency. *There's probably more noise in the public library in Honolulu than in here*, he thought with pride.

"What's the status, XO?" asked Mitchell quietly. His executive officer, Commander Gene Saddler, had the conn.

"We're sitting pretty until Sierra-15 passes us, then we'll move into his baffles and tail him. I don't think he knows we are in the neighborhood. He's behaving very erratically—making more noise than the UVA marching band, Skipper."

"Conn, sonar. We have a new subsurface contact, bearing three-two-zero. It sounds like another Hotel II, sir."

"Sonar, conn. Give me more data, Chief."

"Working on it, XO. We should have it shortly on our current heading."

"Sonar, conn, aye."

"It's getting downright crowded out here," observed Mitchell. "Two boomers, no less, but both of them model Ts. Why deploy them here? Those aging SS-N-5 missiles can only make nine hundred miles or so before they fizzle out."

"Perhaps the subs are in transit," suggested Saddler.

"Yes, Gene, but where to? If they were going to park them off our coast, they would have taken the northern route out of Vlad."

"Guam, perhaps?"

"I suppose so, but that's a lot of expensive firepower for a forward base that a couple dozen cruise missiles could deal with."

"Conn, sonar. New contact is a Hotel-II confirmed. Bearing three-two-one, range by triangulation is approximately forty-two thousand yards."

"Sonar, conn, aye. Designate and send to tracking, Chief."

"Aye, aye, sir. Designating Sierra-16 and sending to tracking."

"Bring us up, Gene, and report it to COMSUBPAC. Something about this seems off."

"Diving officer, bring us to periscope depth."

The *Olympia* raised its AN/BRA-34 mast and sent a burst transmission to a satellite overhead, which then relayed it to Pearl. Less than twenty seconds later the mast was retracted and the submarine returned to depth.

****

The message from the *Olympia* pinballed from COMSUB-PAC to the chief of naval operations to the joint chiefs, finally resulting in a hastily called meeting of select NSC principals.

The CJCS, Admiral Alfred Feldstein, cleared his throat and began. "Mr. Vice President, two hours ago one of our submarines in the East China Sea detected a pair of Soviet Hotel-II class submarines headed into the Philippine Sea. We believe that these submarines were the same ones that the NRO spotted provisioning in Vladivostok about ten days ago."

"I see. Evidently there is something unusual about this otherwise you would not have asked for this meeting," the vice president said.

"Yes, sir. The missile complement carried by these boats is quite limited—three SS-N-5 nuclear missiles, having a range of about nine hundred miles. The Hotels are normally parked off Hawaii or our west coast. When they deploy they usually take a northern route out of Vladivostok, not a southern one, because it gives them a shorter transit to their area of operations. Other than Guam or Subic Bay, there aren't many suitable targets these nukes could reach from the Philippine Sea."

"So why would they go down there?"

"That's the problem, sir. When the boats were provisioning, the NRO observed that they were floating high, indicating that their nukes had been removed. Well, sir, there's nothing much more useless than an old boomer with no missiles. We think that's what we have here."

"And you've asked for this meeting because the National Command Authority mandates that our attack submarines keep track of Soviet ballistic missile submarines?" asked the vice president.

"Correct, sir. We would like to release the *Olympia* from that mandate on this patrol."

"Mr. Vice President," objected national security advisor Moses Tov, "it is never, I repeat, *never* a good idea to lose track of your adversary's SSBNs. These may indeed be the submarine equivalent of a Model-T, sir, but those old nukes are just as deadly as new ones."

"I'm inclined to agree with Moses, sir," said the secretary

of defense.

"There is another possibility, gentlemen," suggested Paul West, the DCI.

"Go ahead, Paul," said the vice president.

"These Hotels are heading for the Philippine Sea. The USS *Midway*'s battle group will be transiting the Philippine Sea in about four days, headed for Yokosuka. What if those two SSBNs are sweepers?"

"What do you mean?" asked Tov.

"Look, the Soviets know that tracking SSBNs is a high priority for our attack submarines. What if those Hotels are meant to lead our SSNs out of the area, giving the Sovs a clear shot at the *Midway* when it passes through?"

"Like decoys?" asked Smithson.

"Precisely."

"What is your opinion of that idea, Al?" asked the vice president.

"To be honest, Mr. Vice President," Admiral Feldstein admitted, "that is the opinion of both the CNO and COMSUBPAC. Personally, I think it is the strongest possibility. I would urge you to give the *Olympia* an exception. Let the Hotels disappear, and allow the *Olympia* to stay in place and see who else comes down the pike. I remind you, sir, that the NRO has also informed us that a pair of Akula-class fast attack SSNs and a Kilo diesel sailed from the Vladivostok provisioning docks about the same time as the Hotels."

"Mel, what do you think?" the vice president asked, looking at the secretary of defense.

"I hadn't thought of the sweeper theory, sir. Normally I'd be dead set against giving these boomers a pass, but the more I think about it, especially considering Ivan's recent provocations against our carrier groups, I have to admit that the sweeper theory sounds quite credible."

"I agree, Mel. Gentlemen, thank you," Bush said, standing up. "The secretary of defense and I will talk to President Reagan, and then I'll contact you, Admiral, to let you know his decision."

****

The messenger of the watch located Captain Mitchell in the wardroom where he was meeting with the engineering officer. "Sir, NAV reports that we are receiving a message from COMSUBPAC on the VLF."

"Very well. Bring it to me in my quarters and have the XO meet me there."

"Aye, aye, sir."

Mitchell turned back to the engineering officer. "Anything else, Barry?"

"No, that's about it, Skipper. I'll post a copy of the revised watch list in the wardroom."

"Excellent. Your division is doing a great job, Barry. Keep it up." Mitchell refilled his coffee cup and negotiated the passageway to his cabin.

A minute later the XO tapped on Mitchell's open door. "Enter and have a seat, Gene. Shut the door behind you," Mitchell directed. "What's the latest on the two antiques?" he asked.

Commander Gene Sadler handed the sealed message envelope to Mitchell as he answered. "Tracking's got 'em locked in. Sonar says they are making so much noise he's surprised we can't hear 'em right through the hull."

"Well, at least they're making it easy on us," Mitchell replied.

He scanned the decoded message, raised his eyebrows, and reread it carefully.

```
IMMEDIATE PRIORITY
DTG 162200Z JAN 89


FROM: COMSUBPAC
TO:   USS OLYMPIA
INFO: CARGRU5
      COMSUBPAC            JCS/JRC
      COMSEVENTHFLT        ONI
      CINCPACFLT           DIRNSA
```

```
                DIRNAVSECGRUPAC    CNO
                NSC

         TOP SECRET
         WESTPAC AO


         1. NCA HAS APPROVED BREAKING OFF
         CONTACT WITH SOVIET HOTEL-CLASS
         SSBNS REPORTED 161800Z JAN 89.
         THOUGHT TO BE DECOYS.
         2. RETURN TO ORIGINAL AO.
         3. ONI CONSIDERS PROBABLE 2 SO-
         VIET AKULA-CLASS SSN AND 1 SOVIET
         KILO-CLASS SS SOON TO ENTER
         ORIGINAL AO. INTENDED TARGET
         THOUGHT TO BE CARGRU5.
         4. ESTABLISH PASSIVE SONAR CON-
         TACT AND TRACK THESE VESSELS.
         5. ACT IN SUPPORT OF CARGRU5.
         6. APPLY ROE ESTABLISHED 162205Z
         DEC 88 BY VESSEL NOT BY FLAG.
```

Mitchell folded the message. "I wondered about that."

"What?"

Mitchell passed the message flimsy to his XO. "COMSUB-PAC says the Hotels are probably decoys. That would explain the noise. Apparently they want to be detected. Anyway, we've got new orders."

Sadler studied the transmission. "What do they mean, apply the ROE to vessels and not the flag?"

"It means that if there are two Soviet submarines in our gunsights, and one launches a weapon and the other does not, we are only authorized to sink the one doing the shooting."

"That makes us a sitting duck, Ben. What's to prevent the second sub from firing on us? After all, we fired at his buddy."

"Gene, you have to remember there is a political aspect to our actions as well as a military one. When the NCA issues a directive like this, they are trying to avoid turning a skirmish into an all-out war."

"Yeah, Skipper, but it's our butts on the line, not the politicians'."

"Uh-huh. But that's what we signed up for, and that's why the government has entrusted us with a commission."

"True," Saddler said, grinning sheepishly. "Sometimes, though, when you get into a knife fight up close and personal, it's hard to remember that."

****

Morning on Saint Lawrence Island dawned gray and cold. Though the temperature was a somewhat moderate thirty-four degrees, the thirty-knot north wind made things very uncomfortable. The ice build-up that normally locks the northern shore of Saint Lawrence Island in a winter vise grip had not yet started.

The sun remained below the horizon, but there was enough ambient light to function. Ned sat in the captain's chair warming up the diesels and nursing a cup of coffee. He was not happy about the wind speed and direction. It was blowing right down the gut of the Bering Strait and would produce some very large swells. At least with the air temp above freezing he wouldn't have to worry about ice build-up on the hull. But he also figured the north wind would bring colder temperatures as the day progressed, and then icing could become a problem.

"Make sure the anchor is dogged down tight, Tommy, then cast off."

His deck hand removed the line from the mooring buoy, coiled it, and stowed it neatly in a locker. Ned throttled up slowly, motoring north.

"Harry," he called over his shoulder, "check the lashings on the skiff. They seem a little loose. When you guys are done, come in and get some coffee."

****

Ned Bascomb's marine band radio crackled to life. "Capitalist Pig, this is Red Commie. Do you read? Capitalist Pig, this is Red Commie, come in please." When he heard that, Bascomb laughed so hard he spilled his coffee. He grabbed the mic and, breaking radio etiquette, transmitted, "So is that what you really think of me, Georgi? After all these years, the truth comes out."

"Well, you know," came the reply, "now that we're legal and can transmit openly, I figured I had to come up with some handles. What do you think? Do you like them?"

Because their operation had been illegal on both coasts, Sukharov and Bascomb had always maintained radio silence for fear of detection. They'd only communicated through a powerful IR link mounted on their masts once they'd gotten close enough.

"This is Capitalist Pig. I *love* 'em, Red Commie. I think I'm going to rename my boat, The Pig. Say, where are you anyway?"

"Seas were very rough coming out this morning. It slowed me down. I have the package. We'll see you in another twenty minutes or so."

"Roger that. Capitalist Pig, out."

Ten minutes later, Harry spotted Sukharov's boat through the glasses. "I see him. He's wallowing pretty badly, Ned."

"At ten feet shorter, his boat is a lot lighter, Harry. And the period of these ocean swells is just the right distance to give him fits. He should have a following sea on the way home, though."

A few minutes later the boats were sailing in tandem, fifty feet apart.

"How do you want to do this?" Georgi asked over the IR link. Using the link was easier than shouting.

"Well, we're not going to be able to tie up in these seas."

"No, indeed," Sukharov agreed. "Why don't I put him in a drysuit and a harness? I'll throw you a line, fix my end to his harness, and toss him overboard. You can haul him in."

"That'll work."

While Jake was clambering into one of Sukharov's spare drysuits, Sukharov's deck hand was tossing a thirty-meter line to the other boat and Georgi was fashioning a harness.

"Look, Major Kelly, you're going to have to get wet. At this water temperature you won't be able to function very long. All you have to do is keep your head above water—let them pull you to their boat. You'll be fine, just wet and cold when you get there."

The two boats pulled to within thirty feet of each other, sailing a parallel course. Kelly stood on the deck and prepared to jump overboard. He turned to Sukharov. "Do you remember telling Bascomb about an American pilot who was shot down by one of your friends several years ago?"

Sukharov looked at him suspiciously. "No one is supposed to know about that."

"Pretty hard for me to not know about it, because I was the guy shot down. I just wanted to say thanks. Your statement saved my bacon."

"It was you?"

"Yep. This is now the second time you've saved my life." He held out his hand, smiling, and Sukharov shook it.

"Will it offend you, Major Sukharov, if I hope to never see you again?" Kelly asked, laughing.

"Not at all," Sukharov said, grinning. "But you've been very profitable to me, Major. Will it offend you if I hope I do see you again?"

"Nope, but it's not likely."

"Would you two majors quit your palavering and get on with it?" Bascomb called from the other boat.

"What is 'palavering'?" Georgi asked.

"It means he wants me to jump in the water. *Do svidaniya,* Major Sukharov."

"*Do svidaniya,* Major Kelly."

Kelly climbed up on the gunwale and dove in. A few minutes later he was sitting in Bascomb's galley, dripping all over the floor, wrapped in blankets, with a cup of steaming coffee in his hand.

Bascomb grinned at him. "Major, how would you like to

go home?"

"Commander, that sounds wonderful."

"Home it is, then. Harry will get you some dry clothes, and there are a couple of bunks down there if you want to stretch out." Bascomb put the helm over and pointed his boat toward Nome.

Chapter 20

Thursday, January 19, 1989, 0315 hours local

"Maybe they're not coming," muttered Petty Officer Emlet to the sonar technician sitting beside him at the console. The *Olympia* had been sailing in large, lazy circles just below the thermocline since returning to her area of operations at the edge of the Asian continental shelf. Captain Mitchell had notified the crew of their new orders and the possibility of tangling with a pair of Akulas.

Emlet glanced at the log and then said, "It's been almost forty-eight hours since we broke contact with the boomers, and nothing at all is happening. Sheesh. This is boring."

"C'mon, Tim," replied his buddy. "In the undersea world things happen at glacial speed. You know that."

"Yeah, until they don't."

"Touché. For my part, I'm glad we're tracking biological whales instead of titanium-hulled sharks." *Akula* in Russian meant shark.

A few hours later, Emlet noticed a bright line on the low frequency spectrum of his sonar display. "Chief, I'm picking up something."

The sonar supervisor stood behind him, watching Emlet's screen. "Yep. Somebody's coming."

Emlet twiddled with the knobs on his console. "Um-hmm. And he's coming out of the same vector the Hotels did."

A moment later a second bright line emerged on the waterfall-like noise on his display. Emlet clapped his headphones to his ears and concentrated. He nodded. "It's them. I've got two probable Akulas, Chief, one along bearing zero-seven-niner, and the other along bearing zero-eight-two."

"Conn, sonar. Reporting two contacts, both are probable Akulas. Bearing zero-seven-niner and zero-eight-two."

"Sonar, conn, aye, designate and send to tracking," the OOD responded.

"Conn, sonar, aye. Designating Sierra-18 and Sierra-19, sending to fire control tracking."

The OOD said, "Messenger of the Watch, inform the captain if you please. Chief of the Boat, rig for ultraquiet. Helm, all stop."

The noise emanating from the *Olympia* dropped to an indiscernible level as the Soviet submarines approached.

Captain Mitchell arrived in the control room and said, "OOD, I have the conn."

"Aye, Captain, you have the conn."

A moment later sonar reported again. "Conn, sonar. Confirm latest contacts as Akula submarines sailing in close company."

"Conn, fire control tracking. Bearing of Sierra-18 and Sierra-19 is now zero-eight-zero and zero-eight-three, respectively. Estimated range by triangulation of both contacts is forty-three thousand yards. Heading two-six-zero, speed fifteen knots, depth two hundred fifty feet."

"Fire control tracking, aye."

Mitchell turned to the navigation officer. "Nav, prepare a SLOT buoy; set it to transmit in two hours. Report to COM-SUBPAC that we are trailing the Akulas out of our designated AO. Include the latest contact information, and report that there is no sign of the Kilo. Launch the buoy as soon as it's ready." The single-use Submarine-Launched-One-way-Transmitter, or SLOT buoy, could be ejected from the submarine at depth. It would float to the surface and after a programmed delay send a burst transmission on a satellite communications channel. When the message was delivered, it would sink, its purpose fulfilled.

"We're going to make like a hole in the water until those bad boys pass by, then we're going to sneak into their baffles and trail 'em, see where they're headed. They'll never hear us while they're doing fifteen knots," Mitchell said quietly to the OOD.

****

The Agency's Gulfstream GIII touched down on Runway 22 at Washington National at dusk and taxied into a private hangar. A worker rolled debarking stairs up to the cabin door and then exited the building. Bill Jensen, Galina Kelly and Roger Carson stepped out of the hangar office and waited at the foot of the stairs. After a few minutes the cabin door opened, and Falcon came down the stairs.

Tears of joy and relief streaming down her face, Galina ran to him. He wrapped his arms around her, holding her tightly. The other two men kept their distance, giving the couple some privacy.

"I was afraid I'd never see you again—I thought I'd lost you forever," Galina said, squeezing him as hard as she could.

"It's over, Galya, and I'm home. It's going to be okay," he whispered in her ear, holding her close.

After giving them a few minutes, Bill said, "Let's all get on the plane. You're not supposed to be here, Jake, and I don't want anyone to see you. There is much I need to explain to you."

They climbed the stairs and entered the Gulfstream. When they were seated, Jensen began. "Jake, the 'Afghan terror attack' was staged to give you a chance to 'escape.' Except for a very small handful of people in the KGB, everyone else over there thinks you are still on the run somewhere in the USSR. It is essential that we let them think that."

"Yes, a KGB captain explained that to me, and why it was necessary."

"It was the only way Geredin was prepared to let you go. Consequently, we must continue the charade. You've got to stay out of circulation and in hiding for another thirty days or so. That way it will appear that you did indeed escape the KGB and then found your own way home without help. The KGB will not be blamed—they have plausible cover due to the supposed Afghan terror attack."

"What do you mean I have to stay in hiding? What about Galina? Listen, Bill, I—"

Jensen held up his hands and interrupted Falcon. "Stop and hear me out before you complain, Jacob. I have booked you both in an exclusive resort in Antigua for the next month as Mr. and Mrs. Jones. You'll be given a CIA credit card that you may use for meals, fun and shopping, up to three hundred dollars per diem."

"Oh. Well, that doesn't sound so bad," Jake admitted.

"Actually, it sounds wonderful," Galina said, smiling brightly at the thought.

Jensen nodded. "Marge, my secretary, has already contacted your school, Galina, to let them know you will be away —they've agreed to get a substitute for your classes.

"Roger Carson is going along as security, just on the off chance the Sovs should track you down and try to reel you in."

"He wasn't much good as security in Khab," Kelly said with some disgust. "He didn't lift a finger when push came to shove."

"Whoa, chief. I acted *exactly* as instructed. The whole plan was to let the KGB grab you. We just didn't count on the GRU interfering with the grab. We knew the GRU was hunting you, but we hadn't figured on them being on the scene."

"WHAT?" Jake exclaimed, looking from Carson to Jensen.

"Oh, Jake," Jensen said, looking at the floor and shaking his head. He looked up at the younger man. "There was no way we could pull off an actual extraction in the time required. Whatever the Soviet Pacific Fleet is going to do, it's going to happen this month—any day now. I needed to come up with a plan to get you to safety as quickly as possible before relations between our countries go in the toilet.

"The best I could come up with was a plan in which the KGB grabbed you before the GRU did. I had to send Roger Carson to smoke you out, because I knew that's who you were looking for. I also realized that Geredin had seen the letter and probably figured it out."

"It was that obvious?" Kelly asked, smiling ruefully.

Jensen nodded. "Yep. Anyway, I believed that if Geredin had you in custody, I could negotiate for your release using the leverage of the scientist-kidnapping disaster. Carson was acting on my orders to just show up. He was not to speak to you, not to help you, and not do anything but stand there like a statue.

"I didn't want to lose Carson, too. That would serve no

purpose at all. As long as he kept his nose clean, I knew they'd let him go since he was traveling on a diplomatic passport.

"What I hadn't figured out—I just didn't think far enough ahead—was that Geredin *couldn't* negotiate with me. It would have played directly into the hands of the coup plotters. So I had to come up with the Afghan terrorist attack."

"That was your idea?"

Jensen nodded. "It gave Geredin room to maneuver. It took some convincing but he finally signed on. And here you are."

Kelly nodded, then looked at Carson. "I'm sorry, Roger. I was wrong about you. I didn't know my lines in this drama, and I've been blaming you."

Carson shrugged. "I think thirty days on the beach soaking up some sun will pretty much even the score, Kelly."

Jensen handed Kelly a briefcase. "This contains your passports, credit cards and driver's licenses, Mr. Jones, as well as some cash. It also has a sat phone with the latest encryption in case I need to contact you, which I probably will. Have fun on Uncle Sam's dime—you've earned it."

"What about airline tickets?"

"Don't need 'em. We're flying you all down on the GIII.

"Roger, you can run home and pack a suitcase. Jake and Galina, give me a list of clothes that you want, with your sizes, and Marge will do some shopping for you. Otherwise, you two are confined to this aircraft until you land in Antigua. Wheels up in," Jensen paused, checking his watch, "four hours."

****

Captain First Rank Boris Sayanovich Mirov bent over the Kilo's plot table, holding a grease pencil and a pair of parallel rulers. Gathered around the plot in the cramped space were the B-445's political officer Captain First Rank Andrei Leonev, executive officer Captain Third Rank Anton Zarubin, and navigation officer Captain Lieutenant Lazar Norin.

"We will hold this course on heading one-niner-seven for

another seven hours, making eight knots. Then it will be time to snorkel. We will come around to a heading of two-seven-three before we do. We'll do seven knots for five hours while recharging the batteries. I do not intend to snorkel again until after confronting the *Midway*."

"Why the course change, comrade Captain?" asked Leonev.

"If we are detected at all, Leonev, it will be while we are snorkeling," Mirov explained. "So we adjust our course in such a way that will not telegraph our true destination. To any onlooker it will appear that we are intending to operate off the coast of Taiwan, far from the *Midway*'s course."

A diesel-electric submarine such as the Soviet Kilo can only run so long on its batteries before it must recharge them. Running the diesel engines to power electrical generators recharges the batteries, a process called snorkeling. It involves coming to periscope depth and raising a snorkel above the surface of the ocean. The snorkel carries oxygen to the diesels and vents their exhaust.

The process is noisy and the snorkel itself can be detected by radar, with the result that a snorkeling submarine is very vulnerable to detection. The Kilo is deadly nonetheless, for when it is submerged and running on its batteries at three knots or less, it is virtually undetectable by passive sonar.

"After we submerge again," Mirov continued, "I intend to set a new course of one-eight-one degrees to bring us into the area through which the *Midway* will pass. We'll do three knots on that leg, holding the course for twenty hours. I doubt the Americans will be able to detect us.

"Finally, we will set a course of two-three-two degrees and hold it for thirty hours at two knots, making adjustments as necessary to meet the *Midway* head on, assuming the intelligence on her intended course is accurate. With this plan we should have plenty of battery left to make our getaway silently."

"How long will we be on station, waiting?" asked Zarubin.

"We won't, if my plan works as it should. Time on station in this case is wasted time which provides the Americans an opportunity to detect us.

"As we draw near to the American carrier, we will make whatever course changes are necessary to evade her escorts. One advantage we hold is that the *Midway* does not carry any fixed-wing ASW aircraft. Unless they employ land-based P-3s, their ASW screen will have pretty short legs, restricted to their helicopters' operational range.

"Fetisov and Gromyko will be detected to the west of the carrier, causing it to turn east, right into our path. We will already be inside the *Midway's* ASW screen. It should be a fairly simple matter at that point to get within eight kilometers of the ship, which is what we have been ordered to do, comrades."

Mirov turned to his navigation officer. "Any questions, Captain Norin?"

"*Nyet*, sir. It seems very straightforward."

****

An insistent, irritating chirping sound intruded into Geredin's troubled sleep and finally dragged him into semi-consciousness. After groping for the lamp switch, he turned on the light and sat up, muttering curses. The chirping continued, and he groggily realized it was coming from the American sat phone passed to him several days earlier.

"*Da*." he grumbled into the phone.

"Kelly just landed in DC."

"Dr. Jensen, I presume?"

"Correct."

"So no speech to the UN."

"Right. No speech. You kept your promise, now I am keeping mine."

"Who killed Admiral Zelenko?" Geredin asked, now fully awake.

"Admiral Shukshin ordered the hit, Anatoly, and he directed Captain Stefan Udom to make the arrangements. Udom contracted with a criminal gang in Vladivostok, offering them thirty thousand rubles to do the job."

"I suspected as much," Geredin muttered. "And you have proof of this?"

"I do. Unfortunately, I cannot elaborate on how I know this particular fact, but on 9 December Shukshin directed Udom to set up a hit on Admiral Zelenko. The reason for the hit was that Zelenko had rescinded Standing Order 17 and had ordered the Pacific Fleet to cease all provocative actions against US naval vessels. Zelenko had also discovered an operation Udom called *Vostochnyy Veter*, and that upset Shukshin."

"I see. And what is Standing Order 17, or Operation *Vostochnyy Veter*?"

"That I don't know, Anatoly. Then, on 11 December, Udom drove to some abandoned warehouses on the Vladivostok waterfront and made contact with a criminal gang. Major Kelly had just transmitted a report to us and was hiding in the area. He actually observed and overheard the negotiation between Udom and the gang, firsthand.

"I might add that Major Kelly is willing to meet with Soviet prosecutors in your embassy and give a video-recorded deposition, as well as answer their questions under oath. This would have to wait until he surfaces in about thirty days, of course."

Geredin sat on the edge of his bed, thinking. "I'd like to hold that option open, but it might not be necessary, Bill. With what you've just told me, I think I can probably extract a confession from Captain Udom."

Jensen shuddered. "I'm sure you can."

****

The P-3C Orion was flying over the Philippine Sea at fifteen hundred feet. Several days earlier the waters had been roiled into a violent maelstrom by a rare winter cyclone. But the winds and seas had calmed as the low-pressure system moved away from the area and high pressure took over. The afternoon sun glittered on the surface of the ocean like a scattered, undulating field of diamonds. Launched from US Naval Base Subic Bay some nine hundred fifty nautical miles away, the Orion could remain on station a total of two and a quarter hours before its relief arrived and it returned to base. The AN/APS-115 maritime surveillance radar scanned the ocean's surface, looking for a returned reflection that might indicate a submarine or periscope.

"Commander, we've got another ninety minutes on station," reported NAVCOM, the P-3C's navigation and communication officer.

"Roger that, NAVCOM. Poke me again when we're down to thirty minutes," requested the plane commander. He queried the senior sensor operator, "SENSO, what can you see out there on the deep blue sea?"

SENSO examined his radar display and shook his head. "Mostly a lot of nothing. Looks like an empty ocean, Skipper."

As the aircraft flew its search pattern over the patrol area, occasionally it would launch an SSQ-53 DIFAR passive sonobuoy into the water. The five-inch diameter buoy contained a sophisticated hydrophone that listened for the telltale sounds generated by a submarine and was equipped with directional circuitry to provide the bearing to contacts.

Ten minutes later, the sensor operator detected a faint radar return. "Commander, we've got a weak return along bearing three-zero-one, range fifty-three miles."

"Roger that, SENSO. NAVCOM, I'm breaking the patrol pattern to check out the contact. Coming around to new heading three-zero-one."

A few minutes later, the aircraft tactical coordinator (TACCO) reported, "Skipper, it is definitely a periscope or snorkel. Bearing is now two-niner-eight, range twenty miles. Working up a TMA."

The plane commander brought the Orion down to two hundred fifty feet as they approached the target. Soon they had a visual on the feather of a wake produced by the submarine's snorkel and ESM mast. The outline of a submarine at periscope depth was easily discerned in the clear water as the aircraft roared overhead.

"Caught him snorkeling. Looks like it might be that Kilo

everyone is searching for. I'm going to make another pass. Drop a DIFAR on it and let's get a good sound signature," said the plane commander.

The sound signature confirmed the submarine as a Kilo-class vessel, and the TMA resolved the Kilo's course as heading two-seven-three, speed seven knots. NAVCOM radioed the contact to *Midway.*

****

"Captain Mirov, we are detected. Are you not going to submerge and change course?" the *zampolit* asked.

"*Nyet,*" Mirov smiled. "Let them detect us. I want them to find us on this leg."

"But why? Do you want this operation to fail?" the political officer asked, speaking loudly enough so that the entire control room could hear the accusation.

"Certainly not, comrade," Mirov replied calmly. "Indeed, the success of this operation depends on our being detected. Come, comrades, let me show you," he said, motioning both the political officer and the XO over to the map plot.

"Surely you must realize that the imperialists' satellites would have caught both SSBNs, plus the *K-284,* the *K-263,* and us at the provisioning docks in Vladivostok. They would also have noted when we disappeared. So they know that five of our submarines are operating in the area. That will draw their attention, and they will mount an effort to find out where we are and what we are up to, especially since the *Midway* and its carrier group are passing through the Philippine Sea.

"By now they've already detected the two SSBNs that sailed ahead of us. Those boats are now lying off the coast of Taiwan. Hopefully, they have drawn away any American attack submarines in the area. It is part of American submarine doctrine that their attack subs' first priority is tracking our ballistic missile submarines.

"But the Americans also know that the two Akulas and our Kilo are still unaccounted for. They will be looking for us.

Fetisov and Gromyko are somewhere in this area at this very moment," Mirov said, pointing to a spot on the map between Okinawa and Taiwan. "If they, too, have been detected, it will appear as if we are going to join them.

"Our present course, if continued, will intersect with the Akulas several hundred miles east of Taiwan, right here," he said, drawing a small circle on the map with the tip of his finger. "That's why I want the Americans to detect us while snorkeling. I am counting on the Americans seeing our present course and concluding that our three submarines are participating in some operation off the coast of Taiwan. I want them to believe that our presence is unrelated to the transit of the *Midway*."

Executive officer Captain Anton Arkadevich Zarubin studied the map and nodded slowly. "*Da*, it is a good plan, Captain Mirov. At the very least it will delay the Americans' reaction until we are much closer to them."

Mirov glared at the political officer with a steely gaze, his blue-gray eyes flashing with anger as he murmured quietly, "I shall not forget your accusation when I write my report, Leonev—a scurrilous slander which you made in the hearing of my entire control room crew."

****

Admiral Stanley Blake stood in the *Midway*'s Combat Information Center and studied the threat plot. The *Olympia* had reported contact with the Akulas several hours earlier via the SSIXS network. Adding to that, a few minutes earlier the CIC had received the report from the P-3C Orion about a snorkeling Kilo submarine.

"What do you think, Admiral?" asked Captain Ernest Skagway.

"I think there's been entirely too much Soviet submarine activity in this part of the ocean, Captain, and I don't like it. First the boomers and now these three attack submarines. They are up to something, and I don't like it when Ivan is up to something and I don't know what it is."

"Do you think they are planning a welcoming party for us, Admiral?"

"Not sure. There's another more likely possibility. I received message traffic last night regarding the *Nimitz* and its carrier group. They are making for the Luzon Strait in the next thirty-six hours or so. Maybe the Sovs are getting in position to harass the *Nimitz*. No offense, Skagway, but a nuclear carrier is a much shinier prize than an old oil-burner like the *Midway*."

"What's up?" asked the air group commander, Clete Simms, who'd just joined them.

"More Soviet sub activity, Commander," replied Admiral Blake. "Okay, here's what we're going to do. So far none of the provocations by the Sovs have involved aircraft, but tomorrow by two bells in the forenoon watch I want the number of Tomcats flying CAP doubled, Commander Simms, just in case. By eight bells, when we're closer to all this sub activity, I want you to double the number of choppers maintaining our ASW screen."

"Aye, sir. I'll redo the duty sheets for our combat air patrols right away. Will you want the choppers loaded out with warshots tomorrow?"

"Yes."

"Very good, sir, I'll see to it."

Admiral Blake turned to the skipper, "Captain Skagway, we have an UNREP scheduled for tomorrow afternoon, do we not?"

"We do, Admiral."

"Move it up to this afternoon. I don't want any messing around with replenishment tomorrow. Please see to it that the whole carrier group is replenished today."

****

"Come in, please," encouraged Anatoly Geredin to the directors of the First and Third KGB directorates. "Sit down. Shut the door, Vladimir. *Spasibo.*" Geredin got up from his chair and limped to the window, looking out on the dirty, melting snow. Moscow was experiencing a brief, unusual warmup, but it was to be short-lived. The forecast included a heavy winter storm bearing down on them from the Norwegian Sea.

Colonels Vasily Vasilyevich Orlov and Vladimir Leonidovich Dobrynin sat facing the old spy, waiting for him to continue. Finally he turned around and faced them. "I am not at liberty to name my source, but I consider the intelligence impeccable and unquestionable. I received confirmation late last night of something that we three have suspected for some time—that Admiral Shukshin had Admiral Zelenko assassinated. Shukshin directed the Pacific Fleet's intelligence officer, Captain Udom, to arrange for the murder. Udom contracted the job to a group of local hooligans for the price of thirty thousand rubles." Geredin hobbled back to his desk and sat heavily in his chair before continuing. "I believe I can extract a confession and full details from Captain Udom. If that is the case, then I will be ready to move against Shukshin, publicly."

The other two men absorbed this information with a mix of sadness and anger. While each of them had at times issued termination orders for Soviet citizens, it was—so they told themselves—in view of the objective good of the *rodina*, not for personal political ambitions. Shukshin, however, had murdered in the name of an illegal coup attempt, and somehow that was beyond the pale. It was a reversion to Stalin's ugly tactics, in which the leopard ate not only his own tail but his whole body until nothing was left.

"How do you plan to do this, Anatoly? You are playing with fire yourself, you know," cautioned Orlov.

"*Pravda.* I have directed Captain Fukina to arrest Udom when he returns home tonight and to secure a recorded confession that lays the blame at Shukshin's feet. If she can secure that, I have directed her to arrest Shukshin immediately."

"She must not go after Shukshin on the base," warned Orlov. "She must wait until he is home as well. We don't know what the loyalties are of the security forces on the base. If she tries to take him there it might quickly turn into a firefight."

"I agree, Anatoly," affirmed Dobrynin. "This is a very dangerous situation—we don't want to light the fuse of the coup ourselves. Wait until he can be arrested out of sight of the base and his security personnel."

"Very well. I hear the wisdom of what you both are saying." Geredin massaged his temples, shaking his head. "Instead of a New Soviet Man, we have a new Soviet mess. I'm getting too old for this."

"What about the coup plans?" Dobrynin asked.

"Whatever naval action Shukshin has planned is going to take place in the next thirty-two hours. At this point we know that he intends to initiate a conflict with the US navy. He's been trying to do it for the last several months, unsuccessfully. The US is refusing to retaliate in the face of the most severe provocation and thus is spoiling Shukshin's grand plan.

"Now that the US has established that record of restraint, I fear what Shukshin might attempt next. It could involve our submarines initiating lethal action. We do know that it's going to happen during the inauguration of the new US president. Shukshin is convinced that conflict with the US will secure most, if not all, of the military behind the coup. I believe he is likely correct in his supposition.

"The disappearance of interior minister Churkin works against us, because it was his voice the troops of the Ministry of the Interior listened to and were loyal to. He could have ordered the troops around Moscow to stand down, or even to defend Gorbachev. The only bright side to the loss of Churkin is that it is so recent that the coup plotters have not yet been able to fill the position with a loyal co-conspirator.

"The clock is ticking, comrades, and our options for fighting this putsch are getting very slender indeed, unless we can take Shukshin out of the picture and countermand whatever orders he has issued to the naval units."

****

"Engineering, conn. Secure from snorkeling and resume running on battery power," Mirov commanded.

A few minutes later, the reply came back. "Conn, engineering. We are secure from snorkeling. Batteries are at one hundred percent. Now running on battery power, Captain."

"Very well." Mirov hung up the phone to the engineering spaces and turned to face the control room. "Down snorkel. Down ESM mast. Down periscope." The wake feather on the surface raised by the *B-445*'s various masts disappeared, eliminating the radar signature detected by the Orion P-3C orbiting the area.

"Helm, make your depth one hundred fifty meters. Hold present course." Mirov turned to his XO and explained his tactics. "When we disappear from their sonobuoys, they will think we have held our course toward Taiwan. We'll get under the layer, cut our speed, and effectively disappear before we change course."

"Our depth is one hundred fifty meters, Captain."

"Very well. Reduce speed to three knots."

"Aye, aye, Captain. Reducing speed to three knots."

"We just disappeared from the American's passive sonar. Next, he'll come and drop an active buoy, trying to resume contact with us. But he's going to drop it in the wrong place," Mirov grinned. He loved the thrill of the contest between the hunter and the hunted.

"Helm, steer a new course for one-eight-one. Planesman, make your depth two hundred twenty meters."

"Aye, aye, comrade Captain. Our course is one-eight-one. Our depth is two hundred twenty meters."

"Rig ship for ultraquiet."

****

Captain Stefan Stefanovich Udom's future was assured. He'd hitched his wagon to Shukshin's rapidly rising star, and with Shukshin as his patron, Udom would do quite well. Fast-track promotions, the most sought-after billets, membership in the *nomenklatura*, political favor and protection upstream—what more could life offer?

He had no interest at all in politics. Retiring from the navy on admiral's pay, that was his goal. He was not anxious to be at sea or in command of a vessel. If possible he would prefer the perks of rank without its attendant responsibilities. Naval intelligence was a perfect fit—it offered him exactly what he wanted out of a naval career and a security classification that made him privy to closely held Soviet secrets.

Udom thought himself loyal to the *rodina*. But in truth, Udom's first loyalty was to Udom. When push came to shove all other loyalties deferred to his own personal best interest.

He was an intelligence officer—not an intelligence operative. His domain was an air-conditioned office where he spent time poring over SIGINT and intelligence reports on the movement and dispositions of the naval vessels of other countries. Of tradecraft he knew nothing. Which explains why he thought nothing of the black Zil parked half a block down from his flat, even though it had never been there before.

Udom fumbled for his keys and unlocked the door. He was looking forward to a quiet meal sitting next to the radiator, reading Sholokhov's celebrated novel, *And Quiet Flows the Don*. He locked the door behind him and hung his heavy cloak on a hook by the door. He flipped the light switch on and turned toward his tiny kitchen. To his shock, he found himself facing a woman wearing the uniform of a KGB captain. Two men, also wearing the uniform of the KGB, flanked her.

"Good evening, Captain Udom," said the woman. "We have some questions we'd like to ask you. I'm afraid you'll have to accompany me to the KGB main headquarters."

Udom's mouth went dry. The way the woman said 'headquarters' worried him. "Here in Vladivostok?" he managed to croak.

She shook her head. "Moscow. The Lubyanka. Your new home."

"May I ask why?" he stuttered.

"Admiral Shukshin is accusing you of the murder of Admiral Zelenko," she lied. "He has corroborated the charge by showing us that thirty thousand rubles are missing from your department's accounts. You, comrade, have a great deal of explaining to do."

Udom's legs went weak and he sank to the floor, his chest pounding. He felt like he could hardly breathe. The room started spinning, and he retched.

"Get him some water, Lieutenant Pankiv," Fukina ordered.

After a moment Udom was able to speak. "No, no! It was Admiral Shukshin who ordered the assassination. Zelenko was interfering with his plans. I was just following orders."

"What plans?"

Captain Udom shut his mouth and tried to gather his wits. In a matter of days, Shukshin would be at the top of the heap and the admiral would be able to order the KGB to release him. And besides, he belatedly realized, Shukshin would never have pointed the finger at him, knowing that Udom could implicate him in Zelenko's death. Surely, Udom decided, this KGB captain was playing him.

"I'm sorry, I have nothing to say to you," he said defiantly.

Fukina just looked at him for a long, silent moment. Without turning her head or breaking her glare, she asked, "Did you get it?"

Lieutenant Bok replied, "Every word."

"Play it."

Bok pulled a small digital recorder out of his pocket, and pressed *PLAY*. Udom heard his own voice protesting, *No, no! It was Admiral Shukshin who ordered the assassination. Zelenko was interfering with his plans.*

Fukina was merciless. "You will have something to say to us when we play that for Admiral Shukshin. I am guessing he does not do the forgiveness thing when it comes to turncoats. In fact, I'd say that the only chance you have to see your next birthday is to talk to us. If you give us the whole story we'll work something out."

Udom shut his eyes, trying to block out the terror that confronted him. *How did it come to this?* he asked himself.

"Hey, you're a navy man, Udom. You should be able to recognize a life preserver when you see one. That's what I'm tossing you."

He held his head in his hands and muttered, "I'll tell you anything you want to know."

****

"I got it. I got a complete confession from Udom," Captain Fukina reported to the KGB director.

"Excellent," exulted Geredin. "There may be time to stop this madness yet. First, make sure that Udom calls in sick tomorrow. No one must suspect that he is in custody.

"Second, arrest Shukshin. Let's see . . . it's after-hours in Vlad, so he should be home by now. Go to his *dacha* as soon as possible and arrest him. Take any bodyguards present into temporary custody as well. If they fight you, arrest them if you can, kill them if you must. Take anyone else in the house —family, children, neighbors—into temporary detention as well. They will be released unharmed within the week.

"But this is critical: no one is to know of Shukshin's arrest. Call me immediately when he is in the bag."

****

It took two hours for Fukina to secure an official naval car as well as a naval officer's uniform that would fit Aleksei Bok. Fukina fitted him with a wire so she could hear the conversation. She picked and armed seven loyal members of her Moscow team and they loaded into two Zils.

Bok pulled into the driveway of Admiral Shukshin's *dacha*, while the two Zils parked down the street. Before Bok emerged from the naval vehicle, he whispered into his mic, "Two armed guards at the door, no others in sight."

He walked up the sidewalk carrying a sealed manila envelope marked in bright red letters, CONFIDENTIAL – EYES ONLY.

The guards were smoking and talking as he approached. Seeing his naval uniform they carelessly waved him past without challenging him. He continued to the door and knocked.

A pretty young woman opened the door. "Can I help you?"

"Lieutenant Bok, from the base communications center

with priority traffic for the admiral."

"He's not here. He's still at the base."

"Oh, sorry, I didn't see him in his office and figured that he'd be here."

"*Nyet*. This morning he packed a bag saying that there was an important operation commencing and he could not leave the base for the next four days."

"Ah. Sorry to have disturbed you, comrade. I'll track him down at the base."

****

"Shukshin was not at home, Director. He's holed up on the base for the next four days. What do you want me to do? Do you want me to try to arrest him there?" Fukina asked.

"Under no circumstances, Kira. Don't set foot on the base. Give me a minute."

Geredin pulled at his lip, thinking. He did not have the political clout to enter a naval base and arrest the commander of the Pacific Fleet. The security troops on the base would never allow it. The only chance to take Shukshin down safely would be off the base and away from his security forces.

"Captain, put the main entrance of the base under surveillance—make sure you are not spotted. If the Admiral leaves the base, tail him and arrest him as soon as it can be done without a firefight. Put his *dacha* under surveillance as well, just in case he uses a different exit and slips past your team at the base.

"I do not want to start a shooting war between the KGB and the naval security forces, so whatever you do, do it quietly and out of sight. I'd rather you lose him than take him with violence in front of witnesses. We're walking the thin edge of a knife blade, Kira, and if we slip up, we'll be the ones who get cut."

Chapter 21

Carrier Group 5 (CARGRU5) steamed through calm seas, making twenty knots on a due north heading. It was a far cry from the weather they had encountered a few days ago. A rare winter cyclone had produced lashing spindrift and mighty rollers. The two *Spruance*-class destroyers received the greatest punishment, occasionally taking water over the bow. The guided-missile cruiser *Bunker Hill*, CG-52, was thirty-eight feet longer and sixteen hundred tons heavier than the destroyers, but it, too, had taken a pounding. The heavy seas gradually subsided as the cyclone and its low-pressure system drifted east. By the morning of 20 January, the Philippine Sea resembled a mill pond.

One hundred sixty miles north of the carrier group, the USS *Louisville*, SSN-724, prowled two hundred forty feet below the surface, unaffected by the weather. The *Louisville* was alternately sprinting and drifting, listening for the telltale sounds of submarines as it sought to protect CARGRU5 from ambush.

Admiral Stanley Blake was in overall command of CAR-GRU5. He was meeting on the flag bridge with the *Midway*'s skipper, Captain Ernest Skagway, and the Air Group Commander (CAG) Clete Simms.

"Get us some coffee, Jeff, and see if you can scare up some of those pastries the cook baked this morning, please," the admiral said to his personal steward.

"Yes, sir."

Blake turned to Skagway. "You wanted to meet with me, Ernie?"

"Yes, sir. Tell him, Clete."

"Admiral, I've inventoried the sonobuoy stores, and we're scraping the bottom of the barrel. We dropped most of our stuff and nearly all of our pingers on the joint ASW exercise we just concluded with the Aussies.

"COMPACFLT has warned us to expect increased Soviet submarine activity in the northern half of the Philippine Sea on this transit. Normally our current stores would be adequate for our return to Yokosuka, but these aren't normal times. I'd like to request a priority COD (Carrier Onboard Delivery) of sonobuoys from Subic."

"I agree, Admiral. Ivan has been getting a little cocky lately. Maybe if we ping him to death we can keep him from trying anything stupid," added Captain Skagway.

Admiral Blake nodded. "Good thinking. Give my staff a list, Clete, and I'll see that it happens."

"Thank you, sir."

"Anything else?"

"Yes, sir," said Captain Skagway, "I'd like to request that the rotation of P-3s out of Subic Bay continue during our transit of the Philippine Sea. Soviet submarines have been on the prod in this region, and intelligence reports tell us something big might be going down in the next day or so. I'd like to keep the extra ASW coverage, sir."

"Yes, I agree, Ernie," responded Admiral Blake. "Okay, I'll contact Subic and see if they can continue to help us out. In the meantime, Clete, get me your supply list and I'll talk 'em into sending us a Greyhound."

****

"See that I am not disturbed—no calls, no visitors," Admiral Shukshin barked to his secretary as he breezed by her and shut his office door behind him.

He looked at the old ship's chronometer on the wall and did a mental calculation. *It's 1400 hours here, it will be 0700 hours in Moscow. If I know Pushkaryov, he will already be in his office.*

He picked up the phone and dialed.

"Pushkaryov," the gravelly voice answered, 6400 kilometers away. The vice president of the Soviet Union had been in his office since 0600, deciding who would be useful in his upcoming regime and who must be cast aside. He was, of course, counting on the success of the coup.

"It's Shukshin. Are you alone?"

"I am. Thanks for calling, Admiral, I was hoping to get the

latest from you."

"In twelve hours the American carrier group will be confronted in such a way that will force them to react," the commander of the Pacific Fleet declared. "Twenty-four hours after that, I anticipate that the conflict will be featured on *TASS* or in *Pravda* above the fold and it will make international news. In two days our ambassador to the UN will be making a very angry speech, accusing the US of recklessness on the high seas. Our military will be ready to act as one, uniting behind a strong voice."

"Whose strong voice?" Pushkaryov asked, knowing the answer.

"Well, mine, of course, Mr. Vice President," Shukshin responded obsequiously. "I will agitate for Mr. Gorbachev to step down. Your name will be brought up, and I will endorse you as the solution to the *rodina*'s problems."

"You know that I am not sold on your plan, Admiral. If this results in a war with the Americans, it will not end well. Our submarines are not going to initiate the attack, are they?"

"Alexander Ivanovich, how often must I reassure you?" Shukshin soothed. "You must trust me, my comrade. Everything is going according to my plan. In just four days, you will be the president of our great motherland, and you can begin the restoration of pure communist doctrine.

"How are things on your end?" Shukshin asked, trying to distract Pushkaryov from posing any more questions.

Pushkaryov noted that the admiral didn't exactly answer his question. But one of the things presidential wannabes lack in the run-up to a coup is clout, and the vice president wisely decided to drop the matter.

"Very well, Admiral. Defense minister Aristov has persuaded the Politburo that a military parade in Moscow on Monday, the twenty-third, would be an appropriate response to the inauguration of America's new president. Consequently Moscow will be brimming with military units hand-picked by Aristov. The Alpha and Vympel special forces units will be there, along with the 2nd and 4th Guards Motor Rifle Divisions and all their armor. Even without Churkin's *militsiya* we'll have enough firepower in the city to take and hold the Kremlin.

"I am scheduled for a televised speech to the *Duma* on Tuesday, at which time I will express outrage over the USA's criminal actions toward our Pacific Fleet and will demand that Gorbachev step down. That will be the signal for General Yegorov to command all loyal Soviet troops to advance on the Kremlin, 'to protect our leaders.' What they will actually do is take control of the Kremlin and hold the members of the Politburo under arrest until they appoint me in a dual role of general secretary and president of the USSR."

"Excellent," said Shukshin. What he didn't say is that he'd worked a deal with Aristov to ensure that Pushkaryov would become a tragic victim of the violence on Tuesday. Aristov would demand that the Politburo select Shukshin for the two offices.

"By the way," Shukshin asked, "whatever became of our beloved interior minister, Yulian Semyonovich Churkin?"

Pushkaryov chuckled. "No one knows. Perhaps the traitor had enough of Moscow's snow and is enjoying close comradeship with some lovely lady on the beach in Cuba."

Shukshin laughed. "Perhaps."

As the two conspirators talked they were wholly unaware that someone—or, more accurately, some *thing*—was listening. The conversation between Vladivostok and Moscow was relayed by Soviet satellites in geostationary orbit 22,236 miles above the earth. The transmissions were intercepted by the radomes of the NSA's Field Station Berlin located in Teufelsberg, in the British sector of West Berlin. From there the signal was retransmitted via satellite to Sugar Grove Station, West Virginia, and then by microwave to Fort Meade, Maryland, where it was absorbed by the NSA's massive computer complex running the ECHELON surveillance system.

ECHELON was designed to process SIGINT gathered from electronic communications traffic around the globe. The ECHELON computer system electronically sorted through and discarded a daily tidal wave of mostly worthless communication traffic. One day's intake of data would have taken hundreds of human eyes months and months to process. ECHELON, however, could keep pace with the daily flood and identify intercepted communications of particular interest.

When the computer system recognized that the origination point of the phone call was the Pacific Fleet headquarters in Vladivostok, and the destination point was the office of the vice president of the Soviet Union, the priority level of the transmission immediately went to the highest level. The Soviet encryption algorithm protecting the phone call was one that had been cracked by NSA cryptologists months before, which meant that the decrypted open recording of the phone call finally wound up on Evelyn Stinson's computer at Fort Meade at 0200 hours, EST. Her pager began to ring, summoning her into the office immediately.

****

"Helm, reduce speed to five knots," Captain Fetisov ordered. He checked the *K-263*'s chronometer on the bulkhead and silently congratulated himself. In two hours they'd be on station, and the Americans would be unaware of their presence.

"Aye, aye, Captain. Making revolutions for five knots."

"Clear the baffles."

The submarine turned slowly to the right in the cold black water. The maneuver put the conformal hydrophones on the hull in a position to hear anything that might be following them.

"Sonar, conn. Report all contacts."

The sonar supervisor polled the three sonar technicians. Their boards were clear. "Conn, sonar. No surface or subsurface contacts."

"Sonar, conn, aye," Captain Fetisov acknowledged. "Diving officer, make your depth one hundred fifty meters. I want to put us below the layer."

The XO remarked quietly, "Strange that there are no surface contacts. The typhoon must have discouraged the commercial shipping from leaving port."

Fetisov nodded. "Probably so."

The black submarine went a few degrees down at the bow and slid below the thermocline. A few minutes later the diving officer reported, "Our depth is one hundred fifty meters, comrade Captain."

"Very well. Helm, make revolutions for fifteen knots."

"Congratulations, comrade Captain," enthused Captain Second Rank Zakhar Rurikovich Khorkov, Fetisov's *zampolit*. "We are almost on station and the imperialists have no clue."

****

Three thousand yards behind *K-263* another black shape glided stealthily through the water as the *Olympia* stalked the Soviet submarine.

"Conn, sonar, target aspect is changing. He's clearing his baffles, sir, coming around to the right."

"Aye, sonar," Captain Mitchell said, practically whispering. "Helm, all stop."

"Aye, aye, Skipper. All stop." The response came back as a whisper.

Mitchell muttered, "Anybody sneezes, you'll be cleaning the heads for a week."

The chief of the boat winked at the helmsman, who grinned back.

"I mean it, COB," hissed Mitchell, a hint of a smile flickering around the corners of his mouth.

After a minute sonar reported, "Conn, sonar. Target aspect is changing again—he's resumed course. His depth is increasing—I'm getting hull-popping noises. Making revolutions for five knots." After a brief pause the sonar supervisor added, "He's dropped below the layer, sir."

"Where is the layer?" Captain Mitchell asked.

"Three hundred feet."

"Helm, take us down to two ninety. Sonar, dangle the TB-23 below the layer. I don't want to lose this guy."

Hours earlier the *Olympia* had detected two Akulas and

designated them Sierra-18 and Sierra-19. They'd lost track of Sierra-18 about four hours ago. Mitchell had elected to continue stalking the contact they still had.

"Conn, sonar. Sierra-19 is now dead ahead, bearing one-two-zero, depth four hundred fifty feet. Screw count has him at fifteen knots, heading one-two-zero."

"Sonar, conn, aye. Helm, make revolutions for fifteen knots, course one-two-zero."

"Sonar, conn. Stay on him. I want to know immediately if he so much as dumps the garbage. Understood?"

"Aye, aye, Cap. We won't let you down."

"NAV, send up a SLOT buoy with the latest. I want CAR-GRU5 to know they'll soon be swimming with sharks."

****

Guided by a yellow-shirted plane handler, the Grumman E-2 taxied to catapult number one, the jet blast deflector behind it rising up. A green shirt hooked the nose gear to the holdback while another hooked the Hawkeye's towbar to the catapult shuttle. The pilot throttled up the powerful Allison/Rolls-Royce turboprops and snapped a salute at the catapult officer. Seconds later the Airborne Early Warning aircraft was in the air, leaving the *Midway* far behind and climbing to its assigned altitude for its four-hour patrol. Four F-14 Tomcats launched immediately after for a CAP.

The air boss's voice came booming over the flight deck loudspeaker, "Respot the flight deck for landing operations!"

This announcement resulted in a new flurry of activity among sailors clad in blue, yellow and green jerseys, each color specifying a different job. The white-shirted Landing Signal Officer (LSO) took his place on the LSO platform on the port side of the ship back toward the fantail. A few minutes later the F-14s returning from their CAP landed in turn and were hustled out of the way by the aircraft handlers. Next down was an E-2 Hawkeye, returning from its patrol.

A communications specialist informed the air boss, "Sir, the Hawkeye we just launched is reporting that we've got an inbound Greyhound for a COD seventy-five miles out. He squawks friendly."

"Acknowledge, and have the Hawkeye hand him off to CATCC (Carrier Air Traffic Control Center)."

A few minutes later, the voice of the Greyhound's pilot came over the radio, "*Midway, Midway, Midway*, this is inbound Greyhound two-seven-niner-five requesting priority in your landing sequence. My starboard engine is acting up, and I'd like to set this crate on the deck before it gets worse."

"Roger that, Greyhound. You are the only aircraft in the lineup at the moment, so you can come straight in."

"Much obliged, *Midway*."

Several minutes later the C-2A Greyhound entered the pattern. As it flew the downwind leg past the carrier, the pilot deployed the landing gear and extended the tail hook. He set his radio frequency to match the LSO's. Several miles downwind, he brought the aircraft around and lined up with the angled deck.

"You're in the groove, Greyhound, looking good. You're about a mile out now. Hope you're bringing the mail," said the LSO.

"Roger that, Paddles. Got the mail and I'm loaded to the gills with sonobuoys. Flying with max gross weight."

"Call the ball, Greyhound."

"Roger, ball."

The Greyhound was now about a half mile behind the stern of the carrier, altitude two hundred feet. The "meatball" on the LSO platform was showing a picture-perfect descent.

At one quarter mile the pilot's cockpit suddenly filled with the sound of warning buzzers. The auto-feather system on the starboard engine failed, feathering the starboard propeller, effectively eliminating one of the aircraft's two engines. This happened just as the heavily loaded C-2A entered the air turbulence created by the carrier's island. The result was a precipitous loss of altitude.

"WAVE OFF! WAVE OFF, GREYHOUND!" shouted the LSO.

The pilot jammed his throttle forward, but it was too late.

The remaining Allison T56-A-425 turboprop engine could not generate sufficient thrust fast enough to lift the aircraft clear of the carrier. The Greyhound hit the fantail and exploded, scattering fiery debris all over the flight deck. What was left of the fuselage slid forward in a fireball and skated off the deck into the water. The LSO dove into the safety net below his platform just before the flaming remains of the aircraft passed over his position.

"Ramp strike! Ramp strike! Firefighting and damage control parties to the after flight deck, on the double." the air boss barked over the flight deck loudspeaker. He repeated the same call over the main communication channel, 1MC.

In seconds, firefighting parties were hosing foam onto flaming portions of the wreckage that hadn't gone overboard, even as damage control parties began assessing the damage to the fantail and the flight deck.

The bodies of the pilot and his three crew members were never found. In addition to the tragedy of losing four good men, the *Midway* also lost the sonobuoys that were to contribute to its protective ASW screen as it transited the Philippine Sea.

****

The men of SPEARGUNS, Antisubmarine Warfare Helicopter Squadron 12 (HS-12), sat somberly in the ready room, waiting for their squadron commander. The fires on the flight deck had been extinguished. In another thirty minutes, sufficient repairs would be effected such that fixed-wing flight operations could resume. The four fatalities reminded the men of HS-12 that the next death could very well be their own. But morbid brooding was not in the nature of these men—at least, not while they were aboard ship on patrol. It helped that the fatalities were names without faces or known personalities: they were stationed at Subic, not on the *Midway*. They would be known—and mourned—there. All the same, no one working aboard the ship was untouched by the tragedy.

"As you were," said CAG, Commander Clete Simms, as he

and the squadron commander, Lieutenant Commander David Olsen, entered the ready room.

"You're all aware the US navy just lost four good men," said Simms. "From all indications it does not appear to be pilot error. The pilot had reported problems with the starboard engine, and a review of video footage of his landing approach appears to indicate that his starboard propeller feathered at the last moment, resulting in a fatal loss of power. The feathering problem is not unknown on the C-2. My observations are not an official conclusion, just my opinion as I watched the video in slo-mo.

"In any case, we still have a job to do. *You* have a job to do —a dangerous job. So put this out of your minds and focus on your job. You're all highly trained professionals. I am confident that the SPEARGUNS can continue to operate at the highest levels of efficiency—in fact, I am counting on it.

"The loss of the Greyhound means our resupply of sonobuoys has also been lost. Lieutenant Commander Olsen is going to brief you on the changes to your mission due to that loss. Good luck to you all."

"Thank you, Commander Simms," said Olsen. Simms nodded, and returned to the bridge. Olsen continued, "Gentlemen, within the last forty-eight hours we know of five Soviet submarines that have been operating on or near our intended course—two Hotel II-class boomers, two Akulas, and a Kilo. In addition we've got two of our own 688s out there somewhere. So there could be plenty of targets for you to track.

"Unfortunately, however, as CAG mentioned, we have a significant sonobuoy shortage. I've checked with the *Bunker Hill*, the *Kinkaid*, and the *Cushing*, and their supply situation is even worse than ours. The upshot of all this is that you will be using your dipping sonar for initial contact detection, which means detection will be hit or miss, and more often miss. Once you've detected a contact, you may use your sonobuoys to attain a positive identification and work up a TMA. Remember that our boys are out there, too, so be positive you are distinguishing friend from foe.

"Intelligence indicates that the Sovs have planned something big in the next eight to ten hours. We just don't know whether we are the target, the *Nimitz*, or someone else. Current thinking upstairs leans toward the *Nimitz*, not us. She will be passing through the Luzon Strait in several hours, and the last report had all the bad boys headed in that direction. We also do not know whether Ivan's provocation is going to involve weapons. It could. That's all I know.

"Because of this, we are breaking with our normal peacetime procedures. You will be flying with live warshots. For some of you, this will be your first time to carry a live weapon since your training evolutions. Remember your training. Remember your procedures.

"Last of all, remember the rules of engagement we've been given. If push comes to shove, you may only launch a weapon at a hostile vessel if it has first launched a weapon at us. You are responding by vessel, not by flag. Don't forget that in the heat of combat, should combat arise!

"I've posted your patrol schedules. We'll have two choppers in the air at all times, and a third chopper and crew on deck in a READY-15 status. You're going to be doing a lot of flying in the next twenty-four hours, so grab sack time whenever you can."

****

Mirov bent over the chart with the *B-445*'s navigation officer, Captain Lieutenant Norin, checking their progress. Concentrating on the chart as he was, it took a moment to realize that the political officer and the XO stood on one side of him and the chief of the boat on the other. He straightened up.

"*Da?*"

"Captain Mirov," said Captain Leonev, the boat's political officer, "I am placing you under arrest. You are clearly conducting this mission in such a manner as to guarantee its failure. I can only conclude that you are intentionally disobeying orders. You leave me no choice."

Every head in the control room looked up in surprise. Mirov was the most highly regarded submariner in the fleet.

He had trained nearly all of them. Mirov's exploits were the talk of the base. The political officer's charge was a shock.

"Indeed," replied Mirov calmly. "And how am I guaranteeing the failure of this mission?"

"By refusing to arrive on station early, which would enable us to be completely silent when the American carrier arrives," answered his XO, Captain Zarubin.

"I see," said Mirov, laying the parallel rulers on the plot table. "Captain Zarubin, how many times has a submarine under your direct command penetrated the ASW screen of an American aircraft carrier?"

Zarubin's face turned red, and he remained silent.

"How many times, Captain?" Mirov repeated. "Go on, tell this control room crew—how many times?"

Zarubin cleared his throat and finally said, "This will be my first."

"I have done it four times, in two different classes of submarine. And you are finding fault with my methods?"

Leonev saw Zarubin faltering and interjected, "Enough of this! As the senior officer, I am placing you under arrest. Chief of the Boat, escort him to his quarters and post a guard. He is not to leave his quarters except by my permission."

"Comrades, this is a mutiny," declared Mirov.

"Will you not fight it, comrade Captain?" asked Norin.

Leonev opened his mouth to respond, but Mirov silenced him with an upraised finger. "Captain Norin, perhaps the most dangerous place on earth to have a fight is in a submerged submarine. No, I will not fight it." He turned to the control room crew. "Each of you is to do his duty. Captains Leonev and Zarubin have mutinied and usurped my authority: let the log show it. Nonetheless, they are now in command, and you must follow their commands as you have followed mine."

"Take him away, Chief," spat Leonev to COB.

The man hesitated until Mirov said gently, "It's okay, Chief. Do your duty."

As Mirov was led away, Captain Zarubin said, "Helm,

make revolutions for five knots."

"But, Anto—ah, Captain, we are not silent at five knots!" Norin objected.

Zarubin looked at the helmsman and said through gritted teeth, "Make revolutions for five knots. NOW!"

The helmsman shot a glance at Norin and shrugged. "Aye, aye, Captain. Making revolutions for five knots."

Zarubin turned on the navigation officer, "Captain Norin! Can you follow my authority or must I arrest you as well?"

Norin glared at him. "I will follow your authority, sir," he said quietly, eyes flashing with anger.

"Very well. Recalculate our arrival time on station maintaining five knots."

"Aye, aye, sir."

****

It was time to receive the second set of orders Admiral Shukshin had spoken of. The *K-263* came to periscope depth and raised its communication antenna. After sending and then receiving a burst transmission, the Akula returned to the depths. The antenna was raised for less than twenty seconds.

Fetisov and his political officer were in his quarters when a messenger from the submarine's communication center brought the decoded message to him.

Fetisov read the message and turned pale. His hands shook as he reread the message. "This is madness," he said to political officer Khorkov. "They want us to sink the American aircraft carrier. We are to engage the American carrier group beginning at 0200 hours on 21 January—just six hours from now."

Khorkov was almost as surprised as his captain. The *zampolit* had been expecting instructions to fire on the Americans—one could hardly infer anything else from the meeting he and the other two political officers had had with Admiral Shukshin. However, he'd not expected the primary target to be an aircraft carrier. It was, indeed, madness.

Fetisov continued, "It says that if I am being prosecuted

by American antisubmarine helicopters, I am instructed to surface and shoot down the helicopter, thus eliminating an immediate threat to my vessel. If *K-284* is also surfaced, I am to contact him and coordinate the attack on the helicopters with him, such that we attack at the same time. I am then instructed to submerge and launch a full complement of torpedoes at the primary target, the carrier. Having done that, we are to return to base. We may fire on any other American vessels that threaten our safety."

Captain Fetisov stared at the message, at a loss for words. He could very well be remembered in history as the man who started World War 3. It was not the sort of legacy he had been hoping for.

"What are you going to do, Captain?" asked Khorkov. Now that it came to it, he desperately hoped he would not have to relieve Fetisov. He did not want to command a submarine under such conditions.

Fetisov considered his answer carefully, unaware that the political officers had met with Shukshin and made a contingency plan to take over the vessel should the captain fail to obey the orders. He sighed. "I will do my duty to the best of my ability, Captain Khorkov, as will you and the rest of the crew. If we die, we die." Meanwhile, thousands of meters northeast of them, Captain Gromyko of *K-284* had just made the same decision.

****

"Come to periscope depth," Captain Anton Zarubin ordered.

B-445 ascended through the dark water until it was seventeen meters below the surface. The high-frequency antenna went up, her position report was transmitted, and new orders were received. In a matter of seconds, the Kilo was resuming its course and five-knot speed as it descended back to two hundred twenty meters.

Zarubin and Leonev made their way to the empty officers' wardroom. Zarubin opened the decoded orders and studied them briefly. "It is as we suspected, comrade. We are to attack the *Midway*. Mirov would never have done this. Admiral Shukshin warned me that we'd have to take him out of the way. According to Shukshin's plan, we were to wait until the last minute before dealing with Mirov—after he'd already gotten us close to the carrier. Admiral Shukshin was not confident I could conn the submarine close enough to the carrier.

"It is best that we dealt with Mirov immediately when we did. Had he seen these orders he would have refused to get in range of the carrier. In any case, if Mirov could get us close undetected then I can, too. I am quite capable of it."

What neither officer realized is that the Kilo's senior chief petty officer, the starshi michman, Oleg Kirovich Titov, was standing in the passageway just outside the wardroom, listening to their conversation. A twenty-five-year veteran of the Soviet submarine service, Titov was the oldest and most senior enlisted man on the boat. The rest of the enlisted crew and even most of the officers esteemed the burly man with a mixture of awe and fear. Titov knew all the complex systems of the Kilo as well as he knew his own personal history.

Titov viewed the submarine officer corps with a mix of cynicism and just enough respect to avoid a reprimand. It was an attitude shared by enlisted men in the uniformed services the world over. Officers were generally regarded by the enlisted as inexperienced individuals lacking common sense: men who needed a steady hand next to them—a steady *enlisted* hand—to keep them from running aground, accidentally diving with a hatch open, or otherwise destroying their own submarine. In the constellation of officers under which Titov had served (which included Shukshin when he was a captain), there were only two exceptions to his otherwise universal disdain of officers. Those exceptions were Admiral Zelenko and Captain First Rank Boris Sayanovich Mirov. These two men Titov held in the highest possible esteem.

Having served with Mirov on nine different patrols, Titov had observed his tactical genius, his absolute mastery of the vessels he commanded, and his deep, genuine care for both the officers and enlisted men serving under his command.

Mirov was stern and demanding, but he got what he demanded from his crews because he gave to them the same level of commitment.

Titov had been sensing a subtle shift in the atmosphere on the submarine base for months and had been unable to put his finger on what exactly was going on. The changes seemed to center around Admiral Shukshin and the entire political officer corps. As a submariner, Titov considered Standing Order 17 a virtual death sentence. The only reason it had not resulted in the loss of a submarine, in his opinion, was the restraint of the Americans. He'd also heard disturbing rumors about Zelenko's death, rumors about the shifting of political winds, even rumors of a planned conflict with the American navy.

Mirov's arrest fit right in with the rest of the politically charged mysteries floating around the submarine service. The accusations against the captain were total fiction. Titov knew that Mirov's tactics were the right ones; he also expected that Zarubin's order to increase speed to five knots would most likely result in the Americans detecting the *B-445*.

Having overheard Zarubin and Leonev, Titov saw that Mirov's arrest was actually part of a much larger nefarious plan—it was not due to any failure on Mirov's part. Shukshin feared that Mirov would not pull the trigger. Titov was also convinced that the whole crazy plan had originated with Shukshin alone, not the high command and certainly not the Politburo. Shukshin was going rogue. It would almost certainly result in the loss of *B-445* and the entire crew, as well as both Akulas.

So what am I going to do about it? Titov asked himself as he returned to his duty in the control room as the chief of the boat.

****

Washington, DC awoke on 20 January to an unusually mild morning. The temperature was in the upper forties and expected to hit fifty by noon. Cloudy and breezy, it was a perfect day for the inauguration. The capital was festooned with red, white, and blue bunting. Canopies and tents were being erected on the west front of the US Capitol building, with seating for the large number of dignitaries and government officials who were anticipated.

But there was critical business to be accomplished before the festivities could begin. An emergency meeting of the National Security Council had been called in light of intelligence received overnight by the NSA.

President-elect George Herbert Walker Bush strode into the meeting room and stood briefly at the lectern. "As you know, I was delegated by President Reagan to chair these meetings for the last several months in light of his weakening health. After today I expect to continue chairing the NSC as president. Over the next several weeks and months the faces around this table will change, as some of you move on to other challenges. I want you to know how grateful I am for the wisdom and ability you each have brought to this council. For those who might be passing off this council, thank you for your excellent service.

"As you may know, I'm a little busier than usual today," Bush said, grinning, "something about a meeting with the Chief Justice." This brought a few chuckles around the table. "So let's get it moving and keep it brief. Paul, you wanted this meeting—why don't you tell us what is going on?"

"Thank you, Mr. Vice President, er, Mr. President-elect—actually I'm not sure what to call you, sir," said the DCI, Paul West.

"Paul, if it makes you feel better, I haven't a clue either," Bush laughed. "Please continue."

"Yes, sir. Overnight a priority intercept came from the NSA, a telephone call between the new admiral of the Pacific Fleet and Alexander Pushkaryov, the vice president of the Soviet Union. This phone call occurred just after midnight, our time."

"You mean this morning?" the vice president asked, surprised.

West nodded. "Hot off the press. It was flagged and went

right to the top of the queue. Our best translator came in at 0200 to translate it. I cannot give you a transcript for security reasons, but several things have become very clear. First, a conflict between their navy and ours will begin at the very hour of your inauguration, sir. It is expected that this conflict will secure the military to the cause of those who are planning to overthrow Gorbachev. Although Admiral Shukshin was a little coy in the conversation, I think we can clearly state that a Russian vessel will attack an American vessel around noon to-day our time, which is 0200 on 21 January, Vladivostok time. Second, the coup itself will take place in about four days in Moscow. The Sovs will be holding a large military parade to send a message on the occasion of your inauguration. This provides a pretext for bringing large numbers of troops into the city. That parade is scheduled for 23 January. The coup is scheduled for 24 January.

"Sir, I must stress this: what I just told you is not the product of intelligence analysis. It was directly and unequivocally stated in that phone conversation."

The vice president leaned back in his chair, laced his fingers together and put them behind his head and stared at the ceiling, thinking. Finally he asked, "Remind me again exactly what they hope to gain by this provocation?"

Admiral Walter Blackstone, director of naval intelligence, answered. "Unity in the ranks, sir."

The chief of naval operations, Admiral Craig Kensington, nodded. "When they hear that the fuse of conflict has been lit, they will put aside political differences and follow a strong voice of leadership."

"And that," Paul West added, "will ensure the success of their coup. Gorbachev will be seen as an appeaser contributing to the decline of the Soviet Union."

"I see. Then we must ensure they never hear that the fuse has been lit," said Bush.

"Sir?"

"Gentlemen, I've got to run—I'm being driven today, on this day of all days, by a schedule I cannot control. Here is what we're going to do. First, if something happens during the inauguration, let it go. Television cameras from across the world are in DC today, so our first blow to the coup plotters' plan is to completely stifle their event. Don't give any publicity to them—don't feed the bear. Do not interrupt the ceremony, don't even try to notify me until the cameras are gone.

"Second, our rules of engagement stand as we last formulated them. No change. Reactive self-defense only. No anticipatory self-defense.

"Third, if they fire on us and either side takes damage, I want a believable explanation for the damage that does not involve either side shooting at the other. I don't know, maybe an accidental collision—something plausible.

"If at all possible, I want to steal from these coup plotters their primary weapon, which is publicity. Their armed forces cannot unite around the conflict if they are unaware that there has been conflict.

"That's our goal, gentlemen. I want to keep a lid on it." The vice president stood and prepared to leave.

Admiral Kensington cleared his throat and said, "Sir, if I may?"

Bush turned toward him. "Go ahead, Admiral."

"If the Soviets adhere to the pattern they have established, they will be going after our carrier battle group with submarines. If their submarines launch a weapon, they will be sunk by our forces—thus, no witnesses. But the Soviets usually also have an intelligence trawler shadowing our battle groups. Unfortunately, that trawler will be a witness to whatever happens. I'd like permission to sink that trawler as soon as any shooting begins—to eliminate witnesses."

"How will you explain the loss of the trawler?"

"I'm not sure yet. Probably the same way we'll have to explain the loss of their submarines. But if we don't sink that trawler, sir, it won't matter what sort of story we spin. The Sovs will find out about the conflict, and our attempt at disinformation will strengthen, not weaken, their hand."

Bush thought for a moment, then nodded his head. "Send it out to the carrier battle groups as an exception to the ROE. If shooting starts, sink any nearby Soviet intelligence trawlers

ASAP."

****

The USS *Louisville*, SSN-724, was ranging to the north and west of the *Midway*'s intended course. It had come to periscope depth several hours prior, and using SSIXS it received the latest intelligence on the detections of the Akulas, as well as the P-3C's detection of the snorkeling Kilo. Captain Randall Boston thus had a clear idea of where the three Soviet submarines were hours ago, but he had no clue as to where they were now. His instincts told him it was the *Midway*, not the *Nimitz*, the Soviets were after.

"We're going to break the sprint-drift pattern, XO. I want to drift on this heading for a full hour with just enough headway for steerage, thirty minutes above the layer, thirty minutes below. Those Soviet subs are out there somewhere, and my gut tells me they are waiting to jump the *Midway*.

"I'll take the conn while you get breakfast. When you're done, you can have the conn while I eat." As executive officer Commander Joshua Wade made his way to the officers' wardroom, Boston grabbed the handset on the bulkhead. "Sonar, conn, report all contacts."

"Conn, sonar. We've got two weak surface contacts headed away from us, a pair of west-bound freighters sailing in company on bearing two-eight-zero. They appear to be headed toward Taiwan and are moving beyond the range of our sonar. I have one very faint surface contact to the south, bearing one-eight-seven, that might be the *Midway*—I think it's coming through the convergence zone. No subsurface contacts."

"Aye, sonar. Keep your ears on."

For the next thirty minutes, the *Louisville* took a zigzag path above the thermocline, idling along at one knot, offering its towed array the maximum opportunity to pick up sounds from all points of the compass.

When the bulkhead timer marked thirty minutes, Captain Boston commanded, "Diving Officer, take us down gradually to three fifty. I want to get below the layer."

"Aye, Skipper, headed for three hundred fifty feet. Planes-man, three degrees down. Make your depth three hundred fifty feet."

"Aye, aye, sir. We are three degrees down at the bow." A few minutes later he reported, "Our depth is three hundred fifty feet."

In the sonar room, Petty Officer Roland Abrams sat bolt upright in his chair, his hands pressing the headphones into his ears. "Got . . ." He stopped, eyes closed, listening intently. Finally, the sonar tech slowly nodded. "Got something, Chief. It is nothing more than a whisper, but I think I actually have a screw count. Give me a sec."

He adjusted the display in front of him and listened intently, turning a few knobs slowly, studying the waterfall-like display with the bare ghosts of white lines showing up.

"Okay," he said finally, exhaling, "Reporting a contact, Chief, a super quiet contact, bearing zero-four-five. There is a screw count, but I can't quite get it. Could I request a course change to one-three-five, then all stop?"

"Conn, sonar. Petty Officer Abrams is hearing ghosts, but thinks it might be a Kilo ghost. Faint subsurface contact on bearing zero-four-five. There is an indiscernible screw count. Requesting new course one-three-five, then all stop."

"Aye, sonar, you got it."

The sonar supervisor, CPO Jurgen Schneider, hung up the phone and looked at Roland Abrams. "Okay, Rolly. You're in command of the boat. You realize, if you detect and track a slow-moving Kilo, you've done what very few sonar operators have ever done? Make us proud, buddy."

Abrams nodded and squeezed his hands against his headset. "Something's there, Chief. I know it."

Fifteen minutes later he was muttering to himself and scribbling observations in his log. "No reactor noise. No machinery noise. Single screw, six blades."

Abrams looked up. "Got him, Chief. It is a definite Kilo. Bearing zero-four-eight, triangulation puts him at range nineteen thousand yards. Screw count has him at five knots. Depth, seven hundred twenty feet."

"Conn, sonar. Rolly's got him, sir. It's the Kilo. Bearing zero-four-eight, range by triangulation calculated to be approximately nineteen thousand yards, speed five knots. Depth, seven hundred twenty feet."

"Sonar, conn. I'll be right there." Captain Boston stepped into the starboard side passageway, forward of the control room, and entered the sonar space.

"Okay, PO Abrams, convince me that you've just done what almost no one else has. You pinned the tail on a Kilo. How sure are you?"

"Positive, Captain."

"Why?"

"Simple, sir. First of all, I can barely hear him, and we have the best sonar in the world. Second, it is a single screw, six blades. I read Kilo, there. Third, he is cruisin' along at five knots with zero reactor or machinery noise. He's definitely a Kilo, sir. No question about it."

Boston stared at the young petty officer, trying to get him to crack. The man just grinned. Finally, Boston grinned back. "Okay, Rolly. I believe you." He turned to the CPO. "Chief Schneider, designate and send to tracking." He looked back at the young sonar man. "By the way, Rolly, have you ever exited a submarine through the torpedo tube?"

Abrams' brow furrowed. "Um, no sir."

"Well, that's what you'll be doing if you're wrong about this. At depth."

Boston returned to the control room. "All stop. COB, rig boat for ultraquiet. We'll let this Kilo pass us and then pull in behind him."

Chapter 22

The SH-3H Sikorsky Sea King helicopter was heavily loaded with everything but sonobuoys, of which it had relatively few. Four lethal Mk-46 acoustic homing torpedoes were attached to its hardpoints. Its mission was to extend and ensure CARGRU5's ASW screen. Two hours into its patrol it had established no contacts.

The full moon was almost directly overhead, just past its zenith, and the pale light glittered on the calm sea below. The four-man crew of the chopper had no time to appreciate the tranquility over which they flew, however. They were hunting for Soviet submarines.

"Lowering the dome," said SENSO (the sensor operator).

"Roger that," responded Lieutenant Sandy Jefferson, the pilot. He concentrated on holding the Sea King steady in light and variable winds. One of the advantages of the full moon above and the glittering sea below was that he didn't have to fight vertigo, a common problem for pilots at night when the horizon was not distinct.

After a few minutes, SENSO said, "Nothing. Not even a whale. I'm retrieving the dome." A moment later, "Dome is secure."

Jefferson flew another two miles further, and the process was repeated. And then again. And then again.

"I think maybe this fishin' hole is empty," Jefferson said. "But cast your line anyway, SENSO, see if you get a strike. Holding her steady at one hundred feet."

"Aye. Lowering dome."

The sonar dome descended through the depths as the cable spooled off the take-up reel. When it reached a depth of one hundred fifty feet, the sensor operator charged the device and send out an omnidirectional acoustical pulse. A weak echo showed up on his display.

"Hey, hey! Got something nibbling on the line," SENSO said. He blasted another acoustic pulse out of the sonar dome and watched his displays. "Yep, I've got an echo. Probable contact, bearing three-four-seven, range five thousand seven hundred yards."

TACCO said to the pilot, "Put us right on top of him, Sandy."

"Roger, TACCO."

Jefferson piloted the Sikorsky to the indicated location, and they started dropping passive sonobuoys on the contact.

"Contact, contact!" cried SENSO. "We've got a submarine. I've got reactor noises and a very slow screw count."

"Let's drop a pinger on this guy and work up a TMA," TACCO said.

The "pinger" is an active sonobuoy, AN/SSQ-62B DICASS (Directional Command Activated Sonobuoy System), which can create an acoustic ping on one of four sonar channels and has hydrophones to receive the echo of the pulse if it bounces off something hard, like a submarine's hull. When the DICASS is deployed, a buoy remains on the surface providing radio communications with the sensor operator. The buoy lowers the transducer on a cable to an initial depth of ninety feet. The sensor operator controls the behavior of the buoy/transducer pair and can give it commands to go active, to let the transducer sink to a deeper depth, and even to scuttle the pair when its job is done.

"DICASS is away," SENSO reported, launching the buoy through the Sea King's sonobuoy ejector tube.

"Ho, I've got three contacts," SENSO reported several minutes later. The active sonobuoy was picking up echos not only from the initial contact, but also from a second one, as well as a very faint subsurface echo coming from something about sixteen thousand yards to the northeast.

TACCO radioed the destroyer *Kinkaid* with the estimated position of the distant northern contact. The destroyer launched one of its SH-30B Seahawks to investigate. By sheer chance the *Kinkaid*'s Seahawk lowered its dipping sonar practically right on top of the northern contact.

Several minutes later, the Sea King identified its two contacts, one as a Soviet Akula and the other as an American *Los Angeles*-class submarine two thousand yards behind the Akula.

The *Kinkaid*'s Seahawk also identified its contact as an Akula.

****

Ever since Mirov's arrest, morale on the *B-445* was worsening. The only two who did not perceive it were the two captains who deposed Captain First Rank Mirov.

As the most senior enlisted man on the vessel, the *starshi michman*, Chief Petty Officer Titov had the run of the boat. The only space he was not permitted to enter unaccompanied, other than the officer's quarters, was the communication center.

Titov made his way aft through the passageways to the engineering spaces, and found the engineering officer, Captain Third Rank Ilya Germanovich Fedin.

"Sir, may I talk to you in private?" he asked Fedin.

"Certainly. Follow me." Fedin led him further aft, through a hatch to the normally unoccupied stern compartment of the Kilo. Fedin closed the hatch behind them and then turned to face Titov. "This is about Captain Mirov, isn't it?"

"Yes, sir. What Captains Zarubin and Leonev did is not only wrong, it was planned before we ever left Vladivostok."

"What? How can you know this?"

"I overheard them talking in the officer's wardroom, Captain Fedin. Zarubin said that Admiral Shukshin warned him to get Mirov out of the way. Shukshin knew Mirov would not follow Shukshin's orders—the ones we received several hours ago."

"The ones that tell us to attack the American aircraft carrier," Fedin mused. "I wondered about that. I don't understand it—why would Admiral Shukshin order us to start World War 3? It makes no sense. It does not sound like something the high command would order us to do."

"Perhaps Captain Mirov *knows* it did not come from the high command, sir. Perhaps that is why Admiral Shukshin knew he would refuse the order," Titov argued.

"Yes. Mirov has connections and sources that go all the way to the Politburo. He might indeed know that this was a rogue order." Fedin looked down at the deck plating, thinking. "So, what are you suggesting, Titov?"

"Sir, I've talked privately to several of the other officers, and they agree—what was done to Mirov was wrong. I've talked to many of the enlisted men, and they are very concerned. They do not have confidence in either Captain Zarubin or Leonev. I think both men should be restrained—tied up and gagged, and put in sickbay. Mirov should be restored to command."

"You realize that if it does not go well, we will be facing a firing squad when we return," said Fedin sternly.

"Sir, we *won't* return if Zarubin attacks the Americans— we'll be sunk. I'd rather die quickly on my home soil in front of a firing squad than contemplate death for ten minutes or so as we slowly sink to a depth that will crush us."

"I see your point. Okay—I'm in. Have you got a plan?"

Titov smiled. "Yes, sir, I do. Have you got a large wrench?"

Fedin smiled back, "Certainly."

****

Zarubin glanced at the *B-445*'s bulkhead chronometer, which read 0150. As far as he was aware, the Americans had not detected his submarine in its current position. He decided to load the torpedoes, flood the tubes, and open the outer doors now while there was no one snooping around. By doing so, he could avoid making all those transient sounds when *Midway* was closer and more likely to detect them.

"Weapons officer, load tubes one through six, flood tubes, and open outer doors," Captain Zarubin ordered.

"But, sir!" the officer objected, "That's—"

"Do it!" Zarubin snapped.

****

The *Louisville* remained motionless in the water, rigged for ultraquiet. Captain Randall Boston muttered silently under his breath. They had lost track of the Kilo, and CARGRU5 was rapidly approaching. Boston felt sure the Kilo was unaware of the *Louisville*'s presence, and he didn't want to give up that advantage by going active with his sonar—at least, not yet.

Irritated, Boston grabbed the handset on the bulkhead. "Sonar, conn. C'mon, Schneider, where is that Kilo?"

"Conn, sonar. Sir, the passive arrays are not telling us anything. It appears he went to all-stop about an hour ago, and he's not radiating any noise. The only thing quieter than a motionless Kilo, sir, is a hole in the water."

"Do you think he could have crept away at maybe one or two knots?"

"It's quite possible, Skipper. We were lucky to hear him at five knots. I don't think we would hear him at all at one or two."

A few minutes later Petty Officer Roland Abrams stiffened. He pressed his headset to his ears and studied his display. "Chief, I think we just located the Kilo. I've got transients at bearing two-three-six. He is flooding his tubes. Based on the signal strength, I think he's pretty doggone close."

"Conn, sonar. Contact bearing two-three-six, close by. We believe it is the Kilo, sir. He's flooding his tubes—wait . . . Rolly reports he's also opening his outer doors."

"Sonar, aye. Good job, boys. Send the information to tracking. Tracking, work up a best-guess firing solution. Fire control, load tubes one and two with Mk-48 ADCAPS, and do it quietly! Do not flood tubes. I just want to be ready."

****

The *Midway* was cruising through a calm sea at twenty knots, leaving a phosphorescent trail of plankton. It was a beautiful night, the full moon riding high and the remainder of the dark but clear sky sprinkled with myriad points of light. High pressure had taken over once the nasty weather had drifted off to the east.

Captain Ernest Skagway stood on the open bridge, enjoying the night air. The activity on the flight deck far below him was, for the moment, subdued. A Sea King sat on the deck below at a READY-15 status, but other than that fixed-wing flight operations were not expected to resume until it was time to replace the current AEW and CAP patrols.

A messenger came up the ladder behind him and requested, "Captain, the watch officer in the CIC asks if you could join him."

Skagway strode into the Combat Information Center and immediately perceived the tension in the room. "What have we got?" he asked Commander Pete Brown, the CIC watch officer.

Brown was studying the threat plot. He turned to Skagway and said, "We've got a pair of Soviet SSNs just north of us, Skipper. Sierra-19 is along bearing three-three-zero, range eight nautical miles, and Sierra-18 is along bearing three-five-four, range thirteen nautical miles. Somehow they slipped through the screen."

"Akulas?"

"Yes, sir. We are pretty much headed straight for them."

"Where's the trawler?"

"Thirty-five miles behind us, Skipper, on bearing one-nine-nine.

Skagway looked at the threat plot for a moment, then said, "Messenger of the Watch, please wake the flag lieutenant, and inform him that the admiral is needed in the CIC."

One of the petty officers manning the communications center said, "Captain, *Kinkaid*, *Cushing*, and *Bunker Hill* are all going active with their sonar. *Kinkaid* is going to investigate Sierra-18."

Skagway glanced at the chronometer on the bulkhead. It was 0155 hours. *I'm not in the mood to take any chances*, he thought sourly. He picked up the phone to the navigation bridge. "OOD, this is the Captain. Change course to zero-three-two, increase speed to flank. Commence zigzagging. Sound General Quarters, and set Material Condition Zebra. Notify the rest of the carrier group."

The relative quiet of the ship was shattered by the alarm bell and announcement over the 1MC: "This is not a drill, this is not a drill. General Quarters, General Quarters. All hands man your battle stations. The route of travel is forward and up to starboard, down and aft to port. Set material condition Zebra throughout the ship. Reason for General Quarters: potentially hostile submarines."

A few minutes later Admiral Blake joined him. A stickler for discipline, the admiral had taken time to shave and his uniform was as crisp as if he'd just received it from the dry cleaners. Skagway appreciated his boss's professionalism—it projected a needed note of certainty and confidence in an uncertain situation. Skagway briefly outlined the measures he'd just taken.

Blake nodded his approval. "Good job, Ernie. Well, it looks like we are the Soviet's target for their latest provocation, not *Nimitz*. According to the recent intelligence, if they're going to do something it will be in the next few minutes."

****

"Pass the word for battle stations, torpedo, COB, but do it quietly!" Fetisov commanded. *K-263* was now ready for combat.

Five minutes later, Fetisov received an update from the sonar room. "Conn, sonar. The American ships have gone active with their sonar. *Midway* appears to have changed course, bearing one-one-five."

"Aye, sonar," Fetisov replied. Suddenly the sound of a sonar ping reverberated through the hull. "Where did that come from, sonar?" Captain Fetisov asked.

"Overhead, sir. It is an active sonobuoy."

"Aye, sonar. Well, we've certainly been detected. Torpedo Room, load torpedo tubes one, two, three, and four."

Fetisov turned to the COB again. "Get two men up here, each with a 9K38 Igla. Have them assemble and load the launchers and stand by for my command." He turned back toward the control stations. "Diving officer, bring us to periscope depth."

A moment later the officer reported, "Captain, we are at periscope depth."

"Very well. Communicator, raise the communications mast and see if you can contact *K-284*."

"Captain, I have *K-284* on the communication channel."

"Put it to my phone."

"Aye, aye, Captain, you should have him now."

Fetisov picked up the handset. "Greetings, Captain Gromyko. Are you ready to die for the *rodina*?"

"I'd rather not, but if it must be so, Captain Fetisov, I am ready to do my duty."

"Do you have any American aircraft threatening you?"

"*Da*. I have a helicopter dropping sonobuoys on me. If he has any idea of what he's doing, he should have a solid firing solution on me by now."

"Do your men have the Igla ready, and are you ready to surface?"

"*Da*."

"Very well. Set a timer for three minutes on my mark. Surface, and when time expires, fire on the helicopter. Ready?"

"Ready."

"Mark."

****

The USS *Olympia* waited quietly, undetected in *K-263*'s baffles, two thousand yards behind Fetisov's Akula. Captain Ben Mitchell shook his head. "I have a bad feeling about this," he said, unconsciously quoting a line from Star Wars. "Fire control, load tubes one through four. Fire control tracking, give me a fresh solution on Sierra-19." Even though the *Olympia* had not used its active sonar, it was able to pull the targeting data from the echoed pulses of the Sea King's sonobuoys.

"Conn, sonar. Hull popping noises. Sierra-19 is ascending." A moment later sonar reported, "Target is at periscope depth, Skipper."

"Aye, sonar. Fire control, match target bearings in tubes one and two."

"Conn, sonar. Target is surfacing."

"What do you think he's doing, Cap?" asked Mitchell's XO, Gene Saddler.

"Not a clue, Gene. He's virtually giving himself up." He thought for a moment then asked, "Sonar, conn. Is that chopper still in the neighborhood?"

"Aye, Skipper. Picking him up loud and clear on the TB-23."

"Sonar, is there any indication Sierra-19 knows we are sitting on his six?"

"Negative, Captain."

Suddenly, a terrible possibility occurred to him. "He thinks his nearest threat is that ASW chopper! Gene, do you remember reading some intelligence reports about six months ago suggesting that Ivan was carrying MANPADS (Man-portable air-defense systems) on their submarines?"

"You mean, like, Stingers?"

"Yep."

"Yeah, I think I did see something about that. Why?"

"Because I think I know what that Akula is about to do. Fire control, stand by. Sonar, stand by for a ranging ping on the target, on my command."

****

George H. W. Bush stepped up to the podium, placed his left hand on the Bible and raised his right hand. "I do solemnly swear that I will faithfully execute the office of President of the United States, and will to the best of my ability, preserve, protect and defend the Constitution of the United States," Bush affirmed. Chief Justice William Rehnquist shook the president's hand, and Bush turned to face the gathered assembly to deliver his inaugural address.

"Mr. Chief Justice, Mr. President, Vice President Quayle, Senator Mitchell, Speaker Wright, Senator Dole, Congressman Michel, and fellow citizens, neighbors, and friends: There is a man here who has earned a lasting place in our hearts and in our history. President Reagan, on behalf of our Nation, I thank you for the wonderful things that you have done for America.

"I have just repeated word for word the oath taken by George Washington 200 years ago, and the Bible on which I placed my hand is the Bible on which he placed his. It is right that the memory of Washington be with us today, not only because this is our Bicentennial Inauguration, but because Washington remains the Father of our Country. And he would, I think, be gladdened by this day; for today is the concrete expression of a stunning fact: our continuity these 200 years since our government began.

"We meet on democracy's front porch, a good place to talk as neighbors and as friends. For this is a day when our nation is made whole, when our differences, for a moment, are suspended . . ."

Dr. William Jensen was seated with the dignitaries, watching the inauguration. As President Bush spoke, Jensen felt a powerful sense of irony. Americans had witnessed a peaceful transfer of power from one chief executive to another forty-one times. It had occurred without riots, without violence, without any threat to the stability of the government.

Yet on this same day, conspirators in the Soviet Union were doing their utmost to foment a coup and were willing to risk war with the USA and even murder their own countrymen in order to accomplish their purposes. It was a revolution without an end in sight—a fundamentally unstable arrangement based on a flawed economic model and an understanding of the nature of man that did not take sin into account.

Jensen's mind wandered as the ceremony continued. *We are not a perfect nation—there are no perfect nations. There remains much work to do to ensure equal opportunity for all of our citizens, whatever their color or creed. It is true that our sins are many—but that is true of all nations, not just ours. When all the variables are weighed fairly, I think we do pretty well. Some nations put a premium on safety; Americans have always put a greater premium on freedom—freedom to fail without interference from the government, freedom to succeed. People line up to get in this country, not to leave it. That's the yardstick that says it all.*

****

The Sea King continued to hover in the moonlight, listening to Fetisov's *K-263* on the sonobuoys.

"Look off to your left, sir," said SENSO suddenly.

"What am I looking for?" the Sea King pilot, Sandy Jefferson, asked.

"The submarine, sir. It's surfacing."

Jefferson turned on his powerful searchlight in time to see the sleek black Akula breaking the surface of the water. He circled the vessel and watched as two men climbed into the sail. They waved at him, with big grins on their faces.

"What are they doing?" asked his copilot.

"Beats me. They keep bending over like they're trying to pick something up. Okay, now they're standing up straight—something in their hands. What's that they are hold—SAM! SAM!"

Jefferson jerked the collective to the right and dropped the Sea King as low as he could get it, desperately jinking, taking evasive action as he raced away at full throttle. Suddenly a fireball appeared miles to the north, but Jefferson forced himself to ignore it and instead concentrate on his flying.

The copilot was in the act of turning his headset selector from intercom to the high-frequency encrypted channel monitored by the *Midway* when the Igla struck the Sea King's tail and exploded. Spinning out of control, the flaming helicopter slammed into the water and broke apart.

****

The two seamen tossed the empty Igla launcher overboard along with the unused one and climbed down the ladder, closing the hatch leading to the sail and dogging it down.

"Hatch is secure, comrade Captain," reported the two seamen, scrambling the rest of the way down the ladder from the *K-263*'s sail.

"The diving board is green, Captain," affirmed the diving

officer, inspecting the display that showed the status of external hatches.

"Aye. Diving officer, take her down to fifty meters. Helm, come to heading one-three-zero, make revolutions for fifteen knots," Fetisov ordered. "Sonar, verify range and bearing to the *Midway*."

A moment later, the fire control tracking officer reported, "We have a solid firing solution for the *Midway*."

"Aye," responded Captain Fetisov. "Fire control, match bearings to the *Midway* in tubes one, two, three, and four. Flood tubes and open outer doors."

"Tubes ready in all respects, comrade Captain."

"Aye. Shoot tubes one through four!"

Four Type 53-65M torpedoes were ejected from their tubes with a blast of compressed air. Immediately their kerosene/hydrogen-peroxide turbine engines began operating, and the four fish accelerated smoothly to forty-four knots. Each carried six hundred sixty-one pounds of high explosive designed to rip through the thick hull-armor of a warship.

"Conn, sonar. Torpedoes are running true."

"Aye. Reload tubes one, two, three, and four."

****

The *Olympia* was loitering behind Fetisov's *K-263*. The explosion of the Sea King could be clearly heard in the control room.

"Conn, sonar. The Sea King was there, and then suddenly it was not, sir. I am picking up transients characteristic of debris falling into the water. It sounds like the chopper was shot down."

Mitchell didn't need sonar to tell him, he could hear the report of the explosion through the hull. He cursed and slapped his leg. "Sonar, conn. Hit Sierra-19 with three ranging pings at full power. I want those boys to know their last day in the land of the living has arrived. Fire control tracking, I want a firing solution ASAP."

The powerful AN/BQS-13 spherical array in the bow of

the *Los Angeles*-class submarine has one thousand two hundred and forty-one sound-producing transducers. It is able to generate acoustical energy so powerful that it produces cavitation bubbles on the bow of the submarine.

"I've always wanted to do one of these," said the sonar supervisor, CPO Stan Lilly, grimly. He nudged one his sonar techs out of the way, saying, "Here, let me do it." Lilly charged the system to maximum power, configured it for a directional beam, and blasted the Akula with a deafening trio of pings.

****

Captain Fetisov stood in the control room of the *K-263* and said, "Time to clear the datum. All ahead flank. Helm, make your heading—"

Fetisov's words were cut off by the reverberation of powerful pings so loud they sounded like fifty men beating on the hull with heavy sledge hammers. The sonar operators screamed curses and clawed their headphones off.

"*Otkuda?* Where did that come from? Where did that come from?" shouted Captain Fetisov.

The deafened sonar techs were still trying to gather their wits, but the sonar supervisor, not wearing headphones and still functioning, gave a quick look at the displays.

"Conn, sonar. Those pings came from directly behind us!"

Fetisov muttered, "How could we not have heard him?" He barked, "Helm, flank speed, course three-one-five. Diving officer, take us down to four hundred eighty meters. Prepare countermeasures."

****

The Kurily was a large 'trawler,' a Vishnya-class Soviet intelligence collection ship. Bristling with antennas, loaded with a surfeit of electronics, its normal mission was to spy on the navies of other nations. Its maximum speed was sixteen knots, which made it impossible to keep up with a carrier group in transit, but it could loiter in an area of operations and collect intelligence all across the electromagnetic spectrum. Admiral Shukshin had assigned the *Kurily* to an area of operations encompassing the region in which CARGRU5 would be attacked.

Minutes before all the shooting began, the captain of the USS *Bunker Hill* stood in the Ticonderoga-class cruiser's Combat Information Center, watching the threat plots while his executive officer conned the ship from the bridge. The Aegis Combat System (ACS) was continuously scanning the environment surrounding the carrier group, detecting and classifying everything within reach of its various long-armed sensors. That included the *Kurily*.

"Fire control, if anybody shoots so much as a BB at one of our assets, that trawler is the first to die, understand?" said the captain.

"Aye, aye, Skipper. Understood."

A minute later the radar contact on the Seahawk disappeared, followed immediately by the disappearance of the Sea King. Up on the bridge, the rumble of two explosions could be heard rolling over the water.

"*Bunker Hill, Bunker Hill,* this is the *Midway.* We just lost two choppers to Ivan's MANPADS. You are at weapons-hold, repeat, weapons-hold," came the announcement over the inter-ship communications channel. "However, you are directed to sink that trawler immediately."

"Let's go active, people," the captain of the *Bunker Hill* said. "Sink that trawler now!"

The fire-control officer selected the trawler as the target and designated four RIM-66 standard missiles to it, and then instructed the ACS to fire.

Four cell covers on the Mk-42 vertical launch system popped open. With a loud *whoosh!* four missiles streaked out of their cells. Initially guided by the AN/SPY-1 surface search radar, as the missiles drew closer to the Kurily their terminal guidance automatically shifted to the AN/SPG-62 fire control radar.

As soon as the *Kurily* detected that it was being painted by targeting radar, its two AK-630 close-in weapons systems went active. Aimed by the MR-123 radar director, each six-barreled 30mm rotary cannon began spraying the incoming missiles with short bursts at a rate of five thousand rounds per minute. Two of the RIM-66s were shredded by the kinetic onslaught and blew up mid-flight, but the brief time necessary for the radar director to switch to the remaining targets resulted in the *Kurily*'s undoing. One missile hit the superstructure, obliterating the bridge, and the other hit the stern AK-630, destroying it.

The ACS on the *Bunker Hill* automatically launched four more RIM-66s, three of which hit the ship, taking out the remaining AK-630, and leaving the entire vessel in flames.

The fire-control officer on the *Bunker Hill* followed up with the manual launch of a single RGM-84 Harpoon missile. The sea-skimming cruise missile hit the *Kurily* at the waterline, dooming the ship. Within three minutes the only trace remaining was a little oil burning on the water.

****

Olympia was tracking the *K-263* as the Soviet submarine began to flee.

The distinctive high-frequency sound of the rapidly spinning screw on a torpedo was unmistakable. "Conn, sonar. The Akula just fired four torpedoes at the *Midway*!"

"Aye, sonar. Nothing we can do for *Midway*, not now. May God help her." Mitchell cursed the ROE that allowed the Akula to take a free shot. He understood that there was a political reason and reality behind the restriction, but he hated it all the same. "Okay, boys, let's put Ivan down in Davy Jones' locker. C'mon, tracking, where's my firing solution?"

"Captain, I have a firing solution for Sierra-19," said the fire control tracking officer.

"Aye. Firing point procedures on Sierra-19. Make tubes one and two ready in all respects. Open outer doors."

"Aye, Captain, tubes one and two are ready in all respects.

Outer doors are open," reported the fire control coordinator

"Fire control, match sonar bearings for Sierra-19, and shoot tubes one and two."

"Aye, Skipper, match bearings for Sierra-19 and shoot tubes one and two," affirmed the fire control coordinator.

"Tubes one and two fired electrically, estimated time to impact, four minutes." reported the combat systems officer.

"Conn, sonar. Torpedoes are running hot, straight, and normal." There was a pause, and then sonar continued, "Conn, sonar. Sierra-19 is running. Relative bearing, dead ahead. Sounds like she's going deeper, Captain."

"We are right on top of her, sonar. She's not going to outrun or outdive an ADCAP," Mitchell said calmly.

A minute later the combat systems officer said, "The torpedoes have gone active and have acquired the Akula."

"Very well. Cut the wires, close the doors, and reload the tubes with Mark 48s."

****

The northern contact that *Kinkaid* was investigating turned out to be Gromyko's *K-284*. Once the K-284 had shot down the Kinkaid's Seahawk and submerged, Captain Gromyko turned his attention to the Midway.

"Sonar, conn. Confirm range and bearing to the *Midway*."

The powerful acoustic pulse bounced off the massive hull of the aircraft carrier, providing accurate targeting data.

"Fire control, match bearings on the *Midway*, and shoot tubes one through four."

The submarine shuddered slightly as rams drove compressed air, ejecting the 53-65M torpedoes from their tubes.

"Now, diving officer, take us down to four hundred meters. Helm, make your heading three-zero-six, make revolutions for thirty-five knots."

Captain Gromyko's concern now was to clear the datum and to get his vessel away from the scene quickly and safely.

****

The *B-445*'s engineering officer, Captain Fedin, called Captain Zarubin from the aft battery access space.

"Conn, engineering. Could you please send Captain Leonev to the aft battery access? I think we may have a potential emergency."

"Engineering, this is the Captain. What is the problem?" Zarubin asked.

"Captain, I'm not even sure I can describe it. I believe that the batteries might be generating a caustic gas that is corroding the compartment. We may have an explosive situation. It certainly looks like something is eating away at the hull. I wanted to get another pair of eyes on it. Begging your pardon, sir, I know it is not a good time for you to be away from the control room, but I thought perhaps you could spare Captain Leonev for a minute?"

"Very well. I'll send him right down." Zarubin looked at Leonev. "Captain Leonev, you are needed in the aft battery access space. Fedin believes he has a problem, and he has asked you to look at the situation. Make it quick."

When Leonev arrived in the aft battery access compartment, Fedin had already removed the access plates. The engineering officer pointed at the open access and said, "Look down in there and to the left—you'll see the corrosion."

Leonev bent over to look in the battery compartment, and Fedin cold-cocked him with a large wrench. Titov came around the corner, and they put restraints and a gag on the unconscious officer, then Titov carried him to sickbay. Fedin passed the wrench to Titov. "Your turn, Chief."

****

Fetisov's *K-263* was just passing thirty knots speed and four hundred meters depth when his sonar room detected the American torpedoes.

"Conn, sonar. We are picking up two American Mk-48 torpedoes, bearing one-three-five. They are active, sir, and have acquired us. Estimated time to impact, ninety-five seconds."

"Release countermeasures. Helm, hard left to course two-two-five.

"Engineering, conn. Go to one hundred ten percent on the reactor, maximum speed."

The *K-263* continued changing course like a writhing snake, leaving knuckles in the water and ejecting noisemakers in the hopes that the torpedoes would be distracted and lock onto the knuckles or noisemakers. Nothing worked. The AD-CAPS continued to chase the submarine relentlessly. The *K-263* was descending beyond four hundred twenty meters when both torpedoes struck it amidships. The point of impact was a mercy, in a way, for between the crushing depth and the incinerating temperature of the reactor core, the crew of *K-263* died instantly.

****

As soon as the two helicopters were shot down, the *Kinkaid* had gone to flank speed and sprinted toward the area where its Seahawk had crashed. The weapons officer launched two ASROC missiles at the coordinates of the contact provided by the Seahawk before it was destroyed. The missiles roared out of the eight-cell launcher. When they approached the area in which the Akula had been detected, a Mk-46 torpedo separated from each of the ASROC boosters and parachuted into the sea. Programmed with a snake-search pattern, the torpedoes quickly locked on to the fleeing *K-284* and accelerated to 40 knots.

****

Captain Second Rank Iosif Fyodorovich Gromyko was mopping the sweat from his forehead with a handkerchief, relieved that he had conned the K-284 away from the scene of the battle successfully, when his sonar supervisor reported torpedoes in the water.

"Conn, sonar. We have been acquired by a pair of Mk-46s, range seven hundred meters, estimated time to impact two minutes twenty-six seconds!"

"Release countermeasures. Full right rudder!"

Between the noisemaker released by the Akula and the knuckle in the water produced by the violent maneuvering, one of the Mk-46s lost its lock on the submarine and detonated on the noisemaker. The other torpedo continued its dogged pursuit.

"Full left rudder."

"Torpedo has reacquired, Captain. Impact in fifteen seconds."

"Emergency blow, diving officer take us to the surface, now!"

But it was too late. The torpedo slammed into the stern and exploded, opening up the engineering spaces to the sea. Gromyko ordered all the ballast tanks in the bow to be filled with compressed air, but the best the submarine could achieve was neutral buoyancy at a steep, stern-down attitude.

A sailor trying to help his comrades escape from a flooding compartment made the mistake of opening the hatch that sealed them off. The sea advanced into yet another compartment. Now at a slightly negative buoyancy, the *K-284* began a long, slow, stern-first slide to the bottom, eighteen thousand feet below.

****

The *B-445*'s chief of the boat, CPO Oleg Kirovich Titov, approached the enlisted man standing guard outside Mirov's quarters. "You are relieved, son. Captain Leonev asked me to keep watch. He said that you are off duty now and may go to your bunk and get some sleep."

When the grateful sailor had disappeared in the direction of the crew quarters, Titov tapped lightly on Mirov's door.

"Enter."

Titov entered the tiny compartment and shut the door.

"Comrade Captain, our officers, aside from Captain Zarubin, and all our enlisted men are requesting that you resume commanding this submarine. We are concerned that the safety of the boat is at stake. We believe that Captains Zarubin and Leonev committed an unlawful act of mutiny, and we are asking you, sir, to return to the control room. The situation has become very dangerous. Just before I knocked on your door, sonar reported torpedoes in the water and distant explosions. We need you now, Captain."

"Where are Captains Zarubin and Leonev?"

"Captain Zarubin presently has the conn. Leonev is indisposed in sickbay."

Mirov eyed the large wrench in Titov's hands. "A headache, I assume?" he asked dryly.

"Yes, sir. I believe so."

"Titov, did you strike an officer?"

Titov assumed an injured expression. "Certainly not, sir! He, ah, tripped and hit his head."

Mirov gave him a look. "I'm glad to hear that you did not strike him. That I could not condone." He stood up, and motioned to the door. "Well, let's be at it, shall we?" The two men returned to the control room.

"Captain Zarubin, you are relieved," Mirov said firmly as he stepped into the control room. "You will be escorted to your quarters, where you will remain until we return to port."

Zarubin turned around, disdain etched across his face. "On whose orders?"

"Mine," replied Captain Mirov.

"You were arrested by Captain Leonev. Your authority on this patrol has ended."

"Captain Leonev raised an illegal mutiny against me. If he thinks he has a case, he can take it up with Admiral Shukshin when we return. If Leonev ever recovers, that is."

"Recovers?" Zarubin asked, turning pale.

"He had a terrible accident, Captain Zarubin," Titov said, tapping the wrench against the palm of his meaty hand. The message was clear.

"Take him away, Chief. Use force only if necessary. Post

two guards outside his door," said Mirov. "I have the conn. Sonar, conn, report all contacts."

"Conn, sonar. Welcome back, sir. We have logged two above-water explosions, bearing two-eight-three and bearing two-six-zero. There were transients following both explosions that sounded like large objects entering the water. This was followed by the launch of four torpedoes along the second bearing. The acoustics fit the signature of our Type 53-65Ms, sir. The tracks of those torpedoes indicate the probable target is the *Midway*. This was followed by two American torpedoes, Mk-48s, entering the water along more or less the same bearing. Those torpedoes appeared to be targeting one of our Akulas.

"Immediately following this, four more torpedoes—again, 53-65Ms—entered the water at bearing two-eight-three. Their tracks indicate that the *Midway* is the target.

"As far as surface contacts go, sir, we are tracking four American warships. The *Midway* is headed straight for us, sir, at thirty-two knots, bearing two-three-zero." The sonar supervisor cycled through the other surface contacts.

"One last, Captain. About two minutes ago there was a distant surface explosion at bearing one-eight-seven, followed by breaking-up noises. Somebody lost a ship, sir."

"Aye, sonar." Mirov shook his head and muttered, "This is madness! Fire control, what is our own status?"

"Tubes one through six are loaded and flooded, sir, with outer doors open," reported the weapons systems officer. "Bearings are matched with the *Midway* sir, and we are ready in all respects to fire."

****

The four torpedoes that had been launched by Gromyko's *K-284* were running straight and true. Five hundred yards ahead of their path, the *Kinkaid* dashed past, dragging a noise-maker, trying to draw the torpedoes away from *Midway*. It was successful. All four fish turned to follow the *Kinkaid*.

The problem was, however, that the torpedoes were not

homing on acoustics. They ignored the noisemaker and shot right past it. The Soviet torpedoes had wake-homing sensor heads, and they followed the wake of the *Kinkaid* right to the ship. Two missed the ship as it maneuvered wildly, but two hit, both amidships. The *Kinkaid* broke in half and sank in less than thirty seconds.

****

In the control room of the *Louisville*, Captain Boston listened to the sounds of the melee all around him. He decided to give up the advantage of surprise on the possibility that he could dissuade the Kilo from firing if it knew its own survival was at stake.

"Battle stations, torpedo," snapped Captain Boston. "We're going to let this bad boy know we are right on his tail. Fire control, what's your status?"

"Tubes one and two are loaded with Mk-48 ADCAPS, but are not flooded, Captain. Standing by."

"Aye, fire control. Sonar, verify range and bearing to that Kilo. Fire control tracking, I want a firing solution yesterday."

The powerful pulse of acoustic energy bounced off the *B-445* and was picked up by the hydrophone conformal arrays on the *Louisville*.

"Conn, sonar, Contact bearing is two-three-seven, range forty-seven hundred sixty yards. No doppler, contact is not moving."

"Captain, we have a firing solution."

Boston nodded. "Aye. Firing point procedures. Fire control, match bearings, Kilo, in tubes one and two. Make tubes one and two ready in all respects. Open outer doors."

"Aye, captain." A few seconds later the fire control officer reported, "Tubes one and two are ready in all respects, sir."

"Aye, fire control, stand by. Sonar, stand by. Now we wait and see what this sucker does."

****

The powerful sonar ping reverberated off the hull of the *B-445*. While using the active sonar gave the *Louisville* the precise position of the *B-445*, it also worked in reverse. Now Mirov's sonar techs knew the exact position of the *Louisville*.

"Conn, sonar!" the breathless sonar supervisor shouted. "We have a contact, bearing zero-five-seven, range forty-three hundred fifty meters. Contact is flooding tubes and opening outer doors."

"*Michman*," Mirov barked. "You are a professional naval warrant officer. Get hold of yourself!" Mirov knew that if panic went unaddressed, it would infect more of the crew.

"Aye, aye, comrade Captain. Forgive me," said the chastened sonar supervisor.

The dull sound of a far-off explosion rumbled through the hull, followed seconds later by another. Mirov stood, thinking. He cursed the fool Zarubin—evidently his haste to arrive on location resulted in their being detected. With that ranging ping, Mirov realized that an American attack submarine had an accurate firing solution for the *B-445* locked into their fire control systems.

"Conn, sonar. Machinery noises identify the contact as a *Los Angeles*-class submarine, sir."

"Very well." Sweat beaded on Mirov's brow. The entire control room crew was looking at him. They knew their lives were now entirely in the hands of their captain. One false move . . .

****

The crew of the *Louisville* were also holding their breath. They'd heard the explosions through the hull, they knew the situation had become deadly.

"What's he doing? Everybody and their brother is launching torpedoes, why isn't he?" Boston muttered mostly to himself, referring to the Kilo submarine. "Fire control, stand by," he said again.

"Aye, Captain, Fire control is standing by."

Boston could feel sweat running between his shoulder

blades. The air in the control room was thick with tension. The sound of a double explosion rumbled through the hull.

"Sonar, conn, was that the *Midway*?"

"Negative, negative. That was . . . that was the *Kinkaid*, sir. Two torpedoes impacted her. I'm getting breaking up noises, sir. She's going down. Rapidly."

Boston cursed, causing the the control room crew to jump.

"Conn, sonar. Four torpedoes have acquired the *Midway*, sir, and are accelerating to terminal speed. Estimated impact in thirty-seven seconds."

They all helplessly watched the bulkhead timer tick off the seconds. Four more explosions sounded through the hull.

Boston's face went white with rage. "Forget the ROE," he spat, "I'll take my chances at a board of inquiry. I'm not letting this sucker get a free shot at the *Midway*, or anyone else for that matter. Sonar, conn, verify range and bearing to the Kilo one more time."

"Conn, sonar, Contact bearing and range verified. Unchanged, sir. Bearing two-three-seven, range forty-seven hundred sixty yards. Contact is not moving."

"Very well. Fire control, match bearings and shoot tubes one and two."

"Conn, sonar, transients! The Kilo is closing his outer doors, repeat, closing outer doors."

"BELAY THAT, fire control, belay that order!" Boston wiped the sweat off his brow with a handkerchief. "Talk to me, Schneider, what's the Kilo doing?" Boston asked the sonar supervisor.

"Not sure, Skipper. But he definitely closed his doors."

"Aye, sonar," Boston acknowledged. He turned to his XO. "What do you think, Commander Wade? He stepped back from the brink, but is he messin' with our minds, or does he want out of the gunplay?"

"I think he's quitting, Skipper. He knows we got the drop on him. He hasn't touched his active sonar. I think he wants to bow out of this dance."

Boston considered that. Finally he nodded. "Okay, let's try something, see how he responds. Fire control, close outer torpedo doors. Ivan will hear that, just like we hear his."

A few minutes later the sonar supervisor broke the tension, "Conn, sonar. Hull popping noises. The Kilo is rising slowly. Bearing is unchanged."

Commander Wade asked, "What now, Skipper?"

"It depends on how far he ascends. He knows we have him boresighted. If he surfaces, he's probably folding his hand. Sonar, conn, hit him again with three pings. Diving officer, put us into a slow, level ascent."

Five minutes later both submarines were on the surface. Boston looked around the control room of the *Louisville*. "Anybody here speak Russian?"

Heads around the room shook in the negative.

"Well, maybe somebody over there speaks English. Communicator, patch the international maritime emergency channel through to my handset."

"Aye, aye, Skipper. You are live . . . now."

"Soviet Kilo submarine, Soviet Kilo submarine, this is the USS *Louisville*. Do not submerge or take hostile action, or you will be sunk. What are your intentions?"

"*Louisville*, this is Captain Mirov of the *B-445*. Our intentions are peaceful."

"Apparently your friends in the area have other intentions." Boston thought for a moment, then continued. "Captain Mirov, you left port with eighteen torpedoes. You will jettison all eighteen immediately. We will be counting."

"*Ne mozhet byt i rechi!* Out of the question, *Louisville*."

"Captain Mirov, this is Captain Boston. Your submarines have already sunk an American ship in the last ten minutes. I have no way of verifying your intentions unless you get rid of your weapons. I am not negotiating with you, I am telling you. You will begin jettisoning all your torpedoes in the next sixty seconds, or I will sink you. Personally, I hope you refuse because right now I'd like nothing better than to send you and your crew right to the bottom. *Louisville*, out." Boston hung up the phone and started one of the digital timers on the bulkhead.

"Sonar, conn. Hit him with three more pings. Fire control,

match bearings on tubes one and two, open outer doors. Stand by, fire control."

****

Mirov's face was red with fury when he hung up the handset. He wasn't sure who he was more angry with, the arrogant captain of the *Louisville*, the two arrogant mutineers, or the arrogant admiral of the Pacific Fleet who'd put him and his crew in this position.

Three loud pings reverberated through the *B-445*'s hull.

"Captain, the American has reopened his outer doors," reported the sonar supervisor.

Mirov struggled with his rage and humiliation. With an iron will he finally brought his emotions under control.

"Aye, *spasibo*, sonar," he said quietly.

"Torpedo room, this is the captain. Disarm and jettison all torpedoes immediately. I repeat, disarm and jettison our entire complement of torpedoes. Be quick about it."

"Conn, torpedo room. Say again?" came the incredulous voice.

"*Da*. Disarm and jettison all torpedoes immediately."

****

Captain Skagway stood in the Combat Information Center of the *Midway* watching the threat plot and relaying ship handling instructions to his executive officer on the navigation bridge. Skagway clenched his fists in frustration. Under his command was a warship with the world's hottest fighter aircraft and the world's best pilots, but the battle he was fighting was almost exclusively under the surface. There was no target against which he could launch an airborne strike. The Sovs were taking potshots at him, and other than his ASW helicopters, he couldn't really strike back. He hoped his escort submarines were scoring. The one surface target available, the Soviet trawler, had been sunk by the *Bunker Hill* a few minutes earlier. *Oh, well,* he thought, *at least without flight operations we are free to take evasive action as necessary without worrying about keeping the wind over the bow.*

A few minutes before, Skagway had ordered that the Nixie be deployed. The AN/SLQ-25A Nixie was a towed decoy system on a long cable which mimicked the sounds of the carrier. It was designed to confuse torpedoes, drawing them away from the warship.

The ambush had turned into a melee resembling a fast-paced knife-fight. Multiple torpedoes were in the water, launched by both sides. The updates in the CIC were coming rapid-fire, without letup.

"Captain, Sierra-18 has launched four torpedoes."

"Captain, the *Kinkaid* just launched two ASROCs targeting Sierra-18."

"Captain, four torpedoes have acquired the *Kinkaid.* It appears that they were originally targeted at us, sir."

"Captain, sonar reports two torpedoes hit the *Kinkaid.*"

"Captain, I regret to inform you that the *Kinkaid* has been sunk."

"Captain, four Soviet torpedoes have acquired us. Impact in less than forty seconds."

Because they were wake-following and not acoustic-homing torpedoes, the four remaining Soviet torpedoes ignored the Nixie and swept toward the carrier. Skagway grabbed the handset on the bulkhead and turned the selector to 1MC. "All hands, this is the captain speaking. Prepare for multiple torpedo impacts in thirty seconds."

The first torpedo hit the port side outboard propeller shaft, bending it and jamming the port rudder, and ripping a large gash in the hull. Shaft alley number four and several of the adjoining spaces flooded, including a small weapons elevator, the cable trunk, and the damage control repair parts storeroom. The concussion could be felt all over the ship, but the great mass of the carrier dampened the shock, so that on the upper decks it felt more like the carrier had collided with something the size of a small tugboat. The next three torpedoes hit on the port side of the hull in rapid succession, each blasting holes in *Midway*'s armored sides.

When the fourth torpedo exploded, it blew through the armored hull, through the voids, and put great tears in the walls of Engine Room number 4, throwing razor-sharp metal splinters through the room like confetti at a party. Five men were in the space at the time. The chief petty officer in the space happened to be standing on the inboard side of the massive gearbox. He was protected from the steel shards flying about the space. But the concussion blew him off the catwalk and into the steel wall on the far side of the space. For a brief moment he lay stunned on the lower deck, until the sounds of the inrushing sea stirred him. Heedless of a broken leg and a compound fracture on his wrist, he dragged his unconscious crew members to the escape trunk as the water level rose.

Fueled by adrenaline, he threw an unconscious man over his shoulder and carried him up the ladder and through a hatch to the fourth deck level. He collapsed on the floor, shouting, "The engine room is flooding. There are three more injured men down there. Got to get 'em out before they drown and before we have to seal this hatch."

Several sailors raced down the ladder, while a burly ensign carried the unconscious man to sickbay and then came back for the wounded petty officer. Similar scenes were repeated through many of the spaces on the aft port side of the ship below the fourth deck level, where the torpedoes had impacted.

Soon the *Midway* was listing five degrees to port and was slightly down by the stern. Up on the bridge, the executive officer was snapping out commands to trim the ship by shifting water ballast from the port to the starboard ballast tanks and from aft to forward.

Damage not withstanding, the *Midway* remained a lethal, if wounded, operational warship, and Captain Skagway was still in the CIC, preparing for any resumption of the ambush.

"Captain, both Akulas are confirmed sunk, sir. The one Kilo has surfaced. We are in radio contact with the *Louisville*, and they are telling us that the Kilo has declared that its intentions are not hostile, and it is jettisoning its torpedoes. There are no live torpedoes in the water at the moment and no hostile surface, subsurface, or air contacts," reported the Combat Information Center watch officer.

"Very well. We will remain at General Quarters for at least another fifteen minutes. I'll be on the bridge handling damage control. Notify me immediately if anything changes."

****

On the *Louisville*, Sonar Petty Officer Roland Abrams was listening intently to the transient sounds coming from the Kilo. He made another tic mark on his log. Abrams counted up the marks and turned to the sonar supervisor. "That makes eighteen, Chief. I can verify he's tossed eighteen fish over the transom."

"Conn, sonar. The Kilo is holding an empty gun, Skipper, all eighteen torps are on their way to Davy Jones' locker."

"Aye, sonar. Communicator, patch me back to the Kilo."

"Aye, Captain . . . you are live."

"Captain Mirov, this is Captain Boston. I am acknowledging that you have jettisoned your weapons. I am requesting that you remain on the surface. There are a lot of people with a finger on the trigger right now, and you don't want to make them nervous, sir.

"Recovery operations are underway, searching for survivors from both navies. We will transfer to the *B-445* any Soviet casualties that we recover."

By this time there were two Seahawks circling the *B-445*, one each from the *Bunker Hill* and the *Cushing*, their powerful searchlights illuminating the submarine. A machine gun was mounted in the side doors of both choppers lest anyone on the Soviet submarine was tempted to use MANPADS. Both aircraft were carrying a full loadout of Mk-46 torpedoes.

Chapter 23

Mirov was briefing his officers and Titov, the senior enlisted man, in the *B-445*'s wardroom. The attempted mutiny was the main topic of conversation with the attack on the American carrier group a close second.

"There will be a naval board of inquiry when we return to port. Some of you will be called upon to testify. Have no fear, just be honest in your answers: tell them what you saw without regard to how it will impact either myself or Captains Zarubin and Leonev. Make written notes while the events and impressions are fresh, but under no circumstance are you to compare notes with anyone else on this vessel. Any written notes you make will be required by the investigators on the board of inquiry."

"Captain, Pacific Fleet headquarters has been trying to raise us for the last several hours. What should I do?" asked the communications officer.

"Maintain absolute radio silence. I believe that there may be a rogue element operating at fleet headquarters. When we give our report, I want to make sure we are giving it to the right people—face to face. We will withhold our report until we return—perhaps more will become clear by then. There will be time enough for the proper authorities to examine the actions of my command and that of Captains Zarubin and Leonev. There is no operational need at present to communicate with the fleet. You may, however, engage in any necessary short-range ship-to-ship communications with the Americans, as required by the search and recovery operations."

The messenger of the watch appeared at the wardroom door. "Captain Mirov, the American captain wishes to speak with you."

"I'll be right there." Mirov turned back to his officers. "Any questions? No? You may return to your duties."

He strode into the control room and picked up the handset. "This is Captain Mirov."

"Captain Boston here. We are shutting down recovery operations, Captain. We have located four survivors from the *Kurily*, and fourteen fatalities. Would you like us to transfer them to your vessel, sir?"

"Captain, as I am sure is true on your submarine also, we do not have space or facilities for the bodies. I would like to request that the dead be transferred to *Midway*. Our representatives will take custody of the bodies upon *Midway*'s arrival at Yokosuka. However, we can accommodate the four survivors."

"That arrangement is fine with us, as I have already discussed the possibility with *Midway*'s captain. I will radio the *Cushing*, and they will send a boat alongside with your survivors. After you have received them, you are free to go."

****

When the search and recovery operations ended at noon the butcher bill for Operation *Tikhookeanskaya Groza* (*Pacific Threat*) became clear. Fourteen dead Soviet sailors were plucked from the water, along with thirty-seven dead US sailors. Four survivors from the *Kurily* were recovered, as well as twenty-nine oil-soaked survivors from the *Kinkaid*.

The Soviet Union lost two nuclear attack submarines and an intelligence trawler, with two hundred eighty-eight total fatalities, of whom two hundred seventy-four were never found.

The United States lost two helicopters and a *Spruance*-class destroyer. The American casualty list included forty-seven injured men and three hundred thirty-six fatalities, two hundred ninety-nine of whom were never found. The damage to the *Midway* would ultimately require a return to Pearl for repairs.

****

"They are not responding, Admiral," replied the fleet communications watch officer to Shukshin's irritated question.

"What do you mean they are not responding?"

"Exactly that, sir. We've sent out a request by ELF to the

B-445, *K-263*, and *K-284* with instructions to come to periscope depth and report. There has been no response. We've also tried to raise the *Kurily*, but without success."

"Keep trying. Let me know as soon as you establish communications with any of them," Admiral Shukshin said.

As he walked back to his office, Shukshin contemplated the terrible possibility that all three of the submarines had been sunk, along with the *Kurily*. Then he realized that such terrible losses would galvanize the military even more than the simple conflict would. His mood changed instantly, and he returned to his office barely able to hide his glee. His plan was working much better than he had anticipated. He hated to lose valuable assets—and by that he was thinking of the submarines, not their crews—but the loss would be an acceptable tradeoff if it unified the navy around the coup. As soon as word got around that the US had sunk three Soviet submarines, which he was now assuming was the case, the sheer outrage would carry the coup to success.

He picked up the phone and dialed vice president Pushkaryov's number.

"Pushkaryov. Speak."

"It's Shukshin. I am happy to report that the conflict between our navy and the US has been engaged. I do not yet have full reports," Shukshin said—actually, he had no reports —"however, I am expecting them momentarily. Has there been any response from the Americans? Has our ambassador been called on the carpet?"

"Not that I am aware, Admiral. I've been watching CNN all morning. The American's inauguration went without a hitch. Our ambassador was present, as well as our, ah, cultural attaché, but they observed nothing unusual. They observed no concern, no attempt by the national security people to communicate with the new president throughout the festivities."

"Nothing?" Shukshin asked, not wanting to believe what he was hearing.

"Not as far as they could tell. Anyway, . . . wait, Admiral. CNN is reporting breaking news. Just a minute."

Shukshin grinned. *Here it comes*, he thought. *And if it is on*

CNN, the news will soon be spread throughout our military.

"Are you still there, Admiral?"

"*Da.*"

"CNN is saying that there are unconfirmed reports that *Midway* and its carrier group encountered a previously unknown World War 2-era minefield in the Philippine Sea. There's been significant damage to the *Midway*, and even reports of a ship sinking. The broadcaster added that there were also some subsurface explosions reported near the carrier that could not be accounted for. One theory is that the detonation of the old mines caused the rest of the minefield to explode."

"But, but, that's impossible!" Shukshin objected.

"Impossible?"

"Ah, no, improbable. Highly improbable that there should be an undiscovered minefield there. There's too much commercial shipping traffic—if there was really a minefield there, someone would have hit the mines long ago," Shukshin insisted. "The Americans are lying. The damage was caused by torpedoes, not mines. They must be trying to hide their aggressions against our submarines."

"What do our submarines say? What have you heard so far?" the vice president asked.

"Nothing yet. I am expecting reports any minute. I'll call you back as soon as I hear anything. Are we still on schedule for the twenty-fourth?"

"Of course. Everything is in place. All we are waiting for now is the news of the conflict with the Americans, news that you promised would unite our military forces around our leadership," Pushkaryov said pointedly.

"Do not fear, Mr. Vice President. I am convinced that all is well. Another twelve hours or so and CNN will be eating its words about this nonexistent minefield."

"You'd better be right, Admiral."

****

Admiral Shukshin sat at his desk, dejected. It was now 1900 hours and there was still no word from any vessel involved in Operation *Pacific Threat*. The Americans had not reacted, but instead were spreading the bogus minefield story. *What is their game?* he wondered. If the real story—or at least the story as it would be altered, massaged and edited by him—did not get out, there was no catalyst for the coup.

He walked over to the windows overlooking the bay and anchorage. The nearly full moon was rising, and a slight breeze was creating riffles on the otherwise calm waters, producing a shimmering effect in the moonlight. The lights of the city on the other side of the water twinkled in the darkness. He heard a long, low blast of a ship's horn. Somewhere nearby a vessel was leaving the anchorage. It was a tranquil scene. Unlike the turmoil inside him.

He walked back to his desk and called the fleet communication center. "I want to know immediately if we hear any word from the submarines or the *Kurily*. I'll be at home. Contact me there," he instructed the watch officer. He then dialed his secretary on the intercom and said, "Have my car brought around in five minutes. If needed, I can be reached at home."

Shukshin had been working on his acceptance speech, to be delivered when the Politburo appointed him to the dual role of general secretary and president of the USSR. According to plan, this would take place following the tragic death of vice president Pushkaryov, who would be inadvertently caught in the crossfire when troops loyal to the coup were taking the Kremlin. Shukshin was counting on defense minister Valentin Valentinovich Aristov's enthusiastic nomination to seal the deal. The admiral stuffed the speech in his briefcase, then gathered the remaining classified documents from his desk and locked them in his safe.

Admiral Shukshin put on his greatcoat, then took the stairs down to his waiting car. As he was driven to his *dacha*, he thought about getting another *dacha* near Moscow. He would need it as an escape from the pressures of governing when he assumed the role of general secretary. *Should I keep this one as well?* he wondered. *After all, I can see myself coming to Vladivostok from time to time. Ah, well, there will be time to decide that later.*

His driver pulled into the driveway. The place was dark—

not a light on anywhere. *That is strange*, Shukshin thought. *My housekeeper, Anna, is usually still up at this hour.*

"Do you want me to go in and check it out, sir, before you leave the car?" asked his driver and bodyguard.

"*Nyet, ne nado.* No need. My housekeeper must have gone out for the evening. Pick me up at 0600 tomorrow."

"Yes, sir."

Shukshin unlocked the front door, entered, and turned on the light. He shrugged off his great coat, and turned up the heat a notch. He stepped into the darkened kitchen to light the samovar for tea, but when he switched on the light, he froze. Sitting at his kitchen table was a woman wearing the uniform of the KGB.

"What is the meaning of this? Who are you?" he asked.

"Captain Fukina, KGB. And you were Admiral Shukshin."

"I *am* Admiral Shukshin."

"*Nyet. Byl.* Now you are nothing, and you will never be anything ever again."

"*Chto za chepukha!* What nonsense! Now get out of my house before I throw you out."

"Again *nyet.* Instead, comrade Shukshin, I am arresting you for the murder of Admiral Pyotr Stefanovich Zelenko."

"What?" Shukshin spluttered. "That's preposterous."

"I agree. That you should even contemplate murdering your superior officer, much less actually carrying it out, is truly preposterous. And yet, here we are."

"Admiral Zelenko was not murdered," Shukshin objected. "He committed suicide. I had nothing to do with that, other than mourning that such a good man and excellent officer died in such an untimely fashion."

"That's funny, because Captain Udom seems to remember a phone call in which you ordered him to kill Zelenko."

Shukshin didn't answer. His mind was racing. If he could just make it through the next four days, he'd be in a place to make these accusations go away. He could bury this arrogant woman and make Udom disappear.

That's the problem with climbing to the top of the heap— you start telling yourself that just one more body will do the trick, and then the killing can stop. There's always *one more*.

Fukina stood, holding a pistol on him. "There's someone who wants to talk to you, Shukshin. I think he might be prepared to offer you a deal. You'll find him in your study. But, comrade," she said, "your sidearm first, please. I wouldn't want you to be tempted to kill again. Hand it to me butt first, please."

Shukshin walked into his study and turned on the light. There was an old man with a cane sitting in his desk chair.

"Anatoly Geredin, to what do I owe the honor of your presence," the admiral said cynically.

"You have had a brilliant career in the navy, Admiral Shukshin," Geredin said, ignoring Shukshin's sardonic welcome. "It would be a shame to mar your illustrious career with a public trial that would convict you of murdering Admiral Zelenko, one of the most popular officers in the navy and a hero of the Soviet Union. So I am offering you a choice."

"You have no proof."

"Oh, but I do. Not only Udom's sworn statement, but I also have a recording of the phone conversation in which you told Udom to do the job." Geredin was lying. He knew that a recording of the phone call existed somewhere in an American intelligence agency, but he also knew he'd never get his hands on it. "I also have an eyewitness who saw and heard Udom contracting the hit. And I know that the contract price, thirty thousand rubles, is missing from Udom's department's accounts. Beyond that, I have circumstantial evidence showing that Zelenko's death was not in fact a suicide, but a homicide, a murder accomplished with cyanide pills disguised to look like his digitalis prescription."

Shukshin sat heavily on the couch. There was no longer any point for bluster or denial—he saw that clearly. "You said a minute ago I have a choice. What are my options?"

"You can deny all this and take your chances with a very public trial in which you will be publicly humiliated. It will be very messy. We will demonstrate how you continually usurped Zelenko's authority over the last several years, finally getting rid of him when he discovered what you were doing. Not a single stone of your record and background will go unturned. When we are through with you, your reputation will be in tatters, both in the eyes of the public as well as in the eyes of the navy, and you will no doubt be executed."

"And what is the other option?" a visibly shaken Shukshin asked.

"You take some of the pills you tricked Zelenko into taking. You won't suffer the humiliation of a trial."

"That's it? Those are my options?"

"What did you expect? You murdered a superior officer in cold blood. What sort of options did you think I would or could offer you?"

Shukshin pulled his last trick from his sleeve. "I need time to think about it, say, four days. I mean, you're asking me to make a decision to end my own life."

Geredin gave him no quarter. "*Nyet.* You must decide now."

****

The morning of 23 January dawned bright, clear, and cold over Moscow. Twelve inches of snow had fallen the night before, but the storm had hurried on to the east, and a strong high pressure system was scooping frigid air into the city. The street crews were only now beginning to deal with the snow-clogged streets.

Alexander Ivanovich Pushkaryov, the vice president of the Soviet Union, got to his office early. He had phone calls to make and meetings to attend before the military parade at noon, to ensure that all the chess pieces were correctly arrayed on the board. Tomorrow was his personal D-Day in which he would topple the criminal government of Mikhail Sergeyevich Gorbachev and then ascend to the seat of power himself.

He was ebullient. Humming the Internationale cheerfully, he hung his great coat and *ushanka* on the coat tree and poured himself a glass of tea from the samovar. His secretary had placed the morning edition of *Pravda* on his desk, and on his side table were half a dozen other newspapers from the important capitals of the world. Pushkaryov's habit was to read the news while sipping his tea before buckling down to his governmental responsibilities each day.

He sat down at his desk and his smile quickly turned to a frown. Two headlines above the fold caught his attention: *Pacific Fleet commander suspected in Zelenko's murder, commits suicide*. He quickly read the article.

> *Admiral Konstantin Grigoriyevich Shukshin, recently appointed to the post of Commander of the Red Banner Pacific Fleet, was found dead in his home this morning by his driver, after having been informed last night by the KGB that he was the prime suspect in the death of Admiral Zelenko. Zelenko's death was initially ruled a suicide, but unnamed sources in the KGB told this reporter that new evidence resulted in the case being reopened as a homicide case.*
>
> *Admiral Pyotr Stefanovich Zelenko, a highly decorated naval officer and a Hero of the Soviet Union, was for many years the commander of the Pacific Fleet and was Shukshin's commanding officer at the time of his death in December. The investigation has also uncovered evidence that Shukshin was implicated in a plot against General Secretary Gorbachev, according to the same unnamed sources in the KGB.*

Pushkaryov put his tea down so hard it sloshed, and grabbed his head in his hands. He wondered who else had been implicated in the investigation. Was his own name on the list? With trepidation he turned his attention to the second headline: *American carrier group hits WW2-era minefield*.

> *An American destroyer was sunk and an aircraft carrier severely damaged when the carrier group blundered into an apparently uncharted Japanese*

> *minefield in the Philippine Sea, a remnant of World War 2. Sources close to the American navy indicate that over three hundred lives were lost in the ensuing explosions.*
>
> *Unconfirmed reports indicate that a Soviet military vessel following the carrier group also hit a mine and may have sunk. Additional underwater explosions could point to the possibility that several submarines have been lost as well, although neither navy is commenting on those reports at the present time.*

That's it, then, thought Pushkaryov. *We cannot proceed with our plans now. Not only is the catalyst for uniting the armed services denied to us by American disinformation, but the architect of that reckless plan is now suspected of Zelenko's murder and has taken his own life.* He massaged his temples trying to ease his sudden splitting headache.

He picked up his phone and reluctantly dialed the defense minister, Valentin Valentinovich Aristov. "Valentin, have you seen *Pravda* yet."

"Just read the front page, Alexander. Are you thinking what I am thinking?"

"*Da.* Call it off."

"I agree, comrade. The window of opportunity just closed. Perhaps it will open again in the future, but for now it is tightly shut. I will call the others and tell them to cancel. You, sir, might want to rewrite your speech to the *Duma*."

"Indeed."

When Pushkaryov finished rewriting his speech to deliver to the *Duma* on the following day, rather than a fiery attack on Gorbachev, it was a speech resigning his office due to his "formidable health problems" which were, in fact, quite imaginary.

****

Two days later, Anatoly Geredin was awakened in the middle of the night by the insistent ringing of his American sat phone.

"Must you always call at ungodly hours?" he groused without even saying hello.

"Last time I checked, Anatoly, you were an atheist—which means all twenty-four hours are ungodly from your perspective," Jensen chuckled.

"I am not in the mood for jokes, Dr. Jensen."

"Sorry. I try to call when I know you are alone. I wanted to give you a rundown of that little dustup in the Philippine Sea, because I'm not sure if you'll be getting any news on it otherwise."

"*Spasibo*, Dr. Jensen. As of this moment, the only news we have is what you people have been leaking. None of the vessels involved have returned."

"We recovered four survivors among your people, Anatoly, and fourteen bodies. The survivors were placed aboard Mirov's *B-445* and are returning to port with that submarine. The bodies are being transported on the *Midway*, and will be turned over to Soviet authorities when the carrier docks at Yokosuka later this morning. Obviously I don't know what your total casualty list is, because most went down with their vessels. On our side, we lost three hundred thirty-six men, most of whom we never found, and forty-seven injured.

"As far as hardware goes, we lost a *Spruance*-class destroyer and two helicopters. The *Midway* sustained significant damage, although I am not at liberty to describe it. You lost two Akula submarines, and one intelligence trawler. By his very cool-headed leadership your Captain Mirov saved his submarine from destruction. It was a very close thing.

"And by the way, Geredin, your people fired first. You told me that wasn't going to happen."

Geredin sighed. "I am truly sorry, Dr. Jensen. I gave you the best intelligence I had. All I can say is that the admiral who ordered this attack was completely rogue. No one here in my organization suspected that he would actually fire on US vessels, unprovoked. Admiral Shukshin, who was behind this rogue operation as well as being a principal member in the conspiracy against the general secretary, committed suicide several nights ago."

"What is the current status of the coup, Anatoly?"

"It has fallen apart. Shukshin is dead, Pushkaryov has resigned his position and has retreated to his yacht on the Black Sea. The other members of the coup have been informed they are under close surveillance. They are stumbling all over themselves in a rush to profess loyalty to Gorbachev. They are lying, of course, but each knows that his life hangs by a thread."

"So the US has been successful in keeping the Soviet devil we know, as opposed to gaining a far worse one that we don't know," Jensen observed.

"You could put it that way, *da*. Pushkaryov would have been a problem for you and for us. But we are uncovering evidence that suggests Pushkaryov would have died during the coup—"

"Accidentally, of course," Jensen interrupted, cynically.

"Of course. Shukshin would have taken over the government. He would have been far worse than even Pushkaryov."

Bill Jensen paused. He knew Geredin would not want to hear what he was about to say. "One more thing, Anatoly. Sooner or later the truth about what happened in the Philippine Sea will come out. When it does, my government will be demanding reparations from the Soviet Union. I encourage you to urge your leadership to comply. We still have the GRU kidnapping scheme to use as leverage, and we will not hesitate to use it. We suffered these losses because we determined it was ultimately in our best interest to support stability in your country. But your people started a shooting war with us, and we will demand satisfaction."

Epilogue

Friday, January 27, 1989

"I'm beginning to feel like a beached whale," Galina groaned, rubbing her very round abdomen with her hands. She was due in little over two months, and she was feeling very pregnant. Jacob and Galina were slathered in suntan lotion and sitting on beach chairs in Antigua, watching the turquoise-hued waves ceaselessly rolling in.

Jake looked at her and chuckled, "Yep. That's about right. But I just love beached whales, especially when they're as pretty as you are, babe."

She smiled at him, then grew serious. "You've changed, Jacob. What happened to you over there?"

"What do you mean, sweetie? How have I changed?"

"I don't know—I'm not sure I can explain it. You—well, you used to make fun of me any time I would talk about God. Or if you saw a Bible lying around, you'd complain about it. I've been reading my Bible every morning since we got here and you've not said a word. I've even seen you reading it several times."

Jacob didn't respond, mostly because he didn't know how to respond. Something *had* changed—something on the inside. It worried him, because he felt like something was going on beyond his power, even beyond his will. Something was happening *to* him—it wasn't something he was doing.

Finally, he said, "Something happened to me while I was on the run. When I got to Khabarovsk I met an old man who let me stay with him, a man named Usilov. I was hiding out— at first he didn't know I was on the run, but eventually he found out. Anyway, Usilov was a Christian, and he shared the gospel with me. One time he was talking about the fact that God required moral perfection from those whom He admitted to heaven. Every person falls short of what God requires. But, Usilov said, God gave up His perfectly obedient Son Jesus Christ to die on the cross. There Jesus paid the penalty and provided an imputed moral perfection on behalf of all who put their faith in Him. Usilov said *what God requires, God*

Himself provides.

"I've never heard that before. It puts everything in a new light for me. I had thought of God, if He existed at all, as some kind of tyrant giving rules that no one could follow and then punishing us when we failed. I never realized that, yes, while He gave us moral laws to live by He also gave us His perfect Son, and credited us with His own Son's perfections when we place our faith in Him.

"It's a radical thought for me, Galina. What God requires, God Himself provides. It—well, it changes everything."

She looked at him and wiped a tear of joy from her eyes. "Well," she said, "I guess I have learned something too, then."

"What did you learn, Galya?"

"That God answers prayer."

****

Sam Bergman sat at his desk, studying the latest NRO photographs of the submarine pens at Vladivostok. A Kilo was being nudged into position against a wharf by several tugs. *I'll bet I know who you are*, he said to himself, poring over the photograph with a magnifying glass.

His phone rang, startling him and causing him to spill his coffee on his desk, luckily not on the photographs. He answered the call while he wiped up the mess. "Bergman."

"Sam, I want to see you in my office right away," said the deputy director of operations.

"What's up, Bill?"

"I've got a new project for you."

Sam groaned inwardly as he hung up the phone. It had been five straight months of very long days, and he was exhausted.

A few minutes later he was knocking on the DDO's door.

"Come on in, Sam, take a seat."

"What's the new project? Is it the Chinese navy this time?" he carped.

Jensen frowned. "Of course not. You're the Soviet analyst, not the Chinese analyst."

"So what's up?"

"You've been pulling some long hours lately. I think it's time you had a break, and your lady friend as well. I've talked to Evelyn's supervisor over at the NSA, pulled a few strings, called in a few favors, and you both have the next two weeks off. Comp time."

Bergman's eyes widened. "Really? You're not kidding me?"

"No, I'm not kidding you. Don't you think it's time you introduced her to your parents? Now get out of here. I don't want to see you for two weeks."

****

When the *B-445* docked at Vladivostok, Captains Mirov, Zarubin, and Leonev were placed under house arrest and restricted to their quarters until a board of inquiry could be convened. The entire crew of the submarine was interrogated, and the orders, plans, and all communications related to Operation *Tikhookeanskaya Groza*, or *Pacific Threat* were carefully examined. In the end, Zarubin and Leonev were executed for mutiny. Mirov was exonerated of all charges and awarded the Nakhimov Medal, a medal for those who exhibit extreme valor and gallantry during sea battles.

****

Upon Anatoly Geredin's announcement of his retirement, the full Politburo approved Colonel Vladimir Leonidovich Dobrynin's appointment as the new head of the KGB. In another two weeks Dobrynin would be promoted to the rank of General Officer.

He walked into his new office—Geredin's old office—as the former spy master was cleaning out his desk. The two friends chatted for a few minutes and then Geredin handed Dobrynin a sat phone.

"What is this?" the new director of the KGB asked.

"It's a direct line to the DDO CIA. Don't misunderstand

me—he's not working for us—he's loyal to his country and always has his nation's best interests at heart. But on rare occasions you might find that the interests of his country and the interests of ours are actually going in the same direction. And when that happens—well, it might be worth a phone call."

The old spy took up his cane, nodded at Dobrynin, and hobbled painfully out the door.

Appendix 1

Cast of Characters

Principal Characters
American
- Jensen, Bill: Deputy Director of Operations, CIA, wife, Susan
- Kelly, Galina: Jake's wife, maiden name was Toporova
- Kelly, Jacob: Major, USAF; pilot, temporarily seconded to the CIA, also known as: Falcon; John Smith; Ilya Ilyich Maslov; Andrei Petrovich Borodin; Yacov Sokolov

Soviet
- Geredin, Anatoly Romanovich: General of the Army, head of the KGB
- Mirov, Boris Sayanovich: Captain First Rank, CO of *K-264* and *B-445*
- Shukshin, Konstantin Grigoriyevich: Admiral, Deputy Commander, Red Banner Pacific Fleet

Secondary Characters
American
- Baker, Larry: Commander, USN, XO of the USS *Honolulu*, SSN-718
- Bascomb, Ned: Commander, USN, ret. Smuggler
- Bergman, Sam: CIA's leading analyst in the Soviet department
- Blake, Stanley: Admiral, USN, CO of CARGRU5
- Boston, Randall: Captain, USN, CO of the USS *Louisville*, SSN-724
- Bridger, John: Rear Admiral, USN, CO of Navy Special Warfare Group One
- Bush, George Herbert Walker: Vice President of the United States
- Carson, Roger: CIA operative and team leader, specializing in direct action
- Feldstein, Alfred: Admiral, USN, Chairman US Joint Chiefs of Staff
- Franks, James T.: General, USAF, CO of the *Hydra*

project
- Mercer, Al: NRO satellite technician
- Mitchell, Ben: Captain, USN, CO of the USS *Olympia*, SSN-717
- Morgan, Ross: Captain, USN, Air Group Commander on the USS *Carl Vinson*
- Raines, Roscoe: Captain, USN, CO of the USS *Honolulu*, SSN-718
- Skagway, Ernest: Captain, USN, CO of the USS *Midway*, CV-41
- Smithson, Melvin: Secretary of Defense
- Stinson, Evelyn: NSA Russian translator
- Waggoner, Bruce: Admiral, USN, CO of CARGRU3
- West, Paul: Director of Central Intelligence, CIA
- Young, Arthur: Captain, USN, CO of the USS *Carl Vinson*

Soviet
- Aristov, Valentin Valentinovich: Defense Minister
- Chernikov, Nikolai Pavlovich: Deceased; Major General, GRU, former commandant of Soviet detention and interrogation facility
- Churkin, Yulian Semyonovich: Interior Minister
- Dobrynin, Vladimir Leonidovich: Colonel, KGB, Chief of the Third Directorate
- Fedin, Ilya Germanovich: Captain Third Rank, engineering officer, *B-445*
- Fetisov, Pyotr Vadimovich: Captain Second Rank, CO of *K-263*
- Fukina, Kira Aleksandrova: Captain, KGB, commands special investigative unit
- Gorbachev, Mikhail Sergeyevich: General Secretary of the Communist Party
- Gromyko, Iosif Fyodorovich: Captain Second Rank, CO of *K-284*
- Khorkov, Zakhar Rurikovich: Captain Second Rank, political officer aboard *K-263*
- Leonev, Andrei Feodoryevich: Captain First Rank, political officer aboard *B-445*
- Nikitin, Roman Romanovich: Major, GRU, commands special investigative unit

- Orlov, Vasily Vasilyevich: Colonel, KGB, Chief of the First Directorate
- Pushkaryov, Alexander Ivanovich: Vice President of the Soviet Union
- Roshchin, Terenti Marlenovich: Captain Second Rank, political officer aboard *K-284*
- Sukharov, Georgi: Major, Air Force, ret., smuggler
- Udom, Stefan Stefanovich: Captain Third Rank, Red Banner Pacific Fleet intelligence officer
- Usilov, Stanislav Fyodoryevich: Soviet boiler maintenance main
- Yegorov, Kirill Ilyich: General, Chief of the General Staff of the Soviet Armed Forces
- Zarubin, Anton Arkadevich: Captain Third Rank, XO of *B-445*
- Zelenko, Pyotr Stefanovich: Admiral, Commander of the Red Banner Pacific Fleet

Appendix 2

Special Terms and Acronyms

1MC: Main communication channel on a navy vessel, heard in every space

21MC: Captain's command communication circuit

688: *Los Angeles*-class fast attack submarine

ACS: Aegis Combat System

ADCAP: Mk-48 Advanced Capability torpedo

AEW: Airborne Early Warning

AFB: Air Force Base

AO: Area of Operations

ASROC: Antisubmarine Rocket

ASW: Antisubmarine Warfare

Baffles: The area directly behind a submarine, in which passive sonar performance is degraded

CAG: Commander, Air Group—in command of all air operations on an aircraft carrier

CAP: Combat Air Patrol

CARGRU3: Carrier Group 3

CARGRU5: Carrier Group 5

CATCC: Carrier Air Traffic Control Center

CCT: Combat Control Team, USAF special operators

CIA: Central Intelligence Agency

CIC: Combat Information Center

CJCS: Chairman of the Joint Chiefs of Staff, US military

CNO: Chief of Naval Operations

CO: Commanding Officer

COB: Chief of the Boat, typically a chief petty officer

COD: Carrier Onboard Delivery, resupply by a carrier-capable transport aircraft

COMPACFLT: Commander, Pacific Fleet

COMSUBPAC: Commander, Submarine Force, US Pacific Fleet

DDO: Deputy Director of Operations, CIA

ELINT: Intelligence gathered from electronic signals not containing speech or text

Gator: Nickname for ship's navigation officer

GRU: Soviet Main Intelligence Directorate, the foreign military intelligence agency of the Soviet Army General Staff

HUMINT: Intelligence gathered by humans as opposed to electronic means

IDF: Israeli Defense Forces

JCS: Joint Chiefs of Staff, US military

KGB: Soviet Committee for State Security

Layer: also "the layer," see Thermocline

LSO: Landing Signal Officer, also known as "Paddles"

Material condition Zebra: A shipboard emergency posture in which all hatches are closed

MVD: Soviet Ministry of Internal Affairs, the Soviet police force was under the MVD

NAV or Nav: Navigation and communication officer

NAVCOM: Navigator and communication officer aboard the Orion P-3C

Non-com: Non-commissioned officer, Petty or Warrant officer

NRO: National Reconnaissance Office

NSA: National Security Agency

NTDS: Naval Tactical Data System, keeps track of contact information

OOD: Officer of the Deck

ONI: Office of Naval Intelligence

Optempo: Operational tempo, the measure of the pace of operations and equipment usage

POTUS: President of The United States

READY-15: Aircraft readiness status, must be ready to launch within 15 minutes

ROE: Rules of Engagement, absent other orders dictates what actions can be taken in event of hostilities

S-3A: Lockheed S-3A Viking, carrier-based ASW aircraft

SAPS: Signal Algorithmic Processing System

SCI: Sensitive Compartmented Information

SCIF: Sensitive Compartmented Information Facility, a completely secure facility in which to discuss or view sensitive intelligence without fear of compromise

SECDEF: Secretary of Defense

SENSO: Sensor operator

SIGINT: Signals intelligence, intelligence gathering by interception of signals

SLBM: Submarine Launched Ballistic Missile

SLOT buoy: Submarine-Launched-One-way-Transmitter, communication device for submerged submarine, transmit only

SSBN: Nuclear ballistic missile submarine

SSN: Nuclear fast-attack submarine

SSIXS: Submarine Satellite Information Exchange Subsystem

TACCO: Tactical coordinator

TB-23: Towed array, a passive sonar receptor on a long tether

TMA: Target Motion Analysis

Thermocline: A horizontal layer in the water created by a sharp change of seawater temperature within a relatively minor change in depth, creates an acoustical barrier

UNREP: Underway replenishment, typically at reduced speed accomplished by vessels pulling alongside

VERTREP: Vertical replenishment, typically accomplished with helicopters

VLF: Very-Low-Frequency communication channel, can communicate with a submerged sub

Warshot: A live weapon, as opposed to dummies or practice weapons

WESTPAC: Western Pacific

XO: Executive officer, 2nd in command

Appendix 3

Russian Terms

Absolyutno: Certainly

Akula: Shark, also the NATO class-name of Soviet fast-attack SSNs

AVIAPOCHTA: Airmail

Chto sluchilos: What happened?

Da: Yes

Dacha: A country cottage, sometimes with elaborate amenities, used as a second home, available to the Soviet *nomenklatura*

Davay: Come on

Do svidaniya: Goodbye

Dogovorilis': We have a deal

Dovol'no: Enough

Glasnost: Openness—Gorbachev adopted *glasnost* as both a political slogan and policy commitment in 1986, as a result, Soviet citizens were permitted to criticize and critique government bodies and policies as well as political figures

Kolbasa: A variety of Russian sausage

Krai: Geographical administrative division of the Soviet Union

Michman: Soviet petty officer or warrant officer

Militsiya: Soviet domestic police force

Ne mozhet byt i rechi: Out of the question

Nomenklatura: Refers to the Soviet ruling elite who possess special privileges

Novyy God: New Year

Nyet: No

Otkuda: Where from?

Perestroika: Restructuring; under *perestroika*, Soviet economic policies were changed to permit some private ownership of the means of production, and there was a move away from economic central planning to greater local control of production

Pravda: True or truth, *Pravda* is also the name of the official Soviet newspaper

Projekt: Project

Proletariat: Soviet working class possessing neither capital nor privileges

Propiska: A work and residency permit

Rodina: Homeland

Soglasno: Agreed

Soviets: Councils

Spasibo: Thank you

Spetsnaz: Name of elite Soviet special operators, combat soldiers similar to American SEALs

Starshi michman: top Soviet enlisted rank, equivalent to Master Chief Petty Officer

Tikhookeanskaya Groza: Pacific Threat

Ushanka: Name for a Russian fur cap with earflaps that can be fastened under the chin or tied up to the crown of the hat

Vostochnyy Veter: East Wind

Ya: I

Za novyy Sovetskiy Soyuz: To the new Soviet Union

Zampolit: Political officer, responsible for the political orthodoxy of the military unit in which he is placed

Acknowledgments

While I am listed as author of this tale, there were many others who contributed. My research relied on the works of many authors and took many forms: declassified CIA and military documents, articles, white papers, websites, books, interviews and personal conversations.

Six beta readers ferreted out many mistakes and typos. I dribbled the tale out to them a chapter at a time. One of them called me a sadist for continually leaving them hanging at the end of each chapter. My wife functioned as a preliminary editor and an invaluable fount of plot ideas, more than once providing a fascinating escape route from the box canyon into which I had written myself. She spotted hundreds of mistakes in the chapters before the betas got their hands on them.

As he has with all my novels, my brother Lou was chief head cheerleader, reading and rereading the manuscript (he's probably sick of it by now!), always providing the enthusiasm and encouragement needed to keep me moving on the project.

My sister Elizabeth is my editor extraordinaire. Her knowledge of grammar and syntax is, to me, nothing short of astounding. When you add her fluency in the Russian language, her knowledge of Russian culture, and her personal and professional experiences in the Soviet Union, she made a mighty contribution to this book—and all as a labor of love.

I am extremely grateful to Captain James Fuqua, USN, ret., who served in the silent service for many years commanding SSBNs and has "been there and done that." He graciously read the manuscript and saved me from multiple inaccuracies and mistakes in the naval scenes.

As always, any remaining errors of fact, grammar or editing are mine and mine alone.

Soli Deo Gloria!

Please help independent authors

Independent authors usually don't have someone managing their books' publicity plan or marketing. We don't have the support of an organization getting our novels in front of retailers who will carry them in their stores. Other than what marketing efforts we can cobble together on our own, we have only one source of publicity that can encourage others to buy our books, and that's *you*, our readers.

Your word-of-mouth recommendation, your Facebook comment, your tweet, your Amazon or Goodreads review is likely the only way an unknown author will get the word out about his or her books.

Let me hasten to admit that the reader is certainly under no obligation. If you don't like the tale, or if the editing was sloppy, or the cover or packaging amateurish then by all means don't encourage someone else to read it. The last thing the independent publishing movement needs are products that fall short of genuine quality.

Even if you think the product is the best work since Bunyan's *Pilgrim's Progress* or Tolkien's *Lord of the Rings*, you still aren't obligated. Art doesn't create a debt or obligation on the part of the viewer. You're free to enjoy it and walk away. Artists take that risk when we create our work.

But if you find a tale you like and you'd like to read more by that author, give him or her a hand by letting your friends and loved ones know where they can get a good story. Post a review, mention it on Facebook, send a few emails, tell a few friends. Once the word gets out, a good story will sell itself; but getting the word out is the challenge. Thanks for your help!

About the Author

C. H. Cobb has a non-stop imagination, identifying with James Thurber's Walter Mitty. His career as a spinner of tall tales began by regaling his small children with the adventures of Moe, the spider that lived in the bathroom fan. He now writes military/espionage novels, dystopian fictions, and political thrillers. Kirkus Reviews has compared his writing to that of Tom Clancy and Dale Brown. His three children are now grown, and he lives with his wife Doris in Ohio where he serves as the counseling pastor of a church.

To find more books by C. H. Cobb you can visit his web site at www.chcobb.com.